Dread Nemesis of Mine

Book Four of the Overworld Chronicles

John Corwin

ISBN- 13 978-0-9850181-4-6

Printed in the U.S.A.

Vampires Drank my Kool-Aid

When Justin's long-lost sister, Ivy, shows up at the funeral for Elyssa's brother, Jack, it seems like the family reunion Justin has long hoped for is finally here. But Ivy isn't interested in playing Barbie or hanging out at the mall with her big brother. She's on a mission against evil, and Justin is at the top of her big-bad-meanies list.

Before Ivy can carry through on her threats, Justin finds out that she's been kidnapped. The kidnapper is none other than Maximus, a self-styled rebel leader of his own army of vampires who once kidnapped Justin's father. He also happens to be a world-class douchebag. Despite Ivy's homicidal inclinations toward Justin, loyalty to family leads him to go after Ivy and settle things with Maximus once and for all. Unfortunately, nothing goes to plan, and Maximus's minions capture Justin.

But even as Justin fights to free himself, he discovers Maximus plans to use Justin's incubus blood to fuel his quest for world domination. And the rogue vampire isn't even at the top of the food chain. Far more powerful forces stand behind him: Daelissa the insane angel, Maximus's vampire sire, and, even worse, Justin's grandparents and, quite possibly, his own mother.

Connect with John Corwin online:
Facebook: http://www.facebook.com/johnhcorwinauthor
Blog: http://blog.johncorwinauthor.com/
Twitter: http://twitter.com/#!/John_Corwin

Books by John Corwin:

Overworld Chronicles:
Sweet Blood of Mine
Dark Light of Mine
Fallen Angel of Mine
Dread Nemesis of Mine

Stand Alone Novels:

No Darker Fate
The Next Thing I Knew
Outsourced
Seventh

To my wonderful support group:

Alana Rock, Kayla Moore, Patrick Yates, Karen Stansbury, Dana Prestridge, Karla Ileana, Keren Hall, Nicole Passante, Anino, and Pat Owens

Thanks so much for all your help and input!

Chapter 1

I was at Jack Borathen's funeral when I saw the young blonde girl watching me as she leaned against a towering gravestone. I noticed the family name etched into the dark marble and shuddered. *Conroy.* My mother's maiden name. The last name of the grandparents who'd stolen my little sister Ivy from us—wrenched her from our lives when I was just a kid. Mom had blurred the memories of my sister from my mind. In fact, I'd never seen her face in real life.

Until now.

Elyssa's hand gripped mine painfully tight as they lowered the casket bearing her brother, Jack's, remains into the ground. Her other brother, Michael, towered in dark silence across from us. My sister— or a girl who looked just like I'd always imagined my sister would look—stood some fifty yards behind him.

I stood frozen with indecision. A funeral was a bad time to dash away without a word. Silent tears streamed down Elyssa's face leaving dark trails of eyeliner against her alabaster skin. I looked back to the other girl. Her bright blonde hair was tied back in a ponytail and she wore a blue dress patterned with flowers. It seemed awfully out of place for winter. She smirked. Her blue eyes glinted. I couldn't tell if they sparked with malice or happiness.

"May his soul rest in the forever, which awaits us all," the Templar priest intoned as he sprinkled the casket with holy water.

I hoped desperately for the ceremony to end so I could excuse myself. But the priest seemed determined to drag things out as long as possible, droning on about the afterlife, God's goodness, and the better place awaiting us all.

I had to call BS. I'd met angels—two of them, in fact. If they were heavenly messengers, the only thing waiting in the afterlife was

1

a world of hurt, and God had hopped on a unicorn and ridden into the sunset a long time ago.

The girl, apparently tired of the long-winded priest, formed an imaginary mouth with her hand, pressing the thumb and fingers together in a talking motion, and gave an exaggerated yawn. She rolled her eyes, and stepped behind the Conroy family headstone. I couldn't let her go. I had to know for sure if she was really my sister, or just some kid who'd wandered off from the funeral. I kissed Elyssa on the cheek and whispered, "I'll be right back."

Her violet eyes widened with confusion as I released her hand and backed away through the crowd. I tried to look casual. And failed. Thankfully, Elyssa's parents were sitting to her right and didn't seem to notice me slip into the crowd right away. The second I cleared the fringe, I sped in a wide arc around the sprawling graveyard and toward the headstone behind which I hoped my sister still waited.

Instead, I found only a note taped to the stone.

It fluttered in a gentle, chilly breeze, taunting me for not coming sooner. I cursed and jerked it free. Unfolded the sheet and looked at the words scrawled on it: *Look behind you.*

I spun, suddenly quite aware I may have walked straight into a trap set by Maximus—a real douche of a vampire who'd once kidnapped my father—or any other number of bad guys. Instead of a group of angry vampires ready to beat me and take me to their rogue leader, Ivy stood there, arms crossed, and a blonde eyebrow arched imperiously.

"Justin?" she asked, her voice still that of a teeny-bopper—cute, but with the sauciness of a fledgling tween. Her big blue eyes and golden hair looked exactly like our mom's, and the resemblance in her face almost took my breath away.

"Ivy," I said, taking a step toward her, arms outstretched for the brother-sister hug I longed for.

She backed away, waggling a finger at me. "Nuh uh, big bro." She stopped and crossed her arms, raking me with a critical eye. "I'm disappointed."

My mouth dropped open and I froze in my tracks. "Not exactly the greeting I was expecting."

"I expected you to look more dangerous. Maybe have a scar or an evil scowl on your face."

2

I wrinkled my nose. "Why in the world would I look evil?"

She snorted and gave me a *yeah right!* look. "Because you *are* evil."

I staggered back a step, my gut feeling like she'd just landed a physical blow with a sledgehammer. "But—but why?" I sputtered.

"You can act innocent if you want, Justin *Slade*, but I know all about you. Grandma and Grandpa told me how your dad tricked Mommy into marrying him and how you got all the demonic genes while I inherited Mommy's. Basically, I'm pure and you're gross."

"He's *your* dad too," I said, anger overcoming my shock. "And our grandparents stole you from Mom and Dad when you were an infant. Did they tell you that?"

She stuck out her lower lip and nodded. "It was to protect me."

"Yeah, then why did Mom stay with Dad all those years, huh? Why not go with them right then?"

"Because she wasn't sure how you'd turn out. Once she figured out you were a spawn, she left."

I opened my mouth to throw a retort in her face, but what if her words were true? What if Mom *had* left me when she did because she saw I was developing incubus powers? Becoming just like Dad? Even if the Conroys had filled Ivy's head with nothing but lies, I had no proof to fight them with. A million retorts flew through my head all at once, but none of them would do a damned thing to keep Ivy from hating me.

Except...why was she here?

Despite the lies and whatever twisted upbringing her—our— grandparents had given her, she'd come here, apparently on her own, to see me face-to-face. Maybe deep down she doubted what they'd told her. Maybe she wanted to decide the truth for herself.

"You can't believe everything they told you if you came here to see me," I said after a few seconds of silence stretched between us. "In fact, I'll bet you're full of doubt."

She giggled and shook her head. "No, I'm not, silly."

"Then why—"

"I came here to get rid of you so I can save the world. Otherwise, you'll have a good chance at wrecking everything we've worked so hard for."

I almost laughed at the idea being harmed by a tiny girl and almost cried because my own sister seemed so sure it was the right thing to do. "Get rid of me?" I shook my head. "Wouldn't that be the evil thing to do?"

"Not if it's for the right reason."

I turned away from her, shaking my head. "I can't believe this. I *cannot* believe my long-lost sister wants to kill me."

She giggled again and dragged the toe of her black tennis shoe in the dirt. "I didn't say *kill* you. I said I'd get rid of you. There's a difference."

"And you're not even going to hug me first? Geez, I realize we didn't get a chance to know each other, but I was hoping for a happier reunion than this."

She grimaced. "Eww. As if I'd touch demon spawn."

"We're related, Ivy. If you know anything about the birds and the bees—"

She waved her hands frantically. "Don't make me think about it! Gross."

I leaned against the tombstone and folded my arms. "Look, before you try to kill or get rid of me, why don't you take some time to get to know me? We could climb trees together, and drink Kool-Aid. I'll cut the hair off your Barbie dolls and you could tell Mom and Dad on me. You know, like real brothers and sisters." Having never known her, I really didn't have a clue what growing up with a sibling would be like, but I did have friends with sisters and remembered some of those Barbie doll incidents pretty clearly. Especially the one we'd dismembered to see if it worked as a voodoo doll. It hadn't.

"I figured you'd try this emotional stuff on me." She blew out a breath. "I mean, if I didn't know you were pure evil, I'd love to have a brother. There are some really mean kids at the school I go to, and I would love to teach them a lesson if I could get away with it."

"Well hey, just point me in their direction and I'll beat them up." I smiled at the thought of coming to my sister's aid, especially if someone was bullying her. I'd been through hell with jackasses who thought nothing of pushing around others simply because they could.

She actually seemed to consider it, pursing her cute little mouth and tilting her head like a puppy, blonde ponytail hanging at an angle. A sigh broke through her lips. "It would be cool to sic a demon spawn on those meanies, but I really can't risk the end of the world just so you can beat up a few idiots."

I tried a different tact. "Why do you think I'll cause the end of the world?"

"Because Grandpa told me."

Biting back a sigh, I asked, "What exactly did he tell you?"

"You're gonna unite the nasties and kill off all the good guys like Grandma and Grandpa. I mean, anyone who's friends with vampires and trannies is messed up."

My forehead pinched. "Trannies?" I had no idea how cross-dressers entered the mix.

"Yeah, the ones who transform into cats and wolves." She made a vague shape with her fingers.

I laughed. "Ivy, it's not *what* you are that makes you good or bad, it's what you *do*."

She opened and closed her fingers and thumb like a mouth as she had earlier. "Blah, blah, blah."

Her mind was sewn tight against my arguments, glued shut with the bigoted lies the Conroys had told her. I wondered if Mom had helped taint my little sister's mind with their propaganda as well.

"You've already corrupted the Templars," Ivy said, interrupting my thoughts. "A whole organization dedicated to the Brilliance and you somehow come along and corrupt it with the Murk."

"Brilliance? Murk?"

"Yeah. Light and Dark. Whatevs."

"First of all, I didn't corrupt anyone. The Divinity did. And once the Templars found out, you might say they saw the light." I grinned at my clever comeback.

"Ha, ha." Ivy glanced to her right.

I glanced in the same direction and saw nothing but headstones and tombs.

Obviously, I wasn't going to change my sister's mind about anything, at least not today. But my goal all this time had been to save her from the Conroys. I looked closer at our surroundings and saw no sign of our grandparents or my mom. Unless they were invisible, Ivy was here *alone*. She was tall, but thin and willowy. She couldn't possibly match me physically. As an added bonus, nearly a hundred Templars stood a scant fifty yards away. I supposed I could grab Ivy

5

and stow her on the Templar compound. Maybe Elyssa and I could figure out how to undo the mind-twisting my dear grandparents had wreaked on her.

"If you think I've really corrupted the Templars, why don't you ask them?" I said, leaning against the Conroy headstone and inching forward with a casual stretch.

"I'm not stupid. The Templars betrayed their sweet angel and she'll make them pay for it, believe me."

A cold spike pierced my spleen. "Angel?" She already knew?

She smirked. "Of course. Daelissa."

I staggered back, losing the few inches I'd closed between the two of us. "Do you realize how dangerous that woman is? She's the real evil behind everything. Did you know she let a very dangerous demon spawn named Vadaemos loose and he killed over a dozen Templars a week ago?" I pounded the bottom of my fist against the tombstone. The blow splintered the marble, sending a crack diagonally up to the edge. "Daelissa may claim to be an angel, but she's a demon."

Ivy shrugged, her eyes exploring the crack I'd opened in the tombstone. "I don't know anything about this Vadaemos man, but when the Templars turned their backs on Daelissa, they got what they deserved."

I gritted my teeth to keep back an angry response. Ivy wasn't in her right mind. Good god, if Daelissa had her claws into her, no wonder she was so messed up. Had the twisted angel also done something to Mom? She must have. It totally explained Mom's behavior the last time I'd seen her in the church parking lot across from the school, telling me she never wanted to see me or Dad again. *Sigh.* Talk about a dysfunctional family. Since then, I'd been transported to Colombia by a malfunctioning magical arch, fought vampiric drug lords, and finally cornered Vadaemos, an evil spawn, in El Dorado, a city where these so-called angels like Daelissa had ruled as gods.

Nightliss was also one of them. Except, she seemed to be good, or at least she'd helped me so far. If it hadn't been for her, Vadaemos would have killed me. He and I had manifested into our demon forms and fought. It hadn't been a contest. Vadaemos's strength and cunning dwarfed my own and only intervention from the dark angel had saved me.

"You look scared," Ivy said. "You should be."

I snapped out of my recollections. Enough was enough. Maybe Nightliss could figure out what to do with my errant little sister. Maybe she could clear her mind of Daelissa's touch just like she'd done for Elyssa. I blurred toward Ivy. Wrapped my arms around— thin air. Ivy's nose was practically touching mine. Except it wasn't. It couldn't. Her body flickered where my hands touched it. A breeze kicked up fallen leaves, sending its cold fingers through my hair. Ivy's hair didn't move a bit.

"I knew you'd try to kidnap me or do something bad," she said, clicking her tongue at me.

"You're a holograph?"

"A projection. Bigdaddy would freak if he knew I was talking to you."

"How did you put this note here then?" I held up the sheet of paper as evidence.

"Mr. Bigglesworth put it there for me."

"Who?"

"You'll meet him soon, big brother. Don't worry. I think I figured out how to get rid of you." She smiled. Waved. Vanished. A misty cloud approximating her shape remained for a second before the wintry breeze scattered it.

I looked at the note again. The words had changed and the original message was gone.

I wish you weren't evil. :(Goodbye.
Smoochies, Ivy

Chapter 2

The funeral had ended. Elyssa stood by the edge of the hole. Her gaze found me the moment I stepped from behind the Conroy family headstone. She looked a little confused. Hurt. Maybe even angry. I didn't blame her. I'd bolted on her in the middle of her brother's funeral. What jackass would do that?

Me, apparently.

Elyssa met me halfway, eyes narrowed. "What happened?"

"My sister."

Her eyes widened. "Sister?"

I nodded. "She was over there." I motioned back where I'd come from. "And she thinks I'm evil."

For a long moment, Elyssa didn't say anything, but the confusion in the arch of her brows told me all I needed to know. Finally she said, "She was here? In this cemetery?"

"Well, not exactly here. She projected, or something weird like that. She wasn't solid when I tried to grab her." I pulled the slip of paper from my front jeans pocket and showed it to her.

Elyssa took it and examined both sides. It was quite obviously blank. "Uh, and this is?" She handed it back.

I flipped the page around, peering at it. Aside from a few creases where I'd folded it, it looked pristine. I couldn't even make out impressions where words might have been. "Or maybe I'm going crazy," I said, feeling even more stupid than usual. "I could have sworn…"

Elyssa gave me an understanding half-smile and shrugged. "Maybe someone is playing a trick on you."

I folded the paper and shoved it back into my pocket, feeling like a complete moron. Could everything have been a bizarre illusion? I'd

8

made my fair share of enemies over the past couple of months as I'd stumbled my way through the politics of the Overworld. Maybe I'd ticked off an Arcane or some other illusionist with the ability to make me see my sister.

Elyssa took my hand and guided us toward the rest of her family as they walked toward a line of black SUVs parked curbside on the winding cemetery road. This place was the final stop for all sorts of beings from the Overworld, warded and guarded against noms in case some of the entities buried here weren't entirely dead. If ghosts existed, this would definitely be the place to find them.

A Templar sprang from one of the SUVs, walked briskly to Thomas, and spoke with him, his gestures urgent. It felt really strange to be on the Borathen family's side of the fence, not to mention openly dating the daughter of the head honcho in Atlanta. Just a week ago, he'd tried to take my head off with a sword.

Thomas turned and motioned us over. Or maybe he was motioning to Elyssa. I followed anyway, trying not to let my nervousness show. When we reached the group, his blue eyes settled on me and narrowed ever so slightly. He pursed his lips and seemed to arrive at some decision, leading us away from the crowd of mourners.

"Colombia is out of control."

"Maximus?" I asked, already knowing it had to be that pompous douche.

He grunted ever so slightly. "Noms in Bogota are starting to notice. He's not even trying to keep his recruitment activities a secret."

"What about here in Atlanta?" Elyssa asked.

"He seems to think he can get away with it down there. Weak local government." Thomas folded his arms and gave me an appraising look. "I'd like to send you down to help Commander Salazar."

Just the thought of going back to Colombia made me shudder. "Did he request me?"

"No. But Maximus seems to have a special hatred for you. It might be enough to draw him out." He looked around as the crowd thinned. "This isn't the place to discuss it. Meet back at the compound

9

in an hour. I plan to put a stop to these rogue vampires once and for all." He turned to go.

"Umm, excuse me?" I said, trying to make my voice sound bold and commanding. Instead, I sounded like a scared kid. "I'm not really an official Templar or anything, so why send me?" Thomas's icy stare focused on me. I swallowed and continued. "Sure, Maximus hates me, but not enough to go out of his way to fall into a trap, if that's what you're planning."

Elyssa's father waited, the sort of learned patience on his face someone employs when hoping an annoying dog will stop barking. When he saw I was done yammering he said, "We'll discuss it at the compound. One hour." With that, he rejoined his wife Leia and headed for an SUV.

"Colombia." Michael grunted.

I turned to face Elyssa's big—actually huge—brother. I hadn't heard him approach, which I'd learned wasn't unusual despite his heavy muscular frame. "Are you going?" I asked, uncertain as to whether it would be a good thing or not. Michael didn't exactly like me, but seemed resigned to the fact I was supposed to date his sister for the good of the world, or so he said.

"Maybe."

"If Justin is going, so am I," Elyssa said, her raised eyebrow daring him to disagree.

I had a really bad feeling about going back to Colombia. I'd made new friends there, led them into ancient vaults beneath a cursed city, and nearly died half a dozen times thanks to a horde of mostly dead angels called husks, giant ley worms, and a half-insane demon spawn. And now Thomas Borathen wanted me to be bait for a crazy rogue vampire? Thanks, but no thanks. The Templars could take care of Maximus on their own. It was time for me to find Ivy, and—if she really was the one who'd contacted me—convince her I wasn't pure evil.

My cell phone rang. I groaned when I saw who it was.

"You need to answer it, Justin," Elyssa said. "You promised him."

I huffed and wrinkled my nose, but answered anyway. "Yeah?"

"Well, hello to you too, sweetheart," Harry Shelton said. "You never call. You never write. And you sure as hell didn't reply to my two texts and phone call."

I glanced at my text log and saw both attempts about an hour apart. I'd promised Shelton and Bella I'd let them teach me all about being an Arcane, a sorcerer, since I'd inherited some of those abilities from my mom's side of the family. I might have super strength, but considering the heavies I'd fought against and those who were likely to come after me in the future, having a few extra tricks in my arsenal couldn't hurt. I put the phone back to my ear. "No, I haven't gone by the Grotto to buy a new phone yet. The funeral just ended."

He snorted. "Damn, those Templar priests like to hear themselves talk."

"Tell me about it."

"Well, it's over now. Grab a new phone—I don't care if it's Orange or MagicSoft—just get it and meet me at Romulus for your magic lessons."

I could never keep the names and locations of his super-secret lairs straight. "Is that the one in Decatur Square, or the one near Centennial Park?"

He sighed. "Decatur."

"Okay, I'll—ah crap."

"Ah crap what?"

"Thomas Borathen called a meeting in an hour. He wants me to go back to Colombia."

Shelton snorted. "Tough titty. He ain't the boss of you."

I gave a dubious laugh. "And you are?"

"Damned right. You promised Bella and me could have our way with you. So unless you want to prove you're a scum-sucking—"

"Fine, fine, I get it. I'll see you later today."

"With a new phone."

"Yes."

"And don't let those salespeople talk you into magical accident insurance."

I didn't even want to think about what that might cover.

Elyssa offered a reassuring smile as I shoved my phone back into my pocket. It was a nom phone, but I really liked it, despite all the cracks and grime it had accumulated from my adventures.

Unfortunately, it couldn't run magic code, so I had to go to Atlanta's super-secret place for all things magical, the Grotto, and snag one capable of running Arc OS—something like a magical version of Windows.

"I'll tell Dad we can't meet him in an hour," Elyssa said.

Thanks to his ghost-ninja skills I'd forgotten Michael, who was standing nearby until he said, "I'll tell him." He tossed Elyssa a key fob. "Take my car."

Her eyes went as wide as giant lollipops. "Are you serious?"

For the first time, I detected the barest sense of uncertainty flicker in Michael's face before he stabbed it with a mind sword. "Yep."

We reached Phipp's Plaza in record time thanks to Michael's black Porsche and Elyssa's supernatural driving skills. I left a handprint embedded in the door handle, happy I hadn't broken it. Sure, a wreck probably wouldn't have killed us thanks to our healing abilities, but I'd lived most of my life as a vulnerable nerd. After a terrifying ride down the spiral driveway into the giant cavern beneath the Phipp's parking garage, Elyssa slid the car into a parking space next to a giant Rolls Royce someone had apparently dipped in purple glitter paint, and adorned with decals of pink unicorns.

"G'day guvnah!" shouted the cheerful lad who cleaned up after the elephants, camels, and other assorted beasts, which arrived in the cavern via the towering Obsidian Arch set in the center of the space.

I waved back.

"Your hands are sweaty," Elyssa said as she wreathed her fingers into mine.

"Gee, I wonder why."

She laughed. "Did you decide which phone you want?"

"Yeah, I'm going with Orange." I watched the dung boy shovel a heap of crap into a wagon. "Who is that kid?"

Elyssa shrugged. "No idea."

"Does he live here? Have family? I mean, who do you have to piss off to get a job like this?"

"Why the curiosity all of a sudden?"

I gave her a questioning look. "All of a sudden? I've only been here three times. It's not like I've had much time to question the socio-economic situation of dung boys in super-secret towns built by angels and used as portals to zip from one side of the world to the other."

A deep throated laugh burst from her mouth. "Where in the world do you come up with this stuff?"

"Quite possibly the very bowels of hell."

We entered the towering doors leading into the Grotto itself. The town—if it could be called such a thing—looked like something right out of the history books. A cobblestone road known as Golden Way led past fancy shops constructed of black marble with green-slate roofs and shiny copper gutters. It had such an old world appeal, it could almost pass for an amusement park or the movie set for a film based in the days of sail-driven galleys and pirates.

Crowds of shoppers strolled casually through the maze of streets, colorful shopping bags in hand. A tired-looking sorceress led a group of excited children dressed in the green robes of elementary grade Arcanes down the street toward a store named Bixby's Arcane Supplies. A large, white wolf with blazing blue eyes nipped at the heels of straggling kids to keep them in line.

"Is that a werewolf?" I asked.

Elyssa followed my gaze. "If it was a normal wolf, it would eat the kids."

"Can you imagine how much better discipline would be at nom schools if we had werewolves?"

"Everyone would be too busy wetting their pants to pay attention," Elyssa said, laughing. She tugged my hand to keep me moving. "No time to sightsee today."

I groaned and continued on.

The sun shone brightly overhead and fluffy clouds drifted on a light breeze despite our location some hundred yards or so underground. The temperature felt pleasantly cool and warmer than the gray chilly city aboveground.

I tried not to stare like a tourist but ended up rubbernecking every few seconds as one bizarre sight after another caught my eyes. This place was just *weird*—juxtaposed between our reality and some other place. A sudden thought hit me like a brick wall and I stopped in my tracks. A hurrying shopper bumped into me and muttered an apology, though her pinched eyebrows and glare said something else entirely.

"What is it?" Elyssa said, turning to look through the window of the shop where we stood. A skimpy outfit made from sheer fabric hung from a very lifelike looking mannequin in the display and left very little to the imagination. "You want me to try it on?"

I imagined Elyssa's athletic curves pressing tight against the scant outfit and felt a blush creeping up my neck. "Um, actually I was thinking of something else."

"*You* want to try it on?" She winked. "I'm sure you'd look sexy."

I laughed uneasily. "Exactly." I took her arm and led her down the sidewalk and away from the distraction. "Actually, I remembered something you told me about this place when I first arrived. About how this place exists in our world and somewhere else."

"What about it?"

"Nightliss's people—angels, or whatever you want to call them—built the framework for this place, right? And supernaturals have added to it over time? What if the Grotto is partly in the same place the angels come from? What if that out there"—I jabbed a finger at the sky—"is the realm of angels?"

Chapter 3

It was Elyssa's turn to stop dead in her tracks. She flicked her gaze to the innocent-looking sky overhead.

"Freaky, right?" I said.

She nodded slowly, eyes never leaving the clouds, as if waiting for a host of angels to burst from behind them and yell, "Surprise!"

"If the environment we see outside the Grotto really belongs to their world, it must look a lot like our own," I said.

Elyssa recovered and motioned me to follow her. "Even if we are partly in their plane, the Grotto is barricaded off from it. I read the history of the place. Looked at images with only the original buildings here. When you get to the edges of the Grotto, there's endless water to the north side, and thick forest on the others. A magical barrier won't let you go any further. The Arcanes tried for years and never succeeded. They ended up using an obfuscation spell so gray mist hides most of the view, supposedly to keep people with more curiosity than brains from trying to break through."

"Or to keep anything on the other side of the barrier from looking in? You said this place is a nexus, like a bubble in between." I imagined it as a full-scale snow globe with alien eyes peering in at us.

She looked inside a dress shop as we walked past it, her eyes settling on one of the complicated Victorian era dresses inside. "I guess it's like a pocket dimension. Maybe this place isn't even visible from the other side."

"Or maybe the sky and everything else is illusion. For all we know, we might be on the moon."

She chuckled. "I guess we're safe then."

"So there's no danger of an invasion sweeping through here?"

"Not unless they built in a back door we don't know about." She shrugged. "Anything is possible, I guess."

I grimaced, imagining an army of insane blonde women like Daelissa lining up to raid the Grotto. "The other thing that occurs to me is how you called this place a *nexus*. Didn't you tell me Daelissa blamed the destruction of the Grand Nexus for turning her people into those creepy cherub things and stranding her here?"

Elyssa threw up a hand as if warding the memories away. "Ugh. I really don't want to talk about the husks, cherubs, whatever you want to call those nasty little things."

The husks—or cherubs as I called them—were the creepy infantile remains of the angels caught up in the destruction of the Grand Nexus, according to Vadaemos. They wobbled around on nubby feet, like toddlers with oversized, ungainly heads and little T-rex arms. But the shiny pitch black skin and nearly featureless head hid horrors beneath. Sometimes when they shrieked, the outline of a face seemed to appear beneath the surface.

I shook my head to clear the images of our last encounter with the cherubs and found my way back to the point I wanted to make. "What makes this place different than Thunder Rock or El Dorado? Was it not connected to this Grand Nexus of theirs? And what about La Casona and the other functioning relics?"

Elyssa quirked an eyebrow. "I have no idea." She tapped a finger to her chin. "But I have a feeling we should pump Nightliss for answers the next time we see her. After all, Foreseeance Forty-Three Eleven says our former rulers were going to come through the Gloom."

We entered an alley and skidded to a halt. In this very alley, we'd had our first encounter with gray men, the creepy golems used by a man we called Mr. Gray for obvious reasons. I'd discovered a large mural of him down in El Dorado and concluded he must be an angel like Nightliss and Daelissa. He apparently wanted me dead or captured, judging from my every encounter with his minions.

"Uh, why don't we take the scenic route?" I backed up a step, remembering the ambush all too clearly. "Not that I'm scared or anything." *Yeah, right.*

"Let's go down another block," Elyssa said, mouth set in a grim line.

We walked down the street a little further and entered a large marble-paved roundabout. A lush, green park sprawled in the center of the huge space. Hardwood trees swayed gently in the breeze, their tops reaching toward the sky. Intricately shaped hedges adorned strategic places inside the park, next to benches and statue fountains.

We continued through the park. My gaze slid over the bizarre buildings surrounding us—one seemingly made from snow-white plastic with shiny stainless-steel balconies, and another patterned in the crosshatch black used in so many carbon fiber designs.

"Why are we always in a hurry to do something when we come here?" I complained. "I'd really like to take you on a real date for once."

Elyssa squeezed my hand. "How about after your magic lessons today?"

"Don't you have Templar duties?"

She shook her head. "I'm still on recovery leave."

"Dinner and a show?" I'd seen a cool Chinese restaurant the first time I'd been here, and Shelton had mentioned a live-action theater he liked to visit.

"How about dancing instead?

Dancing wasn't exactly my forte, but so long as it was with Elyssa, I was willing to give it a shot. "You got it, babe."

A bright smile lit her face. "It's a date."

We left the park and crossed the marble street to the Orange store, bearing a stark white sign with a partially peeled orange emblazoned on it. The building consisted of a similar white material lined with liquid glass, rippling like the surface of a crystalline lake. Across the road from Orange, almost all three stories of the MagicSoft store were made entirely of the liquid glass. I wondered if the floors were too. Unlike the last time we'd been here, there were few people inside either store. We walked up the glowing white stairs, passing a poster which declared, *Now you can compare Apples to Oranges!*

About a half-hour later, we emerged from the store, my shiny new arcphone in hand. Apparently, smartphones were considered dumbphones by Overworld citizens since they couldn't use magic and were limited to traditional cell towers. Arcphones could make use of just about any nom cell signal and the magical cell network. My new toy was wafer thin and no larger than a credit card. I dragged my thumb across the glowing Orange logo on the screen, peeling the fruit and revealing a list of apps. I tapped one of them to reveal a slider and slid it up. The phone expanded until the edge-to-edge screen was nearly seven inches. I pulled the slider down, shrinking the phone to five inches, then three, and back up again.

"Will you stop playing with that thing?" Elyssa said, an amused grin on her face.

"How did I survive all these years without one of these?" I rubbed the smooth, polished surface of the device like a pet. "Nookli, I love you."

"You are the wind beneath my wings," the phone replied in a mellifluous voice.

I laughed. "Awesome!"

Elyssa rolled her eyes.

I played with my phone as we weaved our way back through the Grotto to the parking garage. Despite the magical origins of the new arcphone, it interfaced perfectly with my nom email, and the salesperson had even ported all my saved texts, pictures, and old phone number. I flicked through the few texts in the list. Katie Johnson, my former crush, had texted me several times over the past few days. Ash and Nyte, two Goth guys who, along with Elyssa, had befriended me at an especially low point in my life, had also tried to reach me.

At first, the messages showed up in typical text lingo, with all the associated abbreviations and bad grammar. Then the words shimmered and morphed into something resembling normal sentences with proper punctuation. It was all I could do not to kiss Nookli. What a smart little phone!

I felt guilty about not replying to any of my non-supernatural friends since returning from Colombia, but with the forces of darkness out to kill me, I didn't want to put them in any danger. They couldn't deal with vampires, fallen angels, or hellhounds. I'd barely held my own against most of the threats I'd faced, and I was half demon spawn. Still, didn't my friends deserve at least some small reply? Or would I put them in harm's way somehow?

For what must have been the fifth time, I pulled up Ash's texts and read through them again.

Dude, you still alive?

Seriously, man, holla back.

Katie says you're okay. Me and Nyte gotta show you something cool!

Nyte's texts were similar, going on and on about how he and Ash really wanted to show me some cool new thing—probably a new nose ring or something Goth and gross. Katie's texts were a bit more somber.

Are you alive? Answer me!

Your dad said you're okay. Thank god.

Ash and Nyte keep asking about you. I told them you're okay.

Please, please, please call me when you can. We need to talk!

She'd talked to my dad? How in the hell had she managed that? I wasn't exactly on talking terms with him right now, given his decision to betray Mom and marry a succubus by the name of Kassallandra. My finger hovered over Katie's number. If I could contact anyone, it would be her. She knew about me and the Overworld, thanks to bad timing on her part and a pack of overachieving hellhounds who'd chased Elyssa, Dad, Katie, and me all the way to downtown Atlanta. Maybe it would be okay to call her and ask about my other friends. On the other hand, what if Mr. Gray or one of my other enemies found out about my normal friends and used them against me?

I tucked the phone in my pocket and decided to think about it.

"Don't look now, but we're being followed," Elyssa said, using the shiny surface of her phone like a mirror.

Despite the warning, I almost glanced behind us before turning the motion into a casual stretch of my arms. "How do you know?" Though the walkways weren't teeming with people, they were congested enough to hide any followers.

"I took us through a few side streets we didn't need to use, but the chubby guy with the long black coat and bowler hat is still following us."

I sighed. "We can't have whoever it is trailing us back to Shelton's hideout. How long has he been following?"

"Since we left the Orange store."

"Any idea what kind of super he is?"

She shrugged. "Only one way to tell."

19

My mind rifled through several plans—run, turn and confront, or act casual. Between Elyssa and me, we could handle most threats short of an angel or manifested demon spawn. Using a nearby shop window as a mirror, I spotted the unkempt form of a chubby man close to my height as he regarded us. His expression verged on boredom.

Elyssa led me through a wide alley. We emerged in Founder's Square. Towering effigies of the supernatural founders of the Overworld bordered the sprawling plaza. The massive statue of a demon spawn drew my eye to it and its neighbor, an angel with outstretched wings, hands held low to the sides as though in welcome.

Something seemed off about the two statues. I'd only been to this place once, but the sight had etched itself firmly into memory. "Wait a minute," I said. "The demon spawn statue doesn't have horns anymore, and the angel's wings aren't curled up."

"And the statue of Ezzek Moore is now raising his staff in the air," Elyssa said, pointing out the statue of a man in robes. "These are life statues. They actually move into different positions over time, depending on how the Arcanes charmed them to pose."

"Can they walk?" I imagined turning the Statue of Liberty into a life statue and freaking out the noms.

She nodded. "Sure, I guess."

A crystal-sheathed representation of Earth hovered in the center of the square, rotating slowly. I looked up at the house-sized globe as we passed beneath it, then used the chance to steal a glance back. The man was still following us, not even bothering or trying to hide. Something very strange was going on. Groups of people sparsely populated the wide boundaries of Founder's Square. Enough so if the man were hostile, we could call for help if need be.

I touched Elyssa's arm to stop her and turned to face our stalker. His face never changed expression, nor did he break his ambling stride, walking right up to us and holding out a white marble to me. His irises were so pale as to be almost pink, and his pale skin seemed doughy in spots and rubbery in others. I glanced uneasily at his unnatural-looking fingers and decided I didn't want to touch them.

"That's an ASE," Elyssa said, her brow furrowing.

"A what?"

"An all-seeing eye. Templars use them for holo-recording."

I fixed a stern gaze on the large man, but made no move to take his offering. "Who are you and what do you want?"

The man removed his hat to reveal a shock of bristly white hair, and bowed. "Miss Ivy done sent me, Your Grace," he said in a rough cockney accent.

A hot flush raced through my body. Ivy had sent him? I reached for the all-seeing eye.

Elyssa gripped my arm. "Wait, Justin. It might be a trap."

"It ain't no trap, milady," the man said. He sniggered and flipped his hat several feet into the air. It landed at a jaunty angle on his head as he turned to me. "Truly, Your Excellence, it ain't no trap."

"Then why did you laugh?"

"I'm sorry, Magnificence, but I'm a bit overwhelmed by your presence." His lips curled up ever so slightly as if he were enjoying a big joke at my expense.

I wanted to punch him. "Why do you keep calling me stupid crap like that? Justin will do just fine."

"Whatever pleases you, Your Holiness."

Heat flared in my face in a violent wave of anger. I bared my teeth at him and growled lower than humanly possible. I spoke in deep guttural tones, words in another language. Words I somehow understood. *Do not mock me, filth.*

The man backed up a step, his pale eyes widening ever so slightly. Elyssa jumped back from me, a shocked expression on her face. I looked uneasily at the two of them, unsure what had just happened. I tried to speak the words again, but failed to recall exactly what they were.

"What's your name?" I said, breaking the stunned silence.

The man narrowed his eyes, his lips curling back up with amusement. "If it please Your—you, Justin, my name is Mr. Bigglesworth."

This was the man Ivy had mentioned! "Are you the one who brought me this?" I held out the slip of blank paper from the graveyard.

"Aye, I put it out for you to find."

"Good lord, she really did visit you," Elyssa said.

"Fine, I'll take the ASE," I said, holding out a hand for it and hoping I didn't have to touch Bigglesworth's icky skin.

21

He dropped it into my palm. A smiled crossed his lips briefly before he straightened them. "It's real urgent, sir."

I tucked it into a pocket, unwilling to view it here where everyone could see it. "Where's my sister? What are the Conroys doing to her?"

He shook his head. "It ain't for me to say, no sir. Miss Ivy tells me what to do and I does it, no questions asked."

I stepped toward him, tempted to grab him by the collar despite his revolting skin. "Where do the Conroys keep her?"

Again, he shook his head. "I've done my duty, sir and I can't do no more." He tipped his hat. "G'day to you both." He winked at Elyssa and smirked. Turned on his heel and headed back toward the alley we'd come through a few minutes earlier.

I started after him. "Oh, no, you don't."

The chubby man increased his pace. I jogged after him, not wanting to make a scene. When he reached the alley, Bigglesworth turned. Tipped his cap at me and chortled. His body, clothes, everything, melted into a puddle of pale goop. Elyssa gasped behind me. I watched in utter disgust as the goop funneled into a drainage grating on the side of the alley floor and vanished inside.

Chapter 4

"What," I said, "in the hell was that thing?"

Elyssa shook her head. "Some kind of shifter, but one I'm not familiar with."

I looked at the marble-sized ASE, almost expecting it to melt into goop as well. Thankfully, it seemed quite solid. Still, just knowing Bigglesworth had held it made me want to scrub it and my hands with bleach and steel wool. "How do I turn this thing on?"

"Maybe you should wait until we're somewhere private," Elyssa said.

I turned back toward Founder's Square and noticed horns slowly growing from the forehead of the giant demon spawn statue. "Yeah, you're probably right."

After threading our way through congested afternoon traffic, we reached Decatur and parked behind a donut shop. A red X next to a smelly dumpster marked the spot.

"He chooses the loveliest locations," Elyssa said, holding her nose.

"Better than the one downtown." My nose wrinkled at the memory of the stained mattress in the abandoned building above that hideout.

I turned back to the red X. Imagining a set of stairs in the place of the mark, I said, "Open up, you green-blooded son of a bitch." As usual, my words alone had no effect. I blew out a disgusted breath and made a chalk circle around me. The static feel of trapped magical energy pressed against me. I repeated the spell. The concrete faded away to reveal a set of stairs leading down into a lit hallway.

"Shelton uses some whacked-out pass phrases," Elyssa said as we walked down the stairs.

"You'd have to be a nerd to appreciate it." I hurried down the narrow corridor and entered a large space the size of a school gymnasium, eager to look at Ivy's message. Shelton had partitioned the area into testing grounds, creating a magical gauntlet I hoped to eventually emerge from victorious. At the rate of my learning, that happy occasion probably wouldn't be for another century or so.

On the other side of the testing grounds, we entered a hall and the residential part of his hideout. Shelton had told me he'd carved this entire place out himself with magic. Elyssa and I passed through the hall and found Bella and Shelton lounging at the kitchen table, drinking tea and playing Scrabble.

Shelton groaned as Bella formed the word *zygote* on the board. "Saved by the bell," he grumbled, standing up.

Bella, a petite Arcane I'd met during my time in Colombia, smiled sweetly at him. "And to think, English isn't even my first language."

"Whatever, woman. You've been playing Scrabble a couple hundred years longer than I have."

Bella's violet eyes widened with hurt. "Harry, you should never call a woman out on her age."

Shelton snorted. "Cry me a river, princess. I give you a place to live so we can teach Junior here how to use fairy dust, and you kick my ass at every board game I own."

"Except Candy Land," she said, grinning.

Shelton seemed to bite back a response with visible effort. He blew out a breath and looked at me. "Candy Land my ass. You got the phone, bucko?"

I showed him Nookli. "Yeppers. But first, I need to watch this." I pulled the ASE from my pocket and held it in the palm of my hand.

"What in blazes are you doing with an all-seeing eye?" he said, taking it and holding it up to the light.

"It's a message from Ivy. Some dude named Bigglesworth gave it to me."

His eyebrows pinched. "What kind of stupid name is that?"

I shrugged. "Get this—the dude melted into some kind of pale goo and went down a sewage drain when I tried to chase him down."

Bella gasped. "Are you quite certain?"

I nodded and gestured at Elyssa. "We both saw him do it. Why?"

24

"If this creature is what I think it is, then you have witnessed a very rare breed of supernatural."

"Yeah, well what is it?" Shelton said.

She shook her head. "I do not know if they even have a classification."

"He looked like a creepy version of the Pillsbury Doughboy," I said, shuddering at the thought of his rubbery, doughy skin. "Can he morph into any shape?"

"It sounds to me as though he wasn't trying hard to appear authentic," Bella said. "From the little I know about the species, they often assume the appearance of their last victim."

"Victim?" Elyssa said uneasily.

Bella nodded. "They encase their victims with their bodies—the pale goo you mentioned—and consume the poor soul."

I threw up a little in my mouth at the thought. "On another subject," I said, indicating the ASE, "can you operate the thing?"

"I can do that," Elyssa said, taking it from Shelton and setting it on the table. She tapped the marble three quick times. It started to spin, slowly at first, building momentum until it made an audible hum against the wooden top.

A holographic image sprang into the air above it. Ivy's head crowded the scene, a look of fear emblazoned on her face.

"Justin, I need your help." Tears trickled from her eyes.

The loud clang of metal on metal gonged through the air. Ivy shrieked.

"Let us in you little brat!" Someone shouted, sounding as if they were on the other side of a wall or thick door.

Ivy looked back at me. "Vampires attacked us. I don't know what happened to Mom or Grandma and Granddad." She sniffled and wiped her runny nose with a hand. "I'm in the panic room, but they'll break through any minute. Mr. Bigglesworth is the only person who can get this message to you."

"Why don't you let us in, little girl," said a familiar voice.

A chill prickled down my spine. "Maximus," I growled.

"Come on, sweetness," Maximus said in a sugar coated voice. "We're going on a little trip. You'll love it."

"I'm not going anywhere with you!" Ivy screamed. She turned back to the ASE again. "Please, Justin, help. I don't know when you'll

25

get this or where they're taking me, but nobody else can help me now. I think the vampires killed them all."

A shuddering crack rocked the view and Ivy screamed again as chunks of concrete and white dust filled the air. The holograph blinked out. The rotating ASE slowed to a stop and rolled against a teacup on the table with a *plink*.

Anger and despair welled in my chest, lodged in my throat, and all that emerged was a choked sound. I backed away from the table, my eyes darting back and forth between the concerned faces looking at me. I wanted to rush to Ivy's aid. Do something, *anything* to save her right this instant. Had Maximus taken her to Colombia? Or was he keeping her here and somehow making the Templars think he was in South America? Come to think of it, I didn't even know when this had happened. Yesterday? Today?

Elyssa seemed poised to pin me to the floor if I decided to do something rash and make a break for the door. God knew I'd done such a thing plenty of times. Uncertainty, however, rooted me to the spot. I needed information and Bigglesworth was the only one who had it. Why had he been so casual and mocking when handing it to me? The guy certainly hadn't seemed like someone on a mission of mercy. His relationship to Ivy was unclear to me. Was he a pet? A protector?

"Now don't freak out, Justin," Shelton said. "We'll find her, I promise."

Bella touched my arm. "When did this happen, Justin? Did Bigglesworth say anything more about it?"

"He was a jackass," Elyssa said. "He didn't even say what was on this recording. In fact, he didn't seem particularly concerned about anything."

"It could be due to what he is," Bella said. "Little is known about his kind, but anecdotal evidence would point to them as inhuman in the way they experience emotion, almost like a psychopath. It's highly unlikely he's a friend to Ivy, at least in his view. Ivy, however, may feel quite differently. She is a little girl after all."

I balled my hands into knuckle-cracking fists and stormed away from the table. I wanted to hit something. Break it. Find Maximus and pound him into toothpaste. I took a deep breath. And another. It did little to curb my murderous rage, but the juvenile desire to smash one of Shelton's tables faded. I could do this. I'd faced rough odds before, and when I wasn't jumping headfirst without thinking, I could usually figure my way out.

My gaze went automatically to Elyssa. Her bright eyes met mine. Fierce determination blazed within and she set her jaw in a grim line. She was my strength. My love. Confidence surged within my chest, pushing out the helplessness I'd felt. With her and my friends, I would find Ivy and save her. And if I got to break Maximus's teeth along the way, so much the better.

I smiled. Bella flinched back, eyes wide.

"Do I have broccoli on my teeth or something?" I said.

The Arcane shook her head. "No, but you smiled like a wolf who has cornered a baby deer."

I walked back to the table and took a seat. "Elyssa, I assume the Templars are tracking Maximus. Can they tell me where he is now?"

"I'll make some calls," she said, and walked across the room, phone in hand.

"Shelton, any idea when this recording was made?"

He picked up the ASE and examined it. "Since the video didn't show the date, I'll have to hack into the file system and see if the device date-stamped the recording."

I leaned back, confused. "A file system? But isn't this a magical thingy?"

He groaned. "That's a whole other can of worms, hotshot."

"Give me the abridged version."

"The files are in ArcOS format, just like the spells you can save on your phone."

That much I could understand. "Will you check out the dates for me?"

"Yeah, sure, but it'll take a little while to hook it up." Shelton turned to Bella. "Why don't you give Mr. Bossypants here a lesson while I dig into this?"

Bella took my arm, and turned her violet eyes on me. "Are you up to it, Justin?"

I nodded. "Yeah, it'll help take my mind off…things."

She took me into the large testing room, back to a quiet section. "You've been practicing your circles?"

"Yep. I can get a circle up in no time now." I pulled out my handy-dandy chalk from a plastic pouch on my belt and knelt. In a blur of supernatural speed, I whipped a small circle around me, pressed a thumb against the line, and willed it closed. The air crackled and snapped. Magical energy pressed against me. I rubbed out the line with a foot and felt the energy rush out.

"Excellent," Bella said. "And you've practiced the basic spells?"

Basic was hardly the term I'd use to describe the spells she and Shelton had me practice. One was blowing out a candle. Another was lighting the candle. I'd managed to blow the candle off its pedestal where it set fire to the curtains in Elyssa's bedroom. And while trying to light the candle, I'd managed to melt the wax to a puddle without ever actually lighting the wick.

"Uh, yeah, I did some practicing."

Bella arched an eyebrow. "I take it your fine control is still lacking."

"You might say that."

"You didn't hurt anyone this time, did you?"

I fended off her question with a wave of my hands. "No, nobody lost any hair the last few times."

"Because Shelton wasn't happy about losing his eyebrows. I still don't know how you managed—"

"Can we start? Please?" I looked around the room for the candles I'd been using for practice, but didn't see them.

She smiled. "Today, we'll be entering another phase of control. I hope you've been running through the meditation rituals."

"I haven't really had a chance. It's only been a couple of days."

"Well, you're going to need proper meditation skills to light a candle, Justin. And since you won't be able to rely on circles for everything, you need to learn how to fill your internal well with energy." She touched my stomach just above the naval. "I can't emphasize enough just how important it is you learn to fill your well."

I crossed my arms. "I think you and Shelton have emphasized it nonstop ever since I started taking lessons a week ago."

"Well, today, you're going to learn the steps to filling it."

The demon side of me knew what it felt like to fill a well of energy. When I fed on emotions, it sated a need nothing else could. That energy enhanced my preternatural strength, speed, and other abilities. It also could trigger my ability to manifest or spawn into full demon form. Feeding my incubus side required a certain kind of meditation of its own. Otherwise, my target could be overtaken by lust and do all sorts of embarrassing things. I'd nearly done the deed in the meat department of a grocery store the first time I'd unknowingly tried to feed from a woman.

Bella led me through a series of breathing exercises, telling me to focus on the magical energy in the environment around me. After a while, I thought I felt something, only to realize I was just light headed from all the breathing exercises.

I steadied myself against a wall. "All this is doing is making me dizzy. Isn't there a better way?"

She narrowed her eyes, violet like Elyssa's since she too was a dhampyr, as well as an accomplished Arcane.

Some people are just overachievers.

"Do you remember the first time you learned to whistle? Or snap your fingers?" she asked.

"Uh, not really. I do remember the first time I learned to burp on command by sucking air into my esophagus."

Bella groaned. "Justin, you have to feel the magic around you before you can absorb it."

"I feel it when I make a circle."

"Yes, but you can't always stop and make a circle to fill your well." She gestured at the air around us. "Your well is only so large— a finite container you must constantly replenish from the world around you. Making a circle to do this would be very impractical."

Elyssa appeared from around the corner, a small frown on her face.

I walked to her. "What did you find out?"

"I spoke directly to Commander Salazar. He said Maximus is definitely in Bogota and, as far as he knows, hasn't left."

"Will he help me rescue Ivy?"

She bit her lip. "I don't know. He was planning to hit Maximus before, well, you know."

I raised an eyebrow. "You mean before he sent the Templar army after me when good old Franco, the drug lord, held me captive?"

29

"Yep. Christian said he's holding back on an assault because the number of vampires in Max's stronghold have increased exponentially and he doesn't have enough people."

"Wait a minute, I know Maximus has been recruiting noms, but unless something has changed, he still can't turn them into vampires, right? Is Christian sure they're all vampires?" A chilling thought went through me. "And what about vamplings?"

Elyssa shook her head. "I don't know." She blew out a frustrated breath. "He only told me what he did as a favor."

In any case, I knew exactly where I was headed. No matter how hard I tried to stay out of trouble, it found me. It seemed I had no choice unless I could turn off my emotions and turn my back on the people I cared about. The irony of the situation was very clear.

It looked like Thomas Borathen would get to see me off to Colombia after all.

Chapter 5

Elyssa gripped me in a fierce hug. "It'll be okay. I know you hate it when my dad bosses you around. I'll talk with him and work something out."

I kissed her on her lovely forehead and forced a grin. "I know, babe. I know."

Someone cleared their throat. I turned and saw Bella tapping her foot impatiently.

"We should practice more before you run off, young man." She motioned me back over.

Elyssa nodded. "We're going to need every advantage if what Christian says is true."

"I'll be more of a liability than an asset if I have to rely on magic," I said with a groan. Hard to believe, at one point, I'd wanted to learn magic so badly. But after finding out I couldn't wave a wand, say a silly word, and defeat practitioners of the dark arts, some of the—ahem—magic had gone out of learning.

Bella made me sit down in a chair and resume my meditations. Instead of meditating, I found myself thinking about Elyssa. I sensed her hot, welcoming presence nearby, thanks to my incubus sixth sense. We'd made love for the first time in a dingy hotel room just a week ago. Talk about *magic*. I sent out a questing tendril of incubus essence and found the halo of her aura feet away. She seemed amused with my academic efforts.

I tapped against her halo. She flinched, and for a moment, her defenses sprang up reflexively, cold and impersonal. Then she realized it was me and opened up, even more amused than before. But beneath the surface of her amusement simmered love, spiced with a bit of lust. My demon senses burned with desire to dive right in. But if

I did it without tempering my mood, Elyssa and I might get more than we bargained for. I sure as heck didn't want us to rip each other's clothes off in front of Bella.

Easing back on the throttle, I evened out my emotions, trying to match her amusement, rather than the lust.

"Do you feel anything yet, Justin?" Bella said, seemingly from somewhere far off as I concentrated.

Oh, I felt something all right. I felt a grin spread across my face and quickly tightened my mouth so as not to give myself away. With my incubus senses extended, I could taste some of Bella's emotions, namely frustration and concern. She really cared about me and was worried sick about my abilities. A wave of guilt came over me. Here I was, screwing around while she was dedicating time and energy toward helping me.

Easing back on the emotional throttle, I started slowly withdrawing my senses, trying to focus instead on the magical energy in the air around me. The thread of my essence abruptly tingled in a way it never had before. The feeling was so alien, it shocked me out of my trance and my eyes jolted open.

"What is it?" Bella asked.

"I felt something weird."

"Describe it."

I shrugged. "I dunno. All tingly. It made me feel funny."

"Funny?" She took a seat across from me, gaze intense.

"Well, not funny like when someone touches you in your no-no place, but—"

"Justin, be serious."

I sighed. "Let me see if I can find it again." I closed my eyes and breathed deep. Nothing happened for what seemed an eternity. I realized whatever I'd done had been with my incubus senses extended, so I pushed it out in different directions. Still, nothing happened. Setting aside the emotions emanating from Elyssa and Bella, I forced back my own frustration and probed for the strange sensation again.

All of my senses tingled with such abruptness, I yelped and jerked back. My chair fell over backwards with me in it. Bella leaned down, her violet eyes laughing at me though her mouth held a firm line. She offered a hand and pulled me up with dhampyric strength that belied her petite frame.

"I think you've found the magic," she said, a note of triumph in her voice.

"Did you really?" Elyssa said, eyes wide with delight.

I grinned. "That's magic? It feels nothing like when it's trapped in a circle."

"How does it feel?" Elyssa said. "All I feel when I'm in a circle is pressure in my ears."

"You don't feel the static in the air?" I asked.

She shook her head.

"Strange." I shrugged. "I feel pressure in my ears, too. Depending on the amount of magic in the circle, it's like an electric charge in the air." I set my chair upright and sat again, extending my incubus senses. When I focused on the tingling sensation, it flooded back, nearly overwhelming me. It wasn't unpleasant, just weird.

"Do you feel it?" Bella asked.

I opened my eyes, maintaining my link. Usually when my demonic senses were active, I saw the ghostly, glowing auras of the people around me and sensed their emotions. Looking at Bella and Elyssa, I saw them now, both glowing and healthy with positive emotion. In addition, I noticed a smoky haze in the air and motes of bright light, some drifting lazily, others zipping past like little stars. A bright ball of white the size of my head rotated around a similarly sized ball of glowing black, their twin orbits carrying them down until they vanished into the ground. Tiny capillaries of light pulsating between black, white, and gray ran through the floor and the walls as well. The lines zigged and zagged in places, sometimes broadening into finger width streams before narrowing into a line so thin as to be almost invisible.

I reached my hand for a hazy puff of gray floating before my eyes. It swirled around, insubstantial as a cloud, feeling like nothing to my hand. A spark of flickering ultraviolet passed through Bella's head and out the other side. I snatched at it, but my hand closed on nothing.

"What are you doing?" Bella asked, dodging away.

"The magic. It's all around us!"

She quirked an eyebrow. "Yes, that's generally true."

"And it's like little clouds shooting stars, and lines."

Her other eyebrow climbed even with the first. "What are you talking about?"

"The energy!" I swirled a little cloud with a finger until it resembled a miniature tornado. "This is freaking awesome."

"Justin, you can't actually *see* the magic around us, although you can feel it."

"Are you sure?" I looked at her through my incubus senses, watching her aura cloud gray with doubt. I shrugged. "Maybe it has something to do with the way I'm sensing the magic."

"And how is that exactly?"

I explained it to her.

"You never described it like that before," Elyssa said, frowning ever so slightly after I finished. "I mean, I guess we've never sat down and talked about it."

"Intriguing," Bella said, tapping her chin. "Arcanes have a sixth sense for magical energy. It is possible your incubus sixth sense is entwined with your arcane sense, and it is this which grants you the ability to see the magical energy, or at least a representation of it."

I felt elated. Magic suddenly went from boring and pointless to something I could actually do and see. I flicked my senses on and off, looking at the magical energy. "Maybe I have a sixth and seventh sense. I mean, why does everyone always call it a sixth sense anyway?"

Bella waved my question away with a flick of her hand. "This is fascinating, Justin, it truly is. But whatever it is will have to wait further study. First, you need to learn to store the energy in your well. Otherwise, it really does you no good."

"Can't I channel it straight out of the air? Does it really need to go into storage first?"

"You need to concentrate the energy inside so you can focus and bend it to your will. You can't do that without filling your well. It's the same as making a circle. The more concentrated the energy, the more powerful your spells will be. This is why Shelton and I had you practice blowing out candles and lighting them first. Such a feat is possible even without storing any energy, though we had hoped you might stumble your way into it as many new practitioners do, without us explicitly teaching it."

I looked at her. "You mean most newbs can store energy instinctually?"

She nodded. "Just like your incubus senses triggered without you controlling them. I believe your primary instincts as an incubus have overshadowed your magical abilities. It's really no surprise. In fact, I would surmise from how similar you are in appearance to your father that you inherited more from his side of the family than from the Arcanes on your mother's side."

"I agree," Elyssa said. "He has his mom's nose, judging from the pictures I've seen of her, but everything else looks a lot like his dad."

I touched my nose, trying to remember the shape of my mom's before she abandoned me and Dad to supposedly rescue Ivy from the clutches of her evil parents. "Okay, so how do I store the magic?"

Bella leaned back and balanced her chin on a hand, eyes distant with thought. After a moment, she pursed her lips and said, "How do you fill yourself with emotional energy?"

I shrugged. "I dunno. My tendril sucks it in automatically, like I'm drinking with a straw."

"Perhaps you could do the same with the magical energy?"

"Sure, why not?" I closed my eyes and reached into the place inside where I caged the demon and loosed my senses. When I opened my eyes, I saw the wondrous universe of magical energy again. Extending a tendril, I made contact with a puff of magic. The tingling sensation made me feel giddy as it curled around my probe and melted into it. Other particles of magic drifted toward the curling strand of my essence, drawn to it like a magnet. Soon, the air around it was hazy with energy.

"I'm doing it," I said with a jubilant shout and pumping a fist in the air. "Booyah!"

Bella squeezed my hand. "Great job, Justin."

I glanced at her and saw a similar haze around her aura. "Are you drawing in magic, too?" I asked.

She tilted her head. "How did you know?"

"I can see it melting into you."

"Within a minute or so, you should feel full, as though you've just eaten." She patted her stomach as if to illustrate her point.

"If it's anything like when I feed on emotions, I don't feel full so much as I just don't feel ravenous anymore." I really wasn't feeling full at all from drawing in the magic except the exhilarating rush of energy as it flooded along my senses.

"It shouldn't take long," Bella assured me. "Most new practitioners have a much smaller well which expands with use. You have to stretch it little by little or you might feel sick."

I continued to draw in magic, watching as it flowed from the tiny veins in the floor, up to my tendril, and into me. After another minute, I gave Bella an unsure look. "I don't think I'm doing it right."

She touched my chest and spoke a word, closing her eyes in concentration. "I sense energy in you, but I'm not very good at determining how much magic you've drawn in. Someone versed in arcane healing arts, like Meghan Andretti, could probably tell you more." She opened her eyes and smiled. "In any case, you probably have enough energy to work with."

I closed my eyes and walled up the demon part of me. I wondered sometimes if it was really a part of me, or if I had an alien presence living within. It brought a whole new meaning to the term "inner demons".

"By the way, you need to practice absorbing magic without closing your eyes first."

"But I have to close my eyes so I can concentrate."

Bella offered an apologetic smile. "I don't expect you to get it down pat today, but if you're in a situation requiring fast thinking and magic, you won't be able to close your eyes and concentrate."

My heart sank a little. "Dang. I thought I'd really improved."

She squeezed my hand. "You're doing great, Justin. You just learn differently from anyone else I've ever taught."

"He's definitely different," Elyssa said with a wink.

I stuck out my tongue at her. "Ha, ha."

"I'm going to make some tea and then we'll resume lessons," Bella said, and left the room.

Something prodded my leg from within the front pocket of my jeans. I leapt to my feet and felt inside, finding my new phone. "What the hell?"

"What?" Elyssa said.

"My phone poked me in the leg."

"Oh, you must have it set to poke instead of vibrate."

I glanced at the caller ID, but it was blocked. "Hello?"

"Justin, it's Felicia."

Adam Nosti's little sister, who just so happened to also be a vampire. I sucked in a breath. "Are you okay? Are you still spying on Maximus?"

Static crackled in the receiver, obscuring some of her words. "...don't have time. Maximus has something new for recruiting." More white noise obliterated whatever she said next.

"I can't hear you," I shouted into the microphone. "Reception is really bad." I turned on the speaker so Elyssa could listen in.

Felicia's voice cut in for a second then back out, leaving us in silence. I thought I'd lost her, when suddenly, she was back. "I don't know if you can hear this, Justin, so I'll repeat it again. Maximus has some kind of blood potion. I don't know where he got it, but it turns people into vampires."

Chapter 6

Elyssa and I stared at each other, stunned by Felicia's words.

"Are you sure?" I asked, praying the signal didn't break up again.

"Oh, thank god you're still there." She paused, her breathing fast and panicked. "I don't have long," she hissed. "I'm positive about it. He showed it to one of his top guys. I've been sleeping with him to get information."

I felt my face blanch at the thought of her casual use of sex as a tool. "Felicia, you need to get out of there and go back to your brother."

"Is—is Adam doing okay?" she said, sounding like a little girl. "Will you tell him I love him and miss him?"

"He's very proud of you, Felicia, but you're putting yourself in danger."

"I know. But you, of all people, know I owe some good karma back to the universe."

"Where's Maximus now?" Elyssa said.

"Down here," Felicia said, as if that should be clear to us.

"No, I mean what city?"

"Bogota. He's been using the arch at La Casona to travel, to where, I don't know. Ever since I came back, he hasn't given me a second glance. He has new girlfriends."

"Does he have my sister, Ivy?" I asked, almost face-palming for not having asked that immediately.

"Your sister?" She paused. "I have no idea. So many people come in and out of here all the time, it's impossible to keep up." A noise sounded, like someone knocking on a door. "Crap," she hissed. "Just a minute, hot stuff," she said in a loud voice. "I'm in the bathroom."

"Who is that?" I asked.

"Alvin, the guy I'm sleeping with," she said in a whisper. "Tell the Templars they need to stop Maximus. I don't know who's making the potion, but it doesn't take much to turn a nom into a vampire. Right now, his quantities are limited, but if he figures out how to mass produce it, there won't be anything left in Bogota except a bunch of high school and college-aged vampires who live to serve Maximus. An army."

"We'll stop him," Elyssa said, giving me a look.

"Alvin said it doesn't always work. Sometimes, it turns them into vamplings."

I shuddered. "Oh, crap." Vamplings were part zombie and part vampire, and carried a highly contagious magical virus. One bite could turn a person into a member of the walking dead. I'd seen it happen before, and it wasn't pretty.

"Tell Adam I love him," Felicia said. I'll try to find out about your sister too. Bye, Justin." The connection went dead.

Elyssa pulled out her phone, tapped in a number, and put it to her ear. After a few seconds, she made a face and hung up.

"Who are you calling?"

"Michael. He needs to know about this."

"What about your father?"

Her nose wrinkled. "I'd prefer Michael gave him the news."

"Why? You think your dad won't listen to you?"

Elyssa shrugged. "After mind-wiping me and nearly exiling me to Europe, I don't think I'm the one he'll listen to. And with Jack dead—" She trailed off as a lone tear trickled down her cheek.

I wiped it away with my thumb and caressed her cheek. "You're the best of them," I said. "Talk to him. He'll believe you."

She looked at me, her eyes wet and rimmed with red. "Maybe so, but, ever since Nightliss restored my memories, I've felt so angry at him. Angry and hurt and worthless."

"You're not worthless, Elyssa." I gripped her shoulders and narrowed my eyes. "How could you say that? I mean, you're always so strong-willed about everything. Like the time you nearly took off my head."

A small smile lit her face. "When I found out you were spawn?"

I nodded. "I thought I was a goner."

"I was pissed. Hurt."

"Kind of like now?"

She shook her head. "Now, it's different." She clenched her hands tight and wiped away another tear with the back of her hand. "Anyway, you're right. I'll tell Father. Looks like we have more than one reason to finish Maximus now."

Shelton and Bella walked around the corner, steaming cups of tea in their hands. Bella's eyes looked bright and happy as she spoke to him. Shelton held his arcphone in one hand, studying it, nodding absentmindedly while Bella chattered away.

"Looks like the recording was made this morning around three a.m." He flicked his fingers across the phone and the screen expanded until it was about a foot across. "I also found the location information."

Hope surged in my chest. "You know where they were keeping her?"

"Hold on, hotshot." Shelton held out a hand. "Let me finish my train of thought before you bust in."

"Sorry."

"The location information was partially corrupted." He pointed to a pulsing blue dot in the center of a large circle on a map. The circle took in most of Atlanta, extending out to the northern suburbs. "The bad news is we don't know the exact location where this recording was made. The good news is she was here in Atlanta."

I clenched a hand into a fist. "And the worst news is, she's in Bogota now."

Shelton and Bella exchanged confused looks.

"Bogota?" Bella said. "How do you know?"

I filled them in on Felicia's phone call and Maximus's blood potion. "Looks like I'm headed south."

Bella took my hand. "Justin, you still have a great deal to learn. Give me and Harry a few days to teach you."

I shook my head. "Look, I know it's important, but Maximus has my sister. The devil knows what he plans to do with her. For all I know, it's already too late."

Elyssa took my other hand. "I have to agree with Justin. Once my father hears this, he'll probably mobilize the Templars and move out fast. "

"That'll take at least a day," Shelton said. "Until then, your ass is mine."

"At least let us teach you a couple of defensive spells," Bella said.

"And let me program some useful stuff into your new phone." Shelton minimized his arcphone and jammed it into a pocket. "No sense rushing off to get killed."

"They're right," Elyssa said. She pulled me away from the others until we were alone. "I'll go to Father in person. Make him see how important it is we mobilize quickly. The minute I know something, I'll let you know."

I really didn't want her to go, but the orderly little nerd with angel wings on my right shoulder told me it was for the best if I stuck around and learned a thing or two. The horned demon on my other shoulder agreed since it didn't want to die any more than I did. Pressing Elyssa to the wall with my body, I kissed her hard.

"I wish—"

She gave me a steamy sensual smile and smacked me on the bottom. "Me too. There'll be time later." She kissed me again. "Open the stairs for me?"

As Elyssa vanished up the stairs, a longing tugged at my heart to follow her. To race to the Grotto and take the arch to La Casona in Bogota immediately. The urgency of finding my little sister burrowed into my stomach and weighed it down with dread and helpless frustration. What good would it do me to dash down to Maximus's stronghold without an army backing me up? And what if Thomas Borathen decided her rescue wasn't all that pressing?

Now, more than anything, I needed a snappy montage of happy songs and scenes of uplifting moments from my training so I could learn magic really fast. If only real life were like the movies.

Sigh.

Over the next few hours, Shelton showed me how to store and use spells on my arcphone, digging around in his archives for basic, yet useful spells I could use to get myself out of a bind. Unfortunately, I still had problems drawing in magic without closing my eyes, and even more problems executing a spell with little more than a whimper of power.

"Maybe I'm just too weak," I said. It was late. My eyelids drooped and my tummy felt like I'd just eaten a bowlful of Ebola virus. "Why does my stomach hurt so bad?"

Shelton pocketed his phone and crossed his arms. "It ain't weakness kid. You haven't used your well before. It's like a muscle. The more you use it, the more it can hold. The sick feeling is magic poisoning. Your body isn't used to storing it."

"Is my well a physical part of my body?"

He scrunched up his forehead. "Nah, it's an extension of aura, but it can sure feel like it's a part of your body." He held out a hand and helped me out of my seat. "C'mon. Get some rest and we'll start again in the morning." His phone dinged.

I glanced at the screen and saw an image of Elyssa standing outside the secret entrance. "Um, I would let her in, but I think if I try to do one more spell, I'll puke."

Shelton grinned. "I'll do it."

My heart leapt at the thought of curling up in a nice warm bed with her, even if it was just to sleep. I was too tuckered out to do much more.

Elyssa flew down the stairs the minute the barrier illusion vanished. "Justin, I'm sorry, I really am, but—"

Thomas Borathen came down the stairs, a squad of Templars at his heels. His icy blue eyes bored into me.

"What the hell?" Shelton said.

Elyssa's father ignored Shelton, folding his arms over his chest. "So, young Mr. Slade, are you ready to go?"

"Where?"

"Why, Bogota, of course. Elyssa explained the situation. I communicated with Commander Salazar, and his people are standing by."

I raised an eyebrow. "Just like that?"

He snapped his fingers. "Just like that. We are Templars, young man, not a ragged group of misfits."

"The kid's exhausted," Shelton said. "Can't this wait?"

Thomas glanced coolly at the sorcerer. "He can rest upon his arrival."

"Why are you in such a hurry?" Bella said, appearing from the hallway.

42

Now that the shock was wearing off, some of my earlier depression melted away. "It's fine, Bella." I didn't know why Thomas was so eager to get me on my way, and I didn't care. He was ready to help, and I was ready to go. "I'll pack." I'd stored clothes at a couple of Shelton's hideouts in case of an emergency. Despite Thomas's offer of a place to stay at Big Creek Ranch, aka The Ranch, aka the Templar compound in Atlanta, I didn't feel safe sleeping in a place where he could come by and decapitate me at any moment.

Elyssa followed me back to the bedrooms. "He really surprised me," she said.

"Maybe he wants to get the blood potion off the streets," I replied. "I sincerely doubt he gives two craps about my sister."

"No, he agreed before I even told him about the blood potions."

I shoved a handful of clean underwear into my duffel bag and paused. "Seriously?"

She nodded. "Knowing my dad, he probably wants to move fast before the enemy finds out about his movements."

"How would Maximus know what your dad is up to?"

"He might have vampires watching the compound for all we know." Elyssa crossed her arms. "Keeping the enemy off balance is a favorite tactic of my father's."

"You're going, right?" I grabbed a stack of T-shirts and jammed them next to the underwear.

"Oh, yeah. I made it clear he wasn't keeping me out of this operation."

I smiled. "Good." Some of the worry lifted from my chest. Things would be all right.

"Better pack a little warm," she said. Bogota isn't hot like the south part of the country."

"I don't need sweaters. I'll just cuddle with my smoochie-poo," I said dropping my clothes and taking her in my arms. "How's that, honey boo bear chocolate pie?"

"Sweet Jesus almighty," Shelton said from the doorway, his mouth screwed up in disgust.

My face went red hot. "Uh—"

Elyssa burst into laughter.

43

Shelton waved off my reply. "Look, I ain't about to let an apprentice of mine go wandering off into vampire central without some backup. Me and Bella are coming along."

The embarrassment melted away, replaced by gratitude. I grinned. "Thanks, Shelton."

"Yeah, don't get all mushy on me, kiddo. I just don't want you to be an embarrassment to me by getting your ass kicked." He shook his head and left, muttering.

"Honey boo bear chocolate pie?" Elyssa said with a snort. "I'll need to do some research if I'm ever going to top that one."

I chuckled. "Oh, my head is full of romantic nicknames."

"I think you need to look up the definition of romantic."

My duffel bag bulged with clothes and other supplies. I'd even remembered to pack a toothbrush. As I contemplated the impending journey and hopeful rescue, I thought of Felicia and wondered if we could extract her while we were in there. It made me think of her brother, Adam Nosti. Had she told him anything? Did he even know where she was?

I pulled out my new phone. "Nookli, call Meghan Andretti."

"Do you want me to search the web for *Magic Fishnets*?" my phone replied.

"What? No, *Meghan Andretti*," I said carefully enunciating her name.

Meghan sounded surprised but happy to hear from me. No doubt she was hoping and praying I wasn't about to drag her into yet another mission where mutilation by an enraged demon was a likely possibility.

"Is Adam around?" I asked.

"Sure, he's in his study," she replied, in the voice of someone only just growing used to the quirks of dating someone with an obsession. For Adam, it was finding out who murdered his parents years ago and left him and Felicia orphaned. His obsession had driven Felicia to drugs and eventually to Maximus and life as a vampire. Unlike her brother, she had no arcane talents.

"Justin, what's up?" Adam said, sounding pleased to hear from me.

I hated to burst his happy bubble. "I just heard from your sister."

"You did?" Apprehension tightened his voice.

44

I filled him in.

"Son of a—Justin, she can't stay in that vipers' lair any longer. We've got to get her out."

"I'll have an army of Templars helping, Adam. I'm sure we can do that."

He made a frustrated noise. "I'm coming with you. What? Justin, hang on." The sounds of muffled talking filtered through the receiver. After a moment, I heard his hand slide off the microphone. "Um, *we're* coming."

"Adam, I really don't want to drag you into my mess—"

"Both of our sisters are in trouble, Justin. Hold tight. Meghan and I will meet up with you."

I looked at Elyssa. "Are we taking the Obsidian Arch at the Grotto?"

She nodded and checked the time. "Father says we're shipping out at midnight."

I relayed the information to Adam and ended the call. I knew Adam would want in. I mean, who'd pass up the opportunity to die screaming with me as a traveling companion? At least I'd feel a lot better adding another strong Arcane to the group, not to mention Meghan and her expert healing abilities. Geez, with Bella and Shelton coming along, this promised to be the bestest Justin Party ever. Except I forgot to bring cake. Maybe one of the Arcanes could pull cupcakes from behind our ears. "Your dad has this all planned out, doesn't he?"

Elyssa shrugged. "Commander Borathen doesn't mess around when he makes a decision."

When we rejoined the others near the exit, Bella and Shelton were in a heated discussion with Thomas.

"I take it you have no compunction about taking untrained civilians into this conflict?" Thomas said, his voice deadly calm as always.

"Dude, I'm probably the least trained here and you obviously don't care about tossing me to the wolves." I set my arms akimbo and gave him the look my mom reserved for me when she caught me doing something naughty. "Don't for a minute think you've fooled me into believing you're doing this for my benefit. I'm sure you have some ulterior motive I haven't figured out. Even this morning, you seemed eager to kick me back down to Colombia."

His cool expression didn't flicker as he replied. "What I do is uphold Overworld law, Mr. Slade. For that, I will do anything or sacrifice anyone without compunction. In this instance, our goals coincide. I happen to believe you can play a pivotal role in bringing down Maximus, thanks to your history with that criminal."

There was a moment of uncomfortable silence as we digested Thomas's blunt words. I forced myself to maintain eye contact with his cool, blue gaze and found no shred of doubt lingering within.

I cleared my throat and shifted my feet. "Alrighty, then. Shall we go?"

Thomas turned and left, followed by the rest of us. We piled into the back of a large black SUV, and headed toward the Grotto. I had no idea what to expect once we reached Bogota except for one thing.

Maximus would not go down without a fight.

Chapter 7

Bogota welcomed me with cold, gray arms. Dark clouds scudded overhead, drowning the sunlight. The Obsidian Arch at La Casona sat in the middle of a sprawling plaza in the center of the city, seemingly in plain sight. At the back of the square stood an ordinary wooden door, which—according to Bella—led into the pocket dimension housing La Casona. Since Colombia was her turf, she gave me a quick history lesson as we hustled from the large circle of polished stone beneath the arch.

"Illusion hides this place from the noms, and wards keep them from wandering too close," she said as we crossed the plaza toward a group of waiting Templars.

"We're going into La Casona," Adam said, taking Meghan's hand in his.

"I need some supplies," the Arcane healer added. "We'll meet you at the compound in a couple of hours."

I noticed the way her face hardened every time she looked at Shelton. I also noticed how Shelton kept a healthy distance from Meghan. She'd told me Shelton's hands were dirty when it came to the death of her father. That he'd had dealings with Vadaemos Slade or someone close to him. Even though Meghan had never made any outright threats, I had the feeling it might be best to clear the air between the two just in case. Adam tugged on Meghan's hand and they headed toward the entrance.

Shelton approached the minute Meghan and Adam went through the door to La Casona. He regarded the area with wary eyes. "I've got some contacts in the area. It's possible they'll be able to help."

"Why do you look so uneasy?" I asked.

"Let's just say I haven't made many friends in this part of the world."

Bella raised an eyebrow. "Really, Harry, you didn't tell me that story."

He snorted. "It's a lot more than just one story, darlin'."

"You'll meet us at the compound later?" she asked. "I brought some board games along."

"No more board games," Shelton said, rolling his eyes. "I have something more interesting in mind."

Bella pursed her lips. "Oh, really?" Her voice took on an uncharacteristic sultry flavor. "Do tell."

"Poker."

"Unless it's strip poker, I'm not interested," Bella said, crossing her arms.

Shelton's eyelids went wide, and his face turned a shade of pink.

Elyssa snorted, and I gave Bella a questioning look. Sometimes I had trouble figuring out if she was being serious or not.

"What's wrong with strip poker between consenting adults?" Bella said with a smirk. She tapped Shelton on the nose. "Run along to your contacts, Harry. I'll see *you* back at the compound."

Shelton dug a finger under his collar and tugged on it, as though it felt a bit tight. "Maybe I'll find another place to stay."

Bella laughed. "Don't forget to layer your clothes. I wouldn't want you to lose too quickly."

"Keep in touch," I told Shelton as he hurried to leave. "And be careful."

He tipped his fedora at us and gave us a lopsided grin, his eyes straying to Bella. "I'm always careful."

As he headed for the entrance to La Casona, I noticed Templar guards patrolling the perimeter, and turned to Elyssa. "Didn't Felicia say Maximus used this arch to travel recently?"

She nodded.

"How is that possible with all the security?"

"I don't know." Her eyes latched onto something to our left.

Following her gaze, I saw Commander Christian Salazar, the Templar commander for Colombia, standing at ease, arms folded behind his back, legs shoulder-width apart. Thomas Borathen approached the other man and saluted then took Christian by the elbow and guided him toward the exit while they conversed. I tried to listen in with my super hearing, but the background thrum of the arch as it wound down obliterated their words before they reached my ears.

Salazar glanced back at me with narrowed eyes and shook his head at Thomas. The other man crossed his arms and gave him a withering gaze, but it didn't faze the Colombian. I followed Bella through a long brick archway, and emerged inside a fenced-in lot bordering a street congested with cars, foot traffic, and noise. A thick aroma of burnt diesel and other pollutants crowded my nose. The brick-paved street wound down a long hill between white adobe houses with barred windows and worn terracotta shingles. I looked behind me. The plaza looked like a tall, brick warehouse from the outside. No doubt the razor wire and chain-link fence kept most casual passers-by from trying to get in.

A shadowy flicker in the corner of my eye sent a panicky jolt straight to my heart. I ducked and rolled, eyes scanning for the shadow creature. Instead, I found a gray, cloudy shape drifting around the perimeter. A group of kids were trying to squeeze under the fence. The cloud morphed into a humanoid shape, its ghostly hands brushing the children on the head. The intruders abruptly stood up and wandered down the sidewalk, eyes blank, faces expressionless.

"What is that thing?" I asked with a shudder.

"A minder," Bella said.

"Those things give me the creeps," Elyssa said with a shudder.

I noticed several more of the ghoulish wisps patrolling the fence. "What did that thing do to those kids?"

"Minders twist the thoughts of people." Bella gave a shiver of her own. "Arcanes discovered these things lurking in the Gloom decades ago and, after several disastrous attempts, learned they are sentient to a certain degree."

"They trained them like animals," Elyssa said, eyes angry. "And allow them to feed on noms."

"They feed on normal humans?" I couldn't really muster any outrage, given my need to feed on human emotion.

"When the minder touched those boys, it fed on their thoughts and memories. We still don't know exactly how they do it, but prolonged contact with those things could permanently damage your mind."

I sidestepped farther away from one of the minders as it drifted along the fence in our direction. "They're really that harmful?"

"I would tell you to ask the first Arcanes who discovered them, but they're stark-raving mad now." Bella's violet eyes grew unfocused as if she were looking at a memory of her own.

A line of black SUVs waited outside the fence. Christian and Thomas piled into the lead vehicle, still talking heatedly. Bella and Elyssa climbed into the vehicle behind it. I walked around the back of the same vehicle to toss in my luggage when I felt a cold ping on my supernatural radar. It was close. Maybe fifty feet away. I'd felt that sensation enough to know exactly what it was. I spun to face it.

The Templars felt it, too. Within a split second of the sensation, dozens of swords slid from sheaths. Another cold blip popped up behind me. Another to my side. Followed by another. And another.

"Starfire! Get down!" someone shouted as a ball of white energy the size of my head shot from a rooftop down the road and streaked toward the lead SUV.

"Dad!" Elyssa shouted. She dove from the backseat. Rolled on the pavement and pivoted for her father's SUV. But it was too late.

The fireball slammed into the grill of the vehicle, suffusing the frame with brilliant white light, and exploded. My body left the ground and flew through the air, slamming against the hard brick road. A twisted and charred bumper slammed onto my chest. I sucked in a wheezing breath and heard the whine of tinnitus buzzing in my ears. Screams and shouts echoed as though through a long tunnel.

I shoved the blackened bumper off me and rolled onto my side. Noms scattered in all directions as dozens of dark forms leapt from rooftops and hit the ground running. I pushed myself to my knees. The effort sent waves of agony through my back and ribs. Something hard and sharp brushed against the inside of my arm. I looked and found a blade of shrapnel jutting from my side.

"Justin!" someone screamed.

I saw Elyssa surrounded by a circle of Templars fighting off a mob of vampires. Some of the attackers looked barely out of middle school while others looked college aged. Maximus obviously didn't discriminate by age or gender, because there were plenty of females in the riotous mix. Each attacker wore a red armband around one bicep, each bearing a valentine-shaped heart with two fangs piercing it. Some vampires wore pink shirts with the same heart logo on it.

A flutter of pink drew my attention to the SUV Elyssa had been in. Bella hung halfway out of the backseat. Blood dripped from her outstretched hand, forming a puddle on the ground. I roared with anger. Grabbed the jagged shard of metal in my side and pulled it out. The world faded to black for an instant, and a scream tore from my throat. As the ringing in my ears subsided, I pushed myself to my feet and ran for Bella.

I dragged her from the SUV. She groaned. Her eyelids fluttered.

"Bella?" I said.

"I—I'm okay, Justin."

I watched a slice down her arm slowly heal as her supernatural healing kicked in. "Can you run?"

She nodded.

Strong hands grabbed me by the shoulders and jerked me away. Threw me across the road. I turned my roll into a three-point landing and looked into the red eyes of a gaggle of vampires. One-on-one, I knew I could beat them, but—

Something snapped around my neck. I turned and saw a female vampire smile, her fangs glistening. Bella shouted something.

And the world went black.

Chapter 8

Elyssa

Elyssa stared at the burned-out hull of the SUV in shock. Her father and Christian were in there! Adrenalin burned through her blood. She had to get to them. He couldn't be dead. But he probably was. What sick joke was the universe playing on her to steal her brother and her father from her in the space of a week? She reached for a sword, ready to slice through the mob of vampires surrounding her meager circle of Templars, but her sheath was empty. The sword was in the back of one of the SUVs.

She kicked away one attacker and looked around to see who was in charge. Everyone looked too busy fighting for their lives to think about the chain of command. Considering how many vampires were swarming them, she had to do something.

"Call for reinforcements," she shouted to a local Templar fighting next to her. "I'll cover your position."

He gave her a confused look at first, then seemed to realize who she was. He nodded and backed inside the circle, pulling out a cell phone.

The circle was faltering. Dozens of other Templars were scattered about, fighting individual battles. Considering the odds, they wouldn't last long. Whoever was supposed to have taken charge hadn't. She took a deep breath and bellowed, "Templars, form cohort! Skirmish ranks!"

As if she'd just pushed a button, individual Templars shouted out positions, trading spots and lining up in a wedge, while scattered individuals formed a smaller rank and fought their way toward the main group.

Elyssa backed behind the wedge for a clear view of the battlefield, and checked for Justin. She'd seen him through the throng only a moment ago. Thankfully, the attacking vampires were untrained at hand-to-hand. Maximus was obviously counting on sheer numbers to do the job, but with order restored to the Templar ranks, the tide of battle was turning.

She clubbed the closest vampire in the nose. He yelped. Elyssa thrust a foot straight out, slamming into his chest. He flew back, taking several other vampires tumbling to the ground with him.

With her view momentarily cleared, Elyssa spotted Justin dragging Bella from an SUV. She looked okay, but—Elyssa's eyes caught sight of a group of vampires rushing the two of them. Before he could react, a vampire slapped a sleeper collar on Justin.

"No!" Elyssa shouted. Despite years of training and a sense of duty hanging heavy around her neck, she didn't hesitate a second. She left the protective wedge and ran for him.

The vampire, who'd collared Justin, slung him over her back and dashed down the road. Elyssa dodged a clumsy swing from a vampire and shoved him away. Another charged straight at her. She ducked under his grasp and flipped him over her shoulder. Spun and drove her heel into his neck. A bone cracked and he lay still.

The vampires who'd cornered Justin now blocked the road. The diminutive sorceress, Bella, faced them down, a pale staff in her hand. Though Bella was a dhampyr like Elyssa, she was just an Arcane, not a trained fighter. Elyssa threaded a gauntlet of vampires, racing for Bella and Justin's kidnapper.

Before she could reach Bella, something hard smacked Elyssa in the temple. She rolled sideways to avoid another blow, but her eyesight blurred from the impact. She sprang back to her feet. Her vision cleared just as a muscular woman drove her fist right at the bridge of Elyssa's nose. She caught the fist. Twisted the arm. Drove her elbow into the vampire's arm and heard the crack of bone. The vampire screeched.

Elyssa swept the other woman's legs from under her, grabbed the vampire's neck, and drove her face-first into the brick street with a *crunch*. She looked back at Bella. Several vampires fanned out, encircling the dhampyr. Behind them, Elyssa saw the form of Justin's abductor speeding downhill on foot.

There was no way she'd help Bella with these vampires in time to give chase.

Bella twirled her staff and smacked a vampire in the head. She spun the rod around her waist and, sweeping low, upended the next vampire. The staff whirled over a shoulder, swung down and cracked the downed man in the face. Before the other vampires could react, Bella shouted, "*Kineesi!*" and stabbed the rod into the road. A bright blue light exploded around her, flinging the remaining attackers in all directions. One flew over Elyssa's head and bowled over several of his comrades.

"Holy smokes," Elyssa said. She'd obviously underestimated the woman.

The sorceress saw Elyssa and motioned her over. "We can still catch them!" She rushed to the back of the SUV and grabbed something. Turned and tossed a silver katana hilt-first to Elyssa.

Without another word, the two women sped down the street.

A blinding pulse of energy explodedthe bricks next to Elyssa. Shards of brick stabbed her flesh in countless places. Bella cried out. Somehow, they kept their feet.

"What the hell is that?" Elyssa shouted, looking back over her shoulder.

"There, look," Bella said, turning and pointing at a rooftop in the distance.

Zooming in her sight, Elyssa spotted a man on a roof, holding a sheet of paper in his hand. "Is he an Arcane?"

The other woman grabbed Elyssa by the arm and guided her toward the buildings on the left, taking them out of the man's line of sight. "No, he's a vampire, but he has weaponized scrolls."

And he'd killed her father. Rage boiled in her chest. Part of her wanted to turn around and tear the man to bloody shreds. But her father was dead and there was nothing she could do about it. Right now, she needed to catch the vampire with Justin. Her jaw hurt and Elyssa realized she was clenching her teeth so tight, they felt as though they would crack.

The vampire with Justin vanished around a corner in the distance. Elyssa and Bella blurred after her, whipping past buildings and fleeing pedestrians. They rounded the corner and smacked into a crowd of waiting vampires. Bella tumbled through them, losing the grip on her staff. Elyssa converted her forward momentum into a jump kick, catching one attacker on the chin.

Bella punched one guy in the crotch from her position on the ground. He screamed and went down. She rolled away from a vampire's foot as he tried to stomp her. Elyssa dodged a clumsy lunge by an attacker and, grabbing his shoulders, vaulted over him. Her foot lashed out in a backward kick and sent him stumbling against a brick wall. Bella's staff lay only feet away.

Elyssa swatted aside a punch from a woman dressed in a skintight, leather suit who obviously thought becoming a vampire meant she could live out her Catwoman fantasy.

The woman hissed in Spanish and clawed at Elyssa's eyes. Elyssa gripped the other woman's wrists. Twisted them out and away from each other. Kneed the vampire in the stomach, and finished her with a roundhouse to the face. Catwoman went down in a ragdoll heap.

Bella yelped as one of the vampires landed a punch on her face. She wobbled but managed to keep her feet. Elyssa snatched the staff from the ground. Whirling it, she cleared a path back to Bella, clubbing vampires on the head with it. Though she'd trained with a bo staff, it wasn't her specialty. True, she had the katana Bella had given her, but even as mad as she was, Elyssa couldn't bring herself to start slaughtering these stupid sheep Maximus called followers. They were brainwashed. Not evil.

Bella dodged a furious uppercut from the vampire. Elyssa came up behind the man and swung the staff up hard, nailing him in the crotch with the knobbed end of it. She pushed the staff forward. Bella grabbed the rod. Twirled it. Crushed the man in the balls with a fierce thrust. The vampire howled and fell to the ground, clutching at his injured manhood.

The two women exchanged fierce grins, and dashed past the fallen attackers.

The street dead-ended in two narrow alleys. Elyssa cursed. "Check the left, and I'll check the right," she said over her shoulder as she ran across the road. She reached the end of the alley and looked both ways down a long, deserted street. Bella emerged on the same street on the opposite side of a tall red-brick building.

"No!" Elyssa froze with indecision. Could the woman with Justin have already gotten away? She ran back into the alley and looked up the walls. It was at least three stories to the top and too wide for her to brace against. Elyssa ran up the left wall. About six feet up, she jumped the gap to the other wall. The moment her foot touched the rough brick, she reversed momentum and leapt back across. Within seconds, she reached the lip of the roof and pulled herself up.

The view here was better, but the crowded buildings and snarled alleys hid too much. The only movements she saw were still-fleeing pedestrians and the occasional car or truck in the distance. Police had formed a blockade on one end of the road, but not the other. The vampire with Justin must be headed away from the blockade, but there were too many narrow passageways and side streets for her to lose herself in. For all Elyssa knew, a waiting vehicle had already picked her up and Justin was gone.

"She went that way," Bella shouted from the ground, pointing toward a glowing green line wending down an alley.

"You used a spell?"

The other woman nodded. "We have to hurry. The trail will fade."

It'd take too long to get back down, Elyssa realized. Reversing her ascent wasn't as easy as jumping down the walls. She'd end up breaking her leg or worse, and the time required to recover would be all the time the abductor needed to get away. She looked at the street below. At the trail leading down the alley. She backed up to the opposite edge of the roof. Sprinted toward the ledge. Jumped.

Bella shouted something unladylike from below. Elyssa swung her arms to keep balanced. Already, gravity had her in its clutches. She stretched her foot forward. It barely caught the lip of the roof. Elyssa somehow kept her feet and ran.

"I'm following!" Bella shouted, her voice echoing from the alley.

Dodging right, Elyssa ran along the edge of the roof. The buildings were closer on this side. She jumped each gap without slowing. Ahead, a motor puttered to life. A tire screeched. A tiny green car pulled out from a parking space at the end of the alley. Elyssa saw Justin's limp form slumping in the passenger seat.

"It's him!" Elyssa shouted. She leapt across the alley to a lower building. Vaulted another gap and dropped onto a concrete wall below. Bella streaked past her as Elyssa made it to the alley floor. By the time she reached the street, Bella had pulled out her wand and was looking at the parked vehicles. Most of them were rusted heaps. Something chrome twinkled in the sunlight.

A motorcycle.

"This one!" Elyssa said, rushing to it.

Bella jammed her wand against the ignition. "*Contarte.*"

The engine roared to life.

Bella gripped her staff and shouted another word. It collapsed into a compact rod. She secured it to her waist and hopped on the motorcycle behind Elyssa, gripping her tight. "*Madre de dios,* this is exciting! Let's go."

Elyssa gunned it. The bike was an old Suzuki—a real piece of junk compared to her Harley—but the vampire couldn't hope to outrun it in the compact car she was in. The bike's rear tire squealed and the front end lifted off the ground. Bella squealed.

A figure leapt atop a roof several blocks down. Elyssa saw the person unroll a parchment.

"Another scroll caster," she said, shouting over the noise of the wind and the engine.

The moment she said it, a sheet of ice crackled and crept across the road in front of them. The bike hit it. The tires lost their grip on the nearly frictionless surface. Elyssa let off the gas, but it was too late. They spun out of control and there was nothing she could do about it. If they hit bare asphalt sideways, the bike would flip. Since neither of them were wearing armor, they'd end up with a bloody road rash or worse.

Bella held her wand out and twirled it. A solid blast of air hit the bike, stopping the spin and straightening the bike. Except now they were sliding backwards at breakneck speed. Elyssa slid the katana from the sheath on her back. Stabbed it against the ice and pivoted the bike a hundred and eighty degrees. The bike straightened an instant before the front tire hit pavement. The rubber squealed. The katana sparked against the cobblestones. She slid the sword back into its sheath with one hand while gunning the gas with the other.

A brilliant ball of starfire speared from the figure on the roof. Elyssa leaned hard to the side as a pumpkin-sized globe of white energy turned a nearby dumpster into a heap of glowing slag. The caster tore open another scroll. Another sphere of starfire coalesced and bolted at them. Elyssa sped up, but it was too late to dodge. Her only hope was to lay the bike down and that would hurt. A lot.

At the last minute, Bella shouted and the air overhead shimmered into a mirror-like surface. The energy rebounded like a moonshot. The scroll caster screamed and tried to dive to the side, but he was too slow. The crackling starfire caught him in the chest, vaporizing the right side of his body into blackened mist. His smoldering corpse rolled off the roof and clanged into an empty dumpster.

"Amateurs," Bella said in a loud huff.

Elyssa saw the green car weaving through traffic ahead. She almost smiled. Now that vampire bitch was hers. She split the lane between two cars. Swerved right to avoid another. Bella's grip tightened. The vampire's car broke free of the traffic jam and turned left. Elyssa weaved through the last of the cars and leaned so hard into the turn, her knee almost touched the ground, and the wheels squealed with the effort of holding the road.

The green car screeched through a roundabout, clipping several cars along the way. Elyssa spotted a break in the chain guarding the center of the roundabout and steered through it, cutting the distance between her and the car in half. A truck pulled out from an alley right in front of the car. It swerved away and crunched into another car in the opposite lane.

A lone figure jumped from the car and blurred away down the street, empty-handed. Elyssa braked hard and screeched to a stop. She leapt off the bike. Rushed to the car. Tore the door open and gasped. The passenger seat was empty.

"No." She spun on her heel, searching the nearby traffic. "No!"

Bella came to her side and shouted a stream of Spanish. "The bastards tricked us. They must have pulled him out while we were getting the motorcycle."

"Or skating on ice." Elyssa groaned and pounded her fist against the roof of the car. A tear of frustration and disbelief burned down her cheek. She turned to Bella, weak with the realization of everything that had happened today. More tears gathered in her eyes, though she fought with everything she had to keep them at bay.

"Oh, god, Bella. Oh my god." Her knees went weak and she clutched at the other woman for support. "I've lost Justin. And my dad, he's—he's—" she couldn't say it. How could Thomas Borathen, a man who'd survived wars and everything else the supernatural community had thrown at him, die? It wasn't possible. It couldn't be.

But it was.

Chapter 9

Euphoria filled my body, flooding me with warmth and contentment. A coppery odor filled my nostrils. My eyelids fluttered open. A tall, muscular man, his fangs glistening red in the dim yellow light, grinned.

"Mine at last, boy. Mine at last." Maximus tore a paper towel from a nearby holder and wiped the blood from his lips and his close-cropped goatee.

Horror washed away the euphoric feeling and I strained uselessly against diamond fiber straps securing my arms, legs, torso, and neck to a diamond fiber table. "Did you just drink my blood?" I said, gagging at the thought of his nasty fangs in my body.

"The first drink of many, boy." Maximus slid on a pair of dark wraparound shades and pulled on a tight leather trench coat. "I have tasted spawn blood before, but there is something different, even more spectacular, about yours."

"You nasty perv," I said, squirming with disgust.

"And to think those idiots Franco and Marcel let you get away." His eyes narrowed. "Serves them right for trying to double-cross me."

"Let me go, Maximus."

"Not a chance, boy. You took your spawn father from me, but I do believe I've traded up."

"You won't keep me here for long. The Templars are going to sweep through here and clean house."

He chuckled. "I hope they try." He leaned in close, the metallic odor of my blood on his breath. "I heard a lot of them didn't make it out of the raid on Franco's compound."

"Yeah, right," I hissed between clenched teeth. "You only wish."

"Oh, I don't wish, little spawn—I know. I supplied those weapons to his drug cartel along with a large supply of cursed ammunition."

He clucked his tongue. "I hear those bullets tore right through the much-vaunted Templar Nightingale armor."

My mind flashed back to my wild escape from Franco's compound. The chase. The plane ride from hell. The gunman who shot me and Elyssa. She'd been wearing Templar armor, but the bullets had gone through it like a knife through paper. We'd nearly died thanks to silver poisoning and the harmful spells on those bullets. If Maximus was really the supplier, it likely meant he had stash built up here. If the Templars came, he and his vampire army would mow through them like grass.

Anger flooded my chest. "What do you want with me? Why are you doing this?"

He straightened and crossed his arms across his chest. "You should know why I want you, little fish. Spawn blood will increase the potency of my own so I can finally turn noms."

"Is making more vampires all you care about?" I spat, imagining him sinking his fangs into my flesh over and over again as I grew weaker and unable to do a damned thing about it.

"Turning more noms is only a means to an end." He walked to the other side of the table and put a hand to his chin. "I grant them life eternal and supernatural powers. They will help me overturn the traditional order, the ancients who have ruled us like dogs. Eventually, we will overcome the spawn and turn them into our slaves. Not only will we rid the world of demon spawn, but we will finally be able to live as we were destined."

"As a bunch of blood-sucking parasites?"

The corner of his mouth twisted into a slow grin. "As the rulers of this world."

"No doubt with you as the almighty dictator of all."

"Perhaps." He looked across the large room and the other tables.

The neck strap allowed me to rotate my head just enough to glimpse a part of the room. It was obvious he and his cronies could strap down a hundred people in this place, judging from the length.

"There are those greater even than us who may have a say in who rules, however," the vampire said, eyes focused on something I couldn't see.

"Daelissa," I said. I knew she was involved in this mess. With my mind recovering from the horror of Maximus feeding on my blood, another thought occurred to me. "Where's my sister?" Cold dread laced my skin and plunged into my stomach. *Please let her be okay.*

His eyes snapped to me. "Your sister?"

"Where are you keeping her? Did you hurt her, you son of a bitch?"

Maximus regarded me for a long moment, one eyebrow arching. Understanding lit his expression. Then he threw back his head and laughed.

Bastard! Suffused with rage, I struggled against the bonds, but the diamond fiber resisted. Frustration welled in my chest as Maximus's laughter echoed across the large room. I loosed my inner demon and let it feed on rage, my helplessness. My desire to crush Maximus to a pulp. Stars of pain burst into sight as horns erupted from my forehead. My body swelled. And suddenly, I couldn't breathe. I felt my neck bulge against the straps, biceps and wrists straining at the material. As my body attempted to manifest into full demon form, it was choking me to death.

The world disintegrated before my eyes and my inner demon gave up. Woozy from lack of oxygen, my head lolled as far as the restraints would allow.

"Not going to work, little spawn," Maximus said, still sniggering. "And here I thought you knew how strong diamond fiber is."

"I *will* kill you," I said, in a rasping voice. "Laugh all you want, you filthy, leeching parasite, but I'll kill you and save my sister, you perverted sack of douchebaggery."

The vampire roared with laughter. "That's a good one. I'll have to save it for later." He reached out and casually slapped me on the cheek. "Because I'm feeling mildly compassionate, I'll tell you this, boy. I don't have your sister. The joke's on you."

My mouth dropped open but no words came out. Something in the vampire's eyes told me he wasn't lying. Why would he at this point? I lay completely at his mercy. The bastard hadn't been laughing because he had my sister—he'd been laughing because he didn't. I'd been lured down here. Tricked. Not even my demon form could get me out of this mess, and if the Templars tried to save me, Maximus's minions would tear them apart with enchanted bullets.

Maximus tsked. "Poor little spawn. Looks like Daelissa played you for a fool." He shook his head, speaking in the mocking tone people usually reserved for babies. "Don't worry too much. She does it to everyone, even me. I suggest you rest. I'll be hungry again in a few hours, and you'll need all the energy you can muster to replenish the blood I took earlier." He winked and walked behind me. A door squeaked open. For the first time since awakening, I sensed another cold presence outside the door. A female presence. My lips curled into a tight smile and it was all I could do not to laugh. Maximus was an idiot and I'd be out of here in no time.

I waited until Maximus's footsteps faded down the hallway before making my move. Closing my eyes, I extended a tendril toward the female vampire standing guard outside. I felt her cold aura. Overwhelmingly positive emotions welled from her, mostly adoration mixed with lust. Apparently, she wanted to break her off a piece of Maximus. All the better for me. I could manipulate most females into sexual feelings, thanks to my incubus *skillz*, but with her already feeling the way she did, luring her in here to cut me loose would be a snap.

Equalizing my emotional state with hers took a moment, because I wasn't feeling particularly lustful or happy at the moment. I eased my tendril into her aura, opening the channel to feed.

Alarm spiked. Anger quickly followed. The door banged open and a woman in her early twenties stormed in and stood over me. Long brown hair, matted and tangled, framed a pale homely face. She wore one of the pink T-shirts with the fang-pierced heart I'd seen during the attack and a pair of matching cargo shorts I could just make out with my peripheral vision.

Gripping the table to either side of my head, she leaned into my face, snarling and showing long yellowed fangs. "Try it again, spawn," she said in a girly voice, "and I'll cut these off." She reached a hand down to my crotch and gave a painful squeeze.

I yelped.

She smirked. "You don't think Maximus would put a female down here if she didn't know how to handle herself, did you?"

I looked her up and down with my eyes since I couldn't move my head much. "I don't know, looks like Maximus has pretty low standards for vampires nowadays. Can't you afford designer jeans?"

"We don't need that crap."

"And what's with these stupid hearts on the T-shirts? Did I miss Valentine's day?"

She ran a hand down one of the fangs on the symbol. "It's the symbol for Blood Rush." She pressed sharp fingernails into my stomach. "Maybe I'll tattoo it on your chest."

I squirmed, trying without success to get her hands off me.

She leaned over. Sniffed my neck. Licked it. "Mmm, so sweet. Too bad you belong to Maximus." She sighed. "Maybe he'll get me my own spawn soon." She walked away, slamming the door shut behind her.

Heartbeat thudding in my ears, I writhed uselessly against my bonds until my skin was raw. Lifting my head as far as the neck strap would allow, I looked at my body and flushed from head to toe. I didn't have on anything except boxers. A trickle of dried blood had pooled on my chest between my pectoral muscles. I gagged again, thinking of Maximus's nasty yellow fangs puncturing my skin.

"One requires help," said a calm, almost emotionless voice from somewhere behind me, sounding as though the owner might be in a far back corner.

I would have jumped except for the straps holding me down. "Really, you think so?" I said, unable to keep the sarcasm down to a dull roar.

"This entity believes so."

"This—what? Entity?" I strained my neck but couldn't twist it far enough to see more than a couple of tables to either side. Parts of the room were dark, florescent lights flickering in fitful spurts.

"Yes," replied the same deadpan voice. "This one is also an entity."

My neck felt sore from all the twisting, so I gave up trying to see whoever was speaking. "Okay, Mr. Entity, can you get me out of these straps?"

"This one is unable to do so, other entity."

"Call me Justin."

"This is a designation?"

"It's a name!" Had Maximus stuck me in here with a brain-damaged vampire? Or even worse, someone suffering dementia brought on by the vampling virus? Cold prickles walked down my spine. "Why are you unable to help me?"

"Justin, this one is also bound."

"Why do you keep saying 'this one'? Do you know how to use pronouns?"

"Pronouns—yes. There are many words inside. And some rules for using them."

"Okay, well rule number one, start using pronouns. You sound like an imbecile."

"This one—I will."

"That wasn't so hard, now was it?"

"This one does not feel the 'I' inside—in me."

My brain struggled to decipher what he'd just said and gave up. "What are you?"

"An entity."

I groaned. "What *kind* of entity? You sound male. Are you a vampire?"

"I do not know. I look like the others."

"Like Maximus? The tool bag who was in here talking to me?"

"Yes," he said in the same unfaltering tone. "Therefore, I must be a tool bag."

I would have laughed if not for wanting to cry even more. Great. Just great! Not only was I trussed up as Maximus's personal snack pack, but I had the intellectual equivalent of a lobotomized yak to talk with.

The willpower to talk abandoned me. I had to think, dammit. I closed my eyes and saw Maximus's leering face. When I'd accused him of kidnapping my sister, he'd been completely surprised. He didn't know a thing about it. Could Daelissa be behind this trick? Had she somehow faked the entire video? The memory of Bigglesworth's mocking smile and laughter slapped me in the face. His complete lack of concern for Ivy's kidnapping made sense now. That ball of sludge was in on the joke.

Heartache abruptly stabbed me in the chest as another possibility came to mind. What if Ivy had participated in the sham? What if this was her way of getting rid of me?

Please, no.

Daelissa may have cooked up the idea, but it didn't mean she hadn't used Ivy and the others to stage it. Maximus obviously hadn't lent his voice talent to it, but there were other ways to fake or use recorded versions of his voice. I thought back to the recording on the ASE and tried to remember exactly how Maximus's voice had sounded on it. But my memory was imprecise.

And now, it really didn't matter.

"Are you also a tool bag?" the voice from the back of the room said.

"I'm a tool bag. We're all tool bags." My hands and jaw clenched with rage, frustration, and worst of all, sorrow. My sister thought I was evil. She despised me enough to toss me to the vampires so they could enslave me and drink my blood forever. I felt the hot sting of a tear trickle down my cheek. Betrayal was such a wicked thing. I had tasted it when Mom left. When she told me Dad and I were no longer part of her family. I'd felt it again when Dad told me he was giving up on Mom and marrying Kassallandra. And with this added betrayal, I just felt like crying.

Squeezing my eyes shut, I forced back the tidal wave of pity threatening to flood from beneath my lids. I thought of Elyssa and the Templars and wondered if they'd made it out of the ambush alive. Worry burrowed into my chest.

This isn't helping!

I had to do something. Figure out how to free myself. Sure, this table and the straps were made from what I had been told was nearly unbreakable material. By "nearly" I didn't know if I'd need an atom bomb or just a dragon to part the material. I'd seen Meghan press the ends of a diamond strap against concrete, bonding it to the surface. I'd seen her touch two ends of the material together to form a loop. To open the straps, she'd touched the material. Come to think of it, I'd toyed with it before as well, connecting and disconnecting it with a simple touch.

How did the material know when to bond and when to release? If I could reach one hand over and touch the strap holding the other, would it release me? Or did it somehow magically know I was the prisoner here and I couldn't free myself?

Why in the hell didn't I find out stuff like this until it was too late?

It didn't matter. I didn't have a free hand, and I couldn't slide one of my hands or bend my wrist enough to touch the straps holding them. There had to be another solution, something I was overlooking.

And then it came to me. I might have the answer if I could only figure out how to use it.

Magic.

Chapter 10

Elyssa

Elyssa and Bella trudged down the road back toward La Casona. The motorcycle had apparently given its life during the chase and wouldn't start when Elyssa tried.

"I can hotwire one of these scooters," Bella said as they passed a line of them outside a restaurant.

"Why bother?" Elyssa shook her head as weariness and numbing fatigue settled over her. She felt helpless. Hopeless. This day had taken so much from her. Now all that remained of her loved ones were her mother, Leia, and Michael.

"We'll get him back," Bella said, touching Elyssa on the arm. "I promise you."

How was that possible without her father or Christian to direct the troops? Who'd be in charge now? Michael? A stranger? She slumped onto a set of stairs outside an apartment building and pulled out her arcphone. She touched the screen, but only saw garbled static.

"It appears to be dead," Bella said, taking the arcphone and looking it over. She touched her wand to it. The screen flickered and went blank a moment, then reset and came up normally. "Or maybe it just needed a restart."

Elyssa took the phone. Pulled up Michael's number and stared at it. Should she call him? Maybe he already knew about the day's events.

Bella grabbed Elyssa by the shoulder and jerked her to her feet. The short woman gave Elyssa a stern look. "I know you've been through a lot, young lady, and you're in shock."

Elyssa stared numbly at her. She wanted to say something in her defense, but the words jumbled in her mind and refused to come out.

Was she in shock? She didn't feel the burning surge of anger or the gripping agony of sorrow. She felt nothing.

"We need to get you back," Bella said, and marched Elyssa to a tiny car parked at the curb. She touched a wand to the lock, opened the door, and shoved Elyssa inside. Climbed into the driver seat and hotwired the car with her wand.

A few minutes later they reached a road jammed with cars and people. Bella muttered something and got out. She spoke with a man and got back in the car. "The police have blocked the road. Looks like we'll have to walk the rest of the way."

Elyssa nodded and pulled herself out of the car. Her legs felt leaden. She just wanted to lie down and go to sleep. A fierce look from Bella quashed that notion. The sorceress motioned the Templar to follow. After a long slog through back alleys and side streets, all while dodging police barricades, they made it back to the outskirts of La Casona.

The burnt-out shell of her father's vehicle still gave off plumes of greasy smoke. The front end looked like it had been dipped in molten lava. The SUV Elyssa and Justin had been in looked almost as bad. The other vehicles were gone. A man in a black suit and dark glasses talked to a police officer nearby. Another similarly dressed man caught sight of the two women and approached them.

His eyes gauged Bella, and then Elyssa. He said something in Spanish.

Elyssa didn't understand. "What?"

"I said you'll have to leave this area. It's off-limits during our investigation."

"You're a Custodian?" Elyssa said.

The man's eyes narrowed. "Who are you?"

"Elyssa Borathen."

"Ah." He nodded and pointed toward a black sedan. "The driver will take you to the compound. It's important you don't speak with the local authorities Let us deal with them."

"I understand," Elyssa said.

"What are Custodians?" Bella asked as they approached the waiting car.

"They clean up supernatural incidents so the noms don't notice."

"Mhmm, so these are the same Templars who cleaned up the mess at the Friendly Hotel after Vadaemos's rampage?"

Bella's question reminded her of Jack. Her brother was dead. Her father was dead. "Yes." Elyssa muttered. Even talking was an effort.

The driver pulled out of the cordoned off area and into a blind alley.

"What are you doing?" Bella said, her voice alarmed.

The driver, a woman in the same type of black suit as the men, didn't say a word, but slashed her finger across what looked like an arcphone display in the dashboard. The car rose into the air. Bella gasped. Through the front window, Elyssa saw the hood shimmer into invisibility. Within seconds, they were skimming silently in the air over the jam-packed streets below.

"You Templars get the best toys," the sorceress said, watching the city roll past beneath. "I thought my flying rug was neat. How do you power invisibility for so long?"

"I couldn't say, ma'am," said the driver. "I just work here."

A short time later, the car set down in the center of a compound at the outskirts of the city. A young woman with dark hair, fair skin, and a strong Italian nose met them as they disembarked.

"Trouble follows your boyfriend everywhere," she said with a frown.

"Good to see you too, Fausta," Elyssa said, overcoming the urge to simply grunt at her. "What happens now?"

Fausta bared her teeth. "We kick some vampire ass."

"That's the spirit," Bella said holding her hand out for a fist-bump.

Fausta quirked an eyebrow but didn't leave the enthusiastic Arcane hanging. "I'll take you to the briefing room."

They entered a circular building in the middle of the compound. A guard unsealed the door to the room and let them in. The moment the door opened, Elyssa felt her knees go weak. Fausta and Bella gripped her before she slumped to the floor.

Bella looked up and gasped.

Thomas Borathen met his daughter's gaze for a brief second before continuing his speech. It took everything Elyssa had not to run over and hug him.

He's alive!

Relief and anger collided in her stomach with the force of a locomotive. Why hadn't anyone told her he was alive? Why hadn't he called her?

Bella seemed to know what she was thinking. "We went after Justin in the middle of all the confusion, dear. He probably didn't realize you thought he was dead."

She was right. Elyssa nodded and sucked in a deep breath to combat the flood of tears threatening to shatter her forced composure. She squeezed Bella's hand in gratitude and happiness.

Dad is alive. Justin has to be alive. And I'll save him.

"Maximus has heavy backing," Thomas said, "and he has numbers. Today we saw him attack with scroll casters, nearly a hundred untrained foot soldiers—ammo fodder, in truth.

"He's obviously built a coalition with malcontents from other Overworld factions," Thomas continued. "If we don't attack fast and finish him now, his army will be too large for one Templar legion, and we'll need to ask the Synod for reinforcements."

Christian Salazar stood. "May I have the floor, Commander?"

Thomas replied with a curt nod. "Of course, Commander."

The Colombian Templar faced the room. "Due to unforeseen circumstance, I altered our original plan to attack Maximus's main force. The original attack was scheduled over two weeks ago." His eyes held Elyssa's gaze for a moment.

She remembered. He'd ordered them to divert to capture a high value target. The target turned out to be Justin. Of course, she hadn't even remembered having a boyfriend at the time thanks to taking the White and having her memories of him wiped.

"We'd hoped to keep this conflict strictly non-lethal. It appears Maximus has other plans. We lost three good people in the fight today, and could have lost more if not for Templar Meghan Andretti and Adam Nosti supporting us with their arcane abilities." He gestured toward the couple where they sat near the front.

A loud "HOOAH!" went up from the gathered Templars. Meghan blushed. Adam was busy doing something on his arcphone. Probably programming in a new spell. The guy was gawky and a bit of a nerd, not to mention a conspiracy theorist, but he'd helped her and Justin out before and seemed like a good guy. Meghan, on the other hand, despised most spawn except for Justin. Somehow, her boyfriend had

71

that effect on most people, winning them over despite their prejudices. Unfortunately, there were just as many people who wanted him dead.

"Where's Harry?" Bella asked.

Elyssa couldn't find him in the throng. Then again, he might still be off doing his own thing.

Christian continued. "Operation Staunch will be a two-pronged assault on Maximus's stronghold, located here." He activated an all-seeing eye on the table in front of him. A 3D holograph flickered on in the air above the table, showing an overhead view of the city. Elyssa felt a sudden sense of déjà vu, having seen an almost identical briefing not more than a week or so ago just before they diverted to capture Justin.

Christian continued the briefing, outlining how the attack would commence and calling on his two best infiltration squads to start the assault, followed by a clean-and-sweep from the main force.

"Our infil squads will take out sentries and surveillance with non-lethal force while the main force will surround the compound and contain any escape attempts. We have a high degree of confidence Maximus is on-site." Christian paused and looked around the room. "Any questions?"

A Templar near the front raised his hand. "What if we come under fire from scroll casters or other lethal attack?"

"Use the Lancers to knock out targets whenever possible. If you are under direct threat, lethal force is authorized."

A young woman stood up. "Sir, why are we going non-lethal?" Her fists clenched as she spoke. "They didn't show us any mercy, so why should we?"

Murmurs rose around the room and Elyssa saw quite a few nods of agreement at the Templar's questions.

"We deserve some payback," Fausta said, almost under her breath.

Elyssa agreed with the sentiment in some regards. Maximus didn't deserve to draw another breath. Neither did the scroll casters. But so many of those vampires were hardly her age and had probably been brainwashed or lured in by the romantic notions of being a vampire.

Christian motioned for the murmurs to cease and spoke. "I understand how you feel, Sallah," he said. "I lost a friend and a colleague today. But Maximus has convinced many of his newest followers that we're the evil ones, the ones who want to kill them. He's convinced them we're in league with the Red Syndicate, and want to destroy them. We have no way of countering his blatant lies, but we can fight clean."

From the murmurs in the room, it was clear many Templars didn't agree.

A pale man Elyssa hadn't noticed stood in the front of the room. "Commander, if I may?" His voice oozed with condescension.

Christian looked at the man for a moment before giving a curt nod.

"I am Luciano Pavarotti, special envoy from the Red Syndicate." He smiled, but it was a cold smile, devoid of any real emotion.

Fausta snickered. Elyssa didn't have time to ask her why before the vampire continued.

"My leaders are firmly against Maximus's rogue actions. But they have made it equally clear the Vampire Nation will not tolerate the deaths of innocent vampires who were lured into Blood Rush under false pretenses. The Red Syndicate recognizes all vampires as citizens of our great nation and regrets the loss of life the Templars suffered at the hands of a few isolated terrorists within Maximus's faction."

Sallah jerked to her feet. "A few isolated terrorists? We were swarmed by hundreds of Maximus's terrorists. If the Red Syndicate is so concerned, why haven't your leaders stepped in and stopped them? Why do we have to risk our lives to solve a vampire problem?"

"That will be quite enough," Thomas said, eyes stern.

Elyssa studied his gaze. She could tell he wasn't angry with the Templar, but Thomas set great store by keeping his people in line, no matter what.

Luciano gave Sallah a patronizing smile. "My leaders regret their lack of manpower to deal with the situation, but the Arcanes' unprovoked attack on the Vampire Academy has strained our resources. Once the Templars have taken care of Maximus, we will take control of the orphaned vampires."

Elyssa hadn't heard of an attack on the VA. Only a week or so ago, vampires had attacked the Dallas branch of the Ezzek Moore

School for the Gifted and killed several children before the teachers could kill the attackers. The Arcanes blamed the Red Syndicate. Apparently, the Arcane Council had escalated the conflict. She had a suspicion Maximus's people were behind the attack, pinning the blame on the Reds so they'd be too busy to stop his recruitment efforts.

Adam Nosti, and Meghan with him, stared with open disdain at the vampire.

"This vampire is a liar," Bella said, her voice low and angry.

"About what?" Elyssa said.

"Unprovoked, he says? One of my friends lost a nephew in the attack on the Ezzek Moore School. He was so bright, and so very young." Bella dabbed at an eye.

"I'm sorry," Elyssa said.

"Please know that my leaders greatly appreciate all the Templars do to support the Overworld Conclave," Luciano said. "I am here to monitor the situation and report back once there is a resolution." The thin man smiled once again and took his seat.

Elyssa stood before Christian could open his mouth.

"You realize Maximus has a prisoner, right?" She cast a stern look at her father when she said it. "He has Justin. Is there a plan to get him safely out?"

Christian folded his hands behind his back. "We will rescue him if all goes to plan, Recruit Borathen. Unfortunately, we have no inside knowledge as to where Maximus is keeping him."

"Shouldn't we gather more intel before we strike?" She crossed her arms. "Why don't we commit our full force to an all-out assault instead of stealth? There are too many vampires to—"

Christian held up a hand to silence her. "A full frontal assault would not work for a number of reasons, *recruit*. I suggest everyone get some shuteye. The operation starts at high noon tomorrow. We're expecting a sunny day, and the vampires will be at their weakest then."

Elyssa ground her teeth. It was obvious nobody gave a crap about Justin's safety. Attempting to nullify Maximus with two squads wasn't going to work. Who knew how many vampires stood between the Templars and the leader of Blood Rush? Quite likely too many.

"This will work out, dear." Bella patted Elyssa's hand and smiled.

"Yeah right," Fausta said, standing. "They let Maximus build up and prepare for too long without a response. His activities demand an overwhelming Templar response, not this tip-toeing around."

"That's what I told them," said a familiar voice from the aisle.

Elyssa glanced right as she stood and saw the chiseled face of Beck Andrews grinning at her. "Told who?" she asked. "Yourself in the mirror?"

"Ha, very funny." He crossed his arms. "In case you hadn't noticed, I'm one of Christian's top advisors now. Your father recommended me for the position."

"Define 'top'," Fausta said with a smirk. "Because they obviously didn't listen to your attack plan."

"My father recommended you?" Elyssa felt her eyebrow arch in disbelief. "Payback for telling him about Vadaemos, right?" A group led by Justin had captured a wanted spawn criminal and taken him back to the United States to answer for his crimes. Justin had told her he'd done it to prove spawn weren't responsible for the Thunder Rock massacre all so he could gain her father's approval. Beck, however, had wanted credit for the capture and told her father prematurely. Her father had nearly killed Justin in a duel.

Beck looked away from her. "Sure, I guess that's part of it."

Elyssa got out of her seat and pushed past Beck, resisting, with great effort, the desire to shove him down the auditorium stairs.

"Where are you going?" Bella asked.

"To sleep."

Elyssa stepped out the door, and sensed a cold presence come up next to her.

"Elyssa Borathen," said the cool slithering voice of the vampire envoy, "I'd like a moment of your time." He had an Italian accent, though not as strong as Fausta's could be at times.

She stepped out of the flow of departing Templars and regarded the thin, pale man. What in the world would someone of his standing want with a recruit? "Can I help you, Envoy Pavarotti?"

"I'm quite confident you can, Miss Borathen." He smiled, showing clean white teeth. "Justin Slade has, of late, become a topic of conversation in the capitol."

Elyssa felt a spark of surprise. How would the vaunted politicos of the Overworld know about Justin? Then again, why wouldn't they?

Hadn't he just brought in Vadaemos Slade, one of the most wanted fugitives? And his connections to the most powerful spawn house in the States might also make him a person of great interest. It meant people like Pavarotti might want to use him to their advantage.

"What can I do for you, Envoy?" She tried to keep her voice calm.

"First, let me express my sincere regrets about his kidnapping. Maximus will be brought to justice, I promise you."

"And?"

The vampire smiled. "The Red Syndicate would very much like to meet with Mr. Slade, assuming, of course, his rescue is successful."

Elyssa's stomach knotted. To think they might fail was too painful to even consider. "If the Red Syndicate helped rescue him, he might be willing to meet. Otherwise, I doubt he will."

"Point well taken, Miss Borathen." Pavarotti swept a hand at the crowd of Templars. "I'm highly confident your father will succeed. But I will take your request to the Syndicate and do what can be done from our end." He licked his lips and offered another greasy smile. "It's a very delicate situation, as I'm sure you understand."

A delicate situation would be if she held her razor-sharp katana against his pale throat. She resisted making the comment. "Very well, Envoy. I hope the Syndicate can come through." Any bit of leverage she had was well worth spending if it meant getting Justin back. "And I'm sure my father would feel indebted to the Syndicate for any help rendered." More likely, her father would look at it as interference, but she didn't care.

"Thank you for your time, Miss Borathen." He offered her his hand, giving her the kind of soft, wimpy shake she'd expected from a politician.

Exhausted and cramped with tension, Elyssa went to a guest bunkhouse and tossed her duffel bag on one of the empty bunks. She locked the door behind her, hoping the others would go to one of the other guest quarters in the complex. She'd barely faced away from the door when a knock sounded. Elyssa growled. Unlatched the door, and flung it open. "What—" The words died on her lips.

A large man in a type of scaled armor she had never seen before stood outside. His face was covered by a mask of the same material.

He towered over his comrade, but Elyssa would rather face the big man any day than the person he was with.

Underborn, the most notorious assassin in the Overworld, smiled at her. "Good to see you again, Miss Borathen."

Chapter 11

I would have face-palmed if not for my obvious inability to do so at the present time. Why hadn't I thought of using magic before? True, I could barely light a candle or blow it out, for that matter. And my attempts so far usually ended with disastrous results. Setting myself on fire wouldn't solve anything, and the room appeared to be made of concrete on all sides. A gust of wind wouldn't do me much good either, not unless I could blow myself right out of this hellhole.

Shelton and Bella had taught me quite a bit of general magical knowledge. Willpower was a big deal. So long as I could envision and desire an action with enough focus, I could make it happen. I had no problems with the desiring part, and envisioning wasn't too tough either. Focus was my problem. My mind was like a reel of discombobulated images, constantly fighting for airtime.

Maybe, just maybe, I could figure something out. I thought of the vampire guarding me. Mind control was way above my abilities. Still, someone else might replace her and that person might be easier to manipulate. I had *powers,* dammit. I just had to figure out how to use them.

Closing my eyes, I used my incubus senses to open myself up to the magical energy in the vicinity. I extended a wisp of essence toward a nebula of sparkling power and soaked it in. A tiny galaxy of magic whirled lazily overhead, mesmerizing me with its simple beauty. I wondered if it had magnetic properties causing it to coalesce like that. As I looked around the room with my sixth sense, I noticed darker strands of energy, some of them in similar patterns to the brighter energy.

Lines of magic pulsed up the walls and in the ceiling overhead as well. All in all, the energy patterns looked very similar to what I'd seen at Shelton's hideout. I wondered how it would look in the Grotto,

Thunder Rock, or at another of the angel relics scattered around the planet. Bella had told me about the powerful ley lines running through those places. I'd felt the power rush against me after making a circle in El Dorado. Although some arteries of energy in the ceiling seemed wider than what I'd seen at Shelton's, none of them seemed large enough to be more than just a tributary to the great river of magic I imagined ran through the relics.

I tried to probe down the hallway with my senses. I felt the cold presence of other vampires nearby, and a smattering of normal humans, some female. But they were just out of reach. Even if I managed to lure a female nom down here, the vampire guarding the door would be sure to stop her.

Out of idle boredom, I tried creating magical sparks even though there was nothing to catch on fire. I managed a couple. I heard the guard outside talking on the phone, the other end of the conversation clearly audible to my super hearing. They talked about Maximus and how they'd like to get it on with him.

How could people be so stupid as to fall for someone like Maximus? It made no sense. He was obviously a power-hungry jackass like most politicians, and yet people believed in him and supported him. How could so many humans be so stupid? I growled as a sudden surge of anger exploded in me.

Idiots!

A white fireball the size of my head exploded in the air above. Spots danced in my eyes from the blinding flash of light.

Holy crap. Did I do that?

The door slammed open and the vampire rushed in. "What the hell was that noise?" she said.

I pretended to be asleep, hoping the rapid beat of my heart wouldn't give me away.

"Was it you?" she shouted. "What exploded in here?"

I didn't answer.

"I asked you a question, you nasty thing," she said, her footsteps fading away from me.

"This entity made no explosion," my roommate said in his calm, emotionless voice. "It does not know the source."

The vampire cursed and I heard the sound of a hand smacking flesh. "I don't know why Maximus keeps you around. He should just get it over and end you."

"This entity finds such a prospect undesirable."

"This entity finds such a prospect undesirable, oh, boo hoo hoo," the vampire said in a mocking voice. "Cry me a river, dumbass."

"It is not possible to produce such a quantity of moisture," he replied.

His statement was met with another smack. The vampire stomped toward me and stopped. I heard her breathing right next to me. She must have lowered her head because I felt her breath against my ear. Even worse, I smelled it.

"Are you asleep, snookums?" she cooed in my ear. She sniffed and it was all I could do not to cringe away.

She touched my face. Her skin felt room temperature and soft. Something moist touched my neck and I realized it had to be her tongue. I jerked, eyes opening as I tried to get away from her. She laughed.

"Not asleep anymore, are we, pookie bear?"

"Stay away from me," I said, voice trembling.

She leapt atop the table, straddling me. Her red eyes locked onto my chest. "Hmm, Maximus is so messy." She leaned over, eyes locked onto mine, and grinned with malicious intent. Extending her tongue, she licked the crusted blood from my chest.

I shuddered and writhed. "Get the hell off me!"

"Careful, incubus boy. You might turn me on." She ground against my boxers and moaned. "Maybe I should give you a test ride. Maximus won't mind, so long as I don't drink your blood."

I shook my head and bucked, but couldn't dislodge her. She'd have to inject me with enough Viagra to excite a nursing home because the thought of having sex with her ugly ass made man brain number two shrink up like a stack of dimes. "Get off me, you perv!"

She pushed a clump of matted hair from her face, and smiled. Her fangs retracted, and she looked almost normal, although nowhere near what I'd consider cute. "I can be gentle," she said in her girly voice. "I have lots of experience." She leaned down and nipped my ear, sending a shiver of revulsion through me. "After all, I used to work in a brothel during the California Gold Rush."

Her lips touched mine and she pressed her tongue hard against my mouth, forcing it through my clamped lips. I would have bitten her tongue, but gagged instead at the onslaught of tonsil hockey and her nasty, dead breath.

I convulsed and heaved at her unwanted touch. She leapt off me, quick as a cat.

"I'll have to train you, I see." She tapped a finger against her chin. "Thankfully, I'll have plenty of time to break you in."

A phone, presumably hers, rang, and she walked away to answer it. Before long, she was chattering away about Maximus again.

After my racing heart slowed down, exhaustion flowed through my body, leaving me feeling weak. I had done something amazing, causing a fireball to explode over my head, but what good did it do me here? I couldn't blow a hole through the wall.

Thanks to Maximus drinking my blood, the vampiric prostitute guarding my door, and the moron who shared this room, my future looked terrifying.

"What are you doing here?" my guard said, breaking off her phone conversation.

A female answered. "I'm bringing him food, Amanda. What does it look like?"

The guard snorted. "Trying to get back into Maxi's favor again? Dream on. I never should have taken—"

"As if you're getting any from him," the other woman interrupted.

"Yeah, like Maximus would assign just anybody to guard his new toy, slut. Oh, and you'll have to hand feed him." Amanda laughed. "Maybe you should puree everything next time." The guard resumed her phone conversation, throwing in a few insults about my food handler.

Footsteps approached. I smelled hot bread and other yummy aromas. My stomach gurgled though my heart beat a little faster from uncertainty. I had no idea who this new person was or what they might try to do to me. I felt lips brush against my ear and almost yelped.

"Don't react when you see me," a woman whispered ever so slightly in my ear. "I'll try to get you out of here."

A ray of hope warmed my body. The woman stood and smiled, though her brow wrinkled with worry. My eyes went wide with

81

recognition and it took an effort not to shout with excitement as I smiled back up at Felicia Nosti.

She glanced behind me, toward the door, I figured. Then she touched the strap on my arm. I waited for sweet release. But nothing happened. She touched the strap at my neck. Again nothing. The furrows in her brow deepened.

She leaned down and whispered, "I can't release them. Maximus must have bonded them to himself."

My jaw went tight with frustration. Being so close to freedom only made my bonds chafe worse. Desperation rose in me, and it was all I could do not to freak out and fight the straps, no matter how useless the effort. "Isn't there some way to get me out?" I whispered back in the same low voice.

Felicia held an *empanada* to my mouth. "Here, take a bite and don't take all damned night," she said aloud. She leaned down. "I'm thinking."

I bit and chewed, swallowing carefully so I didn't choke. She put a flexible straw to my mouth. I sucked cool, sweet water down my parched throat. After finishing the meal and most of the water, I felt the urgent call of nature.

"I've really got to use the bathroom," I said. "And not just a number one."

Felicia's eyes widened. "Amanda, he's got to go."

"We put adult diapers on him," the guard said back. "Tell him to go to town. We'll put him in a sleeper collar to clean him up later."

"You have got to be kidding me!" I shouted. "What kind of prison are you running here?"

Amanda burst into laughter and started telling her friend on the phone all about it.

Felicia looked at me with horror and sympathy. "I'll leave you to—uh…" she gagged, and from the look on her face, probably puked in her mouth. When she regained some composure, she leaned down. "I think if I can get a few drops of Maximus's blood, I can open the straps. Don't worry, Justin, we'll get you out of here. I promise." She glanced back in Amanda's direction. "And be careful around her. She's effed in the head."

As if anyone needed to tell me that. I briefly wondered who this "we" was, if maybe there were other vampires who were on our side,

82

but didn't have time to ask before Felicia left. I fought the urge to pee as long as I could, anger and humiliation raging inside me. I felt like a caged, abused animal sitting in dog pound and waiting for the axe to fall. The fury within me surged to the point I could feel my inner demon seeking escape. If I didn't give in, I might try to manifest again. Given what had happened last time, I knew such a thing would only lead to strangulation.

Amanda came in, a leer on her face. She held her phone's camera toward me. "You see him?" she said. "Any minute now and he's gonna crap himself."

Repressed anger exploded. I roared. A deep guttural voice came from my mouth, speaking in the strange language I somehow understood. *You will be first to die*, I translated. My body thrashed. Muscles expanded. My neck pressed hard against the strap, harder and harder. But I no longer cared. I would break my bonds or die trying.

The world collapsed to a tiny circle as my brain burned through its remaining oxygen. But it felt like something was giving. Like the strap might have loosened.

The last thing I saw was Amanda laughing at me.

Chapter 12

Elyssa

"What—how did you get in here?" Elyssa asked as shock rippled through her.

Underborn gave her a lopsided smile. "May we come in before someone notices our presence? I took a considerable risk coming to you."

"You're not coming inside until you explain what the hell you want." This man was responsible for leading Justin through a gauntlet of gray men, hellhounds, and god only knew what else all so he could test his mettle. Underborn's real name was Kevin Sorensen, but he'd also posed as Mr. Turpin, an English teacher at their high school. As a former Templar, this man had survived the massacre at Thunder Rock, unbeknownst to Thomas Borathen, the leader of the ill-fated mission to apprehend Vadaemos all those years ago.

The large man pushed past Elyssa like she was nothing. Underborn followed, slipping in like a greased eel. He pulled a chair from the table in the center of the room, spun it around, and took a seat, propping his arms on the back of it. The big man leaned against a wall and crossed his arms.

"You've got a lot of nerve coming to me," Elyssa said. The desire to smack the smile off Underborn's face threatened to overcome her good sense.

The assassin held up his hands in surrender. "Believe me, Miss Borathen, I did what I did to be sure Justin was up to the task at hand. So far, he has proven himself most capable, if a bit clumsy. He took down *Vadaemos*." Underborn seemed genuinely impressed.

"He wasn't alone." Elyssa didn't care about credit, but Justin wasn't infallible. Nobody was.

"I know, Templar. It is Justin's ability to form the unlikeliest of alliances and forge a resolution that makes him so remarkable." Underborn scratched his head and looked at the silent, looming figure in black for a moment before continuing. "Unfortunately, it appears we have been outsmarted."

"By Maximus?"

Underborn shook his head. "By Daelissa."

Elyssa smacked a fist into her palm. "I just knew that bitch was involved somehow." She narrowed her eyes. "And what do you mean by *we*?"

"Naturally, I mean all of us in the collective sense."

"No." She shook her head. "I know you wanted Justin to take on Maximus. Somehow, you have a hand in this mess, don't you?" She crossed the room and looked down at him. "Did you have something to do with the kidnapping of his sister?"

A grim-lipped smile crossed the assassin's face. "I assure you I had nothing to do with that. However, it would appear the entire kidnapping was an elaborate setup."

Elyssa felt a jolt of surprise. "Ivy wasn't kidnapped?"

Underborn shook his head. "As I said, this entire fiasco has Daelissa's fingerprints all over it."

"What do you suggest we do?"

"The plan your father detailed will not result in the outcome you desire, I'm afraid."

"What do you—wait a minute, the war room's doors are sealed against magical eavesdropping. How do you know what the plan is?"

The former Templar tapped his temple. "I have my resources."

Elyssa brushed aside his reply with a wave of her hand. "Whatever. I don't care. If you have a plan to rescue Justin, I'm all for it."

"That's the spirit, young lady."

Elyssa lashed out lightning-quick toward Underborn's chair with her foot. The man was out of the chair even before her blurring kick connected with it, and watched calmly as her foot splintered the chair into kindling.

He raised an eyebrow at the ruined furniture. "I take it you don't like being patronized."

Though she was shocked at the speed with which he'd moved, Elyssa controlled her expression and gave him an even stare. "You might say that. Treat me like an equal and maybe you'll have someplace to sit next time."

She heard a chuckle from somewhere behind her and turned to see Underborn's looming companion watching the pair of them. "Who's the slab of meat you brought with you?"

Underborn flicked his fingers as if her question were unimportant. "Just some muscle."

As if the assassin needed anyone else. Elyssa had never seen someone move as fast as Underborn. "Fine. Back to my original question. What's the plan?"

"I have resources on the inside, though it took some considerable effort to put them into place. They will free Justin and lead him out. We'll meet them outside the compound and make away with him."

Elyssa crossed her arms. "That simple, huh?"

"Indeed."

She had to admit it sounded pretty simple and doable. No need to sneak in, find him, and rescue him, like she and Justin had to do for his father. Maximus had captured Justin's father, David, and used him as his own special blood reserve. Vampires considered spawn blood something of a delicacy.

Elyssa took a minute to think. Maximus's desire for spawn blood had to be twofold. First, of course, he probably enjoyed the taste. Second, the vampire was too young to turn a nom into one of his kind and most likely thought drinking enough spawn blood might enhance his ability to do so. Elyssa had no idea if Justin's blood could do such a thing or not. She figured Maximus was simply a desperate vampire grasping at straws. Until his blood aged, he'd be unable to turn anyone, and those he tried to turn would be infected with a curse. One that would turn them into a member of the walking dead, a vampling.

"When is the rescue scheduled?" Elyssa asked.

"At four in the morning. Since your father plans to begin the assault at noon, we don't have much time."

"But won't the vampires be at their strongest during the night?"

Underborn nodded. "It can't be helped. We have to get Justin out before the assault or Maximus might move him to a secret location. A place we'd never find him."

The downside to this subterfuge was relying on someone else to rescue her boyfriend. Elyssa itched to get in on the action. To make sure all went to plan. She was a dhampyr, after all. She could hide her heat signature from the vampires and pose as one.

"Believe me, Miss Borathen, things will go more smoothly if you don't try to interfere with the operation."

One word in his sentence piqued her suspicion. *Interfere?* "Why are you telling me this if my only job is to wait around until Justin is led outside? You don't even need me for that." Elyssa searched his expression for a clue, but he was too skilled at hiding his intent behind a poker face. "Tell me what you really want."

Underborn pursed his lips. "It isn't so much what I want as what I *don't* want."

"Maybe you can say that again, but this time, try to make sense."

"The Templars are patrolling the perimeter, keeping eyes on the comings and goings of the vampires."

Elyssa shrugged. "Normal procedure. Our intel would be dangerously outdated if we didn't keep a constant watch."

The assassin nodded. "Unfortunately, it means when we go in to retrieve Justin, those same eyes will be watching us."

"So what?" Elyssa tapped her chin in contemplation as she tried to unravel the weave of Underborn's plot. He had to have ulterior motives. All anecdotal evidence about this man indicated he was exceptional at leading his victims into the exact place he wanted them before ending them. He was known not simply for killing, but for manipulating everyone involved with the deal. And his price was always the most valued possession of the buyer. When Underborn said it would cost an arm and a leg, he wasn't joking.

"I don't wish Templars to see me or my inside agents. While they may not know who I am at first, they would certainly figure it out."

"You want me to clear the perimeter?" Elyssa wasn't sure how to accomplish such a thing. Her father or Christian could give the command to clear the perimeter, but she certainly couldn't. Even if she knew where the lookouts were stationed, distracting one of them wouldn't be enough. The location of Maximus's stronghold left few, if any, concealed approaches thanks to a wide road looping about it and roundabouts on all corners. A tall wall towered over those streets and offered few entrances to anyone wanting inside. From the history

Elyssa had uncovered, the place had once served as a military fort, later converted into a mansion with several outbuildings.

In other words, the Templars using the cluttered buildings around the stronghold would see everyone coming in and out. The vampires on the walls would as well.

Underborn already seemed to know this. "Not feasible, I'm afraid. What we need, however, is nearly as impossible."

Here it comes, Elyssa thought. "Spit it out already."

"What I'm about to tell you may come as a shock."

"After all I've been through lately, your revelation had better be about Godzilla or aliens, because I can't think of much else that would shock me."

Underborn chuckled. "True. After surviving the horrors of El Dorado, fleeing from husks, wraiths, and even facing down leyworms, I don't imagine there is much in the physical realm that could surprise you."

A shudder ran through Elyssa's back at the thought of the husks, short and infant-shaped creatures with smooth oily skin and nothing but a maw of sharp teeth on an otherwise featureless face. Justin called them cherubs which wasn't far from the truth. Vadaemos told them they were the leftover husks of angels nearly killed when the Grand Nexus tying their plane of existence to Earth was destroyed.

She shook the troubled memories from her thoughts and returned to the question at hand. "So tell me then. What's the shocker you have in store for me?"

Underborn seemed to pause for dramatic effect and said, "There is a spy among you."

Elyssa raised an eyebrow. "That's not shocking. It's silly." She glanced at the dark hulk leaning against the wall, and wondered who he was. "Do you agree with him?"

The man didn't respond.

She rolled her eyes. "Maximus has a spy in our ranks? That's your shocking news?" She had no doubt the rogue vampire was spying on them somehow, but to have an actual spy, a member of the Templars, implanted in their ranks hardly seemed feasible. "You realize we can sense vampires, right? I mean, you *were* a Templar."

"I'm quite aware of that, Miss Borathen. However, Maximus has been rather adept lately at avoiding and outsmarting the Templars.

How else do you think he knew about Justin's arrival at La Casona, hmm? Or when, exactly, to hit the convoy? Or how to hide so many vampires from Templar senses until it was time to strike?"

"Easy." Elyssa directed a condescending look at the assassin. "He probably has eyes on La Casona and the Grotto. It's not like we veiled our forces or tried to sneak into Colombia."

Underborn reflected her condescension with a condescending grin of his own. "I would agree with you, except Maximus wouldn't have had enough time to mobilize such a force, not to mention positioning scroll casters in strategic firing locations at a moment's notice. If he had watchers at the Templar compound in Atlanta, he would have had less than thirty minutes to organize before you arrived at La Casona. The cars there to pick you up arrived only moments before you did."

Elyssa ran some calculations through her mind and came to the conclusion Underborn had a point. Unless Maximus maintained a force outside La Casona, he couldn't have mobilized such an organized ambush and kidnapping in so short a time. A chill settled in her stomach. As impossible as it sounded, someone she knew, someone close to the commanders might be a traitor.

"Crap," she said, running a hand through her hair as faces of friends ran through her mind. Could one of them be the spy? She gave Underborn a quizzical look. "Why do you care if there's a spy?"

"If your people see one of my agents inside Maximus's camp bring Justin outside, they'll likely take video with an all-seeing eye and send it up the chain. The Templar spy will see my person and report them to Maximus who will likely torture them until they reveal the identities of my other insiders." He shrugged. "I have spent considerable time and resources putting my agents into place, and can't afford to withdraw any of them at this stage of the game."

"They're just resources to you, aren't they?"

"We're all resources to someone, Miss Borathen." He smiled. "Just ask your father."

Much as she wanted to punch the man in the mouth for his mocking smile, she couldn't disagree. Thomas Borathen had trained her to be a resource more than a daughter. Rather than a father, he'd always been her commanding officer. Had he ever held her as a child and spun her around in his arms, a smile on his face, a gleam in his eye? Had he ever kissed her and told her he loved her no matter what she wanted to do with her life?

The cruel but true answer was no. Any time he'd been proud of her was for her advancement in the Templars. For her fighting prowess. He'd been all too quick to have her mind wiped when she'd stepped out of line and fallen in love with Justin.

Why, then, had her heart ached when she'd thought he was dead? And why had it nearly flown away when she found him alive?

Damn her traitorous heart.

"Do you have any idea who the traitor might be?" she asked.

"I'm afraid not. However, this person is likely close to Commander Salazar or your father. He or she would have to be to gather timely information."

That left very few people. Elyssa's mother, Leia, and her brother, Michael were the two closest to her father. Even so, he rarely told anyone what his plans were until it was nearly time to execute them. As for Christian, she knew Beck was now a top advisor. But who else? "I think I know where to start," she said.

Underborn nodded. "Good. But you'll need to hurry." He checked a pocket watch. "You have five hours until the operation." The assassin withdrew a disposable arcphone and handed it to her. "You can reach me with this once you've succeeded. Don't try to trace the number. It's magically encrypted.

Elyssa took the thin rectangular device. "What if I can't find the traitor in five hours?"

"I said five hours until the operation, Miss Borathen. You have four hours to find the mole."

"Just four hours? Why?"

"Because, young lady, if you don't find them, I will scrub the mission."

Chapter 13

My head throbbed. Every heartbeat sent a dagger straight into my brain. I'd had a horrible hangover before. In fact, the day I'd started down the disastrous road of incubus puberty had been the day of my first and, so far, last hangover. Seriously, one had been enough to make me swear off drinking for life.

"Nyuh," I croaked through chapped lips and a parched throat.

"You are alive," said my roommate in his usual monotone voice.

"Water." My voice rasped like sand across pebbles.

"The guard installed a watering device for you."

I blinked the crust out of my eyes and saw a metal tube just above my face, a drop of water hanging at its tip. I craned my neck up, lips grasping for the precious drop, but couldn't reach it. The droplet hung at the tip of the metal tube, suspended as though by black magic, torturing me with its close but unreachable proximity. As a last resort, I stuck my tongue out. It touched the tip. Sweet water trickled into my dry throat.

Laying back and panting with the effort, I savored the tiny drop. It didn't sate me by any stretch of the imagination, though. I forced my head back up, though the tight strap around my neck choked me. Lapping at the tube with my tongue, I released another trickle of water, but soon had to lean back to rest my throat and neck.

After repeating the process more times than I could remember, I finally conquered some of my thirst. I longed to close my lips around that tube and draw a long gulp of water down my parched throat. No matter how hard I tried, only my tongue could reach it. As I lay gasping from my last effort, I abruptly realized exactly where I'd seen a water dispenser like this—in a hamster cage.

"That bitch," I said, gritting my teeth. Amanda had installed it so I'd have to lick it. On purpose. My incubus hunger growled from its cage. *Great. One more thing to worry about.*

I heard a giggle. Amanda, her phone camera trained on me, came from outside the door.

"You're so pathetic," she said. "Oh no, the big bad spawn is turning into a demon!" She held her hands up and opened her mouth in mock horror. "Please save me!" A nasty grin curled her lips. "Guess what, moron? Even you can't break diamond fiber."

"Must be hard being you," I croaked. "Your life obviously sucks so bad you have to torture someone who can't fight back to feel good about yourself." I forced a grin and glanced at the bird nest she called hair. "Maybe if you owned a hairbrush you could get a date."

Her fist lashed out. My head rocked sideways and fireworks exploded behind my eyes. "Shut up. Shut up! I'll make you sorry you ever opened your mouth."

"Your breath is already making me sorry," I said.

All the air exploded from my lungs as she pounded a fist into my stomach. I opened my eyes and would have shouted had any breath remained in my chest. I saw her face an inch from mine. Her breath smelled of fresh blood. Her eyes gleamed bright with menace and anger. Pissing her off had probably been a bad idea.

"Amanda, what the hell are you doing?" said a familiar voice. "Maximus isn't going to be happy with you beating on his pet spawn."

The guard whirled, hands crooked like claws. Her yellowed fingernails lengthened by an inch. She panted and seemed on the verge of attacking the newcomer.

"Get a hold of yourself," said the voice again.

I *knew* that voice. It wasn't Felicia, though. My mind was too wrapped up in the drama of the moment to run a database search and make a match.

Amanda lowered her hands and growled. "I should suck you dry and blame his bruises on you."

"Yeah, right. As if I was strong enough to hurt a spawn." The owner of the voice stepped around the angry vampire and my jaw went slack.

Katie?

The vampire turned and saw my shocked expression. She laughed. "Guess I punched him too hard." She glanced at the tray of food in Katie's hand. "If he tries to get inside your head, let me know so I can clock him in the face again."

Katie stuck her tongue out at the vampire's back as Amanda turned and left the room, slamming the door shut behind her. Loud music sprang up from somewhere outside the door. Amanda shouted in fury, her voice fading down the hall as she demanded the instigator turn it off.

"What in the hell—no, how in the hell did you get here?" So many words, mostly curses sprang to my head, I had trouble speaking. "Are you effin' crazy?" Somehow, I remembered to whisper my questions, though Amanda probably couldn't hear them over the music. I remembered I was in my underwear with adult diapers beneath, and felt a hot blush creep from my head to my toes.

Tears pooled in my former crush's eyes. Her pretty green eyes. I couldn't believe how much I'd wanted this girl, back when I'd been a hopeless nerd. And then I'd met Elyssa. Katie had stumbled into my world—the Overworld—when she'd come to my house just as hellhounds had attacked. This was far more than stumbling in, however. Had Katie decided to become a vampire?

"Oh, Justin, I can't believe what they've done to you." She kissed my forehead. "I've got to get you out of here." Her eyes wandered across my scantily clothed body.

"Water?" I asked, too thirsty to worry about such trivial things as clothes any longer.

Her eyes brightened, and she nodded, bringing out a bottle of water with a flexible straw. I gulped so fast, I choked and broke into a violent coughing fit. Katie pulled out a phone and looked at it.

"Justin, just keep calm. In a few hours, I'm going to break you out of here."

I gave her a crazy look. "You?" I checked her eyes again to be sure they weren't vampire red. "Are you here to join Maximus's vampire army?"

She shook her head. "No, absolutely not. Something terrible happened, though."

Chewing on a chunk of cheese she put to my mouth, I raised my eyebrows to prompt her to continue.

"I tried to call you. I texted you and left messages, but you never replied."

"Yeah, I was in southern Colombia. No reception."

"I can't even being to understand how or why you ended up down here. I have so many questions." She glanced over her shoulder. Took a deep breath. "Ever since you vanished, I tried to find out where you went and if you were okay. I got ahold of Shelton and your dad talked to me and told me you were fine. Anyway, since you were gone, I started hanging out with Nyte and Ash."

"You hung out with them? As in friends?"

She nodded. "I was lonely. You were gone, and things at school could never be the same after running from those hellhounds, and almost dying and—well, Annie and Jenny would never understand, even if I *could* tell them."

The demonic hunger in me twisted my insides. My eyes closed. When they reopened, I saw Katie's delicious aura hovering around her. *No!* I squeezed my eyes shut and slammed the door on the ravenous feeling. With some effort, I picked up the trail of the conversation again. "Please tell me you didn't talk to Ash and Nyte about the Overworld."

She shook her head. "No. In fact, Ash and I started hanging out more. He's really smart, and cute without all that nasty Goth makeup."

I let out a sigh of relief. "Thank god you didn't tell them anything."

"I didn't, but someone else did. Right after Coach Burgundy and Brad and all those others were killed—" she shuddered. "It was so horrible. Then the huge garbage truck slammed into the police car you were in, and everything happened so fast. You and Elyssa vanished and Ash and Nyte were worried sick about you."

I felt terrible. Not that I'd had much of a chance to call anyone and let them know I was okay, but I knew exactly what it was like to have someone you care about vanish from your life. "Are they okay?"

A fresh tear sparkled in her eye. "These new people showed up at school. I didn't trust them one bit after knowing what you told me about vampire recruiters. They held after-school club meetings, supposedly about finding your true self and the meaning of life, or some crap like that. Ash and Nyte went to one, thinking it would be a big joke. Somewhere along the way, they found out these people were vampires recruiting for Maximus."

My heart sank. Apparently, my attempt at stamping out Maximus's recruiters from my high school hadn't paid off. "Please tell me you stopped them from going."

"At first they laughed about it. Then one of the vampires grew out his fangs and punched a hole through a desk. Most of the people there were like Ash and Nyte—you know, the ones Nathan and his goons call nerds and losers. The ones who want a miracle to make them look cool."

"Oh, god." A sick feeling ballooned in my stomach. "What happened?"

"The vampire told them there was a serum they could take, but it was in limited supply. He took them all on a tour of the Grotto and then down to Colombia."

"And you came with them."

Katie grasped one of my hands and shook her head. Amanda's yelling echoed down the hall. The raucous music still hadn't stopped.

"I let them go, Justin." She sobbed. "I tried to stop them, but they wouldn't listen. And the worst part is—" she hiccupped and wiped at the tears rolling down her cheeks. "I really like Ash. We sort of went out on a date. He told me I shouldn't settle for a weakling like him. He told me that when he came back, he'd be super strong and immortal. And then he'd be worthy of dating me."

I groaned. "I know, I know." She leaned down and whispered. "Then the strangest thing ever happened. Mr. Turpin, the English teacher, came to me and offered me a chance to save them. He said he could get me to Colombia, but that I'd have to spy on Maximus for him all while pretending to be one of his recruits."

"Son of a bitch!" I wormed against my restraints.

"His real name is really weird. Underborn, or something like that." She looked over her shoulder and turned back to me. "He has other people here working for him too."

"You can't trust him," I said. "The man is an assassin." Underborn wouldn't stick out his own neck to rescue anyone. He obviously intended for Katie to be one of his sacrificial lambs should anything go wrong.

The music in the hall switched from pop to Beethoven's Fifth. Katie's eyes widened. "I don't have much more time."

"Is Felicia helping you?"

She quirked an eyebrow. "Who?"

"A vampire—likes to dress geek chic."

Katie shook her head. "No. Another girl is helping me. She's a magician." Her lip curved up at the corner. "She's the one making the music."

"How many of you are there?"

She shrugged. "I don't know. Underborn said he couldn't tell me everything."

I growled. "Don't trust him. Get out while you can. Besides, you can't free me from these straps—not unless you have some of Maximus's blood."

"I'm not leaving you." Her eyes went hard and resolute. "I'll need you to talk Ash and Nyte out of this idiocy, too."

This was spiraling out of control. Scratch that. Events had *already* spiraled out of control. I wanted to grab Katie by the shoulders and give her a stern look. "I'm not giving you an option, Katie. Go now. Don't look back." My stomach growled again. I refused to feed on Katie. I needed her strong and healthy, and able to get the hell out of this place.

She touched my cheek and smoothed my oily, unwashed hair back from my face. "You didn't leave me when the hellhounds came. You could have tossed me away and left me. But you didn't. You saved my life, and now I'm going to save yours."

The music abruptly ended. Katie jerked and tugged on the hamster water bottle until the thin bracket holding it onto the table bent, lowering the tube an inch—just enough for me to suck from it. She kissed my forehead and smiled. "I'll be back soon."

Amanda returned a few minutes after Katie left, her face purple with rage, hair even more frizzed than usual. She leaned down until our noses nearly touched. "Don't think I've forgotten about what you said." She pressed long, yellowed claws against my chest and raked them down the skin, just hard enough to draw blood.

I clenched my teeth and groaned, not wanting to give her the satisfaction of bursting into tears. The sound of approaching voices jerked her upright. Her eyes widened with worry and she dashed off, returning a moment later with a towel and wiped the blood from my chest. My supernatural healing made short work of the light wounds, but I didn't have much juice left for anything else. Hunger clawed again at my incubus stomach. I wished I could drain this spiteful bitch dry.

Surely, Maximus knew he had to feed me essence at some point. Otherwise, I'd descend into madness and probably die. I couldn't remember if anyone had actually told me I could starve to death if I didn't feed the demon inside, but considering how awful it felt to go hungry, common sense told me it would be a painful way to go.

As the voices grew closer, I knew why Amanda looked so worried. The voices belonged to Maximus and another male.

"Greetings Lord Maximus," Amanda said as the lead vampire's voice grew closer.

Maximus replied. "What was your name again?"

"Amanda, my Lord."

I imagined her curtseying and swooning like a lovesick puppy. *Lord Maximus?*

"Guard the door at the top of the stairs and make sure no one enters until I return."

"Yes, yes, Lord Maximus. And if I can do anything for you—I mean *anything* at all, please let me know."

"I believe I just did."

"I'm so sorry, sir!" Her feet scrambled away.

Maximus and another man chuckled.

"I daresay she would pluck her own eyes out and stew them for you, Maximus," said a man in the kind of British accent I associated with royalty.

"As would most of my followers." Maximus, as usual, had zero self-doubt in his voice, maintaining his perfect one-hundred percent douche bag average.

"*That's* the spawn?" said someone else, a third man.

Footsteps tread closer until I saw Maximus and a tall, thin man with an oiled mustache and monocle over his right eye look down at me. A chunky guy, young looking despite a head of unnaturally white hair, appeared at the end of the table. He alternatively studied me and scribbled with his stylus on the tablet computer in his hand—an arctablet, I figured, or maybe just an arcphone expanded to tablet size.

John Corwin

"Showing me off to your best buds?" I said to Maximus.

"I'll need some samples," the white-haired nerd said.

Maximus nodded. "Take what you need, Dash."

"Dash?" I said with a laugh. "What kind of name is that?"

Dash rolled his eyes and walked away. When he returned, he held something in his fleshy hands. Before I could make another smart remark, he jammed a ball gag in my mouth and strapped it around my head. I bit down, thinking I'd crush it with my preternatural strength, but it was apparently made of diamond fiber because I nearly broke a tooth.

"Don't be too rough on the poor chap," the man with the monocle said. "I wouldn't want to spoil him with too much stress. Cortisone levels and all that rubbish, you know."

"Would you like a taste, Master?" Maximus said.

The other man raised an eyebrow and looked at me. "He looks a bit unwashed."

Master? The word caught me off guard. I'd never heard Maximus defer to anyone. Could this be the mystery vampire helping him turn people?

Dash came around to my neck and squeezed hand sanitizer from a bottle. I felt the cold gel as he rubbed it against my neck. "There you go, sir. All clean."

The Master took off his monocle, leaned down and sniffed. "I daresay he's a tad ripe, Maximus, but his blood practically sings, doesn't it?"

"Exactly, sir. And that's why I think he's the solution to our supply problems."

The needle prick of fangs pressed into my skin. I jerked, but the Master gripped my head tight and held it. Either I'd already lost a great deal of strength, or he was much stronger than most vampires I'd fought. Probably both. I thrashed with my body to no avail. My breaths came in rapid pants through my nose. Despite my horror, a rush of pleasure flooded through me like a drug.

I'd never done hard drugs, but I imagined they would feel a lot like this. And it scared the hell out of me, because I never wanted the euphoria to end.

The Master pulled back and wiped daintily at his red lips with a handkerchief. "Marvelous. Magnificent." He looked with amazement

98

at Maximus. "You didn't tell me he was so much better than other Daemos."

The rogue leader gave a feral grin. "At first, I thought it was just me. But there's definitely something about this kid, isn't there?"

"Night and day, young man."

"Give me time and I'll quantify and qualify the differences," Dash said, holding a slim wand to my wrist. He twirled it once, and drew it away. Blood squeezed from a pore in my skin until a globule the size of a quarter hovered in the air. Another spin from the wand caused the sphere to rotate faster and faster until the plasma separated from the red blood cells. A separate layer of glowing blue liquid formed. Dash held out a vial and pointed into it with his wand. The blue liquid drained from the sphere. He filled two more vials with the remaining fluids.

"What is that?" Maximus asked, looking at the glowing blue.

A slow grin spread across the Arcane's face. "If I'm right—and I usually am—this is the answer to our problems."

The Master cleared his throat. "Meaning what, exactly?"

"I can advance Maximus's blood potency *and* increase the amount of blood serum we're producing. Soon we'll have enough to turn thousands of mortals into vampires."

Chapter 14

Elyssa

Elyssa hated short deadlines.

It meant she had to hurry, and hurrying usually led to mistakes. In this case, she had no room for error. She watched through the window as Underborn and his hulking companion headed toward a tool shed behind the guest bunkhouses where a very small man waited on them.

Phissilinth.

She'd met him the first time Justin had sought out Underborn to make him call off a hit on his father. While the small man seemed harmless enough, she knew without a doubt he was every bit as deadly as Underborn.

Phissilinth pulled out a key, inserted it into the tool shed door lock, and opened it. Through the opening, Elyssa saw a hanging chandelier and a rich red rug running down a long hall lined with portraits. She didn't need to ask where it led because she'd been there before. It was Underborn's lair. As to where the lair actually was, she had no idea. The key Phissilinth used could apparently be used to open doors and take them almost anywhere.

Her mouth dropped open as a thought occurred to her. She blurred outside before the three men crossed the threshold, and jumped in front of Phissilinth.

"Good day, Madame." He bowed with a flourish.

"Hello, Phissilinth."

"I'm pleased you remember my name, Miss Borathen."

She smiled. "It's a hard one to forget."

"What do you need?" Underborn said, gazing warily at the lightly wooded surroundings. Elyssa noticed few Templars came to this part of the compound, because it was so far removed from the main barracks and the central buildings. "We shouldn't tarry, and you have a job to do."

"I want the key," Elyssa said, pointing to the simple brass skeleton key in Phissilinth's child-like hand.

"What do you propose to do with it?" Underborn said. "Rescue Justin? Open a doorway straight into the lion's den and snatch him from their grasp?"

"Couldn't have put it better myself." She narrowed her eyes. "Why risk everyone when I could just use that?" Anger flared at Underborn's cavalier attitude, but she held it at bay with some effort. For all she knew, this was another of his tests.

The assassin put on an oily smile. "If it were so simple, I would have done it myself." He took the key from Phissilinth and held it up. "This key is one of the seven Relics of Juranthemon. It is priceless, of course, and very powerful. As a price for such power, it can be very difficult to control."

Elyssa huffed out a breath. "First of all, Juranthemon sounds like a word you just made up. Second, I don't give a damn how hard it is to control. Tell me how to use it and I swear I'll return it to you."

"You don't understand, Miss Borathen." Underborn's smile went from oily to downright condescending. "The key can open virtually any location, so long as another door opens at the other end. But to go to an unexplored place means you must first show the key where you want to go on the Map of Juranthemon."

"Then get the map and show it."

"I do not possess it. I do, however, have a very extensive list of places the key goes to. Maximus's compound, unfortunately, is not one of them."

"And a tool shed is?" She waved at the old stone structure.

"This tool shed was formerly a small chapel used by a small, forgotten sect of Indians who inhabited this area." He indicated some of the other ancient structures in the area. "These building were preserved by Arcanes and repurposed by the Templars. The original door has been replaced many times over the years, but that doesn't matter to the key. Unless you can steal the map from whoever owns it, I can't create a new path into Maximus's compound."

Elyssa didn't believe him for a second. A last-ditch, desperate plan formed in her head. Underborn would probably kill her for trying it, but he left her no choice.

"In fact," Underborn continued, "the key was not originally a key at all. It tends to present itself as a different object, depending on the user's expectations." He held it in his palm and reverently traced a finger along the metal.

"Really? That's amazing." Elyssa leaned closer. "It looks like a skeleton key."

"Indeed. It's fascinating."

Elyssa looked behind Underborn and opened her eyes in alarm.

The assassin turned his head to look. Elyssa snatched at the key. A gloved hand gripped her wrist too late. The cold metal of the key pressed against the inside of her palm. All she had to do was escape three trained assassins.

Easy, peasy, lemon squeezy. Well, more like difficult, difficult, lemon difficult.

Elyssa twisted her arm from the big man's grasp. Opened her mouth to shout for help. A heavy foot caught her in the back. She somehow kept her balance and spun sideways as the same foot whooshed by her head. Underborn and Phissilinth stood nearby. The tiny man's face held an expression of concern. The assassin looked entertained. The big man in black lunged for her arm again.

Elyssa jumped away and jammed the key into her jeans pocket. The big man's arms blurred for her. She fell back on learned instinct, blocking and diverting his blows. He was fast, but she was faster, unencumbered by all that muscle. In fact, every move he used seemed familiar. This was, in itself, strange, considering most people learned the same moves and executed them with their own unique mannerisms. Everyone had their own tics and nuances, even masters of the fighting arts.

Her mind flashed back a few years. She'd fought this man before. In fact, she'd fought him many times before. No one else moved like—no—it couldn't be! Disgust and betrayal welled inside her. Rage broke the surface in the form of a snarl on her lips. The man's foot lashed out. Elyssa threw her hands down in a blocking motion, simultaneously using the power of her opponent's kick as a springboard, launching her straight up. Twisting in midair, she slammed the side of his face with a brutal kick. Landed lightly on her feet. Danced back.

The big man staggered back a foot, grabbing his jaw.

Elyssa bared her teeth. "Come get me, traitor."

"Oh dear," Phissilinth said. "Perhaps you should—"

Underborn laughed. "And spoil the fun?"

The big man's fists tightened. He straightened and stared at the assassin. "Get your own key, Sorenson," he said in an unnaturally deep voice, one which Elyssa knew to be magically altered.

But he could talk like a midget for all she cared. She knew who he was now. And her heart ached.

Another laugh erupted from the assassin. "Why do I need to retrieve that which I already possess?" He pulled another key from his pocket.

Elyssa looked at the skeleton key in her hand. "You're lying."

Underborn shut the door to the tool shed. Put the key in the lock and twisted. The door opened to a grassy glade. Birds twittered and butterflies danced in the sunlight. He shut the door. Opened it again. The hallway once again presented itself.

"The key you possess opens a footlocker in my bedroom." Underborn smiled. "I knew you couldn't resist."

His brawny companion cracked his knuckles and said, "Enough with the games, Underborn." He turned to Elyssa. "I know how you must feel now, but I'm doing this for the greater good. I'm not a traitor, no matter what you think."

"Just get the hell out of here." Elyssa's throat was raw with anger and grief. How could he go over to this man, this evil, psycho killer? "The next time I see you, I'll break your jaw."

Underborn and Phissilinth stepped through the doorway. The big man hesitated at the threshold. "You can try, Ninjette." He closed the door behind him, leaving Elyssa alone in the dark.

She sank to her knees and let the tears flow. So many emotions assaulted her at once—hope, fear, anger, betrayal—she hardly knew what she was feeling. He had to have his reasons. He *couldn't* be a traitor. He'd helped her before, tried to help her escape her father when he'd wanted to make her take the White. She took deep breaths to banish the tears. He had to have a reason for this.

Think logically, damn it!

The jumble of emotions cleared and her breathing eased. Now she felt foolish. What if she'd blown his cover? What if he was working against Underborn and now she'd exposed him? She jerked to her feet.

No, Underborn knew who he was. It should come as no surprise whatsoever that he would use Michael, her own brother, against her. Until she had time to dig deeper, she had to remain focused on the task at hand.

Gripping the key, she cocked her arm back to throw it over the wall surrounding the Templar compound.

"What are you doing back here?" Fausta said.

Elyssa jerked and looked at the other woman. "Thinking."

"Haven't you heard? We're not supposed to do that. That's what the commanders are for." Fausta wrinkled her nose. "I do not like this plan of attack. Stealth squads? Your father is wrong. Dead wrong. It's the stupidest plan ever."

"For once, we agree," Elyssa said slipping the key into her pocket. She regarded the strong-nosed woman for a moment. They'd only met recently, but Elyssa had been through hell and back with her in Justin's quest to apprehend Vadaemos. Finding the traitor in their midst would require help, and Fausta might have inside knowledge of Christian's organization.

"There's something more going on with you," Fausta said. "I can see it in your eyes."

The Italian woman was nothing, if not blunt, and Elyssa didn't have time to be anything but straightforward. "I need a list of anyone who'd know about our arrival yesterday."

"Practically everyone in the compound."

"Yes, but how long before we arrived did they know?"

Fausta shrugged. "Christian announced the motor pool duties only half an hour before, so probably around that time."

"How far in advance did Christian know about our arrival?"

"I wouldn't know. Beck might." Her eyes narrowed. "Wait a minute. You think someone set us up?"

Elyssa folded her arms. "Don't you?"

Fausta tapped her chin. "Things happened so fast, I really didn't give it much thought. Christian said Maximus has been watching La Casona. I'm sure he has eyes everywhere."

"Yeah, but would he assign a vampire army complete with scroll casters to watch the place? No way. You can't hide that many vampires for a long time, especially raw recruits. I think they used a scroll spell to mask their presence."

The other woman leaned against the stone wall of the tool shed. "You think someone on Christian's advisory council betrayed us." Her eyes hardened. "But of course you believe your father's council is blameless."

"That's because I know how my father operates."

"And because you think nobody in your legion could possibly betray you, right?" Sarcasm dripped from her words.

"Absolutely not." Elyssa slashed a hand through the air. "My father's advisory council consists of my brother, Michael, when he's around, and my mother. He hardly tells them anything. Most of the time he keeps his plans close to his chest and springs them at the last moment."

"And you think he told Christian his plans to come down here in advance?"

"He must have. Christian wouldn't appreciate another commander popping in unannounced, especially when he wants to convince him to start a joint military operation against the vampires. That requires a lot of planning."

Fausta held up a hand. "Fine, fine. Your father is paranoid. Assuming this is true, we can concentrate on Christian's council."

"Has he had problems with other operations?"

"Problems, yes. But I wouldn't point to a traitor as the cause for those problems."

Elyssa pursed her lips. "Hmm, so nothing stands out to you?"

"No."

Elyssa had hoped to discount Beck as a traitor, but if this was the first disaster Fausta could point to as the possible product of betrayal, her question might have done the opposite and pointed to him as the likeliest candidate for a good ass-kicking. Beck had sold them out to Thomas Borathen after they'd captured Vadaemos, all so he could earn a few brownie points, no doubt. That had led to a duel between Thomas and Justin. Then Daelissa had shown up and freed Vadaemos. The demon spawn had killed several Templars, including her brother, Jack, that night. Her chest tightened. What if Beck hadn't called her father to win favor, but to start a fight so Vadaemos could escape?

His actions had led to chaos. Or would Daelissa have shown up anyway? Elyssa couldn't say. She conveyed her suspicions to Fausta.

The Italian woman arched an eyebrow. "Beck is a *culo*, sure, but I don't think he would betray us."

"What if he resents my father for sending his family away from Atlanta?"

"For kissing you?" Fausta snorted. "So your father is paranoid and overprotective. Are you sure he's fit for duty?"

Elyssa held back an angry retort. "Okay, fine. If it's not Beck, who else is on the council?"

"Lieutenants Jean-Claude Ville, Gigi Martinez, and Ludovico Maracci."

"Three people?" The task ahead seemed even harder, especially given the time limit involved.

Fausta shook her head. "Ludovico died in the ambush, so I sincerely doubt he was involved."

"Definitely dead and not disappeared?"

"I saw his body. It was him."

"We need to question the other two. Check their stories."

"What makes you think they'll help?"

Fausta had a point. These people might give Elyssa the time of day simply because of her last name. But if she started questioning them about treachery, they'd boot her out and probably complain to Christian and Thomas as well.

"The wheels are spinning," Fausta said. "Who are you going to beat up first?"

"This isn't time to be joking," Elyssa said. "In case you don't remember, we're supposed to be attacking Maximus tomorrow. What if he already knows we're coming?"

A curse escaped Fausta's lips, and her face sobered. "Come on." She motioned for Elyssa to follow.

"Where are we going?"

"We have no time for, how do you Americans say it—pussy-jumping around."

Elyssa chuckled. "I think you mean pussy-footing." She jogged to catch up to Fausta. "Who are we going to first?"

"We don't have time for games, so we're going to be direct." Fausta looked back over her shoulder and smiled. "We'll break into their rooms and search them."

Bella walked around the corner and Fausta nearly plowed right over her.

"Goodness!" said the short Arcane. "What..." She looked from Fausta to Elyssa and back again. "Oh. Something really bad must be happening for you two to be taking a walk together." She smiled and rubbed her hands together. "Where are we going? Are we going to rough anybody up?"

"No way," Fausta said, shaking her head. "We'll attract too much attention with so many people."

Elyssa pursed her lips and regarded Bella. Thought about how she'd hotwired cars in seconds. "I think she'll be perfect for what we have in mind. Think about it—who'd be better at opening locks than an Arcane?"

"Oh yes, I'm an old hand at larceny," Bella said. "During my younger years I excelled at breaking and entering."

"Younger years? You still look like a child," Fausta said, towering over the other woman.

"Don't be so mean," Bella said with a frown. "I'm only a head shorter than you. Besides, *botte piccola fa vino buono*."

Fausta laughed. "I hope you're right."

"What does that mean?" Elyssa asked.

The Arcane woman winked. "It's an old Italian saying: A small cask makes good wine."

Elyssa already knew Bella was more powerful than her size indicated. "If we're searching rooms, we'll need all the help we can get." She gave Bella an appraising look. "I have a feeling our sorceress friend here makes very good wine when she mixes magic and subterfuge."

Bella beamed at her. "After so many boring years in *Ciudad De Los Angeles*, it will be wonderful to live life in the fast lane again."

"Fine, fine," Fausta said. "Let's go." She stalked toward the officers' barracks.

Bella followed close in her wake.

Worry still gnawed at Elyssa as she caught up to her partners in crime, but at least she knew one thing for sure. Things were about to get interesting.

Chapter 15

I grinned lazily—even though grinning was hard with a gag in my mouth—at the three men standing over me as Dash withdrew a long needle from my arm.

"Don't give him too much," said Maximus.

"I daresay he already has," said the Master.

Dash didn't look concerned. "It's only temporary. I need to undo one of his straps to get the IV in."

The big vampire touched a finger to the strap on my forearm and the one securing my bicep. My arm flopped loose. Dash rearranged my arm. I felt a sharp prick in my wrist.

"Okay, tighten the straps now," he said.

Tension pressed against my arm. But I felt way too good to care.

You're drugged, moron! Snap out of it!

"Why?" I tried to say around the hard ball in my mouth. "I want Mommy."

"He's drooling," said the man with the funky mustache.

"I've set the blood drip so it won't drain him faster than he can regenerate," Dash said.

Maximus nodded. "How much blood can we expect daily?"

"Maybe a liter. But he needs to feed."

"Already taken care of," Maximus said, and looked at the British vampire. "How much blood can you spare for the serum, Master?"

The Master adjusted his monocle. "A liter will be no problem."

Dash nodded. "Once I've diluted the serum, I could quadruple our production."

"Excellent work, chaps. I believe our little plan will pay big dividends in the end."

Their conversation droned on, but I was too out of it to comprehend everything they were saying.

"...but what if Daelissa changes her mind again?" Dash waved his arms as if to indicate the room. "All this work will be for nothing."

Mention of the rogue angel's name snapped me from my haze. I focused on the conspirators and tried to take in whatever they said.

"It doesn't matter if she changes her mind," Maximus said. "She's crazy half the time anyway. We figure out how to reprogram those things and Methuselah can send all he wants. We'll just make 'em part of the army."

"Bloody good, chaps," said the Master. He pulled a pocket watch from his cloak and glanced at it. "My contacts tell me the Syndicate is meeting to discuss their difficulties with the Arcanes. They even sent an envoy to the Templars, if you can believe it."

"Are they still arguing about what to do with me?" Maximus grinned.

"Indeed, my young apprentice. But our people have enough votes to keep the Syndicate running in circles."

"And Vlad?"

"He's been beyond caring about the mortal world for centuries." The Master polished his monocle and held it up to the light for inspection. "I believe full-scale war with the Arcanes is imminent, wouldn't you say, Mr. Armstrong?" He replaced the monocle on his eye and headed for the door.

Dash nodded and followed him. "My contacts told me the council is pushing hard for retribution. They've tripled security on arcane schools, and are calling in the battle mages."

"That should keep the Templars off our backs," Maximus said. He leered down at me for a few seconds before turning and leading the others out of the room and away until their conversation faded.

Whatever Dash had injected me with lost its hold some indeterminable time later, and I lapsed back into coherence. I felt tired. So very tired. Hopelessness pressed against me like a suffocating wave.

"Those entities seem intent on doing bad things," said the calm voice of my companion.

I almost cussed him out for stating the obvious, but felt way too exhausted to make the effort. Besides, for all I knew, they had him on the same drugs Dash had doped me with. Anyone would be stupid with that crap in their veins.

"Ungh," I said. It took everything to get one syllable out, not that it mattered with the ball gag in my mouth.

"I do not have a greater context to understand their motives. Perhaps if a library were made available to me I could understand their puzzling desire to cause you harm."

At least he cared.

A hot tear trickled down my cheek. I closed my eyes against the pain. Elyssa's face filled the void. I looked longingly at her full lips, her bright violet eyes, her porcelain skin. I might never again touch those lips or feel her warmth press tight against me.

I miss you.

I groaned.

Someone made a noise to my right. I looked and saw a middle-aged woman I didn't recognize standing there. "I'm supposed to come here," she said, looking around. "Uh, Maximus sent—"

My demon surged for her so fast she didn't have time to complete the sentence. My essence latched onto hers and drew long and hard, an alcoholic having the first drink of the day. She moaned and rubbed her hands up and down her body. I felt the feverish hunger in me burning in my eyes. The woman straddled me and pressed her lips to my face, my chest.

I was out of control. Part of my mind watched in fascinated horror. Another part was too angry and tired to give a damn. Energy flooded into me, rich, warm, and fulfilling. Within minutes, the woman slumped and rolled off me, thudding on the floor. Guilt stabbed into me and I jerked control from the demonic force within before it killed this woman. She might love Maximus and want to be a vampire, for all I knew, but killing her wouldn't solve a thing.

Maximus was the first in a short list of people who needed killing.

Amanda appeared, an evil grin on her face. "Enjoy your dinner, spawn?"

I glared at her. It was all I could do with the gag in my mouth. She tossed the woman over a shoulder, and carried her away down the hall.

Fully refueled, but thoroughly depressed, I stared at the ceiling and wondered how long I would suffer this fate. My only choice would be to let myself die. But would my demonic urges allow me to do such a thing or would it take control at the last minute?

A hand gripped something on the back of my head and the gag popped loose. I spat it out and looked into Maximus's eyes.

"What are you doing down here again?" I said. "Come to gloat more?"

He leaned against the wall to my side and regarded me with a serious look. "Who is your mother?"

"As if you don't know already."

"Humor me."

I considered telling him to screw himself, but saw no harm in telling him something Daelissa must have already told him. "Alice Conroy."

"Are you certain?"

"Go screw yourself." I felt marginally better going with my first instinct.

He smiled. "I'm genuinely curious. You are mixed spawn and human which should make your blood worse than a pureblood, and yet even Dash agrees your blood is far superior."

"Have you ever met someone with my pedigree?"

"No. So for all we know, the assumption that a human-spawn mix is inferior might be wrong." He shrugged. "Dash finds you fascinating. I suspect he would like to take you apart to satisfy his magical curiosity."

"Thank heavens you're such a good, caring person."

Maximus pulled up a stool and sat down. "You realize we don't have to be enemies, Justin. Although I have cooperated with Daelissa, she is far from being a true ally. If anything, I'm just a tool for her."

"Then why help her? She plans to let her other angel friends into this world, and guess who they won't need anymore?"

"I'm not a fool. You think I don't know her plans? I'm a diversion, nothing more. I know she has true allies who are far more involved in her plans, but I don't know who they are. The Master is my true ally, my mentor, and there are several Arcanes who also believe in our cause."

"To do what? Form a vampire army and rule the world?" I snorted. "Maybe you could be a little less cliché with your plans for world domination. Hey, I have an idea—how about you and your vampires sponsor a roadside trash pickup? You can save the environment and feel great about yourselves."

"I don't have a diabolical plan to rule the world, little man." Maximus leaned over me and showed his fangs. "Not that I should expect anyone of your limited years to understand. I want a better world. We have the gift of immortality. Imagine it! Mankind could live forever. Think of the achievements we could make."

His coppery breath was making me nauseous. "With you as the Grand Poobah, right?"

He shrugged. "Perhaps temporarily. The Master has already indicated he has no desire to rule. He would advise me."

"What happens when there are no more humans to feed the vampires? What about the people who don't want to be vampires? The Red Syndicate keeps your numbers low so they don't run out of food, not because they don't want everyone having the gift of immortality." I felt dirty just defending the vampire nation. "Face it, Maximus, you want power, plain and simple. Your whole Vampire's Revolution is just the kind of crap you know people will listen to so you can justify a massive power grab."

"Food will be no issue. Even now we only accept those with the desire to see deeper into themselves. To become more than they are. Those noms who are sheep, who don't care about advancing, will be used as cattle because they deserve nothing more."

"So you get to choose who's predator and prey? Who receives immortality and who gets to be a vampiric pincushion?" I pulled my mouth into a sneer. "You're not a god. You're a sicko."

Maximus opened his mouth as if to argue then clamped his teeth shut with a click. His fist pounded the table right next to my head. "Obviously, you're beyond reason. I'd hoped to convince you I'm right. Perhaps then you'd donate blood to the cause, and I could free you."

Son of a bitch, I could have gotten free!

Talk about screwing myself over. "Uh, actually, you are making sense," I said. "Maybe I was just angry and felt the need to lash out."

Maximus laughed. "Too late." He leaned in close. "Too late. I gave you a chance and you slapped my helping hand away. Perhaps in another year or so I'll reconsider. If it isn't too late by then."

I ground my teeth.

The vampire sat back down on his stool. "I know a little of your history, Justin Slade. Your former classmate Brad Nichols had plenty to say about you."

"Yeah, great job turning him into a vampling, by the way." Brad hadn't been my BFF or anything, but I wouldn't wish turning into one of the walking dead on anyone.

"I regret our original serum was unable to fully turn him, but he accepted the risk. I knew people like this Brad Nichols when I was young. Kids who thought they were better than everyone else and took what they wanted from the weak. I, too, was bullied and harassed."

I gave him an incredulous look. "Dude, you're huge. Who would mess with you?"

"Believe it or not, I was short and scrawny. I grew up in New York and attended a Jewish school. This wasn't popular with the Catholic kids in my neighborhood."

"You're Jewish?"

"I was adopted by Jewish immigrants who found me abandoned when they arrived at port. My real parents left me behind a rat-infested warehouse. I probably would have been eaten to the bones had not my adopted father gone around the back to urinate and found me naked on the ground."

I grimaced. "That's horrible. What kind of people would do that to a baby?"

The look he returned sent chills down my spine. "Believe me, I asked them the same question when I found them." His fangs slid out an inch.

Somehow, I managed not to gulp. "What made you decide to become a vampire?"

"The Master, persecuted by his brethren, fled here from Britain and took a teaching position at my school. He saw how poorly my peers treated me and took me under his wing. When I reached a mature age after university, he offered me the chance for immortality." Maximus held out his hands. "And here I am."

Try as I might, I couldn't make myself hate the guy. After all, he hadn't really kidnapped my sister, although, yeah, I guess he'd kidnapped me and my father. But it wasn't for an evil cause or anything. In fact, the more I thought about his crimes, the more reasonable they seemed. Maximus was an all right guy who wanted what was best for me and everyone else. And he had the prettiest glowing red eyes.

Something from recent memory prompted me to look away from those glinting rubies and squeeze my eyes shut. The positive feelings I had for him faded and a dull ache settled into my head. "Stop using your little vampire tricks on me," I said. "Maybe you had a rotten childhood. Maybe rats almost ate you. It's sad—tragic even. But it's no excuse to kidnap me or my father and start Overworld War One or whichever war you guys are on now." I opened my eyes and looked him full on. "So cut it out."

A surprised look crossed his face. "How did you—" He shook his head. "You're right. Compulsion is obviously not the way to convince you. Perhaps one day you'll see and agree with me. Until then, I regret to say, you must be confined. Once we've dealt with the impending Templar attack, I'll see about relocating you to more comfortable quarters."

"Templar attack?"

"Oh, yes." He smiled. "Their fearless leader, Thomas Borathen, has a very sneaky plan in mind."

"And you know this how?"

"How else? Daelissa has eyes and ears everywhere. One of her minions delivered the details to me. I regret to say we'll have to kill any Templar who sets foot in my domain."

Fear stabbed into my chest. Would Elyssa be in the attacking force? "What do they plan to do?"

"How about this—I'll tell you all about it for your next bedtime story." He checked the time on his phone. "In fact, we have only a few more hours until our uninvited guests show up."

"No, please, Maximus. I'll do whatever you want. Don't kill them."

He leaned down until his face was half an inch from mine. "You spurned my offer earlier, Slade. I may be kind to my allies, but I am unforgiving to my enemies. Bear this in mind for future reference."

With that, he left the room.

"I think your friends are in dire trouble," said the nearly monotone voice of my roommate after a moment of silence.

I couldn't have said it better myself.

Chapter 16

Elyssa

Bella opened Jean-Claude's apartment with a swish of her wand.

"Finally," Fausta said and pushed past the other woman. "Took you long enough."

"They had wards protecting this place." Bella followed her in. "If I'd opened it without disarming them, every Templar in the compound would have come running."

Elyssa touched Bella's arm. "Can you check the locks on the other apartments? Maybe disarm them in advance?"

The Arcane smiled. "What a wonderful idea, Elyssa. I'll be back soon."

As soon as the other woman vanished, Elyssa stormed over to Fausta and jerked her away from the kitchen drawer she was rifling. "What the hell's your problem with Bella?"

"Let me go before I—"

"Before you what? Start a fight in an officer's apartment, which you've just illegally broken into?"

Fausta freed her arm and resumed looking through the drawer. "Fine. I'll treat her nice." She flicked her eyes to Elyssa. "Happy?"

Elyssa rolled her eyes. "Whatever. I swear you're the grumpiest, most volatile Templar I've met."

"I'm not grumpy!"

"You'd never even know how pretty you are with that frown always on your face. It's like someone pees in your oatmeal every morning."

"I don't frown all the—wait, you think I'm pretty?" A look of astonishment crossed Fausta's face.

Elyssa felt acutely uncomfortable. "Uh, yeah—but don't let it go to your head."

"Well, well, what have we here?" said a male voice from the door.

The two women jumped.

Adam Nosti waved from his position where he casually leaned on the doorframe. He arched an eyebrow. "I knew you guys had that furtive look to you." He pushed off the jamb and glanced around the room. "Isn't this one of the officer's quarters?"

"Shhh," Elyssa said and snatched him by the arm, jerking him further inside. Half a dozen lies ran through her head before she decided to tell him the truth. Adam, after all, was quite the conspiracy theorist, so he might believe her. "We think there's a traitor in Christian's upper brass."

"A traitor?" said a horrified voice from the doorway. Meghan came inside, eyes wide.

"*Madre de dios*," Bella said, coming in behind Meghan. "Who let the dogs out?"

All eyes settled on her, and for a brief moment, there was absolute silence.

"Does that not mean what I think it does?" the Arcane said, her eyes uncertain. "I'm practicing my American idioms."

"If they know we're in here, who else is going to just stumble in?" Fausta demanded, arms akimbo. "We haven't even searched the first apartment yet."

"Looking for incriminating evidence?" Adam said, a mischievous twinkle in his eye. "I have a practiced hand at that."

Meghan crossed her arms and glared at the others. "Nobody's doing a thing until you explain what in the world is going on in here."

Elyssa gave her the short version, leaving out the details about Underborn's involvement.

"I can't possibly believe a Templar would do such a thing," the healer replied. "And even if they did, what do you expect to find in their living quarters? A signed invitation from Maximus to betray Christian? Emails? A video of the suspect calling the vampires and telling them what to do?" She shook her head. "You need to question the suspects and find out what they know."

118

"Honey, you never know," Adam said in a placating voice. "Sometimes, if you look hard enough, you can find all sorts of telltale signs people leave behind."

"We don't have time to round them up and play twenty questions." Elyssa resisted the urge to stomp her foot like a child. "Justin's in trouble, his sister is in trouble, and if Maximus knows about our upcoming attack, the vampires will slaughter our people."

"For the sake of argument, you think this betrayal happened within the past few days?" Meghan asked.

"It must have. My father probably told Christian a day or two in advance that we were coming."

"Very well." The Arcane healer sighed and pulled out her wand. "I may have a spell for such a thing, provided any communications happened no more than three days ago, and they happened here."

Adam's eyebrows shot up. "Whoa, what spell are you talking about?"

She offered him a sly smile. "A girl's got to have some secrets."

Bella took a seat. "This should be fascinating."

"Get up!" Fausta said. "You might shed hair, and Jean-Claude will know someone was here."

The Arcane pulled a long strand of hair from the back of the couch. "I think someone already beat me to it."

"You know how you wondered what the walls would say if they could talk?" Meghan said, weaving her wand in an intricate pattern around the room.

"You can bring inanimate objects to life?" Bella asked.

Meghan smiled. "Not exactly." Her wand emitted blue particles of light, which dusted the room in a cold glow. "Everything absorbs energy, and the energy leaves behind a pattern. This spell pulls the sound patterns back out and plays them."

"Holy mother," Adam said. "Do you know what I could do with a spell like that? How much it would help my investigations?"

Meghan's eyes hardened. "Save the discussion for another time, Adam." She opened her mouth to say something else when the faint sound of voices echoed in the room—voices that belonged to someone other than the intruders.

"Oh, Jean-Claude, you naughty man. What are you going to do to me on this couch?" said a female in a sultry voice.

"Let's just say we'll be cleaning up afterward," said a low, French voice.

Bella leapt off the couch, brushing at her clothes as if they were on fire.

Meghan's face burned bright red. "Those were the earlier conversations. Let me forward through to the more current patterns."

Elyssa went to the door to stand watch as Meghan worked her magic. Thankfully, the officers were still in preparations for the upcoming operation. They might not even return to their quarters for the evening. But if Elyssa couldn't find the traitor, she planned to stop the operation one way or the other. No Templar blood would be spilled if she could help it.

Adam appeared at her side. "I need to talk to you."

"Then talk."

He motioned her into the hallway. Elyssa reluctantly stepped outside the door, looking toward the building lobby to be sure they weren't visible to anyone who happened by outside.

"My sister is in Maximus's compound."

"I know."

"She hasn't always been perfect, but she's all the family I have left in the world." He took a deep breath. "Look, there's something you're not telling us. I've been at this investigation gig for too long not to be able to tell when someone is keeping secrets."

Elyssa crossed her arms, her mind searching for reasons not to tell Adam about Underborn. The Arcane geek had helped her and Justin a lot in the short time they'd known him. He'd even given them instructions for finding the assassin. While she definitely didn't want to tell Christian or her father, Adam deserved to know. "It's not really a secret, but I don't want other Templars to know."

"Know what?"

"Underborn has a plan to get Justin out, but he won't commit unless I find the Templar mole. He claims the spy would compromise his people inside Maximus's compound."

Adam swore and furrowed his brow. "Can he get my sister out?"

"We can ask."

"No, we have to insist. Even if we have to lie about the mole, we've got to make him get Felicia out of there."

"You want to lie to the Overworld's deadliest assassin?"

He looked straight into her eyes. "Without a doubt. If it saves her, then damned be the consequences."

A twinge of doubt plucked at Elyssa's nerves. "I don't think Meghan would like to hear you talking that way."

He smiled. "Then let's be sure we find the mole." His gaze darted toward the apartment. "I'll go help her."

Elyssa watched him go back inside. She hadn't thought about lying to Underborn, but since Adam mentioned it, she felt slightly more assured about their mission. If it meant saving Justin, she'd lie to Underborn in a heartbeat. She checked the time. Less than two hours until deadline. If she could do this right, she would, otherwise, she'd lie.

After what seemed hours, but was in reality only half an hour, Meghan worked through the sound patterns while Adam recorded them on his arcphone so he could search them for key phrases. Despite having a lot of crazy sex, nothing indicated Jean-Claude was the traitor.

They moved on to Gigi's quarters.

"I'm filtering out random noises," Meghan said, after several moments of spell casting failed to produce any talking. "So I guess Gigi doesn't talk much."

A ghostly female voice emanated from the bedroom. Meghan walked inside. Adam followed with his phone. Elyssa stayed by the door, anxiety growing as she waited for them to finish and hopefully find something, anything. The next person on the list would be Beck. He was a new officer, promoted only recently, so he didn't have his quarters here yet. Instead, he'd probably been staying in general quarters or, at best, one of the cottages normally reserved for grounds keeping. Could he really be the traitor?

Adam and Meghan emerged. Adam shook his head. "She talks in her sleep," he explained in answer to the querying looks of the others. "Mostly nonsense." He gave a nervous laugh, his eyes looking a bit unsettled.

"What's wrong?" Elyssa said.

He rubbed the back of his neck. "Nothing I can put my finger on. I guess I feel bad for the woman. Didn't you hear the screaming?"

Elyssa nodded. She'd heard a lot of weird noises coming from the bedroom while searching the rest of the apartment, but had discarded them as useless. A sigh escaped her lips. "There's only one person left. Beck."

"What about Ludovico?" Fausta said. "Maybe he was the traitor and they accidentally killed him." She shrugged. "Stranger things have happened."

"We should be thorough," Meghan agreed.

The group walked down the hallway to the next apartment. The building wasn't large—just enough to accommodate up to five apartments, and didn't offer many places to hide should someone enter the main lobby. Elyssa had already scouted the other hallways and found two emergency exits they could use. The problem would be escaping notice in the wide-open corridors.

"So freaky," Adam was saying to Bella. "Like the poor woman has nightmares every time she sleeps."

"She wrote about them in her diary," Fausta said, rolling her eyes. "In great detail. I think she's obsessed with her dreams."

"You went through her diary?" Bella said.

Fausta sighed. "Where else would I look for clues?"

"Wait, she wrote about her nightmares?" Adam gave her a curious look. "What the heck was she dreaming about that scared her so much?"

The Templar dismissed his question with a backhanded wave. "Oh, stupid things like a statue that came to life and a house where it was always raining and foggy in the backyard and sunny out front." She shrugged. "What's so scary about that?"

Adam frowned. "A statue?"

"Yes. Go read her stupid diary if you're so interested."

Elyssa's feet jerked to a halt. She almost didn't realize she was no longer moving until she looked down. Something in Fausta's statement had jolted her memory. Something about a house with—oh, crap. "Where's the diary?"

"It was stupid," Fausta said, reiterating her words slowly as if Elyssa wouldn't understand otherwise. "And there wasn't anything else interesting in there, not like Jean-Claude's quarters."

Bella's face turned red at the mention of *those* noises, and she brushed at her clothes.

"Where is it?" Elyssa asked.

"The top drawer of her nightstand has a fake bottom."

Elyssa ran back, thankful Bella hadn't rearmed the wards yet and found the nightstand in question. She dumped the miscellaneous items from the drawer, and knocked the bottom until a panel fell out along with a black, leather-bound diary. The first several pages chronicled Gigi's early days at the Templar Academy until she apparently grew tired of writing every day and stopped. The next section was short, but chilling.

The same nightmare again. I'm afraid to tell anyone or they might think I'm going crazy. Who is the woman in the statue? Why can't I see her face? And what's in the fog outside the back window? I know I saw someone out there. But I can't open the sliding glass door.

Elyssa looked at the date of the entry. It was more than ten years ago. She thumbed through a few more pages, each one detailing other iterations of the same dream, scattered randomly over the past decade. But once she reached more recent dates, it seemed the woman had suffered the same nightmare at least once a week. In the past month, Gigi noted the same dream almost every night.

I'm crazy. I have to be. I'm unfit for duty. But how can I tell Christian? Other than these dreams, I feel fine and in control. I asked Healer Delgado about recurring dreams, and she said most of the time they come from childhood trauma. I wish I could remember more of the dream. I wish I could remember what happens when I walk out the front door and into the sunshine.

A horrible realization crept over Elyssa as a similar scene replayed in her mind. After she'd taken the White and had the memories of the previous two months erased, she'd had the dream of being inside a house with a fog-shrouded backyard and a sunny front. She'd seen her own face in the fog outside the back and assumed in retrospect the entire thing had something to do with her memories trying to resurface.

Maybe her reasoning was partially correct. Or maybe it had something to do with the Templar Divinity, the self-proclaimed angel, Daelissa, who was, apparently, behind most of the trouble lately. Daelissa had spoken to Elyssa of gifts her people had given humanity. Among those supernatural gifts were the ones Templars received as part of the Blessed and Novice rituals. The rogue angel herself was the one who gave them. But what if they came with a Trojan Horse buried inside? What if nobody was a traitor, but Daelissa could spy on everyone through their dreams because she was the one who blessed them? The one who touched their minds to wipe all memory of the rituals?

She bolted to her feet. They had to find Gigi immediately and question her. Put her under hypnosis, if necessary, and question every aspect of her dreams. But if Daelissa really could come to any Templar in their dreams, what good would planning do? The woman could find out anything she wanted.

Elyssa found the others still inside Ludovico's apartment. "We've got big trouble."

Bella's eyes widened. "The officers are returning?"

"God, I wish it was that simple." Elyssa waved at the others and told Meghan and Adam to stop what they were doing.

"This had better be good," Fausta said, crossing her arms and tapping her foot. "Because we're running out of time."

"You'd better make time." Elyssa held up the diary. "Because if Daelissa can do what I think she can, the Templars won't be able to keep anything from her, and Maximus can roll over us any time he wants."

Chapter 17

Time ticked by at a snail's pace. Worry gnawed at my insides, leaving me with a sick, hollow feeling. I couldn't do a damned thing to help Elyssa or the Templars. Hell, I couldn't even scratch my nose. I was sick to death of being tied down and feeling useless. Though Maximus had been gone a while, Amanda hadn't returned from wherever he'd sent her, which was something of a respite. I'd been unable to resist struggling against my bonds, but succeeded only in chafing myself raw.

The scrape of a foot in the hallway drew my attention, but the angle of the table limited my view. Felicia's head poked around the corner. She looked around the room and rushed inside.

"I have it," she whispered, voice full of excitement and nervousness.

"Have what?"

"Maximus's blood."

"Should I ask what you had to do to get it?"

She smiled. "Nothing terrible. I changed out his razor blade for one with a jagged edge, so he cut himself shaving. Then I sneaked in and grabbed the tissues he used to blot the cuts from the trashcan." She held up a wad of tissue with a couple spots of blood on it.

"He's not much of a bleeder," I said.

She pulled the IV from my arm and stared at the container of blood Maximus had collected. Her nostrils flared, and I could tell it took a lot of effort for her to ignore it. Shaking her head like someone awaking from a daze, Felicia took the tissue and pressed it against the bond on my arm. It parted.

We both heaved big sighs of relief.

"Get me out of here and you can have all the blood they took from me."

Her eyes widened. "Really?"

"As if I could put it back inside me."

She smiled and worked on the remaining bonds. The last few seconds of imprisonment were torturous. When she finally separated the last strap I sprang off the table and stretched. My knees almost went out from under me, probably due to such a long period of inactivity. Felicia jumped and hugged me.

"I did it!" She kissed my cheek. "I can't believe I rescued you." She pointed to a bundle on a nearby chair. "I even remembered to get all your stuff."

I was so happy to see clothes again, I forgot to be embarrassed about being in my underwear. I didn't even want to think about all the potty breaks I'd taken in those adult diapers Amanda kept me in. She hadn't put another pair on me since putting me to sleep to clean out the last pair, no doubt because she had some other horrific way of demeaning me in mind. I wasted no time pulling on my pants, Felicia, for her part, wasted no time taking a sip of my blood. She sighed in pleasure. I shuddered and looked away. "Adam would be very proud," I said as I stuffed my arcphone into a pocket and threw on a shirt. "In fact, I think you should tell him what you did yourself."

A gasp came from the door. I spun, expecting to see Amanda. Instead, Katie stood at the doorway, mouth wide with shock.

"Who—what?" she said.

I waved her in. "Katie, this is Felicia. Felicia, Katie."

Felicia wiped a smidge of blood off her lips with the back of her hand, and then shook Katie's.

An overwhelming sense of relief settled into me as I realized I could kill—or save—two birds with one stone. Naturally, I still had to find Ash and Nyte and get them out of here as well, but my manly sense of duty demanded I rescue the women first.

"Justin, oh my god," Katie said, hugging me tight. "Underborn told me he might have to call off your rescue because there's a spy in the Templars, but I was like, hell to the no! And then I told him he could go eff himself with broken glass because I wasn't going to leave you in here. But I couldn't figure out a way to get Maximus's blood for the straps, and the Arcane who's supposed to help me said she wouldn't do anything until she got the okay from Underborn and—"

I put a finger to her lips. "Katie, it's all good." I took her gently by the shoulders. "But now you and Felicia need to get out of here. Is there a way I can get out without being seen?"

Katie and Felicia nodded.

"I know of two ways out," Katie said.

"Technically, there are three viable exits," Felicia said, sounding a lot smarter than I remembered her being. Then again, Adam had told me she was a whiz in school who practically disintegrated when her family was murdered.

I peered into the hallway, checking for signs of anyone coming. No telling how long I had before Amanda reared her ugly hairdo again. "Lead me to the closest one. We have to warn the Templars about the spy." I gripped Felicia's hand. "I want you to come with me. You've more than made up for past mistakes as far as I'm concerned."

She shook her head. "But I helped kidnap your father. I almost killed you and Elyssa with the vamplings."

"Felicia." I took her other hand. "Look at me."

She met my eyes with reluctance.

"I forgive you. It's time to stop letting the past rule your life and time to make your brother do the same. Maybe we can solve the mystery of your parents' murders and put an end to his obsession together."

A tear trickled down her cheek. "You—you really think it's possible?"

"Anything is possible."

She took off the horn-rimmed, geeky glasses she favored and tossed them on the floor. Crushed them underfoot. "I always dressed in these short skirts and nerdy clothes because Maximus wanted me to. Said it turned him on. I'm through being someone's pet."

I squeezed her hand. "If there's anything I learned over the past few months, you just have to be yourself and to hell with those who don't like it."

"Thanks, Justin." Felicia dropped her hand from mine. "If we get out of this alive, that's exactly what I plan to do."

I glanced at Katie. "Where are Ash and Nyte? Do they know I'm here?"

She shook her head. "I just found out they're not here anymore. Maximus sent a whole group back to Atlanta."

I wanted to ask her how and why, but my questions could wait until we were clear of this hellhole.

"I'll need to scout ahead," Felicia said. "Katie, you know the exit by the dumpsters?"

Katie nodded. "I'll take him through the cellar."

"That's a great idea. It'd be too risky taking him up top." Felicia held up a finger and trotted down the hall. She returned with a sword encased in a leather scabbard. "I got you this in case you run into trouble." She held it out to me.

I took it and fumbled with the straps, trying to figure out which way it went. Before long, both women took over, strapping it over my shoulder. Katie closed the buckle and stood back a step.

"Reminds me of that time I went to see you fight all those other nerds in Kings and Castles." She smiled.

A grin caught me off guard as that unfortunate day came to mind. "Wasn't that the same day I got drunk and said all sorts of nasty things about you online?" Talk about bottom of the barrel. It had been the day before I'd hit incubus puberty.

"We really don't have time for this," Felicia said in a low hiss. "I'll go draw the guards off the cellar door. Follow me in fifteen minutes, and I'll meet you at the dumpsters. I doubt anyone will be back there. The odor is awful, especially with a supernatural sense of smell."

"They haven't been dumping bodies there have they?" I asked, horror constricting my chest at the thought of what all the vampires had been feeding on.

Felicia shook her head. "No, even Maximus isn't stupid enough to let his followers drain the locals. All the noms who want to be vampires have to let the others feed off them in the meantime. Otherwise, we'd have the cops busting down our doors." She checked the time on her phone and showed it to us. "Fifteen minutes, then you follow, okay?"

I nodded. Katie and I watched Felicia climb the spiral stairs and leave. Katie took my hand and gripped it tight.

"I'm nervous." Sweat dampened her palm.

I gave her a sideways hug. "We'll be fine." I sniffed my armpits. "Eww. I can't wait to take a proper shower."

"Oh, man," I said as a thought hit me.

"What's wrong?" Sweat dampened Katie's blonde hair. She tied it back to keep it out of her face.

I checked the time. Ten minutes to go. "Wait here. I'll be right back." I jogged into the room where Maximus held me prisoner. A panicked sense of claustrophobia struck me full on at the sight of my table. Taking a deep breath, I surveyed the room, looking at the long rows of tables. In a far, dark corner, I saw a shadowy hump atop one and strode to it. In the dim light, I made out the form of a man, still fully dressed in a suit, lying on the surface.

He stared blankly into space. I snapped my fingers and he jerked. My blue-tinged night vision hadn't come on yet, so I couldn't make out his features, just his general outlines.

"You will help me?" he said.

"Are you a vampire?"

"I am still unsure of my designation."

Whatever was wrong with this guy might slow me down, but my conscience told me it would be wrong to leave a poor, lobotomized dude tied down like this. Touching the straps restraining him didn't do anything, so I had to run back across the room to retrieve the bloody tissue Felicia had used to free me. I brushed it against each strap and they parted. The man sat up. Pivoted and set his feet on the ground. He stood in one fluid motion and looked at me.

"Thank you." His voice remained dull and almost without inflection.

"You're welcome. Want to escape with us?"

He nodded. "It seems the next prudent move."

Man, I really had some questions for this guy. Maximus must have given him electro-shock therapy or really strong drugs. I didn't understand how his vocabulary could be so good with such obvious brain damage, though. I motioned him to follow me, walking around the outside edge of the room. My night-vision kicked on and off as I looked around the half-lit room.

Katie came in and hit something on the wall. The lights in my section flicked on.

"What are you doing?" she said. "It's almost time."

I came to an abrupt halt as the flickering light revealed a heap of arms, legs, hands, and heads. A sick feeling came over me. Good god, it was a pile of bodies!

Maximus, you sick bastard.

I spun to warn my former roommate. Shock froze me in place. I fumbled at the sword, but the girls had strapped it on at such an awkward angle, I couldn't get it out of the scabbard on my back in time.

"What is wrong?" asked the man I'd just rescued.

Except he wasn't a man at all. He was a golem. A gray man.

Chapter 18

Elyssa

A klaxon wailed in the Templar compound.

"Crap, crap, crap!" Elyssa said as she and the others left the officers' quarters. "Why are they sounding the assembly?"

Fausta shook her head. "No idea. But maybe it's a good thing. We need to warn Christian."

And I need to tell Underborn about our discovery, Elyssa thought. But would it do any good to tell him every Templar was a potential spy?

"Is Healer Delgado stationed on this base?" Bella asked Fausta.

The Italian woman nodded. "Yes. Why?"

"I want to consult her patient file on Lieutenant Martinez. Perhaps something in there will shed light on matters."

"Why don't you ask her yourself?"

Bella shrugged. "It would probably be faster if we continued our criminal activities."

Fausta looked toward the brightly lit assembly area, a large paved area as big as a football field. "I'm going to warn Christian first. Maybe he'll check into it himself."

Elyssa wasn't all that sure how Christian would react upon hearing their report. What if he didn't believe them? What if he had them arrested? They *had* to convince him. Find evidence to support their claim. "I'm going with Bella."

"Me too," said Adam, face grim.

"I can't go tell Christian one of his lieutenants is a mole all by myself," Fausta grumbled. "I'll look like an idiot."

"I'll go with Fausta," Meghan said. "I'm a healer, after all. Perhaps I can run a diagnostic on Gigi and find out how vulnerable we are to Daelissa." Her lips tightened. "I did *not* join the Templars to be used for evil."

The two groups set off in opposite directions. Healer Delgado's office was located just outside the center of the compound next to the armory. The building was dark, but Bella detected no wards guarding the door. Elyssa looked around the deserted area, assuming everyone had responded to the assembly signal.

Bella unlocked the door within a few seconds. They filed inside and looked through the building until Elyssa found the door with Delgado's name on it. The room was devoid of filing cabinets or any paperwork for that matter. A quick search revealed a complete lack of such mundane things.

Adam found a slim tablet on the Healer's desk and turned it on. An orange logo appeared, but a flick of his finger to peel it met with an error.

Warning: This device is property of Healer Delgado and cannot be accessed without her permission. Any further attempts to access this device will be met with unpleasant countermeasures.

Elyssa cursed.

Bella looked the device over and gave a helpless shake of her head. "I'm not so good with these fancy gadgets."

"Just happens to be my specialty," Adam said, pushing thick glasses up his generous nose. He pulled out an arcphone and held it next to the tablet. "It uses a face print," he said after a moment. He looked around the desk and found a picture frame lying flat on the surface. He touched the edge and a holographic image, presumably of Healer Delgado and her family, flickered on above the frame. Adam smiled. "Perfect."

He activated a spell on his arcphone. A pale light wrapped around the three-dimensional holograph of Delgado's head, taking in her auburn hair, brown eyes, and fair skin. He stared at his phone for a moment, and grunted. Elyssa forced herself to remain patient, though she couldn't help stalking back and forth while he worked. After that failed to keep her anxiety at bay, she pulled out Gigi's journal and read more of the entries to see if anything else stood out to her. Bella watched over Adam's shoulder, apparently fascinated with his process as she oohed and aahed.

Adam sat in the chair before the desk. He said a few words, closed his eyes, brow furrowed in concentration, and drew his fingers in a wavy pattern across the surface of his arcphone. A beam of light speared from the phone and struck him in the head. His face screwed up in what Elyssa guessed might be pain, though he didn't scream or shout. The blinding light from the phone covered his face in a red glow then faded, leaving spots in Elyssa's vision.

She hoped nobody had happened to look at the office over the past few minutes. They'd have to be blind not to have seen the glow coming from the spell. The dancing colors in her eyes faded and Elyssa sucked in a breath as Healer Delgado looked back at her and smiled.

"Adam?"

He nodded. "Hang on. This effect won't last long, and it hurts like hell." He flicked the tablet on.

"Good evening, Healer Delgado," the tablet said in a soothing female voice. "How can I help you?"

"Grant full privileges to Bella—uh, what's your last name?"

The Arcane smiled at him. "Bella will do just fine."

"Are you sure you'd like to add Bella Will Do Just Fine to your list of administrators?" the tablet said.

"Yes," Adam said, his face tightening and twitching.

An orb of light spun from the tablet screen and settled around Bella's face. "Welcome, Bella Will Do Just Fine. I am now yours to command."

Adam lurched from the chair and ran down the hall, hands pressed tight against his face. Elyssa stared after him in alarm.

"It's a side effect of the spell, dear," Bella said. She motioned Elyssa closer. "Let's see what we have here." She held up the tablet. "Computer, please show me all files on Gigi Martinez."

"There are ten recordings, ranging from two hours in length, to thirty minutes. Which would you like to see?" A holographic list sprang into the air in front of Bella's face. She jerked back and almost dropped the tablet.

Elyssa took the device and laid it flat on the desk so she could see the list. Bella gave her a sheepish grin.

"Did Healer Delgado come to a conclusion or guess as to what was wrong with Gigi?" Elyssa said.

"Bella, would you like me to answer the question from *Unauthorized Individual*?" The disembodied voice spoke the last two words in a robotic monotone.

"Please answer all of her questions," Bella said.

"Very well. Here are excerpts from recordings made by Healer Delgado as to the cause of Lieutenant Martinez's medical issue."

Delgado's face flickered on in place of the holographic list. "In conclusion," she said, "I prescribed her a potion from the apothecary made up of fish oil and green tea, and recommended a series of treatments with Healer Arroyo, who specializes in treating dysfunctions of the mind. I do not think this issue will persist. It's likely caused by stress."

The image vanished to be replaced by another. "Lieutenant Martinez's issue has persisted for quite some time. According to Healer Arroyo, his many sessions with her have failed to pinpoint any specific trauma, save for one. When she was still a raw recruit, she escorted a group of Arcanes into El Dorado to map out the caverns beneath the cursed city. Lieutenant Martinez was one of two survivors of the expedition and was so scarred by the experience, she requested the White from then Commander Anise Pratt, who, with great reluctance, granted this request."

Healer Delgado looked down, as if consulting something and then back up. "I can only assume the trauma from this scarring event continues to haunt the officer despite taking the White. Since we know so little about what happens in the communionary, or the effects of taking the White, I can only theorize it did not completely wipe away her memories. Healer Arroyo observed a much greater gap in Lieutenant Martinez's memory than just the expedition, however. Indeed, she was missing almost two months' worth of memories. For now, I have no easy answer to this issue, but maintain Lieutenant Martinez is still fit for duty as these dreams have not, so far, affected her exemplary performance."

They watched through the remaining excerpts, but the healer had no further clues as to the cause of Gigi's dreams. Elyssa, however, had a sinking feeling she knew what caused it. The White. It was a rare ritual, but using it for Gigi's purpose—to forget a traumatic experience—was not unheard of. Elyssa had no idea how many people had taken it. She wasn't even sure if the Templars kept records on such a thing. Daelissa obviously tampered with the memories of anyone who underwent the rituals, even the Blessed or Novice, because nobody remembered a thing about what happened during them. Elyssa was an exception, thanks to Nightliss, the dark angel and friend of Justin's, who opposed Daelissa.

But the memory gaps so typical after rituals were short, hours at most as opposed to months. If the nightmares Gigi had were indicative of Daelissa's probes for information, Elyssa could ask her father or Christian to have anyone who'd experienced such dreams to step forward. But maybe Daelissa couldn't invade just anyone's dreams. She might be powerful, but she wasn't omnipotent. What if she could spy on the thoughts of those people whose long-term memory she'd affected? That meant anyone who'd taken the White was susceptible. It meant Elyssa was susceptible.

Not good.

She shuddered. Good news, bad news. Either way, she was far more informed than she had been an hour ago. Even if it meant she could no longer be a Templar, at least the vast majority of her comrades would be safe from the rogue angel's touch.

Adam returned. His face had returned to its normal gawky appearance, though his skin glowed sunburn red. "Now I remember why I hate using that spell unless I really, really need to."

"You must bring me up to date on these gadgets," Bella said. "It makes me feel like an old ninny when I have to look up something on my arcphone. Sad to say, I use the gizmo mostly for phone calls and pinning pictures on social media instead of using it for magic."

He offered her a strained smile. "Any time."

Elyssa grabbed the tablet off the desk. "We have to get this information to my father and Christian."

"You saw something incriminating?" Bella asked.

"The White." Cold prickles ran up Elyssa's back at the mention of it. "I think Daelissa can reach Martinez because she had her mind wiped. At least, I hope so. Otherwise, it means Daelissa can enter the dreams of any Templar."

Adam gave her a curious look. "Didn't you take…" he didn't finish the thought.

"Yeah. I took the White." Elyssa's voice came out rough with emotion despite her best efforts. She'd squandered her childhood, devoted almost every moment of her life for the Templars. But if she was a danger to their secrecy, she couldn't stay. Even her father would be forced to agree to her resignation.

They raced across the compound to the assembly area. Nearly two hundred Templars stood in perfect rows as a tall man with a long red robe walked along the large stage in the front and spoke. Elyssa wondered where the rest of the legion complement was, or if her quick assessment of the crowd's size was wrong.

"Who in blazes is that?" Adam said, pointing at the man on the stage.

"Oh, goodness." Bella's eyes widened. "I believe it's Artemis Coronus, the Seneschal to the Grand Master of the Templar Synod."

And a Templar Knight. Elyssa almost stumbled with the realization as they jogged along the perimeter of the assemblage looking for her father. Very few of the Knights Templar remained, and almost no one in recent memory had been granted the ultimate honor. Even the great Thomas Borathen had never been offered the position, though he was known throughout the Overworld for his military victories over the centuries. For one of them to be here meant something serious was going on. For the Seneschal to be here meant—well, she didn't know what it meant, except major political forces were in motion.

Artemis held up a gloved fist. "The days of pitchforks and persecution are over. While the Synod does not agree with the actions of the rogue vampires known as Blood Rush, we strongly advise against a military course of action."

"You've got to be kidding," Adam said. "Since when would a Templar Knight back down from a fight?"

A deep chill gripped Elyssa's chest. The Synod could command the local legion to stand down if they brought it to a vote. They spoke for the Divinity. Supposedly, they were the only ones who had personally spoken to her—and remembered it. Elyssa didn't know the truth of the matter, but seeing how the Divinity and Daelissa were one and the same, it didn't much matter to her. If the Synod still trusted the Divinity, it probably meant they'd work against the Templars.

"There's your father," Bella said, pointing to Thomas. Fausta and Meghan stood nearby, engrossed in conversation with the

Commander Salazar while Thomas looked on as Artemis continued to rail against the decision to attack.

"You two run ahead," Adam said, stopping and panting. "I don't have supernatural endurance. I'm gonna puke if I don't take a break." He gave Elyssa another look. "And let me know when you talk to the other guy.

Underborn. "I will."

Bella and Elyssa blurred around the perimeter, reaching Christian within seconds.

The Templar commander looked at them expectantly. "*Recruit* Borathen, you'd better have an excellent reason for not being in formation right now."

"I told you she was getting proof," Fausta said, and spun to Elyssa. "You got proof right?"

Elyssa put on her best poker face and held out the tablet to Christian. "I don't know how much they told you, but here it is in a nutshell: Daelissa has been invading Lieutenant Martinez's dreams to spy on the Templars. It's possible she can do that to any Templar, but I think she's more limited than that. After examining the Lieutenant's records, I believe I have reached an explanation. Daelissa can do it because Lieutenant Martinez took the White."

Christian's jaw tightened. He folded his arms and narrowed his eyes. "Fausta, maybe you'd better tell me again exactly what you did. I know for a fact Healer Delgado is here at assembly, and only she, Lieutenant Martinez, and I know about her taking the White."

Fausta's face went white. "Uh, we..." She cleared her throat, looked down and said in a rush, "Broke into the officers' quarters where Meghan Andretti made sounds come out of the walls and figured out that Lieutenant Martinez was having bad dreams, and Elyssa read her diary, and then we—"

Commander Salazar held up a hand, his eyes going cold with disbelief and anger. "Slow down and back up. You forcibly and illegally entered the officers' quarters, and read Lieutenant Martinez's confidential journal?"

Elyssa decided Fausta wasn't doing a very good job of explaining things. "I think you're overlooking the importance of my discovery, sir."

Christian's stern eyes locked onto Elyssa. "You expect me to believe Lieutenant Martinez is a mole?"

His angry look only hardened her resolve. "I expect you to believe Daelissa can use Lieutenant Martinez to find out our plans in advance. Daelissa is helping the vampires, and Maximus probably knows we're coming."

"How would you know that?"

Elyssa took out the diary and turned to the last page. She read an entry she'd discovered while waiting on Adam to break into Healer Delgado's tablet. "*This dream was much different than the others. At first, I was in the House. As usual it was foggy and rainy through the sliding glass door in the back, but outside the front door, the weather appeared beautiful and sunny. I walked out the door, toward the sunshine, and suddenly found myself reliving the briefing with Christian and the other officers as we discussed Thomas Borathen's plans to come via arch to La Casona. It felt like a lucid dream, except I couldn't control myself. I practically relived every conversation I had with Christian and the other officers from the day, but skipped everything in between. Usually, I don't remember every little thing about a dream, but this one I do. Maybe because it was almost an exact repeat of my day? I don't know. I don't feel stressed, but maybe this new war Thomas Borathen wants to start scares me more than I want to admit.*"

Elyssa turned to the next page. "*Another strange dream. I started in the house, and after walking out the front door, found myself in the briefing with Christian, Thomas Borathen, and the other officers. In fact, this dream was exactly like the one from my previous entry—I relived briefings and several conversations from the day. This is too strange to be coincidence. It's almost like something is forcing me to relive this. Is it my troubled conscience? I never wanted war with the vampires, but after the ambush on our convoy, we don't have much choice. In my dream, I kept looking at Ludovico's empty chair and feeling the anger and pain. He shouldn't have died. How did the vampires know to be there?*"

Elyssa looked up from the diary. "I think Daelissa is somehow pushing her to dream about Templar briefings. It would explain how the vampires knew about our arrival at La Casona."

"They're dreams, recruit." Christian made an exasperated noise. " Lieutenant Martinez is obviously under great stress. Most officers, including myself, probably dream about briefings." His eyes hardened to steel. "As for you and Fausta, you'll both have nightmares once we determine the punishment for your actions tonight."

Chapter 19

I gave up trying to draw the sword, and readied my fists for a fight. Gray emotionless eyes regarded me. The golem tilted his—its—head ever so slightly to the right.

"Has this entity offended you?" it said.

"What's wrong with him?" Katie asked, staring at the gray hue of the golem's skin. "Did Maximus do something to the poor man?"

Words finally came to my tongue. "You're a golem. A gray man."

It held its hands out, inspecting them as if for the first time. "This entity—I—am gray. Is it wrong to be this color?"

My adrenaline rush faded. Either this gray man meant me no harm, or it was playing nice until I let my guard down. I'd fought these things before and knew I could take them one-on-one. Still, I wasn't about to turn my back on the thing. Positioning myself behind one of the tables, I nodded a head at the pile of bodies. "What did Maximus do to those people?"

The golem approached the pile and knelt, taking a limp hand in his. "They are also gray."

Tearing my eyes off the golem, I soaked in details I'd missed earlier. Some bodies in the pile wore gray suits. Some were without clothing. Without exception, they were all gray.

"Whoa, that's sick," Katie said, kneeling next to one of the bodies. Part of the skull hung open, revealing shiny metal inside.

I snatched Katie away from the golem. "Don't go near him."

The gray man stood and faced me. "I cannot harm you, Justin. You preserved my existence; therefore, I am bound to your service."

"Bound to my service? Like a slave?"

"I am required to follow your directives."

"What if I told you to jump off a cliff?"

The golem paused to regard me for a moment with its gray eyes. "How tall is this cliff?"

"I don't know." I shrugged. "Like a thousand feet tall."

"Would there be obstructions such as rocks or other debris at the bottom, or would there be deep water?"

"Jagged rocks."

Again, the gray man seemed to ponder the question. "The probability that such a jump would end this entity's—my—existence would likely result in declining such an order."

I couldn't help it. I burst into laughter.

"Are you expressing merriment or pain?" it asked.

I stifled another bout of laughter and took a deep breath. "I was laughing."

"You are amused at the proposition of my demise from a long fall?"

"No, no, no. It's *how* you refused that made me laugh." This thing was just too bizarre to destroy. It might be lying, but for now, I could put it to use. If we ran into any vampires, I might need a helping hand. "What happened to the other golems?"

"Such information is not inside me. I recall our group approaching this place and entering, but nothing more. Another entity—person—stood over me after an indeterminate period of blackout. It said, 'This one might work.' Another person replied with, 'It had better. It's the last one.'"

Judging from the pile of ten or more bodies, I guessed Maximus might have been trying to reprogram the golems for his own uses. Something odd occurred to me about the pile of inanimate bodies. Golems usually broke down into gray sludge when they died. Whether that was a normal thing or something their creator built in, I didn't know. These gray men had somehow remained whole, maybe because of Maximus's tampering.

Katie knelt again and looked inside the panel on one of the golem's heads. "Ooh, look at this."

I squatted beside her. A light flickered like a candle in a gentle breeze from within the cavity. I peered inside the door. The compartment was rounded and about the size of a tennis ball. A tiny globe of wavering light hovered within, equidistant from the sides. Tiny threads of energy sparked against the metallic surface inside.

"So that's what makes them tick," I said. "I guess it explains why they die if their heads are cut off."

"I have a light within me?" said a voice inches from my ear.

I jerked upright and backed away.

The gray man tilted his head at me. "I apologize if I startled you."

Taking a deep breath, I shook my head. "Guess it'll take some getting used to, having you around." I gestured at the spark. "If your comrade is any indication, yeah, you have one inside you too."

"And this is life?" he said.

Try as I might to think of this golem as an "it", I couldn't stop thinking of the thing as a "he" even though I doubted his creator had bestowed him anything between the legs. "Artificial life," I said. "Not real."

"So, I am not really alive."

"Uh, Justin, we don't have time for existential discussions." Katie pushed herself up and grabbed my hand. "We've got to meet Felicia and get out of here."

A flash of panic raced through me as I realized we'd been dawdling. "Crap, how long has it been?"

"We're going to be overdue if we don't hurry."

"How far?"

She shrugged. "I don't know, but pretty far. Like a couple hundred yards maybe."

I sighed. "Might be faster if you hitched a piggy-back ride."

Katie smiled and hopped on my proffered back. "Thought you'd never ask."

"Come with us and watch our backs," I told the golem, hoping it wasn't a mistake trusting the thing.

"I assume that is an idiom since I will have difficulty seeing your back through the person perched upon it." The golem's tone never wavered from a calm monotone.

"Uh, yeah." I resisted a face-palm. "It means protect us."

"I will."

We ran.

Not more than twenty feet later, we ran into trouble. Literally. Racing up the spiral staircase, I slammed into Amanda and sent her sprawling. She sprang to her feet in an instant, eyes wide, fangs extended at the sight of me.

"How the hell?" She bent her fingers like claws. Looked at Katie and smiled. "Oh. The little morsel helped you. I guess she fell prey to your incubus charms."

Katie slid off my back. I held my hands in what I hoped was a good fighting position. Self-defense remained one of those things I should probably have learned at some point, but the bad guys hadn't given me much breathing room.

Amanda grinned. "I'm going to make short work of you." She flashed forward.

I dodged back, but not before her sharp fingernails raked my hide, leaving bloody trails along my arm. I growled and lunged. Her body swayed left. She grabbed my arm. Twisted it, and used my momentum to drive me into the stone wall. Fireworks burst into my eyes.

"Leave him alone!" Katie yelled.

I looked up in time to see Amanda smack her against the wall like a doll.

A rough hand clawed into my hair and dragged me up. Amanda kneed me in the stomach and followed with a flurry of blows to my chest. Every breath of air exploded from my lungs. I sucked and heaved for oxygen. The vampire kicked my feet out from under me and pinned me to the floor.

"You didn't think Maximus chose me just because I can resist your incubus powers did you?" Her yellowed fangs glittered in the light. "I've studied martial arts for over a hundred years."

"Martial arts this, bitch," said Katie and dumped a flask of silver liquid on Amanda's head.

The vampire screamed as the substance burned the skin on her face. She flailed at Katie, but a gray hand caught the vampire's and held it.

"These martial arts are interesting," said the golem.

Amanda twisted away from the gray man and backed off, wiping the silver liquid from her face. It left angry red welts where it had been. "You think a little silver is going to kill me?" she screamed at Katie. "I'm going to drain you dry, you little tramp."

"I cannot allow such a thing," the gray man said, and stood between her and Katie.

I jumped to my feet and stood beside the golem. "Think you can take on two of us, Amanda?"

"Does a bear crap in the woods?" She lunged.

I let go of my body, and let instinct take control. Her fist flashed for my face. I dodged and felt the wind from its passing. The gray man grabbed her wrist. I grabbed her other arm as she overextended from the missed punch. Together, we drove our knees into her stomach and slammed her against the wall. She recovered faster than I thought possible. Kicked off the wall and flipped forward, twisting at the same time. Her arms slipped from our grasps. Amanda ran back up the stairs and vanished.

Katie stood up, rubbing her bottom, a pained look on her face. "Oh, crap."

"We're going to have company." I looked at the golem. "Where were you at the beginning of the fight?"

"I had returned to our prison room for a moment. I am sorry for the delay."

"Yeah, well keep close from here on out."

Katie clambered onto my back and wrapped her legs around my waist. "Let's go."

At the top of the spiral staircase, a long hall ran to the left and right, wide enough for four people to walk abreast. The stone construction looked old but sturdy. Doors lined the corridor to our right. To the left, the tunnel ended at a red metal door with skull and crossbones on it.

"What's in there?" I asked.

"No idea. They keep it locked all the time." Katie motioned to the right. "That way."

I jogged in down the corridor, and peered inside the first open door. It had obviously been a prison cell, converted into a room complete with a bunk bed and rug.

"This used to be a dungeon," Katie said as we raced down the hall. "This is where most of the vampires live, but thankfully, it's still dark topside, so they're probably all up there."

A young woman stepped from a doorway and yelped as we almost ran her over.

Katie motioned with her hand as we approached a junction. "Take a left at the fork."

I nearly plowed into a guy and girl who were making out hot and heavy just outside a doorway. Ahead, a group of people mingled, drinking, laughing, and talking. Loud music started up.

"Act casual," Katie said.

"With you on my back?"

"Yes."

All eyes settled on the gray man as our group pushed through the crowded hall. From what I could tell, they were all noms—normal humans.

"What's wrong with him?" asked a girl, the alcohol on her breath concentrated enough to start a fire. She grabbed at the golem's hand.

"Too much alcohol," Katie said, and then yelled, "Giddy up, horsey!"

I made a whinnying sound and the crowd burst into laughter as we galloped away. A moment later, we reached a set of stairs leading up to an open archway.

"We have to be careful here," Katie whispered in my ear. She climbed off my back. "It'll be better if we walk. At the top of the stairs is the courtyard. We'll need to take a right and go through a tunnel to reach the dumpsters."

I nodded and looked at the golem. Unless it was pitch black, he'd stand out like a sore thumb in his gray suit. I looked inside a couple of the rooms and found an open suitcase with clothes about his size. I grabbed a pair of jeans, a T-shirt, and a baseball cap. "Put these on."

"They do not match, Justin."

"I don't care. Now hurry!"

He stripped down to a pair of gray boxers while Katie watched with uneasy fascination. His hairless body appeared lean and muscular, his skin the same bloodless gray as his face. He slid on the jeans and the orange soccer jersey, sliding the baseball cap over his slicked-down, silvery hair last. Katie stood on her tiptoes and spun the hat around backwards, then slid a pair of wraparound shades on the golem's face.

She dusted off her hands. "Perfect."

The golem's expression never changed, but I figured if he had a miserable look, this was it.

"Am I sufficiently disguised?" he said.

"Yeah." I ducked into a room and grabbed a ball cap and shades for myself, slid them on. I waved toward the stairs. "Lead on, Katie."

She went up to the archway and peered through. Motioned us to follow. "Clear."

The compound looked like a fortress. A tall wall ran around the perimeter. Adobe buildings of varying size crowded the edges while a large brick-paved courtyard held the center. The shadowy forms of vampires patrolled the tops of the walls, and the courtyard was full of vampires. I'd expected them to be partying it up like the humans below, but they were all business.

Several long lines wended through the area. At the end of each one stood vampires handing out rifles and ammunition while yet another shouted squad assignments. Almost without exception, each vampire wore a band around their arm with the pierced heart of Blood Rush emblazoned upon it. No matter how raw these recruits might be, this place was obviously built with defensive capabilities. The Templars were walking into a slaughter. I had to get out of here and warn them.

Gunfire erupted from somewhere across the courtyard. Vampires shouted and raced toward the conflict, rifles at the ready.

"Oh no," I breathed. "I think the Templars are here already."

"We can get out and warn the others," Katie said, tugging my hand. "That's about all we can do."

"What the hell are you newbs doing out of the dungeon?" said an angry male voice from behind.

I turned and came face-to-face with an armed vampire. "Just wanted to see what's going on, sir."

He grabbed my shirt and pulled me close. "We told you—wait a minute. You don't smell human." His eyes went wide and he opened his mouth.

A gray hand gripped his throat and squeezed. The vampire struggled, but couldn't dislodge the hand. I walloped him in the face and he went limp. Katie took the rifle from his shoulder and slung it over hers.

"Carry him," I told the golem. "We can't leave him here."

The gray man tossed the unconscious vampire over his shoulder.

146

Somehow, we made it to the short tunnel and emerged in the middle of overflowing dumpsters. Despite Felicia's assurances, I spotted an arm poking out from one and shuddered.

The gray man tossed his unconscious passenger in an open dumpster and closed the lid.

"Where is Felicia?" Katie said, looking around the dumpsters while pinching her nose tight.

I checked the time. We were five minutes past due, but surely that wasn't enough time for her to assume something terrible had gone wrong and go looking for us, was it? Katie vanished behind a dumpster. A moment later she made an excited noise and reappeared.

"I found the exit Underborn told me about and opened it. We can go."

"Not without Adam's sister."

"At least don't stand out in the open—" Katie's mouth dropped open.

Amanda and a cluster of vampires rounded the corner, guns drawn. Some had rifles. Others held pistols. They all looked ready for blood.

Chapter 20

Elyssa

Fausta clenched her fists. "Punishment? Commander, have you ever known me to do something stupid for no reason?"

He shook his head. "And that's what has me so puzzled. You *were* on track to become an officer. But you've thrown it all away by recklessly acting on misguided notions. You'll be lucky to ever make up for it." Christian turned his gaze on Elyssa. "And *you*." He shook his head. "You've been given more chances than most."

Meghan appeared with Healer Delgado in tow. "Before you condemn these loyal Templars, perhaps you should defer to the experts, Commander."

He looked at Healer Delgado. "Do you have anything to add?"

The woman looked a bit off balance, Elyssa thought. Hardly surprising considering what Meghan might have told her on the way over.

"I'd like to hear a full recitation of events," Healer Delgado said after taking in the faces of the others in the group. "Healer Andretti explained a few things on the way over, but I'm afraid my mind is a bit discombobulated from all the commotion."

Christian set his jaw but let Elyssa explain everything, including her own experience with taking the White and the dreams she'd had about the house with fog and rain in the back and sunshine in the front. She also gave the healer the inside scoop on Daelissa, the blonde so-called angel whose sanity seemed to hang by a thread.

"Why have I heard nothing about this Daelissa person being the Divinity?" Delgado said. "My god, if everything Recruit Borathen says is true, we're in terrible danger."

"Our discovery about Daelissa was very recent," Christian said. "Commander Borathen and I were discussing how to proceed with the information. As you can imagine, this revelation would be a shock to Templars."

The healer's eyes tightened. "Better to shock them now than lead them to their deaths, Commander. We need to question everyone and discover if these dreams are plaguing anyone else, or if they're limited to Lieutenant Martinez."

"But they're just dreams," Christian said, shaking his head. "I can't recall and abort a mission based solely on one officer's unusual dreams."

"Wait," Elyssa said with a gasp. "Did you say *recall*? You mean, the assets are already in the field?"

Christian paused as if considering whether he should answer the question, but relented. "Commander Borathen got wind of Artemis's unofficial visit and knew he might try to stop our offensive. In case you hadn't noticed, nearly half the legion isn't here. We sent the stealth teams ahead and the remainder of the force is waiting in the wings."

"Crap!" Elyssa's chest tightened. "You have to recall them now. They're walking into an ambush."

"What is going on over here?" Thomas Borathen said in a low voice as he pushed into the circle. He looked Elyssa and the others over with his cold blue eyes.

Christian pondered the question for a moment before turning to Elyssa. "Perhaps you should explain. Again."

Elyssa wanted to throttle him. "We don't have time. When are they going in? Is it too late?"

"Someone had better explain the meaning of this immediately." Despite the blaze of his eyes, Thomas's voice was low and calm but not without menace.

Seeing no alternative, Elyssa spit out the story once again, taking time to read the diary entries. Her emotions warred within her as she read. Would Underborn still go ahead with his rescue mission? Elyssa traced the outline in her pocket of the arcphone Underborn had given her. She had to contact him immediately and tell him what was happening. But she couldn't let hundreds of Templars walk into a deadly ambush. This legion had already lost good people during the

149

attack on the drug lord, Franco's, compound barely more than a week ago while trying to apprehend Justin. Sadness nearly choked her as she read the diary entry. Poor Justin. He'd been kidnapped by Franco, only to have Maximus do the same thing to him.

The thought knocked loose the memory of a conversation she'd had with Justin a few days ago. He'd recounted his imprisonment at Franco's compound. How he'd nearly been beaten to death before tricking them into bringing him a woman so he could feed and regain his supernatural strength.

Franco and his right-hand man, Marcel—both of them vampires—had supposedly kidnapped Justin for Maximus. In return, Maximus was supplying them with weapons and ammunition. *Ammunition.* The cursed bullets Franco's thugs had used tore through the Templar's Nightingale armor like it wasn't even there. Elyssa cursed. So much had happened between that conversation and now, but it was no excuse. Forgetting to tell them about the cursed ammo was a deadly oversight.

"What is it?" Meghan asked.

Elyssa shook her head. "The ammo Franco and his gang used to penetrate our armor wasn't something they made. It was supplied to them by Maximus."

"Our people are still investigating those bullets," Christian said. "We still don't know where they originated, so how in the world could you know?"

She shook her head. "Justin told me. He said Franco was bragging about Maximus being their supplier. If that's the case, it doesn't matter if Daelissa knows our plan of attack. Our armor can't stop those bullets, and our people don't know it. They'll never even know what hit them."

Christian cursed.

Thomas pursed his lips. "Recall them," he said. "Now."

The Colombian commander put an arcphone to his ear. "Lieutenant Martinez, the operation is Foxtrot Utah. Do you copy?" He gritted his teeth. "I don't care. Do what you have to do." Christian lowered the phone. "We might be too late."

Gigi Martinez was in charge of the attack? This was worse than Elyssa had imagined. True, just because Daelissa had invaded her dreams didn't mean the woman was under the angel's direct control.

But Commander Salazar obviously didn't believe Elyssa's warning about the diary enough to remove Martinez from command.

Thomas nodded. His eyes betrayed not a lick of uncertainty or stress as he said, "Sergeant Gaetano, I'm placing you in charge of a rescue team."

Fausta stiffened and saluted with a fist over her heart. "Yes, Commander."

"Healers Andretti and Delgado will be part of the team. You choose the others and get to the front. Understood?"

She nodded. "Borathen, you're with me."

"Add me to your number," said a deep voice. Michael Borathen appeared, two katana hilts protruding diagonally above his muscled shoulders.

"No way in hell," Elyssa snarled, as anger boiled up inside her. It took all her control not to fly at him with everything she had. Unfortunately, it would mean she'd have to explain her reasons. Now was not the time to settle this. Rescue Justin first. Beat the crap out of Michael second.

"Explain yourself, recruit," Christian said, eyes puzzled.

Elyssa stammered. "I—uh, I think he's too tall for a stealth mission."

"This isn't stealth," Fausta said, her eyes looking the hulking figure up and down. "This is search and rescue, and I could use a big man with big swords. Hell yes, Michael. You're on the team!" She took a quick headcount. "This should be good for now. I'll pull from the main force at the front if I need any more bodies."

Christian nodded.

They rushed to a slider disguised as a helicopter and hopped in. Adam Nosti climbed in behind Meghan.

"Wait for me!" came another voice outside and Bella clambered into the cabin.

"Oh, no, you don't." Fausta shook her head. "You two aren't Templars."

Adam clenched his teeth. "My sister is in Maximus's compound. You're not keeping me off this mission."

"I can vouch for him," Meghan said. "He can take care of himself."

"And I can vouch for myself, young lady." Bella took a seat and belted in. "Heaven knows I've been through more than you could ever imagine."

Fausta shrugged. "Fine, but if either of you gets fragged, don't come dragging your broken, bloody bodies to me." She dropped into the pilot's seat and hovered a hand over a control. The illusionary rotors on the slider turned on, mimicking a chopper warming up as they spun increasingly faster. "Buckle in, people. This is going to be bumpy." The Italian woman didn't wait a second longer, and took them into the air fast enough to press the passengers hard into the seats. Pressing forward on the control stick, she catapulted them toward the compound.

Elyssa glared at Michael. He returned her burning gaze with a raised eyebrow.

"What do you want me to say?" he said at last.

"There's nothing you *can* say. Does *you-know-who* know about you coming along?"

"I already told him about the spy issue. You only repeated your story three times." The barest hint of a smile lifted the corner of his mouth. "He said your findings were too vague. In other words, he's not risking his assets. So I told him to go to hell."

Cold fear settled into Elyssa. It was all on her now. As usual, Underborn couldn't be counted on to do the right thing. Anger and disappointment clawed at her throat and it was all she could do not to scream curses at her brother. "How could you work for him? How *could* you?"

Michael glanced around at the other curious eyes in the cabin and shook his head. "Not now, Ninjette. We'll discuss this at a more appropriate time."

Adam's eyes lit with understanding as he met Elyssa's. But he kept his mouth shut and didn't say a word.

"Now is always an appropriate time for gossip," Bella said, her violet eyes bright with curiosity.

Elyssa saw no further reason to hide the truth. If anything, she felt guilty for holding back on them. "Underborn is the one who told me there might be a spy in the first place. He told me he had people inside Maximus's compound who could rescue Justin, but he wouldn't go through with it until I found the spy."

152

Fausta's head whipped around. "Everything we did tonight was just to save your boyfriend?"

"Oh, Elyssa." Bella tutted. "Why didn't you mention this before?"

Elyssa's heart sank. She'd been selfish. But telling the others about Underborn might have cut out a lot of the unnecessary wrangling and explaining. Thanks to her discretion, a lot of Templars might die. "I'm sorry. I should have told you all from the start."

Fausta slapped the console. "*Figlio di Troia!* If you ever bring me into something like this again, you'd better tell me everything." Her voice was low and harsh.

Bella touched Elyssa's arm. "Now, now. Don't be too hard on yourself. Judging from the way Commanders Borathen and Salazar run things, they probably wouldn't have listened to you if you'd mentioned Underborn. If anything, they'd be running a top-to-bottom search for the scoundrel."

"She's right," Michael said. "You know Thomas would have overreacted, especially if he knew Underborn had come to you."

"You did the right thing," Adam said.

"Stop enabling her," Fausta said.

Meghan simply narrowed her eyes, as if trying to discern how someone could be so stupid.

Before Elyssa could say another word, the slider bumped down in a courtyard. She noted that none of the Templars present except Michael wore armor, not that it mattered if cursed bullets hit them, but she still felt naked without it.

"Speaking of Underborn," Michael said as they piled out of the cabin. "I know of two secret entrances we can use to get inside the compound."

Fausta threw her hands into the air. "Why do you people not tell me these things before we go?" Her Italian accent was stronger than Elyssa had ever heard it. Fausta retrieved her arcphone and activated a three-dimensional map of the surrounding area. "Show me."

Using his fingers to rotate and zoom the image, he homed in on an alleyway across from the compound, and marked it with a red "X". "There's a hidden hatch in the ground there." He flicked the image and went to the other side of the building where he marked a building. "In the basement, there's a door behind a set of lockers that opens into a tunnel as well."

153

"If Underborn planned on having his spies use these secret tunnels, why didn't he just have them leave Justin at the exit? Nobody ever would have seen them."

Michael indicated several points on the map right next to the hidden hatches. "There are Templars sentries stationed right next to them. They'd report the hatches and the mole would find out. Should that happen, Maximus would be sure to seal them off."

While his argument made sense, Elyssa couldn't help but feel Underborn was playing at something else. Something bigger. What it was, she couldn't say.

Fausta considered the map. "We are closest to the alley, so we'll take that route." She picked up her phone, configured it into wireless radio mode, and contacted the main force of Templars near the compound. After a moment, she got through to Lieutenant Martinez.

"Commander Salazar told me you're leading in a rescue team," the officer said. "I'm ready to commit the rest of our forces, but he told me to wait on your go-ahead." An exasperated note sounded in her voice.

Fausta's eyes gleamed in triumph. "I'm transmitting the location of a secret entrance to you. I suggest you send a force there. My group will enter via a tunnel on the other side. On my signal, we can flank them, and once we have their attention, you can lead the main assault."

"Where did you get this information?" Lieutenant Martinez replied after a brief pause. "Why wasn't I informed?"

"It's new intel." Fausta sent the coordinates. "What's the status of our squads on the inside?"

"The stealth squads went in before the command came down to withdraw. They're surrounded and cut off. We had no idea about these cursed bullets the commander told me about."

"No time to waste then," Fausta replied. "Get your people in position and tell me when they're ready."

"I don't think the lieutenant is happy taking orders from a sergeant," Bella said.

Fausta grinned. "I know. Isn't it great?"

Michael unlatched a compartment on the bottom of the slider and slid it out to reveal an array of weaponry.

Fausta grabbed a pair of katanas, and fastened the sheaths on her back in less than thirty seconds, then raised an eyebrow at Elyssa as if daring her to do better.

Elyssa ignored the other woman, deciding on a pair of sai swords, a couple of flash grenades, and a lancer on each wrist. The darts would incapacitate anyone who got in their way.

Fausta groaned. "Sai swords again?" She looked appreciatively at Michael's katanas. "At least your brother has good taste in swords."

Meghan and the others grabbed lancers as well. Adam pshawed and pulled out a pair of automatic pistols.

"We're trying to keep casualties low," Elyssa said.

Fausta shook her head. "Not if I can help it." She slapped the compartment shut and motioned the group on. "Those bastards are taking out Templars. Friends of mine. I plan on getting some payback."

Elyssa had mixed feelings about it. "Most of Maximus's recruits are probably kids or young adults no older than me. In case you've forgotten, he has a knack for brainwashing people and using vampire compulsion to make them do what he wants."

"Are you saying his rogue army is full of innocent wittle kiddies?" Fausta said, her tone mocking. "Maybe we can tell their parents."

"Elyssa has a point," Michael said. "Maximus and his lieutenants are responsible for this. Let's not indiscriminately kill everyone until we sort things out."

Adam took a polished wooden rod about six inches long from a pouch on his side and shook it. It sprang into a staff. "I'm looking forward to sorting this out." With the automatic pistols in holsters at his side and thick glasses on his nose, he looked like an odd cross between a cowboy, wizard, and geek. He pulled the glasses off and stuffed them into the pouch.

"Don't you need those?" Elyssa asked.

Adam chuckled. "My eyes are perfectly fine. Those are just for show." He winked. "Don't tell anyone."

They reached the alley. Michael hunted around on the paved ground until he found a brick embossed with the tiny symbol of an eye. He pressed the symbol three quick times and a hatch popped open, revealing a ladder.

"Ladies first," said Fausta as she slid down the ladder.

Elyssa followed close behind, swallowing the ball of nerves in her throat, and followed Fausta into the dark. The Italian woman shouted.

Elyssa turned just as someone rammed Fausta and sent her tumbling back.

Chapter 21

Katie screamed bloody murder.

She whipped out the automatic rifle she'd taken from the vampire. Pressed it against her hip. And unleashed a hail of bullets at the vampires. Her entire body shook with the explosive kickback. Vampires dove left and right. One screamed as a bullet struck his leg. Another dropped lifeless to the ground as crimson blossomed on his forehead. I could only stand in stunned silence watching Katie rampage like a Mafioso with a Tommy gun, spraying the vampires' positions until the gun clicked empty.

She stood frozen, her breath coming in ragged pants before apparently realizing there were no more bullets. Her eyes grew wide as she took in the bodies, the blood, the carnage. The gun dropped from her hands. Vampires poked their heads from behind cover. I jerked Katie behind the dumpsters as they returned fire.

Bullets dinged and ricocheted off the dull green metal. We crawled through the smelly refuse on the ground toward an open hatch protruding from the ground. Its top was lined with bricks. When closed, it would blend in with the surrounding pavers—perfect camouflage. The gray man appeared ahead of us. His hat was gone, as were his Jersey-boy shades, but I didn't notice any bullet holes in him.

I'd been in danger before. Giant dragon worms had nearly run me down; creepy, dark, cherub creatures had tried to drain me, and even shadow people had taken a shot at sending me to an early grave. But there was something about being shot at that made my bowels turn to water. I crawled at top speed along the ground, like a baby whose diapers were on fire. God knew I'd need diapers if I didn't get down that hole in a hurry.

"Stop firing, you idiots!" Amanda screamed from somewhere behind us. "They're out of ammo. Go get them!"

Katie trembled as she reached the open hatch and climbed down a ladder inside. I saw tears streaming down her face as she vanished into the darkness below. I waved the gray man to go ahead of me and followed him down, closing the hatch with a click as the sounds of running footsteps approached. With any luck, the vampires wouldn't find it. I didn't plan on waiting around to find out.

"I didn't think, Justin." Katie sobbed and almost dropped to her knees in the cramped tunnel. "Oh, god, they're dead."

I grabbed her before she collapsed and surveyed the darkness with the aid of my night vision. Flashlights hung on a rack nearby, but I didn't bother with them. The tunnel was dry, roughly hewn from rock. We could stand, but judging from the irregular ceiling, I didn't dare put Katie on my back and run. One of the crags in the roof might brain one of us.

"Can you see in the dark?" I asked the gray man.

"Yes."

I looked at his eyes, but unlike most supers, his didn't glow in the dark.

Katie sniffed and wiped her nose with the back of her hand. "Oh, god, I'm such a mess. I go all vampire slayer and then fall to pieces."

"It'll be okay. Just hold it together until we get out of here, okay?"

She nodded.

Placing her hand on my shoulder, I guided Katie down what was, for her, a pitch-black tunnel. Her breathing grew rapid, and I heard her struggling to keep her sobs under control. It was a fight to keep my own fear subdued as I listened for sounds of pursuit. We jogged down the tunnel, despite Katie's blindness in the pitch. She kept her head low and hand against my back.

Light appeared ahead from a hole. I stopped. Katie ran into my back.

"Is that light?" she asked.

I heard voices ahead. We had nowhere to go but back, and damned if I was going to go back. The light from outside was dim—probably from a street lamp—but it was enough to make my night vision flicker wildly. A figure dropped down the ladder, followed by another.

Vampires.

It had to be. They must have already known about this exit. Amanda could have radioed ahead to cut us off. If they wanted to take me back in, they'd pay dearly for it.

I took Katie's hand and transferred it. "Katie, hang on to the golem."

"But—"

I didn't listen. I launched myself at the shadow ahead. Crashed into it. A female yelled in surprise. I bulldozed her back into the one following her, roaring like a crazed beast. I had to get up the ladder. Had to escape.

The first vampire gripped my neck. I punched her in what felt like the face.

"Oh dear, what's going on down there?" said a very familiar voice.

I reared back my fist again just as a bright light illuminated the person I straddled. I caught a glimpse of Fausta's face just before her fist eclipsed it and slammed me against the ceiling. I thudded face down in the dirt.

"Justin?"

"Elyssa?" I woozily crawled forward and saw her lying beneath Fausta.

"Oh, god!" Tears sprang into her eyes. "It's Justin!"

Elyssa tried to get around Fausta, but the tunnel was too tight.

"Ugh, can't you wait to get aboveground before getting all smoochy?" Fausta said, motioning for Elyssa to ascend the ladder behind her. She followed.

I climbed up after, breathing free air at last with the compound a hundred yards or so behind me. Elyssa launched herself into my arms, planting kisses all over my face. I felt like I'd just won the Kings and Castles Grand Tourney, even if I did smell a bit ripe from captivity.

"Are you hurt?" I asked. "I thought you guys were vampires."

Elyssa's full lips spread into a beautiful smile. "Hurt? You're alive. If you want, I can fly."

Just the sound of her voice sent a wonderful chill down my back.

"Oh no, dear, what's wrong?" Bella said from somewhere behind.

John Corwin

I turned to see Katie pulling herself out of hole, sobbing. She shook her head. "I—I—"

The gray man emerged behind Katie.

"Son of a—!" Elyssa ripped her sword from its sheath.

I jumped in front of him and threw up my hands to ward off his quick dismemberment. Strong arms gripped my waist. Before I could get out a word, he flung me over a shoulder and ran.

"Stop!" I shouted as he rushed down an alley at breakneck speed. I looked up to see Elyssa and several others in hot pursuit. "Where are you going?"

"The other entity wishes you great harm, Justin," he said, his voice not the least bit strained from exertion. "Her sword could be detrimental to your health."

"Stop, stop, stop! She's not trying to kill me. She's my girlfriend."

"Are you certain? She appears dangerous."

"She's not after me. She's after you."

He stopped so suddenly, I was surprised I didn't fly off his shoulder. "Should I leave you and continue to flee?"

I sighed. "Put me down. I'll save you."

He placed me on my feet a split second before Elyssa and Fausta, swords drawn, reached us. I held up my hands. "Wait. He's with me!"

Elyssa's violet eyes blazed. "Justin, he's a freaking golem. How can he be with you?"

"Trust me on this." I noticed the golem edging away from us ever so slightly, and motioned him back over. "I'll explain it when we get back to the group."

"This is one of the golems you told me of?" Fausta said to Elyssa.

"Yeah." My girlfriend shook her head and furrowed her lovely brow. "How do you do it, Justin?"

I caressed her cheek with a hand and pressed a kiss to her lips before whispering, "I'm just a badass."

Fausta groaned. "In case you don't remember, we're on a mission to save Templars, people. We can't waste any more time on lovesick teenagers."

"Wait, you're going in *there*?" I said, jabbing a finger at Maximus's fortress.

Elyssa nodded. "I'll explain on the way back."

We jogged back to the hatch and Elyssa told me about their plan of attack.

"Ugh, this is not how I envisioned spending my first day of freedom." I took Elyssa's hand. "But there's no way in the world I'm letting you go back in there without me."

"Justin," said a sharp male voice and Adam Nosti appeared. "Where's Felicia?"

A knot of dread caught in my throat. "She freed me, and was supposed to meet us so we could all leave at once. But she didn't show up."

"And you left her in there?" he stared incredulously at the walled compound.

"I didn't have a choice," I said. "A group of vampires was shooting at us. We had to get out of there."

"So you're saying that tunnel could be full of vampires?" Fausta said. "*Merda!*"

I shook my head. "No, I don't think they found the hatch. I closed it behind us and it's pretty well hidden."

Fausta lowered her ear to the open portal and listened. "I don't hear anything. Maybe you're right." She pulled out her phone and started issuing commands.

I turned and saw Bella hugging a distraught Katie who still shook with sobs. Someone gripped my shoulder. I turned to see Adam all up in my face.

"How could you?" Adam said, his face crimson. "We talked about this, man. Both our sisters are in trouble."

"No. Mine wasn't in there," I said. "It was a lie."

"My sister saved you, and you didn't even make sure she got out okay?" His eyes glinted with anger. "Son of a bitch."

"Adam, it's not his fault." Meghan took his arm. "We can still save her."

"Look, man," I said, staring into the geeky Arcane's furious gaze. "I'm going back in. We'll save her. I promise."

His eyes reddened. He bit back on what might have been a sob or a shout of frustration. "She's all the family I have, Justin." He turned away. Clenched his fists tight. "Look, I'm sorry. I didn't mean to blame you."

161

I put a hand on his shoulder. "Believe me, I understand. I know how you feel."

He looked back. "Yeah, I guess you would."

I walked over to Katie and Bella.

Elyssa stood nearby, a helpless look on her face. "What's wrong with her?"

Katie took a shuddering breath and looked at Elyssa. "Nothing. I'm sorry I'm such a wimp." She wiped at her tear-stained eyes.

"She shot some vampires," I said.

"Shot them?" Disbelief took Elyssa's voice up an octave.

"I couldn't help it, okay?" Katie broke into new tears. "The gun fired so fast. I think I killed at least five of them."

"More like two," I said. "You just seriously wounded the others."

"But I had to save you, Justin. Screw that jackass Underborn. He's a first class bastard."

"Wait a minute," Elyssa said, mouth dropping open. "You were one of Underborn's moles?"

Katie gave a miserable nod.

"The poor girl has been through hell," Bella said.

Elyssa walked up to Katie, mouth set in a firm line—and hugged her.

I felt my eyebrows try to climb off my forehead. I'd expected to meet a fairy riding a flying dragon before seeing this.

"Thank you," Elyssa said, and pulled away after a moment.

Katie's green eyes looked a bit shell shocked as she nodded. "I did what was right."

"You did good." My girlfriend looked at the other woman as if seeing some hidden potential. Or maybe she was just looking for a reason to punch her anyway.

"And now, back to me," Fausta said, pressing a thumb to her chest and gazing expectantly at the rest of us. "Got your attention? Good. The other rescue team just entered their tunnel. We've got to move out now."

I turned to see a large figure emerge from the shadows. The breath caught in my throat. Michael gave me his trademarked, calm look.

Offering him a nod, I said, "'Sup?" and tried to keep it real.

He grunted.

162

The gray man stood nearby, watching as Fausta began her descent into the tunnel.

"Can you stay and watch Katie?" I asked it—him—whatever.

"I will, Justin."

Katie offered me a tear-stained smile. "Be careful. Don't get shot."

I smiled. "You know me, I'm always careful."

Elyssa snorted and followed Michael and the others in the tunnel. Noticing I was the last person, I quickly followed her down.

"Uh, so we're gonna go in blasting?" I asked, trying to readjust the sword on my back so I could actually use it if need be.

Just ahead of Elyssa, Michael pulled something from a holster and passed it back to Elyssa who gave it to me. A gun. A big one. I looked it over, my night vision allowing me to see it with nearly perfect clarity. "A Desert Eagle. Nice." All my knowledge about guns came from video games. I'd blasted a virtual zombie or two with a gun like this. Thinking back to Katie's traumatic breakdown, real life promised to make it an unforgettable experience that would scar my very soul.

"I'm having flashbacks to El Dorado," Bella said. "You sure there aren't any shadow people down here?"

"Shut up back there," said Fausta in a harsh whisper.

Elyssa passed me a couple of clips for the gun. I shoved them in my pockets. We scurried down the tunnel in silence and drew to a stop right back where I'd come from—Maximus's godforsaken compound. I couldn't see much past Michael's over-muscled form, but caught a glimpse of Fausta climbing a ladder.

My nerves knotted. What if all the vamps were still waiting up there, guns drawn, and ready to blast anyone who came out? Then again, if they'd found the hatch, I felt certain they would have chased me. The line started moving again. Before long, I was able to climb the ladder. Three unconscious vampires lay nearby.

Fausta gripped one and motioned to Meghan. "Can you wake him up? I want to ask some questions."

Meghan nodded, made some flippity-do patterns with her wand before touching it to the vampire's head. His eyes jerked open. He opened his mouth wide. Meghan touched his throat with the wand and only a whisper emerged.

"Where are the others?" Fausta asked.

He clamped his mouth shut.

Meghan ran the wand along his skin, and blood seeped from the vampire's pores. He tried to scream, but again, only a hoarse whisper escaped.

Fausta gripped his shirt and put her knee on his groin. "You better speak up before I turn you into a eunuch for the rest of eternity."

A horrified look crossed his face. "They left us here to find the secret exit. Amanda left to report to Maximus."

My phone dinged. Everyone glared at me. I turned down the volume, and looked at the notification. There was a text message from an unknown sender. I almost ignored it since I was, you know, breaking into a vampire fortress and all, but satisfying my curiosity was only a thumb-flick away. The text appeared, and my stomach lurched.

I have Felicia. Return to me or she dies. –Maximus

Chapter 22

My heart dropped, bounced off my liver, and gave me a queasy feeling. I almost blurted out Maximus's demand, but one look at Adam's tormented face told me it would be a bad idea. He was already skirting the edge of sanity. I'd been there before and knew how it felt. Pushing him now might be the final straw.

I replied: *Don't hurt her! I'll come back!*

I hoped my text might give the rogue vampire pause. By the time the Templar surprise attack started, he might not have a chance to hurt her. My phone vibrated. I checked for a response.

You have thirty minutes, spawn.

I responded again and told him I would. Now all I had to do was hope Fausta's plan was brilliant.

Gunfire echoed from ahead, popping and snapping like fireworks.

Fausta motioned us close. "The vamps have two Templar squads pinned down. We'll sneak up behind and take out the attackers."

"How many OPFORs?" Elyssa asked.

"No idea. A hundred or more. They've got the place warded against fly-eyes, so I can't get exact positions."

Adam's lip curled into a snarl. "I'll take care of that." He pulled out his arcphone. Several long seconds passed. "Damn it. Whoever set up these wards knows what they're doing. Looks like there's a magic power source keeping me from overriding it."

Bella's hands, wrapped tight around her staff, eyes closed in concentration nodded. "Maximus has a very powerful source of supernatural power somewhere below us." Her eyes opened. "The wards are barely draining it. I have a terrible feeling there is an Arcane working for them, and whoever it is might have even more in store for us."

"Dash Armstrong," I said. "At least, I think that's his name. It sounds almost too stupid to be a real name."

Adam wrinkled his forehead. "You've got to be kidding me."

"I kid you not. The dude's name really sounds like some kind of action figure from the fifties."

"No, that's not what I meant," Adam said, shaking his head. "Dash is one of the Dream Team from the Arcane Tourney. He studied under Aston Beaumont himself."

"Why does that name seem familiar?"

"Beaumont is the one who lost an arm as payment to Underborn."

My mind flashed back to before I'd ever met the slimy asshat. "Beaumont's the sorcerer who won the tourney every year, right?"

"Yeah, until Folder Reeves came along, and Beaumont had Underborn kill him."

Fausta held up a hand. "Can you stop this Dash Armstrong?"

Adam's eyes blazed with determination. "If he stands between me and Felicia, he's a dead man."

Bella extended her wand and turned in a slow circle before stopping, the tip angled slightly down. "I have the source located." She looked at Adam. "You stay with Fausta. I will take care of the source. Get a fly-eye up the moment I do."

"Why don't we do this the old-fashioned way?" Elyssa said. "And use our eyes. Chasing after that power source might be a waste of time."

"Maybe," Fausta said, a distant look of concentration on her face. "But there are other reasons to take down the wards."

I waved off their arguments. "I'll go with Bella. If we don't have the power source down within fifteen minutes, go ahead with the attack."

"I'll scout around the old-fashioned way," Michael said, his eyes meeting Elyssa's. "We need to know their positions and numbers if this doesn't work."

Fausta narrowed her eyes. Nodded and pointed at the wall. "Okay. Recruit Borathen, it looks like you could climb the wall and keep cover behind the buildings. Use it for a scouting position and tell me what you find." She looked at Michael. "See if you can find our trapped squads. If you can take any attackers out without detection, go for it. Meanwhile, I'll sneak around to the left side of the courtyard

166

and see what I can see. Meet here in fifteen and we'll go with whatever option is left to us."

Elyssa gripped my hand and squeezed three times. *I love you.* It was our top-secret code.

I squeezed back and smiled. "Kick ass, baby."

She raised an eyebrow. "Don't I always?"

I motioned to Bella and led her to the exit of the dumpster corral. The area was clear. We sneaked down the stairs. The same groups of noms were still below, partying it up, somehow oblivious to the battle raging topside. One kid with a mop of curly hair offered us a toke on a joint the size of a cigar as we passed. I waved him off.

"How interesting," Bella said as we made our way down a side hall. "Instead of donkeys, these kids turn into vampires."

"Donkeys?"

She led me around a corner and shook her head. "Kids these days."

"Did I miss some reference?"

She rolled the wand between her fingers in an absent-minded motion. "What do you think about Harry?"

Women and their ability to change the subject. "You mean Shelton?"

"Who else, dear?"

"Uh, well, he's quite a character." I wasn't sure what she was getting at. "I mean, I think you can trust him even though he definitely has secrets."

"Hmm." Bella stopped all of a sudden, and I almost bowled her over. The hall terminated in a stone wall. The short Arcane said a few words, and let go of her wand. Instead of falling, it hovered in midair. She thumped the narrow end, spinning it. It spun slower and slower until, like a compass drawn to the north, pointed right at the wall.

"It must be on this level," she said. "Or it would point down."

"Illusion?" I asked.

She picked up a loose bit of mortar and tossed it at the wall. It bounced off with a convincing *thunk*. "It could be a solid illusion." She sighed. "I could use the path-finding spell I used under El Dorado, but it might give us away to the Arcane."

"Maybe there's an easier way," I said, walking the remaining length of the hall while trailing my fingers down it. A third of the way on the other side of the corridor, my fingers went through the stone. "Aha!"

"Excellent work, Justin." Bella patted me on the arm. "Sometimes, we Arcanes forget there are many ways to skin a goat."

"Are there really that many ways?"

She nodded and walked toward the fake wall. "But one way is usually better than the others." She held a finger to her lips and vanished into the fake wall.

I followed. We'd gone about a hundred yards down the dark passage when the rumbling growl of what sounded like a wounded animal echoed off the stone walls. My eyes met Bella's glowing peepers. I motioned her behind me and crept to the corner. Light flickered from beneath a closed door. The handle turned without noise and I eased it open. Inside was a laboratory straight out of a mad scientist's wet dreams.

Opened crates were scattered everywhere. A large stack of them leaned ponderously against the wall next to the entrance. I saw a partially disassembled gray man strapped to a worktable in the corner to our left. Metal cages, all empty from what I could tell, cluttered the back of the room.

Dash sat before a large aluminum table, manipulating a three-dimensional holograph of the courtyard upstairs, zooming in and out to look at two groups of Templars, which looked like they were pinned behind one of the stone buildings in the courtyard. He circled a group of vampires in the image and they glowed. As he dragged his finger from one location to the other, I saw one of the vampires touch a headset and motion for his group to go to the location.

Good god, it's like a freaking video game.

As Dash zoomed into another area, I saw inert bodies of black-armored Templars mingled with those of vampires in an open space between the building and the vampire army. I realized if I could take over Dash's display, I could pinpoint all the enemy locations. Not only that, but I could tell them to move into strategically bad areas to give the Templars an even better chance at beating them.

I whispered my idea to Bella. She jabbed a finger at a huge Tesla coil in the center of the room, streaks of black and white energy racing around its edges as it occasionally gave off a burst of radiance in all directions.

"Is that the source?" I whispered.

She shook her head. "No, it's only a focus."

Another bellow of pain echoed from somewhere in the room, but a quick glance revealed nothing, thanks to all the stone columns holding up the ceiling. The bellow sounded somewhat familiar to me.

"Does he have a crazy supernatural animal guarding him?" I thought back to Yolo, Vadaemos's companion beneath El Dorado. The strange animal turned out to have more bark than bite, and I hoped Dash hadn't captured the poor thing.

Bella shrugged. "I don't know. But whatever is powering the coil must be attached to it somehow." She pointed to a thick cable running across the floor and behind a thick column. "It must be behind there. You sneak up to it and detach the cables." She held a hand out as the tesla coil spilled another flash of energy into the air. "Dash has attuned his focus, the coil, so it benefits only him with the energy. If it's not disabled, he'll be able to replenish his magical energy at a rate I can't hope to compete with."

I nodded. "I'm on it."

Hard-soled shoes echoed in the hallway we'd just come through. I grabbed Bella and pulled her behind the closest stack of crates.

She whispered something and waved her wand. I hoped she was cloaking us in invisibility, though it didn't seem to be the case.

"Why haven't you moved our forces in for the kill?" said Maximus.

I poked my head up and saw the rogue vampire towering over Dash's seat.

Dash looked up at him. "I guess it depends on how many soldiers you want to lose. They're cornered but still dangerous."

"We have far more soldiers than they do. Send them in. This isn't one of your games where you have to get it perfect." Maximus's eyes wandered somewhere to his right. "Have you finished with the potion?"

"It came out perfect. Even though we didn't have much of the spawn's blood left to work with, it diluted a lot better than I thought it would."

Maximus nodded. "Excellent." He motioned at the screen. "Finish them off. I'll deliver this batch of potion to Atlanta."

"Is the next attack still on schedule?"

169

Maximus paused in his turn. "Two more days. By then, we'll have the spawn back and can resume production of the potion."

Dash looked uncertain. "You really think he'll show?"

"He has a weakness for weakness." A grin split the vampire's red lips. "The girl is broken and worthless, but I have no doubt he'll return to claim her."

I sure didn't like the sound of that and hoped Felicia was really okay.

He checked his watch. "I'll be back soon. I expect the Templars to be in body bags when I return. "With that, Maximus walked behind a column.

The Tesla coil hummed louder and louder, energy flashing off it in waves. The air crackled and the smell of ozone permeated the place. It flashed bright one last time and the hum faded and died.

"What the hell?" I said in the lowest whisper possible.

"An arch," Bella whispered back. "Good heavens, they have one here."

If that was true, Maximus was gone, probably back to Atlanta. No wonder Christian's people hadn't seen him using La Casona. This was bad. Really bad. This meant Maximus could set up arches in other cities. He could distribute the vampire potion all over the world. I gritted my teeth. Not on my watch, damn it.

I motioned toward the Tesla coil and made a breaking gesture with my hands. Bella nodded. Slipping out from behind the crates, I stayed low and skulked my way toward the other side of the thick columns in the middle of the room. I probably could have stalked over with a marching band behind me and Dash, absorbed in annihilation, never would have noticed, but I took no chances. Using a column for cover, I peeked around it and saw the arch. It wasn't a large one, just wide and tall enough for a car to drive through, embedded in a pedestal of polished black stone like the huge ones. Obviously, it wasn't like the portable, expanding ones Kassallandra and Pokito had used.

Either Dash knew how to make the things or, more likely, Daelissa had helped him move one from another location, and showed him how to attune it. Hopefully disabling the power source for the Tesla would render the arch unusable. I didn't want to worry about Maximus returning with reinforcements.

"What the hell?" Dash said.

I glanced at the holograph and saw him zoom in on Elyssa, perched on the wall and peering out across the buildings toward the gunfire. He studied her for a moment, and flicked the view, searching until he found the rest of the group hiding out near the dumpster corral.

"Son of a—" he centered the image on a group of patrolling vamps and highlighted them.

I couldn't waste any more time. Keeping low, I followed the thick cables back toward the cages in the back of the room. Something hissed to my right and clanged hard against the cage. I looked up in time to see a vampire—no a vampling—straining against the bars to reach me, its eyes glazed with death, rotting lips peeled back from broken teeth. I backed away and heard a cooing noise behind me. I spun.

"Da nah," said a cherub from inside a barred cage of some kind of clear material.

The dark creature's skin glistened like oil. A round orifice lined with sharp teeth opened on its otherwise featureless face. My knees went weak at the sight and I almost fell on my butt and back into the vampling's arms in an effort to avoid the thing, even though it probably couldn't reach me through the strange container imprisoning it.

My foot found the thick cable, however, and I tumbled to the ground. Rolling away from the danger zone, I pushed myself up and looked at the creatures. What the hell was Dash doing with these things? Was he experimenting on them? I didn't have time to ponder. Turning, I followed the cables where they led into a small room in the back.

I raced through the doorway. Giant jaws snapped in my face as I nearly smacked into a creature the size of a really, really big snake strapped to the floor with diamond fiber. The breath caught in my throat as I looked down the glowing maw of the monster. It was nowhere near full size—a baby perhaps? Whatever the case, I now knew where the power was coming from.

A leyworm.

Chapter 23

Daelissa must have given Maximus more help than anyone realized, I thought as I regarded the beast. It would take some kind of crazy, supernatural powers to capture this thing. Red parietal eyes the size of my head gleamed at me above a long, lean muzzle more like that of a crocodile than a snake, complete with ridged forehead and two horns curving back atop it. It bellowed like a wounded bear, revealing a maw of obsidian shards and the bright glow of energy from deep inside its throat.

I ran down its length, all fifteen feet or so and found why the poor thing was bellowing in pain. Its scaly hide had been gouged down to raw flesh. The cables were attached to two large, silver terminals someone had plunged into the leyworm's body. It made me wince just looking at them. I reached out a hand to touch one of the terminals. Sparks flashed in my face. A magnetic force backhanded me against the wall.

What the hell?

Dazed, I staggered to my feet, grabbed a wooden rod off the floor and extended it toward the terminal rods. Either Dash had a protective spell around them, or the energy channeling through them was too much for the wood to handle. It splintered and broke without ever making contact.

Ignoring the terminals, I bent down and pulled on the cable. A wave of dizziness passed over me and a nauseous feeling clawed up my throat. My stomach felt engorged with hot acid. My head pulsed with a static feeling, as though a cat were licking my brain. I dropped the cable and staggered away before I succumbed to the madness lurking in that energy. I felt disoriented and drunk. Sick with too much power, like a go-cart burning rocket fuel.

My knees hit the floor and my vision faded to static. Forcing back the barf crawling up my throat, I tried to shake off the nausea. After a long moment, my hands against the rough stone floor came into focus. Blood welled from the palms of each one where I'd gripped the cable. Tiny bolts of lightning seemed to dance across the spots of blood.

Wiping the blood from my hands, I staggered to my feet and regarded the oversized garden snake. I couldn't free the beast. Maybe only Dash could. I peeked around the corner. The Arcane's attention lay solely on his display, monitoring a group of vampires as they raced toward Elyssa and the other Templars. I was out of time. I considered shooting him with the gun Michael had given me, but it seemed overkill when I could probably sneak up and knock him out.

Making my way past the cages outside the leyworm's room, I stepped over the cable and dashed for Dash. Ten feet. Seven. Five. I raised my fist. An alarm wailed. I smacked into something very invisible and very solid, rebounding like a baby off a sliding glass door.

The Arcane jumped out of his chair and turned to me, one hand extended in front of him. His eyes widened. He smiled. "You came back to us, I see." He flicked his wrist and a cage in the back area opened. Another flick of the wrist sent my gun flying to land on the table behind him. "I'll just put you away and deal with you later."

An unseen force clamped around me. I couldn't move. I could hardly breathe. It pushed me toward the cages, and there wasn't a thing I could do to stop it

A beam of brilliant purple speared toward Dash. It hit his invisible barrier and slowed, burrowing through after a second, and struck him between the shoulder blades, knocking him to the floor. The pressure on me vanished. I stood and saw Bella, staff extended, continue to blast Dash with the purple light.

The man, still crouched, waved a hand through the air. Bella's energy refracted and washed across the barrier, no longer penetrating it. Dash stood up, teeth bared in anger, his white hair standing straight on end like static-charged cotton. "Think you can come into my house and beat me, bitch?" He held a hand toward the Tesla coil. A jagged bolt of bright light raced to meet his fingers. He aimed his other hand at Bella. Energy crackled from his fingertips. Bella ducked behind a crate as the beams splintered wood and blasted parts of the stone floor to dust.

I knew there was no way I could help. My magic skills were crap, and I couldn't physically reach him. I considered letting the vampling and cherub loose, but they'd probably chase me in circles before going for him, and then what? I'd be toast.

On the other hand—a suicidal notion gripped me, but I could think of no other way to cut the Arcane off from his source. I just had to hope it worked. I ran back into the back room and offered an uneasy smile to the leyworm.

"Hey there, buddy. I can help you out if you promise not to eat me or my friend. Can you do that?"

It roared in my face hard enough to blow my hair straight back.

I suddenly wished I still had on adult diapers. "I'm going to take that for a yes." I examined the straps. They were a foot wide and layered with jagged edges that bit into the leyworm's scales and kept it from slithering out. I stood at the edge of the closest strap and prepared to flee the moment it was loose. Leaning down, I extended a finger. Touched the strap. Leapt away. The creature's eyes swiveled to follow me. The strap, however, remained in place.

The big red eye rotated to meet my gaze. The pupil shrank to an angry pinpoint of black.

The leyworm made a strange growling noise like a dog trying to speak humanese. Or maybe it was just hungry. I touched the strap with the palm of my hand. Still nothing. It was all I could do not to shout in frustration. I might need Maximus's or Dash's blood to open the stupid thing. Gripping the strap in both hands, I tugged.

And almost fell on my butt when it parted.

The leyworm twisted, but still couldn't get free. I jumped back as its flailing body nearly slammed into me. The next strap split, but only after I touched the entire width of it where I wanted it to part. Before the creature could use its new freedom to gobble me up, I raced to the last strap and slashed my hand across it.

The snakelike dragon roared and twisted. The terminals swiveled and rocked with sick, wet sounds in the monster's flesh. The creature's eyes widened, probably in agony. I found the farthest corner of the room and watched in sick fascination as it struggled. It jerked once, twice, three times. The bladed terminals slid from the leyworm's body

174

in a spray of crimson, and clanked to the floor. I heard the Tesla coil snap, crackle, and pop one last time before it faded to black with a low hum.

Dash's eyes flicked toward the device. He screamed profanities.

Bella jumped from behind the splintered remains of her dwindling cover. "Got you now, punk!" She aimed the staff and blasted him with purple energy. Dash ducked the first blast and grabbed his own staff off the floor.

"I can still kick your ass," he said and retorted with a bolt of black light.

Their attacks, beams of pure crackling energy, met in the center, pulsating and pushing back and forth against one another, undulating up and down like two snakes furiously French kissing. Rock and wood disintegrated to dust where the two forces touched them. I didn't want to see what would happen should either force touch one of the Arcanes. Bella gritted her teeth in determination. Dash growled as sweat gathered at his brow. Slowly, he reached a hand back toward the table where the holographic image hovered, hand grasping at my gun.

I charged toward Dash, shouting a warning for Bella, when something bowled me over and flattened me against the ground. The breath whooshed from my lungs and I thought for sure I was dead. The pressure vanished. I staggered to my feet and saw Dash lift the gun.

"Die, you stupid—aghh!"

And then the leyworm ate him.

Bella screamed.

"Holy crap!" I shouted as the earth dragon's jaws chomped down on the sorcerer, spraying the vicinity with gouts of blood and all sorts of nasty tidbits.

Before I could move, the creature opened its bloody maw wide and came right at me. I froze, my life flashing before my eyes. The creature whizzed past close enough to make me spin in place. It burrowed through the stone wall like hot butter, made a sharp turn, and vanished.

"Oh dear," Bella said, staring at the puddle of bloody chunks where Dash had met his grisly end. "No matter how many times you see something like this, you never get used to it."

I gagged and looked away. "How many times exactly have you seen a leyworm eat a person?"

"A person? I believe this is the first time."

Walking wide of the blood, I went to Dash's holographic display and zoomed in on Elyssa and the others. The vampires were standing just around the corner from them, apparently plotting out their plan of attack. My allies had their backs to the enemy. They'd be wide open. Elyssa dropped off the wall she'd climbed earlier and walked toward the others, unaware of the danger. I pulled out my phone and told it to call her.

She looked at her phone when it chirped at her and answered. "Justin?"

"Get ready. You have vampires at six o'clock!"

The vampires piled around the corner, guns at the ready just as Elyssa shouted a warning. White light speared from behind the cover of a crate, slashing across the attackers. Guns dropped from nerveless hands as the surprised vampires gripped their smoking flesh and dropped dead, their bodies sliding into halves. Somehow, their leader used the butt of his assault rifle to hold himself up. Adam appeared from behind the crates and kicked the lone survivor in the chest. The surprised vampire's torso slid off, spilling innards all over the ground.

"Good heavens," Bella said, violet eyes wide. "I believe Mr. Nosti might be upset."

It was all I could do not to puke. "Ya think?" I scrolled around the battlefield and focused on the pinned-down Templars. There were too many vampires between Fausta's force and theirs. "Still there, Elyssa?" I said into my phone.

"How did you know about the vampires?" she asked.

"A leyworm just ate Dash. He's got an eagle-eye view of the entire place on his tablet, so I can see everything."

"Ate him?" She made a gagging noise. "What about the Templar force coming in from the other secret tunnel?"

I found them hunkered down on the opposite side. They seemed to have a better shot at getting past the vampires than our side did. Somehow we had to find a way past. Could we go under? Over? I spotted another group of evil-doers flanking the pinned-down Templars and realized it was only a matter of minutes before all this planning was moot. With the force coming up behind them, they'd be overwhelmed in no time. Somehow, I had to contact them. If only I had a way to—it suddenly occurred to me I was standing in front of Dash's control interface, and not just a simple overhead view of the situation.

I face palmed. "Stupid, Justin. Real stupid."

Bella watched me curiously. "What is it?"

I circled the group of flanking vampires with a finger, lighting them up on the display. Using the method I'd seen Dash use, I streaked a finger across the map, leading them back to Elyssa and the others. One of the vampires stopped, pressed a finger into his ear and nodded. He waved his finger in a circle in the air and motioned the vampires toward the route I'd indicated.

"Elyssa, I know how we're gonna win this thing."

"Oh?"

I told her my plan. "Can your people handle it?"

She nodded. "What happens if the bad guys catch on?"

I shrugged even though she couldn't see me. "Let's hope they don't."

The first group of vampires I'd re-routed closed fast on Elyssa's position. Using my finger, I drew a new circuitous route while Elyssa filled in the others. I panned the view until I found a side entrance and group of fifty armed vamps guarding it. I highlighted a few at a time and sent them to various places in the compound until only a few remained. Then I located any sentries on that side of the compound and sent them to the top of the wall opposite.

"Ready?" I asked Elyssa.

"Reinforcements are on the way."

Flicking the view to the side, I spotted a small squad of Templars sneaking up to the now lightly guarded entrance. Within the space of a minute, they downed the guards with lancers and secured them. I sent small groups of vamps to the entrance, one at a time, watching as the Templars secured each squad in a quiet, efficient manner. I lost count of how many vampires I sent to their non-lethal doom, but no matter how many were out of action, scores more remained.

Maximus had organized his people into military squads, and the leader of each one seemed outfitted with some kind of device enabling Dash's gizmo to give them orders. In fact, the level of organization was almost frightening. True, most of the vampires were just untrained kids, but it reminded me a lot of the dog soldiers in Africa. How long until Maximus brainwashed even more people into killing for no other reason than he simply wanted them to? Vampires already held a considerable advantage over noms with their supernatural strength and agility. If he decided to use his army against a civilian population, they'd be hard to stop.

The size of the vampire force had shrunk by almost two-thirds, thanks to my redirection, when I saw a sizeable group break off from the main force and head away. I zoomed in and saw a familiar face—Amanda. She looked *pissed*. According to my aerial view of the compound, she was headed for Dash's hideout. Toward the only way into this place.

And it was too late for us to escape.

Chapter 24

I looked around Dash's super-secret lab and saw no other way out. There was, no doubt, a hidden passage lurking around here somewhere, but I didn't have time to find it. Scrambling over the wreckage of crates and equipment left after Dash's fight with Bella, I approached the hole the leyworm had made. The edges of the stone cracked and broke off, brittle to my touch where the creature had slammed through it.

"What are you doing?" Bella asked.

"We've got about five minutes before thirty vamps storm this place."

Her brow furrowed. "But how—"

"Amanda. I think she figured out Dash wasn't in control anymore."

"Oh dear."

"Yeah, you could say that." I peered into the dark gap. My night vision popped on, granting me a better glimpse of the path the leyworm had left. About ten feet into the solid rock behind the stone wall, the creature had taken a sharp left before diving straight down to parts unknown, leaving a neat round hole and a terrifying drop my night vision lacked the range to fully see. Across from the hole was a wall of crumbling rock, probably where the leyworm had made the turn.

Bella knelt beside me and sent a globe of light wandering down the tunnel. It turned into a pinprick before finding the bottom. "I don't think this is a viable route."

Measuring the space with my eyes, I estimated I could brace my hands and feet against the sides of the hole and walk myself down, but the going would be painfully slow, and one misstep would mean depositing my broken body into the bowels of the earth. Bella was just too short to even attempt my idea.

"Bella, Can you blend us in to the surroundings?"

"Like camouflage? Of course. But I must warn you, I'm exhausted. Dash took nearly everything I had."

"How long could you maintain the spell?"

"Perhaps half an hour. Beyond that, I'll probably pass out." She sighed. "I do have a levitation spell that might work to gently lower us down the shaft. How much do you weigh?"

I shrugged. "I have no idea. Two hundred pounds maybe?" I'd lost all of my chunky bits during my transformation from nerd to incubus, but had put on height and muscle, so my net weight had increased. But I hadn't exactly weighed myself lately to see the exact results.

"Goodness." She looked up, muttering calculations.

I pulled out my phone and gave Elyssa a rundown on the situation.

"Why the hell didn't you tell me sooner?" Elyssa said, and barked out commands to her comrades.

"What do you think you're doing?" I heard Fausta say in the background.

Elyssa gave the other Templar a terse reply and ended the call. I ran back to the overhead display and scrolled to my companions just as Fausta threw up her hands like an angry Italian, and motioned for Elyssa to lead the way. My phone chirped with an incoming call from an unknown number. I'd added Maximus's number to my contact list, so I knew it wasn't him.

I answered, and an unfamiliar voice said, "This is Sergeant Itchi. Fausta gave me your number. She wants you to guide us to the remaining OPFORs in the compound."

Since there wasn't much more I could do before Amanda and her goons burst inside, I rattled out a list of directions, took a couple of pictures with my phone, and sent them to Itchi. At any other time, I would have also tossed in a few jokes about his name as well, but decided to devote the time to staying alive until help arrived. I looked at the display and watched the main force of Templars enter via the side entrance they'd secured and head toward their pinned-down comrades. I noticed the squad entering via the other secret tunnel also moving in and felt a wash of relief.

"Justin, my spell won't work." Bella's eyes looked empty of hope. "You're too heavy for me to lower that far. I don't know what to do."

I heard scuffling noises echo from outside the door to the lab and panic took hold. If only we could hold out for a few minutes, it might give Elyssa and the others time to reach us. I spotted the huge pile of crates near the door and zipped over to them. Despite the strength granted through my demon spawn genes, the crates hardly budged. I resorted to pushing them one at a time with more success until the door was blocked.

Someone pounded on the metal door. "Slade! I know you're in there, you son of a bitch! Let me in!" It was Amanda.

"I'm sorry, my mom told me not to open the door for strangers."

She screamed a flurry of curse words at me, pounding on the door. "Give it here, you idiot," she shouted at someone. I heard her maniacal laugh. "Let's see how you like this, Slade."

The echo of quickly retreating feet alerted me something very bad was about to happen. I grabbed Bella and jerked her away from the door. An explosion rocked the room. The door blasted through the crates. Whistled through the air about a foot from my head. Clanged off a support beam.

Amanda hooted with laughter and appeared at the doorway. "Here, catch!" She threw a square package my way. It landed on the floor and skidded next to my feet.

"Oh, fudge." I gripped Bella's hand and dove for the tunnel left by the leyworm.

A hot blast ripped through the air, slapping me like a red-headed stepchild. I lost my grip on Bella and skidded down the tunnel, ricocheting around the corner. My frantic hands grabbed at the rock. I shouted as the rough surface tore into my skin. I hit the crushed rock at the back edge of the hole and bounced off the rim in a shower of gravel. There was nothing below me but empty air.

I fell into the dark. Somehow, my hand caught on a shard of rock protruding from the side of the shaft. Agony sliced into my hand. Blood dripped into my face as it dribbled down the rock from this latest injury. I heard a crack. Pebbles skittered from beneath my handhold, falling into the pit. With my free hand, I reached for the lip of the hole. Too far. I swung out my feet, trying to brace against the sides. The tiny ledge crumbled, leaving only enough room for my fingertips to hang on.

No. It can't end. Not like this!

Using all my concentration, I summoned my focus and willed myself to rise toward the ledge. Something tingled in the back of my mind, working its way forward until it seemed to press against the inside of my skull. A presence brushed against my feet.

Up. Push me up.

A slight pressure grew against the soles of my shoes. It was working! I willed it to push harder and harder. The weight of the world seemed to drop onto my shoulders. My focus vanished at the shock. The strain on my shoulders vanished.

The ledge gave way. Gravity grabbed my ankles and jerked. My stomach lurched and I stifled the scream threatening to rip from my throat. Eyes squeezed shut, I waited for the end.

"Justin, I can't hold this for long," came Bella's strained voice. "My fight with Dash tired me more than I thought."

I opened an eyelid and looked up. Sweat beaded on her forehead and her hands trembled. Instead of falling, I hovered. Bella held her staff tight as she raised her hands toward the ceiling. My feet didn't feel like there was anything solid beneath them. I tried jumping, but my legs kicked against thin air.

"Please…don't do that," Bella said in harsh whisper. "Wait for the ledge."

I looked up and stretched out a hand. The lip of the hole remained at least an inch away.

Amanda's voice echoed down the tunnel. "Bring me the bodies."

The sound of feet tramping through the room reached my ears. Bella clenched her teeth. Sweat beaded on her forehead. A low moan scraped through her throat.

The ledge grew inexorably closer, each second feeling like an hour.

"What the hell?" someone said from very close by. "There's a hole here, but part of the wall collapsed on it."

"Well clear it and check it," Amanda said. "Now!"

My fingers grasped the lip. In one big heave, I pulled myself to solid ground. Bella moaned in relief. Her staff clattered to the floor.

182

The dhampyr toppled straight toward the hole. I dove to the ground and barely caught her arm before she slid over the edge.

Voices grew louder from down the tunnel. We were screwed. I dug with desperation into my magical education, grasping at straws. On the other side of the hole, I noticed the crushed rock was partially gone, leaving a divot and a pile of rocks. There was just enough room for us to crouch on the other side of the jumbled stone and, with any luck, hide. If I could camouflage us, it might just work.

"I heard a noise in the tunnel," someone shouted.

With Bella held tight under one arm, I jumped the gap and ducked under the unbroken shelf of stone just above the ledge. I scraped the remaining stones into a higher pile. It wasn't much, but it was better than nothing. I put Bella down, and ducked beside her, praying the pile of rocks would hide us, willing with all my might for it to happen.

A familiar tingle touched my mind, as it had when I'd tried to push myself out of the hole. I knew I was capable of magic, but how in the hell could I stop an onslaught of vampires? Unlike Shelton, I couldn't form a magical barrier. I couldn't zap vampires with a magical light beam like Adam. Unless I could figure out how to summon a fireball like I'd done while Maximus's prisoner, Bella and I didn't have much of a chance.

Then again, who said magic had to be all about brute strength? Maybe I could cloak the two of us. But if a vampire jumped the hole, they'd land right on us, and that would be that. I might be able to fight off a couple, shove them down the hole, but if they had guns, I might as well jump down the shaft with Bella.

In a flash of inspiration, I raised my head and focused. The tingling grew stronger, thicker, and nauseating in my stomach. It was all I could do not to heave. Footsteps echoed ahead. I didn't have time to see if my little spell had worked before two vampires rounded the corner and came straight toward us. I ducked, forcing my mind to concentrate on my intentions instead of the panic welling inside me.

"I know I heard something back here," said a male voice. "Clear as day."

"You know what I'm going to do, *hermano*? I'm going to drill a bullet right through that spawn's demon skull." The unseen speaker made a popping noise. "Gonna drop him like a sack of dirt, man.

"Not if I do it first, bro."

"Do you see anything?" Amanda yelled from somewhere down the tunnel.

"Not yet," one of the men yelled back.

"That is one ugly chick," said the first guy and chuckled.

"I wouldn't even put a bag over that *chica's* head and fu—w-w-hoa!"

"What th—"

The vampiric wonder twin's screams faded into the distance as they plummeted down the shaft.

I glanced over the pile of rocks hiding us and saw with pride what looked like a solid floor. My spell had worked!

More footsteps rushed down the hall. I ducked back down.

"Where'd they—ahh!" The latest newcomer joined his comrades.

"Holy mother! Oh my god," said another voice, this one sounding much younger. "They just dropped straight into solid rock."

"You idiot," Amanda said, "They're using magic. Probably set up a trap and hid somewhere. Throw rocks at the wall to see if it's solid."

"Yes sir." A rock clattered off the wall behind me.

"Keep testing the walls you morons! First one to find that little spawn bastard gets a taste of his blood." Footsteps stomped away from us.

Several more rocks clacked against the floor and walls before the guy tossing them shuffled away. Sweat beaded my brow as I tried to hold my concentration, but it was like grasping a slick rope with sweaty hands. As my focus waned, the tingling subsided along with the nausea.

I heard a soft gasp. Bella's eyes lit up in the dim light and looked into mine. She pressed her hands against my chest. "Where are we?"

"Hiding." I glanced over the makeshift stack of rocks. The hole was visible again. "I think we're safe for now." I couldn't help but brag about my little feat of magic.

A smile lit her face. "I'm proud of you. It is true when they say necessity is the mother of magic."

Someone shouted. Gunfire echoed from the main chamber.

"Justin!" Elyssa shouted.

"Maybe you should stay here," I told Bella.

She tried to rise and groaned, pressing a hand to her head. "Perhaps you are right."

I jumped the hole and sneaked around the corner to the chamber. Several vampires lay unconscious in the middle of the floor. The rest had taken cover behind the columns in the back of the room, popping out at random and spraying bullets toward Elyssa's position. The vampling and cherub strained against their cages toward the nearby vampires. It would be very bad if either got loose. The infant-like cherub would drain the light out of anyone it caught and turn them into a shadow person. The vampling might start an epidemic if it bit anyone.

How Dash had procured the cherub, I had no idea. Daelissa must have done it. *Why* she'd done it was a mystery. The leyworm made sense, being a source of magical power, but why a cherub? Had he been studying ways to harness the power of these creatures? To enslave them? No, there had to be another explanation.

"Where's Maximus?" someone roared in anger. I poked my head out and saw Adam, his face red as he emerged from behind cover, staff held out in front of him. "Where's my sister, Felicia?"

A vampire sprayed bullets at Adam. Inches from hitting him, the air rippled with the impacts. Bullets clattered to the floor.

"Felicia is your sister?" Amanda laughed. "Maximus found out she'd betrayed him. Taught that bitch a lesson."

Adam's face went white. His jaw clenched and rage burned in his face. "Where is she?"

"Dead, you idiot!" Amanda threw something at Adam, a blur of brown that hit his shield and fell to the ground at his feet.

It only took me a split second to identify the rectangular package. It was the same explosive she'd thrown at me.

Chapter 25

Adam looked down. That was all he had time to do before the blast.

"No!" I shouted, arm extended toward him as if I could prevent his death with the force of my will. Nauseating sickness swept through my body and I felt as though I were holding a superheated bubble of molten liquid in my hand.

Adam flew back a foot, landing in the ruins of a crate. The air in front of his shield rippled like water disturbed by a thousand tiny rocks.

The pain and pressure in my hand increased. Almost by reflex, I flicked my hand away from Adam and toward Amanda's position. A concussive blast shattered stone and wood, sending vampires flying back against the cages. Adam sat up on his elbows and looked at me with pure astonishment.

Fausta yelled, "Frag out!" Tossed two metallic spheres at the vampires' position, and turned her face away. Blinding light flashed through the room. Spots danced in my eyes. I fell to my knees, gagging and heaving while my stomach groaned. I wondered if I'd eaten something spoiled, though this sensation felt much different from spicy Indian food surprise. Half-blinded, I pushed to my feet and saw Elyssa and Fausta pumping vampires full of the silvery lancer darts as the fallen bloodsuckers moaned and wallowed on the floor, severely weakened by the flash grenades.

Adam strode into the fray and found Amanda. He stood over her, feet planted to either side of her body, and pulled her partially upright by her pink T-shirt. "Where's Felicia?"

Amanda let out a weak snarl. "Go to hell, Arcane."

He punched her in the face, wincing as he did. Dropped his staff and jerked her shirt with two hands. "Tell me, you bitch."

She spat blood in his face.

Adam roared and slammed her head against the floor. His fists pummeled her face as an animalistic cry ripped free from his lungs. Elyssa and Fausta grabbed him by either arm and pulled him, kicking and flailing, off the bloodied vampire.

"Adam!" Shock filled Meghan's face. "What's wrong with you?"

Tears streamed down stricken man's face. He slumped in the grasp of the two Templars holding him. Elyssa gave Fausta a sad look and nodded. They let him go as Meghan rushed to his side.

"I failed her," Adam said, wiping at his face, hands clenched into white-knuckled fists. He stood, breathing heavily, obviously fighting the pain.

My heart almost broke looking at the man. I *knew* how he felt. I understood what he was going through. Felicia had died saving me. I walked toward Adam, my throat constricted with guilt. I remembered Maximus's text to me. Had he been lying, and already killed Felicia? Or might she still be alive somewhere? Maybe Amanda was just trying to push our buttons and had lied.

I didn't know if I should tell him and give him hope, or let him grieve. What would be worse, I wondered—having hope and finding her dead, or never knowing? I knew what my choice would be. I'd want to know. For me to keep this from him would be wrong, so very wrong. I'd been an idiot to keep it from him earlier.

"Adam, I—"

He turned on me. "You could have saved her," he said, voice quiet and broken.

His words stabbed my heart. I knew if he was angry now, he'd be even angrier when I showed him Maximus's texts. Pulling out my arcphone, I retrieved the messages and held it out to him. "I'm sorry. I should have showed this to you earlier. Amanda might be lying. Maybe Maximus locked her up somewhere and she's okay."

"Why the hell would you keep this from me?" Adam stared with disbelief at the phone before flinging it back at me.

I caught it before it bounced off my chest. "I was afraid you'd go over the edge, man. I didn't know whether it would matter or not."

He turned away, taking deep deliberate breaths. "We have to find her then." His voice broke. "Or find her body. I can't leave her here. I have to take her home."

"Wait a minute," Fausta said. "Maximus is gone?"

"Through the arch there." I pointed to the obsidian structure. "But when I freed the leyworm Dash had hooked up for its energy, it took the power with it."

"Where did he go?"

"Atlanta, I think."

Fausta cursed. She pulled out her phone and walked away, speaking in urgent tones.

Elyssa squeezed my shoulder. Kissed me on the cheek. "Are you okay?"

I nodded.

"This place is a mess," Bella said, leaning against her staff as she emerged from the tunnel. "And I'm pooped."

Healer Delgado knelt beside her, running a wand over her. "You've overextended yourself." She shook her head. "You'd better rest or you might burn out."

Bella nodded with a resigned sigh. "I know."

Michael appeared in the large hole which had been the original entrance before Amanda blasted it wide open.

"Where have you been?" Fausta said.

He took in the destruction without so much as batting an eyelash. "We've got another problem."

"Another one? Haven't the others subdued the remaining OPFORs?"

Michael nodded. "Some escaped into the tunnels beneath us. I saw them breaking the lock on a metal door. They got it open before I could stop them."

Fausta bit her lip. "And what's on the other side?"

"Let's just say this place is about to be overrun. By vamplings."

Screams echoed from far down the tunnel. My blood went cold, and the hairs on my neck bristled. Elyssa's porcelain skin went a shade whiter. She took a step back, hands grasping the hilts of her sai swords in a manic grip.

I put a hand on her wrist. "Are you okay?"

Her pupils were wide and dilated. "I—I'm sorry. The memories. Almost dying..."

I enclosed her in my arms. "I'll save you again if I have to."

She managed a weak smile. "You'd like that, wouldn't you? Another gold star for your fridge?"

I replied with a long deep kiss. "I don't need gold stars, just the touch of your lips."

"I really must write that down for the romance novel I'm writing," Bella said.

Embarrassment flushed my face and I pulled away, having forgotten the world didn't really stop when I kissed Elyssa. "We'd better move out."

"We need to contain these things ourselves," Michael said, face grim. "The space is too narrow to bring down a large force of Templars." His eyes locked onto the cages at the back of the room and the vampling there. In a few quick steps, he closed the distance, and impaled the zombified vampire's head. The vampling hissed and flailed, despite the sword jutting from its skull. Michael slid his sword free and stared at the creature. "They don't die easily."

"Da nah!" screamed the cherub, its nubby arms grasping at Michael's legs.

He ran it through with his sword.

A shrill scream tore from the creature's mouth. A tortured face appeared beneath the smooth oily surface on its head where the nose and eyes should have been. Smoky black wings, insubstantial apparitions unfolded from its back. Despite the scream, it didn't die.

Michael slid his sword from the cherub's flesh with a sick, wet sound. His eyes met mine. For a moment, I almost sensed understanding in his gaze. Respect. And then the moment was gone.

I looked around for my lost gun, but settled for an assault rifle left by a fallen vampire. If I could avoid shooting myself or my companions, it might come in handy. Elyssa adjusted the straps on my scabbard, tilting the sword so I could reach it.

"Thanks."

She kissed me on the cheek. "Michael and I will take point. You help guard the rear."

Fausta raised an eyebrow. "Unless I'm mistaken, I'm the one in charge here, Borathen."

189

Elyssa rolled her eyes. "Fine. Orders, sir?"

"Michael and *I* will take point. Bella, you and the Healers will barricade yourselves in here and keep an eye on the prisoners. Borathen, you and incubus boy guard our flank. I've ordered squads to block all the exits so the vamplings can't escape and infect the populace."

"Sir, yes, sir!" Elyssa said, tossing in a sarcastic salute.

"You really don't make a good soldier," I said in a low voice. "You're too used to bossing everyone around."

A confident smile spread her lips. "Because I'm usually right."

"Move out," Fausta said.

"I'm coming, too," Adam said, anger burning in his eyes. "I've got plenty of juice left."

Fausta nodded. "Let's do it."

We headed for the door, leaving Meghan and Bella behind. Then my stomach heaved and cold sweat broke out on my face. I staggered, taking deep breaths to keep from upchucking all over the place.

"What's wrong?" Elyssa said, gripping my arm to keep me upright.

Meghan came to my side, and ran her wand along my body. "Magic poisoning." She took my chin and turned my gaze into her blue eyes. "Did you do any spells recently?"

"Yeah." I told her about the camouflaged hole.

"I think he saved me from that explosion earlier too," Adam said. "Because my shield wouldn't have done a thing to protect me from a blast like that."

Meghan's eyes grew wide. "A complete novice containing an explosion? Impossible."

"The boy has potential," Bella said.

"Can you make me feel better until we get through this?" I asked, though the nausea seemed to be fading again.

Meghan sighed and pulled a piece of bubblegum from a pouch on her side. "Chew this. I give it to first-timers to help with the sickness. But they usually don't have it this bad." She pulled out another piece. "On second thought, have two."

I tossed them in my mouth and chewed. "Minty."

"Is he okay to fight?" Fausta asked, eyes narrowed.

190

"The gum will help." Meghan pursed her lips. "And he has more spirit than most, anyway. Considering what he's been through, I wouldn't hesitate to trust him with my life."

I felt my face flush. "Uh, wow. Thanks, Meghan."

"If you're the best of your kind, there is still hope for the world." She smiled. "Good luck."

Adam pecked her on the lips. "I'll be back."

Her smiled vanished, replaced by a worried frown. "Keep your mind, Adam."

I wasn't sure what she meant by that, and didn't have time to ponder as Fausta stomped her foot and waved us on. We ran down the tunnel. Screams and shouts echoed from ahead. Once we reached myriad hallways, grunts, shouts, and shrieks seem to come from all sides. We came to the bottom of the stairs leading into the courtyard. A groups of Templars in black Nightingale armor stood, swords ready, at the top. Fausta saluted them, and we moved on.

We found the first bodies a couple-hundred feet in. I recognized the care-free kids who'd been smoking weed from earlier. Their throats were torn open, their mouths open with horror in the final moments of life. Four vamplings with mouths fastened to the dead, sucked the blood from their veins with greedy slurping sounds. One of the vamplings, formerly a female, as evidenced by the filthy tattered skirt and blouse she wore, slurped at a pool of blood on the floor.

None of the undead creatures looked as bad or smelled as ripe as the ones Elyssa and I had faced when saving my father from Maximus. These couldn't have been turned for long. Michael's sword blurred, taking the head of the nearest creature. Fausta flashed the other way, dropping two as Elyssa's brother finished off the last one. The headless bodies thrashed wildly, arms groping. The head of the female vampling landed in the pool of blood. Her tongue continued to lick at it, as though nothing had changed.

"Templars are still immune to the vampling virus right?" I asked Elyssa as Michael and Fausta beheaded the people murdered by the vamplings, and then dismembered the undead, even as their body parts continued to struggle.

She nodded. "Far as I can tell, once the Divinity—Daelissa—granted us our abilities, she couldn't just take them away, or I think we'd have noticed."

A shuffling noise sounded behind us. We turned and saw two more of the walking dead shambling our way. Elyssa grunted twice, her sword a silver blur, and both vamplings dropped headless to the floor, their fanged mouths snarling as they bounced off the stone. The bodies squirmed, hands grasping blindly while gouts of thick rancid smelling blood drained from the necks. I'd hoped they would go still and just die. Instead, we had to butcher them as Fausta and Michael had done the others.

My heart pounded like mad and sweat broke out on my forehead. These things were relentless. Why wouldn't they just die? A flashback from the fight in the catacombs beneath Maximus's Atlanta lair gripped me with claustrophobia. The stench. The press of fetid bodies. The pure rot. The grunting and hissing and biting. They just kept coming and coming and coming and they never ever stopped.

"Justin, are you okay?"

I jerked back into focus on the present and Elyssa's concerned face. I nodded. "Yeah. Sorry. Guess it freaked me out more than I thought it would."

A nod. "Me too." She touched my hand. "I hate these things."

Even Fausta's look of grim determination couldn't hide her shaking hands as she and Michael walked past the still-twitching bodies on the floor. Adam put a hand over his mouth and looked away from the slaughter. Looking away did nothing to help me. I still smelled the coppery scent of death, the blood of the newly fallen, and the stagnant blood of the vamplings.

Our progress turned into a slog. Fausta called in other squads of Templars to clear any side halls, making sure to clear every room and passage of the foul creatures as we made slow progress down flights of stairs and toward the room the things had originated. I remembered the red metal door from my escape with Katie. Now, at least, I knew why Maximus had kept it shut.

I wondered if he could really be so power hungry as to unleash a vampling plague on the world. Remembering our little talk and his grand sense of ego, I realized how stupid a question that was. Of course he would. If he couldn't win, nobody would.

The hallway ended at the now warped and broken red door. The hinges and lock had been blasted off. Groans, shuffling feet, and most of all, the stench gave away the occupants of the room beyond. Several feet behind me on the left, a familiar spiral staircase led down to the room where Maximus had imprisoned me, now dark.

"We'll contain them at this chokepoint," Fausta said, nodding toward the broken door. "No sense going in that hellhole." She pulled out her phone. "I'll call for the Custodians to come down and clean up the mess with some flamethrowers."

"They don't need flamethrowers with me around," Adam said, brandishing his staff. He gestured, and a glowing white ball hovered in the air before him. With a wave, he sent it inside the room.

Something roared. A vampling lunged from the doorway.

Michael's sword flashed, cutting the thing's arms off before it could reach Adam. The Arcane jumped back with a shout.

More snarls echoed as Adam's globe of light hovered a few feet inside the doorframe.

"Turn it off!" Fausta hissed.

It blinked out.

"It's not the light," Michael said. "They smell our blood."

Pattering feet sounded from within. Shuffles, heaves, and groans built into a growing cacophony as the monsters felt the draw of the life force pumping through our veins and homed in on it.

"Positions," Fausta commanded, readying her sword.

Michael took up a position opposite her while Elyssa took up the center.

The creatures attacked in a mob. Fausta and Michael butchered scores of them as they reached the door, forced back only by the volume of bodies as they stacked up at the door—dismembered heads, arms, and legs thrashing thanks to the unholy magic giving them false life.

I took a few steps back down the hall toward the spiral staircase to give the Templars more room. Adam growled out a command and shot a fireball from his staff. It turned the fallen bodies into a roiling pyre. The sickly sweet odor of burning flesh filled the air.

Something cold grabbed my ankle and jerked. I tumbled backwards down the stairs, rolling to a stop partway down. A sharp agonizing pain lanced into my calf. I jerked my leg, but failed to free it. A rush of fire seared my veins, seeming to catch my entire body on fire. I looked up and saw with horror the source of the agony.

A vampling, feasting on my blood.

Chapter 26

Unlike the sensation when Maximus had fed upon me, there was no pleasure whatsoever from the vampling bite. Only pain and agony. Using every last ounce of willpower, I bent back my other leg and kicked the thing's head.

Something cracked. The creature's head snapped back at a terrible angle. Slammed into the curved wall. The vampling pushed off it, landed on all fours, and hissed. A pair of broken glasses dangled from its nose. A soccer T-shirt and shorts, torn and bloody were the only other reminders of the humanity the undead creature had once possessed.

Despite the withdrawal of its fangs, the agony in my veins persisted. Desperation lent me the strength to roll backwards down the stairs while the vampling, running on hands and feet like an animal, chased me. I tried to lurch to my feet. Dizziness pulled me back to the floor. I resorted to crawling as the venom in my blood betrayed all sense of balance.

Cold hands gripped me. The vampling's teeth went for my ankle. A frightened yelp escaped me as I jerked my foot free and kicked my pursuer in the head. The kick propelled me head-over-heels, backwards down the remaining stairs. At the bottom, I hit the wall to the side of the stairwell. The hilt of my sword clanged against the stone. Somewhere during my flight, I'd lost the assault rifle. Bracing my back on the stone surface, I pushed to my feet, drew my sword, and turned right to face my attacker.

The vampling snarled. Dove at me.

Reflex kicked in. I dodged to the left. Swept my sword down in a cutting motion. Steel met bone, cleaving through it like hot butter. One of the vampling's arms flopped to the ground. I jerked my sword from the creature's ribs and sliced down again and again, chopping the thing into bits.

A groan sounded in the hallway behind me.

I spun and faced two more undead. Steadier on my feet now, I mustered all my strength and sliced both their heads off in one clean sweep. Reversed my swing and took off their legs. More groans warned of another attack. Vamplings shambled out of the room where Maximus had strapped me down like an animal. Horror, hatred, and anger suffused my heart and burned into my veins.

Even more creatures appeared behind me. I had nowhere to go.

Fear vanished, erased by the certainty that, here, I would die. Blinding anger burned through the fear, boiling into fury.

"*Xhi kakini xhe keyalla!*" I shouted in a guttural voice. *I will kill you all*!

Demonic instinct overwhelmed me, and my sword flashed like lightning among my enemies.

"Justin?" A warm hand caressed my jaw.

My eyes fluttered open. I flinched back with a shout.

"It's me, Justin. Elyssa."

"Holy Mary, what happened down here?" Fausta looked around the room, eyes wide. Blood spattered her face and clothing, but she otherwise looked no worse for wear.

I held out a blood-coated hand to Elyssa. She pulled me to my feet. I felt weak, but not completely drained. Dismembered, twitching bodies lay everywhere. Dark vampling blood covered the floor in a spreading lake of death.

"I don't remember." Pressing my hands to my head, I tried to recall the battle, but found only fleeting images and roars. Had I manifested into my demon form? My sword lay at my feet, and the bodies looked as though I'd run them down with a lawnmower.

"Remind me not to piss you off," Fausta said. She looked up the spiral stairs. "I think we're done here."

I followed her and Elyssa up the stairs, still feeling woozy and disoriented. The gagging stench of charred flesh and hair made me double over as I neared the top. It was all I could do to push it away as my supernatural senses soaked it all in.

A gentle breeze carried the smoke toward the chamber from which the vamplings had come. Adam, his face sweaty and covered in soot, appeared to be the source of the wind, his staff waving in circles. When he saw us, he stopped, mouth dropping open as he looked at me.

I looked down and noticed my blood-soaked clothing and my crimson hands. "Oh, god."

Michael, his own face splotched here and there with red, raised an eyebrow. "What happened?"

"He went crazy or something and killed—I don't know—twenty vamplings?" Fausta shook her head. "It was hard to tell with all the body parts."

Michael nodded his head toward the stairs. "Is it clear down there?"

Elyssa took my hand and squeezed. "Yes."

"What about in there?" I pointed at the chamber beyond the red door.

Michael nodded. "Looks like it. We were about to go check it out."

Adam sent a globe of light inside the room. Piles of roasted bodies and dismembered limbs lay at the entrance and beyond. A tar-like substance I identified as burnt blood covered the floor.

"I really don't want to go in there," Fausta said with a shudder. "Maybe we should wait on the Custodians."

Taking a deep breath, and instantly regretting it, thanks to the odor, I stepped past the charred bodies and inside the room. If the cells in the tunnels had been where the former dungeon wards had kept most of the prisoners, this room must have been where they put the vilest criminals, or at least the ones they wanted to suffer the most.

The room was large and filled with crude torture devices. They looked old, rusted, and unusable. Along the edges of the room were windowless, iron doors. I heard a moan and jumped back, ripping my sword from its sheath. The weak moan came again. I looked around the room, but couldn't find the source. Then I looked up. Cages hung from the ceiling by thick chains. In the glow of Adam's light, I made out a pale form lying in a heap inside one of them.

It groaned.

"Lower the cage," Michael said. "We need to burn it with the others."

A crank on the wall secured the chain. I spun it around, lowering the cage as the poor creature inside moaned. The cage clanked to the floor. A thick padlock secured the barred door.

"I've got it," Adam said, touching his staff to it. The padlock snapped open a few seconds later.

The cage door squealed open with a firm pull of my hand. The vampling huddled in the fetal position, shivering under a pile of blood-stained clothes.

"That's odd," I said.

Michael grabbed at some loose cloth and dragged the vampling out. Let go and backed away. The body sprawled. Red eyes looked up into mine from a blood-stained face. Blackened veins riddled the skin, writhing like snakes beneath the surface. I gasped and dropped to a knee.

"Help me," the infected vampire rasped. "Please, Justin."

I stared in horror at the vampire. At the young woman I knew. At Felicia.

Adam cried out. His staff clattered to the floor as he fell to his knees beside me. "Felicia! Oh, god. What the hell did Maximus do to you? That son of a bitch!"

She gripped his shirt with a pale hand already darkening with infection. "Adam?" She smiled. Shuddered and gasped. "Brother, you're here?"

"For you, sis. I came for you."

"You—you finally came for me." A tear trickled down her cheek.

Tears poured down Adam's face. He bent over his sister and hugged her tight as agonized cries tore from his throat. "All my fault. All my fault. Don't leave me, Felicia. Please don't die."

She sucked in a breath as her body bucked with spasms. "You have to kill me. No choice."

"Isn't there anything we can do?" I asked Michael. "Some kind of Templar cure?"

He looked on, his eyes troubled. "I'm sorry."

Elyssa appeared in the doorway, holding Meghan in her arms. She set her down. "She's over there. Please try to help."

Meghan knelt, placing a hand over Felicia's forehead. Eyes full of tears, she looked at Adam and shook her head. "There is no cure. Nothing I can do."

"Can my blood do anything?" I asked. "Like it helped Stacey with the hellhound venom?"

"I'm afraid not," Meghan said. She wiped the moisture from her eyes and took Felicia's hand.

"Take care of my brother," Felicia said. "Marry him and keep him out of trouble. He's a handful."

Meghan sniffed and nodded. "I will."

"He'll blame himself. Always does." Felicia sucked in a harsh breath. "Not his fault. I…made choices."

"I should have been there for you," Adam said.

"Love you anyway," she said, panting as pain filled her eyes.

Wiping away the cloud of moisture in my own eyes, I stood up and walked away, anger boiling within. Why had I let her go off by herself? Why hadn't I insisted she stay with me and Katie? Wasn't there someone who could stop this infection? Cure her?

Daelissa!

The insane angel somehow prevented Templars from succumbing to the virus. Could she cure them? The question was moot. She didn't give a crap about saving anyone, only about restoring the rule of her people by any means necessary. But there was another person who might be able to help. First, I'd have to find her. I looked at Felicia's slim figure, writhing as it battled the vampling curse, losing inch by inch.

"Meghan." I touched her shoulder and pulled her aside to leave Adam still hugging his sister.

"Yes, Justin?" She wiped her red nose with a tissue.

"I think—hope—I know someone who can cure her."

She shook her head. "It's not possible, Justin. We've tried to find a cure in the past, but it just doesn't exist. The vampling curse is the blackest part of the vampire curse, dark and ancient magic far beyond arcane knowledge."

"If Daelissa can inoculate Templars against it, maybe she can heal the virus."

"After what you've uncovered about her, why would she help?" Meghan shook her head. "She's mad."

"No, not her. There's another."

Meghan's eyes widened. "The dark angel?"

"Nightliss."

The Arcane considered this information for a moment. "She helped you defeat Vadaemos. She's very powerful."

"I think she can cure Felicia, but I need time to find her."

Meghan's eyes narrowed. "Why would Nightliss leave you? If she's so powerful, why isn't she here helping right now? Do you know how many lives we could have saved?"

"I get the feeling there's a lot more going on than just me," I said. "It took everything she had the last time she helped. For all I know, she's recovering."

A sigh escaped her lips. "Well, whatever her reasons, I hope they're good ones. All I can give you is more time." Meghan looked at Felicia and shook her head. "But it won't be much. Days at most." She gripped her wand and seemed to steel herself with a deep breath. "I'd better do it now."

I walked over to Adam and placed a hand on his shoulder. "We might have a chance at beating this." I took Felicia's hand in mine and offered her a hopeful smile. "I'm going to find Nightliss. Just hang in there, okay?"

"You really think there's a chance?" Felicia asked, hope rising in her pained voice.

I squeezed her hand. "There's always hope."

Meghan waved me and Adam away, kneeling behind Felicia, and putting the petite vampire's head in her lap. Murmuring in a low voice, she stroked the wand through the air over Felicia's body while the rest of us stood and watched. A gentle white glow settled around Adam's sister, and her convulsing body went limp and relaxed, eyes closing as if in the bliss of relief from pain.

By the time she'd finished, Custodians had appeared, wearing large silver tanks on their backs like something out of an old sci-fi movie.

"What are those for?" I asked Michael.

"Quicksilver."

"I can't believe they have that much of it," Elyssa said as she came to stand next to us.

"This is probably all of it," Michael said. "Nobody knows how to make it anymore, or where to find the ingredients."

I remembered the stuff. Underborn had used it after Brad Nichols and his infected group of vampires had tried to kill me at my school. "Is there any other way to prevent the spread of infection?" I asked.

"Fire works, to a degree." Michael shrugged. "But quicksilver is far more effective."

A great idea occurred to me. "What if we injected Felicia with it? Would it cure the virus?"

He raised an eyebrow. "It'd kill her. Back in the day, before we used non-lethal methods, Templars used to dip their arrows in quicksilver to take out vamplings and vampires alike." Michael grunted. "Dhampyrs have some protection thanks to their human side, but it wouldn't be pretty."

A Custodian administered a shimmering squirt of quicksilver on a puddle of blood. The mercurial substance flashed through the dark liquid, following the streams and tendrils wherever it had leaked, leaving behind bright crimson.

I looked at the sticky red mess on my hands and clothes. "What about the blood on us?"

Elyssa motioned to a nearby Custodian and took a small spray bottle from him. "Hold out your hands. This is a diluted potion, but it'll still sting."

She sprayed a tiny amount into each of my palms. Silvery lightning burned its way across my skin, jumping the patches clean of blood, reaching every little splotch. Clenching my teeth, I watched it devour the dark infection along my arms, leaving behind red, irritated skin and clean blood. Hands balled into fists, I endured the brief pain as it seared across my face and neck.

"Wow, that hurt."

Elyssa gave me a sympathetic look. "You look like death incarnate."

"I feel like poop."

Each of the others used the potion to clean their skin. Michael, stoic as usual, didn't so much as flinch as the diluted solution disinfected his few patches of exposed skin and his uniform.

Meghan motioned to Adam. "I used a sleeping beauty spell on Felicia. It will slow the infection, but not stop it."

201

The tall Arcane knelt and picked up his sister, cradling her limp form to his chest.

"Let's move out," Fausta said after giving the Custodians a heads-up about the mess I'd left downstairs. She gave Felicia's limp form a concerned look and put a hand on Adam's arm. "You realize, if she turns vampling, we'll have to put her down, right?"

"I know," Adam said, voice rough. "So kindly shut up and get the hell out of my way."

Fausta raised her hands and stepped aside. "Put her someplace secure. I won't risk her infecting anyone else."

After negotiating bodies, blood, and a small army of Custodians as they cleaned up the aftermath of the bloodbath, we emerged outside into the breaking dawn. We were taken into private tents, provided fresh clothes, and given one more burning spray of quicksilver to be sure before they cleared us to leave.

Fausta came out of a tent near mine. She offered me one of her rare smiles and handed me a key. "Christian promoted me to Lieutenant."

"Congrats!" I said, unsure if I should try to hug her, or if that would lead to a swift disembowelment.

"I am the youngest female to ever hold this rank." She sighed. "Everyone had thought Elyssa would be the first. And then you came along."

My heart sank. "Just when I think you're not a bitch, you go and say something like that."

Fausta shrugged. "I don't avoid the truth."

"Yeah, but you could have some tact." I held up the key. "So why did you give me this?"

"It goes to my new quarters—a private cabin at the compound. But I can wait before moving in." She laid a hand on my shoulder. "There's more to you than meets the eye. When I first met you, I thought you were soft and weak, not to mention an untrustworthy demon spawn."

I raised an eyebrow. "Why didn't you just say all that with flowers?"

Her hand dropped and she gave me a genuine smile. Her resemblance to Elyssa was uncanny, despite her larger nose. "Enjoy the cabin. Just wash the sheets before you leave."

I groaned. "Don't take this the wrong way, Fausta, but you have beauty lurking behind your bitch shield. Maybe even deep down, you have a good heart." I leaned close and whispered, "But don't worry, I won't tell anyone."

A laugh burst from her mouth. She clamped both hands over her face, trapping her mirth, and regaining her composure. "I would appreciate it if you kept that a secret." She walked away.

Elyssa emerged from her tent a moment later and smiled. We climbed inside a slider. I showed her the key and grinned. "I scored us a private cabin."

She leaned her head against my shoulder, closed her eyes, and sighed. "I love you."

I squeezed her tight against me and tried to pretend everything was all right. Worry tangled my nerves. My calf throbbed where the vampling had bitten it. I was infected. Meghan had as much told me my blood was no defense or cure for the virus, and since I was half-human, it would ravage me every bit as much as it had Felicia.

Guilt pressed against my chest. I should have told the others. But I hadn't. I couldn't. There was only one person I could trust with this for now. And what would I tell her? How could I explain to the love of my life that unless I could find Nightliss and she could cure me, our future together would be cut short? If Nightliss couldn't cleanse the infection, I had at least one more duty to fulfill.

I would kill Maximus.

Chapter 27

The truth hurts. Especially when you have to tell someone you love your future as a member of the walking dead is only days or hours away. But I wouldn't let pain prevent me from telling the woman I loved. After all we'd been through, I owed her that.

Elyssa's eyes widened as though I'd just stabbed her in the heart when I gave her the lowdown. "Let me see right this instant, Justin."

I pulled up my pants leg to reveal two blackened puncture wounds surrounded by pale flesh. I usually healed within minutes, depending on the severity of the wound. Not this time. A shudder ran up my back at the realization of how deadly serious this situation was. Time was ticking. Every beat of my heart carried infection further into my body.

Tears ran down Elyssa's cheeks as she knelt to examine the wound. Her face tightened with anger. "Why didn't you tell Meghan?" She stood, arms akimbo, lips trembling. "We have to tell her this instant!"

"There's no cure," I said, reaching a hand to caress her cheek.

She slapped my hand away. "How—how could this happen?" Her hand wiped away the tears. "I'm not going to just let you die. Meghan can put you to sleep like Felicia. I'll find Nightliss myself."

"And if my fallen angel can't heal me, what then?" I gripped her shoulders. "I'm not going into suspended animation. If Nightliss can't heal me, I want to be awake and fighting until the end." An inhuman growl vibrated deep in my chest as sudden anger surged. "Maximus is mine to kill."

Elyssa's eyes widened. She backed away a step. "Is that what you really want? To kill him? Even if it kills you?"

I pictured Maximus's leering face leaning over me as I lay strapped and helpless, his blood slave for eternity. He'd kidnapped my father. Infected Felicia. Killed scores of Templars. He was an egomaniac, born and bred for destruction by Daelissa herself. A cancerous tumor on the Earth. He had to die.

"Yes," I said, my voice oddly calm despite the sea of boiling rage building in my chest. "I do."

She blanched. "I'm not saying you're wrong. Maximus is rotten to the core. But why do you sound so bloodthirsty? It's not like you."

Maximus laughs. He stands back from the table and points at me as he, Dash, and the Master laugh until they cry while I struggle with futility against the bonds. Rage. Fury. Frustration. My emotions roil through me in a tidal wave. I will destroy—

"Justin?"

I gasped and looked at Elyssa, the vision of my tormentors vanishing like smoke. "I—I don't know." The anger washed away, draining back into the dark depths from which it came. "Maybe I'm just tired. We've been through so much crap. And the dead—god, I don't even want to think about it."

Color returned to her cheeks. She graced me with a wan smile and hugged me, pressing her head against my chest. "We've all been through too much. I don't want to lose you."

"I don't want to lose me either."

She looked up at me. "We'll rest. And then we'll talk to Meghan."

"It won't do any good."

"Please."

I sighed. "If it'll make you feel better. But Nightliss might know a cure."

She nodded. Smiled. "Thanks."

After a long hot shower, I called Stacey. Nightliss had been hanging with my felycan friend during her days as a little black cat. I hoped she might know where the angel was.

"Justin, you sound absolutely awful, love," Stacey said in her British drawl. "Whatever is the matter?"

"Oh, a little bit of this, a little bit of that." I recited a five-minute summary of the past few days.

She took in a sharp breath. "Why the bloody hell didn't you ask me and Ryland to come help? You know I do so enjoy fisticuffs against those vile bloodsuckers."

I laughed. "I might still need your help. Maximus escaped. We think he's back in Atlanta."

"Well then, lamb, we shall have to be sure his return is short-lived." She sniffed. "Now, as for Nightliss, Ryland and I will scour the area for her. I'll have my friends—"

"Your cats?"

"Indeed. They form quite an informative network. Ryland can ask his doggie friends for help."

"Hey now, cupcake," came a gruff voice from the phone. "They're wolves, not dogs."

"Hey, Ryland," I said.

"Howdy," he replied, his voice growing louder in the speaker. "I see you managed to go almost a week before stirring up trouble again."

A smile caught my lips. "I get bored easily."

"Ain't that the truth." He paused. "I do have news of your little angel friend."

Breath caught in my throat. "You do?"

"Wait a bloody moment," Stacey said. "How do *you* have news?"

"Wolves are smarter than cats for one thing," he said.

Stacey made a cute growling noise. "Someone doesn't want cuddle time tonight."

It was time to steer the conversation back on track. "Uh, guys, back to Nightliss. What do you know?"

Ryland cleared his throat. "A group of dark Arcanes was killing off supernaturals in San Francisco with nasty black magic. Rumor has it a young Arcane woman formed a coalition of supers to fight back. They were losing the fight until a woman matching Nightliss's description swooped in and helped them win."

"When was this?" I asked.

"About a day ago. Heard it from a lycan buddy of mine who was involved. He said she came outta nowhere, like an avenging angel."

"Anything else?"

"Not that I know of, but I'll have him ask the Arcane. Maybe she knows."

"Please do. It's literally a matter of life or death."

"Ain't it always?"

I spoke with them a few more minutes and ended the call after promising to contact them when I returned to Atlanta. Because I hadn't heard a word from Shelton during all this mess, I gave him a call next. He answered after several rings.

"Where the hell have you been?" I asked.

"Too much to explain." He sounded weary. "The past caught up to me, and I've trying to outrun it ever since. Should have known not to go back there, damn it."

"Crap, Shelton, why didn't you come to the Templar compound?"

He snorted. "Once I found out about the ambush the vamps pulled on you, I tried. It would've been a suicide mission." He sighed. "Look, I hate to be a disappointment and all, but I took the arch back to Atlanta. I had to pull a lot of favors just to do that."

Disbelief went through me. "Back in Atlanta? What's going on with you? Are you okay?"

"Too much to explain. Let's just say I didn't have a choice."

"Wow. Okay, I guess." I shook my head, wondering just who didn't like Shelton around these parts. Then again, considering he'd been in league with some dark people, including Vadaemos Slade at one point, he probably had as many enemies as I did.

Shelton apparently took my silence for his cue to say something. "Since you're talking on the phone, I assume you survived the ambush."

"I think my story is as long as yours," I said, and gave him an abbreviated account of events.

He blew out a low whistle. "And I thought I had it bad. Geez kid, you don't go halfway."

"We have to find Nightliss, Shelton. I know you just went through some kind of escapade yourself, but—"

"Hey, I'm on it." He chuckled. "Not a boring moment with you around."

"Tell me about it."

"Well…" he trailed off. "I guess I'll go."

"Glad you're okay." I remembered something. "Oh, and Bella's been asking about you—Harry."

"Uh, how nice."

"Is there something going on I should know about?" It took some effort not to laugh at his obvious discomfort. I just wished I could have asked him face-to-face.

"She's cute."

"Yeah?"

"Yeah." Another pause. "I'm gonna go now and hunt down an angel, okay?"

"Thanks."

"No problemo." He ended the call.

Elyssa emerged from the shower, a towel wrapped around her body. Leaning her head to the side as she dried her hair with another towel, she said, "Any luck?"

I nodded and relayed what I'd found out.

"Well, it's a start." She pressed her hands to my face and kissed me. "I'm so tired. It's always one thing after another."

"It never ends."

"I just want to forget everything. The pain, the anger. I want to let it all go." Her kisses became more insistent. "Just for one night."

I ran a hand up her neck, gripping her damp hair tight as need and desire swept me in a flood. "I just want you." My voice came out rough. "You're all I ever wanted."

She tore off my shirt. Pushed me onto the bed, and straddled me. Leaned down, her hair hanging in damp, tangled braids to both sides, violet eyes glowing with hunger. Her soft lips pressed against mine. I felt her fangs nip my lower lip. She ran kisses down my neck, groaning softly.

I gripped the towel and pulled it off, flinging it away to reveal her slender, athletic body. With a twist, I flipped us around, pinning her beneath me.

"You won't be needing these," she said, unbuckling my pants and pushing them down.

Brushing aside the raven dark hair from her face, I looked down upon her full lips, at the fangs protruding ever so slightly from beneath. I kissed her upper lip. Her bottom lip. Leaned into her neck and drew in the heady scent that drove me wild.

"You smell so…amazing," I said and pulled the sheets over us.

I woke up to the sound of someone knocking on the door. I pulled on my pants before answering.

"Oh!" Katie stood there, face blushing red, eyes wide as she stared at me. She reached a hand toward my stomach. Pulled it back, as if reconsidering. "God, I just want to touch your six-pack."

"Hello, Justin," said a calm, familiar voice.

I flinched, spotting the gray man as he stood motionless in the twilight outside. "What time is it?"

"Almost evening," Katie said. "The Templars brought us back here, although I had to convince them not to take poor—uh—whatever his name is and toss him into a cell." She jerked a thumb toward the golem. "I slept like a rock. Holy crap was I tired." Her eyes wandered up my torso. "Anyway, when I woke up, I came over here and found him sitting outside on that bench over there." She pointed out a wooden bench along a path leading through the compound. "It was kind of creepy."

"I did not intend any creepiness," the golem said.

"Weren't you bored?" Katie asked.

"I'm not familiar with being bored. Is this something I should attempt?"

"Not if you want to be bored," I said.

His head tilted. "I do not know enough about being bored to either want or not want it."

"Poor thing," Katie said, shaking her head. "He doesn't know much."

"Hang on," I said, and went back inside to grab a shirt.

"Is that Katie?" Elyssa asked, sitting up in bed.

"And the gray man."

She groaned. "Let me get dressed."

After we were properly clothed, I invited Katie and the golem inside and told her about my efforts to find Nightliss in the hopes Felicia could be saved.

Katie snapped her fingers. "Wait a minute. Now it makes more sense."

"What does?"

She pulled out an arctablet and accessed a document. "Underborn gave me access to a ton of information, like Templar crime reports, stuff like that, when I was studying for my undercover role. I found reports from all over the world where bad guys were being mean and all, and then a mystery woman showed up to save the day. But there were some weird cases where they described a blonde woman helping. Nightliss is short, has an olive complexion, and black hair, right?"

"Yeah, unless she can change her appearance, Daelissa is the only blonde angel I know of," I said, "and I can't imagine her being helpful to anyone. Back up for a minute—you're saying Nightliss has been spotted all over the world by the Templars?"

Katie gave a nod. "Mostly Templars. There were reports from normal sources too, like random people with cameras or posting to social websites. Ireland, Paris, and Johannesburg, I remember for sure."

"And you're sure Nightliss is the person in these reports?"

"The descriptions are so similar it'd have to be a big coincidence. Plus, some reports mention dark, smoky wings."

"Yeah, that about nails it," I said. The angel didn't have wings per se, but when she was using her magic, smoky apparitions in the shape of wings appeared, spreading from her back.

"Your angel has been a busy little bee," Elyssa said. "Didn't she give you some way to contact her?"

Katie arched her eyebrows. "Yeah, like a phone number? Email address?"

"No." I sighed. "Not even a friend request. She wanted me to choose a side. Her side. Then she could give me a gift, which I assume meant I could contact her whenever."

"And you didn't decide?" Elyssa said, brow wrinkled. "After all the times she's helped us?"

I pushed away from the table and paced. "I know, I know. Seems like a big mistake in hindsight." My gaze found Elyssa. "But what if I choose wrong? What if Nightliss isn't what she seems to be?"

"Seems like a slam dunk," Katie said. "At least from what you've told me."

I dropped back into my seat. "Yeah. Maybe it is." I definitely regretted my indecisiveness now. Time was against me and Felicia. To make matters worse, Maximus was still free and probably up to his old games. Every minute I sat here was another minute my nemesis could fortify his position and another heartbeat closer Felicia and I were to un-death. I'd been inside his Atlanta compound while saving my father. While it wasn't built like a fort, there were only few ways inside. Risking open war with him might expose the Overworld. The Templar Custodians had barely kept things under control in Bogota. In Atlanta, it would be almost impossible.

If noms discovered the existence of the supernatural in their midst, all hell would break loose. At this stage of the game, however, it might not matter, especially if Daelissa managed to restore the Grand Nexus and allow her people back into our world. Their reemergence would give a whole new meaning to hell on Earth.

"Why didn't Nightliss help us with Maximus?" Katie said. "All the stuff she's done, and she didn't lift a finger to help. You could have died."

I had to admit, it worried me a little bit. Nightliss had proven herself powerful and capable. But she'd also told me she wasn't fully recovered from the destruction of the Grand Nexus centuries ago. She might be overextending herself. Sitting here was no longer an option. I *had* to find her. I had to stop Maximus.

My calf throbbed, sending a jolt of pain up my body.

I struggle against the tight bonds. Dash leans toward me, his eyes wild and crazy. He throws back his head and laughs. Skin flakes from his cheeks, his nose, his mouth, leaving raw muscle and bone. Blood streams from his eyes and ears, trailing down his throat. Still, he continues his hysterical laughter as I look up, helpless.

Fury burns through me. Blinding pain jabs into my skull. I will kill them. Kill them all. The table beneath me groans. Bends. Snaps in two. I am free. Free!

"Justin!"

My face stung. Rubbing my cheek, I looked at Elyssa. She and Katie's expressions were filled with uncertainty—maybe even fear. "What—where?"

"You were shaking. Yelling." Katie looked down.

I looked at the table. I'd gripped it so tight, the metal had bent. "Uh." Words failed me. "I guess I'm stressed out more than I thought."

"That would be putting it mildly," Katie said.

Elyssa touched my hand. "We need to talk with Meghan."

"Can't it wait?"

Her eyes went hard. "You promised."

I jerked my hand out from beneath hers. "Fine. Let's go."

"If it is acceptable to you, Justin, I will remain here." The gray man had hardly spoken a word since taking a seat in the corner of the room.

I nodded. "Sure."

"Perhaps I will attempt being bored as you suggested earlier. It sounds interesting."

"It's not all that interesting," I said. "Why don't you practice being happy instead? We could all use a little more happiness right now."

He tilted his head. "I will consider it, Justin."

We left him in his corner, and walked to the infirmary where we found a team of healers treating Templars wounded from the day before. Meghan saw us and approached.

"Any luck finding Nightliss?" she asked.

"Not yet." I sighed. "Can we speak somewhere private?"

Her eyebrow quirked. "Sure." She led us outside the squat adobe building and took us behind it. Turned to face me. "What's on your mind?"

"Show her," Elyssa said, voice tight.

"What's wrong?" Katie asked. "Justin?"

I pulled up my pants leg.

Meghan's eyes went wide. "Oh no."

Katie gasped. "Justin. Please don't tell me that's—"

"It's a vampling bite." The punctures were as black as the day before. The skin around them looked slightly bruised.

"Do you want me to suspend you?" Meghan asked, kneeling to run her wand over my skin. "The rate of infection seems much slower than usual, so you might have more than a few days before—before the end."

I glared at Elyssa. "See? No cure. Waste of time."

Her jaw went tight. "It is not a waste of time. Now we know your infection isn't spreading fast. We have time to find Nightliss."

I wanted to feel reassured, I really did. Instead, the clock in my head just ticked louder.

Nightliss, damn it, where are you?

212

I wanted nothing more than to see her. To know help had arrived. A wave of dizziness washed over me. It took everything I had not to stagger as my balance teetered on the brink. I didn't want to give Elyssa any excuse to make me take the Sleeping Beauty option from Meghan. I might have days or a week, but the truth was obvious now. This infection was as relentless as the vamplings.

And it wouldn't stop until I was dead.

Chapter 28

Katie shrieked when we walked into the cabin.

The gray man still sat where I'd left him, a frightening leer plastered on his face. The god-awful expression vanished as his lips resumed their normal flat state. "I have been practicing being happy, Justin," he said in his calm voice. "It is not easy."

"You call that being happy?" Katie said, a hand pressed to her heart. "Smiling like that?"

He nodded. "From what I understand, smiling is an important part of being happy. But smiling is very difficult."

"It is when you're not happy," I said, frowning. "How do you know all this stuff? Do you have a bunch of information programmed into you?"

He tilted his head. "I am not programmed like a computer. My spark contains a great deal of data, although I do not know its origination. Some of this data is already organized into information, linking it to what I have seen in the world. Other parts are quite raw and scattered, and I must research them."

"Such as how to be happy?"

He nodded. "Emotions are very hard to understand. From what I have gathered, one must experience such things to understand them."

"Get a girlfriend. You'll figure out a lot of emotions really quick."

"Hey now," Elyssa said, punching me on the arm.

The gray man looked from me to Elyssa. "Finding someone who wishes to be with me in that sense would be very difficult, Justin. I believe many here would rather see me burned to ash and forgotten."

"Like little gray cinders on the wind," Katie said. "How sad."

The golem studied Katie for a moment. "I have decided my name."

I cocked my head. "Really? Is it George?"

"How about Dexter?" Katie said. "I love that name."

"No. It is Cinder."

"Huh?" I said, failing to see why he'd choose such a name.

"After Katie mentioned the word, I looked it up. It describes me rather accurately. I am gray. I am not a full being in any sense of the word, but an ashen representation of a human. I am but gray dust molded into form."

I stared at him dumbfounded for a moment. "That was almost poetic. But isn't a cinder hot ash?"

"I do have a spark inside me. While it is not hot, I believe the name will suffice."

I stood up and walked across the room to him, held out a hand. He stared at it for a moment before standing and extending his own.

I gripped his hand and shook it. "Nice to meet you, Cinder."

He looked at me. I caught the twitch in his eyes, almost too slight for anyone without supernatural senses to have seen. "Thank you, Justin."

"Congratulations, Cinder!" Katie said, clapping her hands.

Elyssa stared at us like we were crazy. "Yay. The golem has a name. Now, instead of wasting time, let's do something to find Nightliss."

"I believe I have pertinent information regarding this entity," Cinder said, flicking his fingers across the arctablet Katie had used earlier.

A picture of the dark angel hovered above the table. Rustic buildings, roofs laden with snow lay behind her as she stared somewhere off into the distance while swirling snow surrounded her. She wore only a simple black dress despite the sub-zero temperatures. The shadowy outline of wings hung from her back, and her black hair billowed. Beneath the image was a caption: *Crazy beautiful girl with wings. Not Photoshopped!*

"Where was this?" I asked leaning forward for a better view.

"In Breckenridge, Colorado," Cinder said. "When I discovered the image, it triggered memories in my spark, uncovering a series of directives we were given regarding this entity."

215

"Mr. Gray knows about Nightliss?" My insides went cold. Cinder's creator was—as far as I knew—in league with Daelissa. As Ivy had put it, a Brightling.

"I do not know a Mr. Gray. From what little I can recover of my previous instructions, Nightliss is a person of great interest. This revelation led to a chain of thought which revealed even more." Cinder tilted his head slightly. "You are a person of great interest to my creator as well, Justin."

Elyssa jumped in front of me, arms splayed protectively. "I knew keeping him around wasn't a good idea. How long until you act on those instructions, golem?"

The golem regarded her in silence for a moment, then said, "I have no intention of acting on any prior directives. Justin saved my spark, my continued existence. There is no higher price to repay."

"It's hard to believe that little light is life." Katie said.

"It's not life. It's what animates these things," Elyssa said. "Sometimes it's in the chest. Sometimes, the head. Disconnect the spark from the body, and they drop dead." She took a step toward him. "It may look more lifelike than any golem I've ever seen, but it's still just an inanimate object. I say we end this charade now before Frankenstein's monster turns on us. For all we know, he's a spy."

"Leave him alone." I grabbed Elyssa's arm and pulled her back. "He hasn't done anything to show he's a danger."

My girlfriend's blazing eyes turned on me. "You're taking sides with that thing over me?"

I took an involuntary step back, hands held up protectively. "No. But I know how it is to be judged and found guilty just because of who and what I am. Things happen for a reason."

She took a deep breath, pinching the bridge of her nose and closing her eyes. "I know. I'm sorry. But we're on a timer, Justin. You are dying, minute-by-minute, and diversions like this—this *thing* are only getting in our way."

"Perhaps this is one of those emotional girlfriend things you spoke of earlier," Cinder said, his voice as calm and polite as if Elyssa hadn't just discussed destroying him. "Although, I am unsure if it is awakening emotions in me."

"I'll show you emotions," Elyssa said, going for her sword.

"Whoa!" I shouted, taking her arm. "Remember the whole not killing thing we just talked about?"

"I believe I may be of help," the golem continued, gray eyes studying Elyssa. "Before my awakening, I believe my mind was part of a collective consciousness shared by me and those of my kind. We were tracking the movements of this being." He waved away the photograph and replaced it with an overhead map of the world. His finger touched various locations around the globe, including one in Atlanta and southern Colombia.

"These are places she's been seen?"

"With some frequency, though most sightings came here." He pointed to Atlanta.

"Because of me?" I asked. "Was she watching me?"

"More specifically, she visited the abandoned granite quarry called Thunder Rock." The golem zoomed in on the area.

"Where did she go in Colombia?"

"The dead city, El Dorado."

Elyssa pinched the image, zooming it back out to the world map. "And these other places?" She pointed to the red dots. "Are they abandoned angel relics, too?"

"They are uninhabited," Cinder said. "Interdicted by the Arcane Council, according to the records."

"I really don't want to go back to Thunder Rock," I said with a shudder. It hadn't been so long ago I'd been lost there, nearly devoured by cherubs, and shot through a series of malfunctioning Obsidian Arches, only to end up in El Dorado where shadow people had tried to suck me dry.

"So it's possible we could find her there," Elyssa said.

Cinder gave a stiff nod, as if he weren't accustomed to using body language for expression. "My memories are not complete. Only shards remain, though more may come back to me with proper triggers. Still, Thunder Rock appears to be a place of some significance for the...angel."

I raised an eyebrow at the uncertainty in his otherwise calm voice. "I don't have time to sit around Thunder Rock, hoping that Nightliss will show up."

A thud sounded against the door.

Elyssa groaned. "Great. Probably Fausta. My father is already mobilizing forces for an assault on Maximus in Atlanta." She swung open the door and gasped.

A petite woman with olive skin and dark hair lay outside the door, her skin cut and bruised in so many places, it looked like she'd been beaten and left for dead. Elyssa pulled the hair away to reveal a bloodied face with several deep cuts. Even so, I recognized her instantly.

"Nightliss!" I dropped to her side. "Oh, god, what happened to her?"

"I'll get Meghan," Katie said, gingerly stepping over the prostrate angel and running toward the infirmary.

I tore the sheets off the bed and covered it with towels. Elyssa set Nightliss down atop them. Kneeling by her side, I took the angel's hand and pressed a palm to her forehead. She felt cool. I put an ear to her mouth and detected the barest hint of breath.

"Nightliss?" I said. "Can you hear me?"

She didn't even twitch.

Meghan showed up a moment later, a white bag decorated with purple flowers in one hand. "Clear away from her," she commanded, drawing her wand and running it along the angel's still form. Wisps of smoky vapor drifted from her body, forming a ghostly outline. Some of the vapors were green. Most were orange or red.

The healer shook her head. "I don't even know how she's still alive." She reached in her bag and withdrew a mason jar filled with glowing white light. "Justin, you'd better back further away. This is soul essence. I don't want you accidentally siphoning any away."

Too stunned by the oddity of soul essence in a jar to say anything, I backed all the way into the kitchen and watched as Meghan unscrewed the lid and held it beneath Nightliss's nose. My incubus senses tingled. I felt the demonic part of me strain against my control as the halo of light drifted toward the angel's face like a lazy snowflake.

Nightliss groaned. Her eyelids fluttered. Her chest heaved, and she took in a deep breath. The light swirled into her mouth, unwinding like a ball of yarn until the last wisp vanished. The angel coughed. Black fluid bubbled from her mouth. Meghan turned her over, holding the other woman's head over the edge of the bed.

Nightliss convulsed. A guttural noise started deep in her throat, a gagging, choking sound. More of the dark liquid dribbled onto the tiled floor.

Katie and Elyssa jumped back, their mouths clenched with disgust.

Meghan ran her wand up the angel's back, chanting under her breath. The wand glowed brighter and brighter until, with one gut-wrenching convulsion, Nightliss expelled a gout of oily black goop. It splattered all over the place, soaking into the bed mattress and Meghan's plain blue dress.

Forget cleaning the sheets. Fausta was going to need a new mattress.

Seemingly oblivious to the foul-smelling fluid, Meghan took a towel and wiped Nightliss's mouth and face with it before turning the angel back down on the bed.

"What," said Katie, pinching her nose, "is that stuff?"

Meghan shook her head. "I have no idea." She looked at me. "Is there a bucket in the kitchen somewhere?"

I looked under the sink and found a plastic trash can. Pulled the bag out of it and handed it to the Arcane. She muttered an incantation, twirling the wand in a tight circle. The dark fluid whirled, forming a funnel. Droplets of it struggled free of the mattress, towels, and Meghan's clothes. She altered the pattern of her wand. The liquid formed a floating sphere, shimmering in the incandescent light. I picked up the trash can, enclosing the liquid in it.

Meghan lowered her wand, and wiped beaded sweat from her forehead. "Don't dump that down the sink until we figure out what it is."

I nodded and put a lid over it.

"Will she survive?" Cinder said, his eyes never leaving Nightliss.

"I believe she has a slim—" Meghan broke off as Nightliss coughed, eyes blinking open.

"Jared?" the angel said, eyelids drooping. "Please don't leave me." She drifted asleep, breathing easy.

"I think I'll upgrade her chances from slim to good," Meghan said after the surprise faded from her face.

"Who's Jared?" I asked.

Elyssa smiled and crossed her arms. "I hope you don't expect an answer to that."

"Yeah, but—"

My girlfriend crossed the room in a blur. Gripped me in a fierce hug. Tears trickled down her cheeks. "Nightliss is going to be okay. You're going to be okay."

Warmth spread from the very center of my being as my thoughts shifted back to the impending doom infecting my blood. "Yeah." I grinned. "Maybe you're right." *Provided Nightliss can actually cure me.* The joy faded at the possible reality she may not. As if to remind me, an icy cold ache dug deep into my calf muscle, causing me to wince.

Meghan went into the kitchen and poured a cup of water from the faucet. Dark circles underscored her eyes. For the first time, I realized how haggard she looked.

"Are you okay, Meghan?" I asked.

She offered a wan smile. "Just exhausted. We've been treating casualties non-stop since yesterday. Commander Salazar requested Healers from other legions, so hopefully we'll have a break soon." Her gaze shifted to Nightliss. "Let her rest. Whatever you do, don't try to wake her." She finished her water and headed for the door. "I'll return to check on her soon."

"How's Adam?" I asked.

She turned from the door, worry lines in her brow deepening. "He hasn't left Felicia's side." A tear glistened in the corner of her eye. "Will you talk to him, Justin? Make him see it's not his fault?"

"Sure," I said, my throat suddenly dry. I couldn't help but feel I was to blame. Sure, it was irrational. Following Felicia's instructions had seemed the smart thing to do at the time. But hindsight dug into my gut with a vicious twist, showing me how I could have prevented this outcome.

"You can't save everyone," Elyssa said, squeezing my hand.

"I guess if nobody else is going to say it, I will," Katie said, her eyes fixed on Nightliss.

"Say what?" I raised an eyebrow as a female mind once again succeeded in confusing me.

"How very convenient the one person you need suddenly shows up on your doorstep." She crossed her arms and gave me a look that dared contradiction.

Elyssa groaned. "Damn it, she's right. I didn't want to say anything but…"

"Does it matter how she got here?" I said.

"I was so happy to see her, to think you might be cured, Justin." Elyssa shook her head. "But miracles like this don't just happen. Not in the real world."

"Since when was the Overworld the real world?" I said, crossing my arms tight against my chest to keep my hands from shaking, even though deep inside, I knew they were right.

"Maybe she was already looking for you," Katie said. "Maybe she got in trouble and you're the only person she could turn to." She shrugged. "It doesn't explain how she knew where you were, of course. But we need to be careful. Someone messed her up bad. That same person might have done something to her and dumped her here as a trap."

"You're sounding as paranoid as me," I said. "Cripes, I guess it's contagious."

"Justin—" Elyssa started.

"I don't want to talk about it anymore." I slashed my hand through the air and suppressed a growl threatening to rise out of my chest. "She's here, and that's all that matters. Whether she's the answer to all our prayers remains to be seen."

"I found this outside," Cinder said, appearing at the doorway. He held up a clump of blonde hairs that looked as though someone had grabbed a handful and yanked them out. "They were caught in the grass outside the door where your friend was."

"Meghan's a blonde," Elyssa said, then glanced at Katie. "And so are you."

"Yeah, but someone tore these out," Katie said. "I sure didn't see any bald patches on Meghan.

"An angelic cat fight," I said. "I'll bet they're Daelissa's."

"So Daelissa brought her here?" Elyssa's eyebrows pinched.

My stomach rumbled. *Not good.* "We'll just have to ask her when she wakes up." The happiness I'd felt upon first seeing my prayers answered all but evaporated. I could see the hope fading in Elyssa's eyes as well.

Katie wiped her eyes. "I'm sorry, Justin. I hope I'm wrong. I just don't want anyone to get hurt." She sniffled and turned. "I'm going to take a walk. It's stuffy in here."

Elyssa watched her go. "I'll keep an eye on Nightliss. Maybe you should go talk to Adam. Make sure he doesn't get too—you know."

"Too excited? Overly optimistic?" I sighed. "Story of my life."

She gave me a sad smile, and nodded.

I kissed her on the forehead. "I'll go talk to Adam. Let me know if anything changes."

"May I go?" Cinder said, rising from his seat.

"Sure." I motioned him along and stepped outside into the dark chilly night.

We headed for the long Quonset the Templars were using to temporarily house the injured. I figured they hadn't had to deal with such a large number of casualties as this before. Then again, nobody had expected an army of vampires armed with cursed bullets.

"Justin, is Nightliss truly an angel?"

I stopped and looked at Cinder, surprised by the uncertainty in his typically deadpan voice. "I think so, though not in the biblical sense of the word. Just like vampires aren't exactly how most books portray them."

"Do you believe she is a being of great power?"

I nodded. "No doubt. Why?"

His gray eyes focused on something in the distance. "Can she make me real?"

"Real? But you are—" My mouth dropped open as my slow wits picked up on the significance of his remark. "You want to be like me?"

"Perhaps not a demon spawn," he said. "Real flesh and blood would be enough."

"Why?"

"I believe my grasp on emotions is improving." He pressed a hand to his midsection. "Based on the way something inside me reacts to Elyssa's willingness to end my existence makes me desire humanity. I do not wish to elicit negative emotions in others because I am magically animated and not, according to most standards, real."

I put a hand on his shoulder. "I understand what you're going through. I've been there." Glancing back at the cabin where the angel rested, I wondered what she would think of his request. "I have no idea if Nightliss can turn you into a human. Your creator, Mr. Gray, might know the answer."

"The Mr. Gray you mentioned earlier...he made me?"

I grimaced, realizing I hadn't exactly sat the poor golem down and explained my history with the gray men. "Uh, I think so. From what I know, he's an angel like Nightliss."

"Oh." Cinder looked at the ground. "Then perhaps it is impossible. Otherwise, why did he not make me more human?"

Aside from gray being his creator's favorite color, I had no answer for him. "Look, let's talk about this later." I motioned him onward. "Once Nightliss is up and about, she can tell you for sure."

He stayed where he was. "Justin, I am sorry for deceiving you."

My chest went cold. "What do you mean?"

"I did not actually desire to accompany you to Adam. Instead, I wished only to ask you this question in private."

I sighed in relief that his following me wasn't part of an evil plot. "You don't have to come."

"Perhaps I will practice being bored as you suggested earlier. It may further my understanding of emotions."

"Are you sure you actually *feel*?" I asked.

"According to definition, I believe I do." He held out his hands and looked at them. "I also sense things by touch, smell, sight, and sound." His arms dropped to his sides. "It appears, however, I was not meant to experience or utilize emotions. It was not until I *awoke* in Maximus's lab that the first tingling of awareness or emotion entered into me. Whatever caused such a change was not part of my original composition."

"Did Maximus do something to you?"

He opened his mouth, and then with robotic precision, shrugged. "I do not know."

"Look, we'll talk about this. Just practice your emotions, preferably somewhere away from Elyssa for now. Okay?"

He nodded. "Thank you for listening, Justin."

"No problem." I left him standing there and headed for the corrugated steel building with a semi-circular roof at the other side of the complex. A familiar figure emerged from the front door and stormed toward one of the two-story dorm buildings. *Adam.*

I hurried to catch up to him, following inside where he slid a key into a door lock.

"Adam," I said.

He jerked. Looked at me. "Oh, Justin." He opened the door. "Come on in."

I followed him into the dorm room. Two unopened suitcases sat atop a still made bed. He moved them to the floor then opened a duffel bag and dug out a memory card. I hoped for a cue to start my talk, but he didn't say anything else, content to keep messing with his arcphone, popping the memory card in and looking at something on the screen.

"What you got there?" I asked.

He grunted. Flicked his finger and activated the holographic display. A dizzying array of symbols filled the air. Something about them seemed awfully familiar. He waved his hand across the sea of symbols, arriving at a complicated pattern I felt certain I'd seen before.

"Remember this?" he said.

I narrowed my eyes, trying to recall. "I think I do."

"The spells you took from your mom's computer. You asked me and Shelton to look them over."

My heart clenched. "The spells of mass destruction? The ones someone could use to wipe out an entire race of supernaturals?"

"Time we put it to use, Justin." He turned off the display and shoved the phone in his pocket. "I deciphered the runes for one of the spells. Got them all in place. Now all I need to do is power the spell."

"You mean you're going to—"

"Yeah. We're going to wipe out every vampire in Atlanta."

Chapter 29

"Adam, this is a really, really bad idea." I held out my hand. "Why don't you give me the memory card, and we'll figure out a safer way to contain Maximus?"

His eyes flared. "After all the evil Maximus and his army have done, you just want to let him go?"

"I never said that."

"No, but you might as well." He crossed his arms. "Think about it. Maximus knows by now about what happened here. He'll also know the Templars will make a play for him in Atlanta. I'm sure his brainwashed minions are ready to go toe-to-toe with Templars again, especially armed with those bullets."

"Yeah, but he won't have Dash to help him. He's out of places to run."

"He still has Daelissa on his side. And there's nothing more dangerous than a cornered animal." Adam threw his hands up. "Think about it, Justin! What's worse—losing more Templars, or taking the vamps down without a fight?"

"Not every one of them is evil. And like you said, he's brainwashed a lot of them." I shook my head. "And what about other vampires—those who aren't even involved with Maximus? That spell will kill them as well."

"Maybe they deserve it. They're bloodsucking parasites."

Deep down, I really didn't have a soft spot for vampires, but Felicia had proven not all of them were bad people. "What if somebody else's sister is in there? Someone's brother? Someone's kid? You'll be killing them. Felicia showed us people can change, even vampires." I held out a hand imploringly. "Adam, everyone deserves a chance to prove they're not a monster."

His eyes reddened. "It's the only way. The best way."

"Deep down in your heart, do you really believe that?" I ran a hand down my face. "Believe me, if I had a spell I could target Maximus with, I would do it. He needs to die. Anyone who'd risk a vampling plague to advance his own power isn't someone you want to keep sucking breath. Or blood, for that matter."

Adam leaned against the door and slid down it until he sat on the floor. "I don't know what to feel anymore. Or believe," he said in a whisper. "I used to think I'd be okay with Felicia ending up dead. After all the horrible things she'd done to her body, I figured I'd get a phone call in the middle of the night. Find out she was dead. Instead, she became a vampire."

"It's not your fault."

"No, no, no, Justin. That's where you're wrong." He gave a hollow laugh. "If I hadn't become so obsessed with finding my parents' murderer, I wouldn't have ignored her. She needed love and attention. I gave her nothing except the bare minimum." He sighed. "Everything else, every emotion, every hour of every day, I spent searching for the killer and training myself to end them." His eyes met mine. "I drove her to this. I might as well have thrown her in that room full of vamplings myself."

I walked over to him and held out my hand. "Take it."

He looked up, puzzled, and gripped my hand.

I pulled him to his feet. "What's done is done. The important thing is that we make the right decisions from here on out. Slaughtering vampires en masse is probably not one of them."

He sighed. Pulled the memory card from his phone. Handed it to me. I looked at the innocuous sliver of plastic for a moment before handing it back. "I trust you not to use it," I said. "But it may have other uses."

His eyebrow perked up. "Oh?"

"Can you modify it to knock out or disable vampires instead of kill them?"

He pursed his lips and stared into the distance. "The spell goes after the magical DNA vampires rely on to live. It strips it out one tiny part of the equation, and kills them. It's possible, with enough study, I could figure out how to alter the runes, make it nonlethal, but that might take months."

I shrugged. "Well, it might be useful in the future."

He held up the chip. "The spells on here are so advanced, I find it hard to believe even your mom could have written them. It took me and Shelton some serious computer time to decode even a couple of runes."

"If that's true, who's capable of such complex spells?"

"It's not just about writing them, Justin. It's also about powering them." He slid the phone into his front pocket. "Even if you hadn't talked me out of this, I'd have to find a heavy-duty arc generator and be able to focus the energy from it to pull off a spell of this magnitude. There are only a couple of individuals I know with that kind of power, and one of them has helped us before."

"Nightliss and Daelissa." I thought back to the display of power the dark angel had shown during my fight with Vadaemos. It also reminded me why I'd come to find Adam in the first place. "Nightliss is here."

His eyes went wide. "Here?" A look of wonder lit his face. "Can she help?"

I grimaced and explained the situation. "Meghan is helping her—or trying to. Nothing is certain yet."

His face fell. "Oh. Please let me know the instant you find out."

"Of course. Hopefully we'll know something soon." I had more to say, but pain spiked in my calf. I clenched my teeth. Dark smoky tendrils carved the air before me. A bright coppery scent filled my nostrils. I lost all sense of balance, and fell hard onto my back.

Maximus leers down at me. He extends a hand. A flare of anger energizes me. With a roar, I spring to my feet and ram a fist at the vampire's face. I miss and hit the wall behind him. Concrete dust billows from the hole my fist makes. Maximus yells. Fear shows in his face. I lunge. An invisible force stops me inches from his throat. A blinding flash of light seems to explode in my head and I fall back, staggering, and squeezing my temples.

"Justin, stop! It's me!"

I looked up to see Adam, staff glowing bright before him.

"Wh—what happened?" My head ached. Sharp pains raced up and down my leg.

"You yelled something about Maximus and nearly caved in my skull." He backed into the hallway, clearly not taking any chances. "Dude, you must be suffering some kind of post-traumatic stress. Have you talked to Meghan about it?"

A sinking feeling in my guts told me it had nothing to do with stress. The vampling curse was doing something to my mind. Bad enough it might kill me, but if it made me a danger to everyone around, that would be much worse. I nodded. "Yeah. Maybe I should see if she has something I can take."

"Probably a good idea." He lowered his staff. The glow winked out. "I'll study the runes some more and let you know if I figure anything out. Okay?"

"Yeah." I pinched the bridge of my nose to fight back a throbbing headache and left the room. "Sorry about, uh, you know." I waved at the hole in the wall.

Rather than return to the cabin, I took a long walk around the Templar compound, breathing the night air, giving my head time to clear, and the headache time to fade. My guts twisted inside me as I considered the inevitable conclusion to the vampling infection. An occasional wave of hope took the sting of fear away as I meandered the complex, but uncertainty kept dealing it a deathblow before it could stick.

I walked past the edge of the central buildings toward a grassy area where a few trees grew. An old stone shed sat in the center, the wear and tear on it giving it the appearance of being much older than most of the other buildings in the area. Cinder sat at the base of the outbuilding with a glazed expression on his impassive features. Even though the moon gave off some light, I probably wouldn't have seen him without my night vision.

He looked at me. "I think I have 'gotten a handle', as you say, on being bored. At first I found the new environment to be most stimulating, but after achieving a great deal of familiarity with it by sitting here for over an hour, I sensed an uncomfortable lack of newness which urged me to seek out new stimuli. But I deemed it best to stay here away from the other Templars lest they decide I am a threat."

"I don't think I've ever heard boredom described quite that way, but you've nailed it on the head." I studied him for a moment. "I should send you to a speech therapist."

"Are my vocal communications garbled?"

"No, but you hardly use any inflections so I can't tell if you're happy, sad, bored, or what. Maybe I should sit you down in front of some soap operas for a while. You'll hear all sorts of inflections then."

"I would be grateful, Justin."

Something about his calm manner brought a sense of peace to me. I took a seat on the grass across from him, questions about this strange being bubbling in my mind. My phone chimed with a text message from Elyssa before I had a chance to ask him anything.

Nightliss is awake.

I sprang to my feet.

"Have I offended you in some way?" Cinder asked.

I shook my head. "Nightliss is conscious."

"May I speak with her?" The faintest hint of hope registered in his voice.

"I don't know if she has her strength back yet. Let's see what's going on before we assault her with a ton of questions, okay?"

He stood. Gave a stiff nod. "This is acceptable."

When we reached the cabin, Elyssa waited outside. She spared Cinder a cursory glance and stopped me. "She's still weak, Justin. Meghan didn't want her seeing anyone yet, but she keeps asking for you." Her lip trembled. "I hope she can help."

The fear reawakened in me, burning through my stomach and inciting a cold sweat on my forehead. "Me too, babe."

Cinder walked a short distance to a bench. "I will sit and await your return."

Inside, Meghan spoke with Nightliss in low tones. The angel, reclining on pillows in the bed, looked up at me. Her lips curved up. She squeezed Meghan's hand.

"I must speak with him alone."

Meghan nodded. "Take it easy. You've been through a lot." She looked at me. "Did you talk to Adam?"

"Yeah. Told him I'd talk to Nightliss."

Meghan nodded and left.

Nightliss patted the chair next to the bed. "Come sit."

I dropped into the seat and took the angel's petite hands in mind. "What in the hell happened to you?"

A tear sparkled down her cheek. "I tried to reverse the irreversible."

"I don't understand."

"I tried to convince Daelissa her course of action is rash and dangerous." Her green eyes looked sad. "She took the chance to ambush me. I am still no match for her."

My hands trembled as I considered my next question. "Look, I know you've been through a lot, but I have to know something. How did you get here?"

Her eyes looked up, as though accessing memories. "I only remember bits and pieces."

"Anything you can remember will be helpful."

Her eyes widened. "Justin, you look worried."

"We really needed to find you, and then *poof* you appeared right outside the door."

She shook her head. "And you think I may be part of some trap."

"I'm sorry—"

"Justin, I would never hurt you." She touched my hand, and the shaking in it stopped.

"I'm sorry." I looked down, unable to meet her eyes. "I don't want to believe it. But it's too convenient."

"I will tell you what I can." She touched a finger to her chin. "I fought Daelissa. Just when I thought I would die, there was a loud boom. A scream." Her eyes flared with fear. "Someone grabbed me, but the world was dark. I clawed at them. Tried to free myself. And then I must have fainted." She gasped and looked at me. "Perhaps Daelissa brought me here. She may have done something terrible to me, Justin."

I gripped her hands. "You're safe now. If she did anything, I promise we'll try to help you."

Tears welled in her eyes. "Perhaps it's best if I go away in case—"

"No!" I said, my voice louder than I'd meant it to be. "No," I repeated in a whisper. "We need you here."

"Why?" She asked in a tremulous voice. "I might be...*dangerous*."

"A vampling infected Adam's sister, Felicia. She's dying."

Nightliss's eyes widened. "She has the curse?"

"Yes."

"Is she human?"

"She's a vampire."

The angel wiped a tear from her cheek and looked away in thought. "I can help, but I will need the blood of her sire."

"Uh, what's a sire? Her dad?"

"The vampire who turned her."

My heart dropped. I didn't have a clue who her sire was. She'd once told me it was Maximus, but from what I understood, he hadn't been a vampire long enough to change others without the severe risk of killing them and making them vamplings. I hoped Adam knew.

"What are the odds you can heal her?" I asked.

"Very good." Her lip curled into a cute snarl. "I remember when my kind gave the *gift* of immortality to humans. The Brightlings—those like Daelissa—ever spiteful of beings they considered their lessers, insisted it come with a price. They cursed the gift so the bearer must drink the blood of others to survive. And should a human try to pass the gift, they would, instead, pass on the vampling curse."

My brow furrowed. "But vampires *can* turn humans."

She nodded. "Yes. Humans are very good at bending reality to their will. It appears somewhere in history, a vampire was able to overcome the curse, but only after a certain length of time. Much like anything with humans, it requires force of will and focus."

A sense of relief warmed me in a gentle flood. Felicia could be saved. That had to mean I could also be saved. "Nightliss, I was bitten, too. I'm infected."

Her eyes went even wider. "No, Justin. Please tell me this is not true."

My heart went cold at the alarm in her eyes. "You can heal me though, right?"

Tears gathered in her eyes. She pressed herself against me in a fierce hug. "You are demon spawn. Your kind is much different from humans."

"But I'm half human."

She looked up at me with a tear-stained face. "It does not matter. My kind has tried to interfere with the work of demons. But the magic

231

is different." She took deep breaths and leaned back, wiping the moisture from her face. When she regained some composure, she looked back at me. "I am so sorry, but I cannot help you, Justin."

Chapter 30

Cold nausea nearly overwhelmed me. I gagged and turned away, panting with the effort of not barfing all over the place.

She laid a comforting hand on my shoulder. "There is so much I can't remember. I know how to rid a human or vampire of the vampling curse, but demons and demon spawn are beyond my abilities."

"Can't you poke around?" I asked. "Maybe you'll get lucky."

She offered a rueful smile. "More likely, I would kill you, or destroy your mind."

A humorless laugh burst from my mouth. "Wow, all sorts of great choices."

"Perhaps the curse will not affect you in the same way as a human." She shrugged. "Perhaps, like my kind, you have some sort of natural defense against such curses."

"It's definitely doing something to me." I told her about my hallucinations and the episode with Adam. "If the curse doesn't kill me, it might drive me crazy."

Nightliss pressed a hand to my cheek. "I promise I will find a way to save you, Justin. As I said, I don't remember everything from my past. Perhaps there is an answer. If only I could convince Daelissa to listen to me, she might also know a cure."

A tiny sliver of hope lodged in my chest. "Thanks," I said, voice dry. "Looks like I'd better get a move on if I want to help Felicia."

"I am sorry I was not there for you, Justin."

"You can't be everywhere at once."

She gave a sad shake of her head. "I was so foolish to try to talk to Daelissa. Otherwise, I would have been there to help you with Maximus. You might not have been bitten."

"It sounds like you've been really busy. All-over-the-world busy."

"Yes. There are many pieces to this puzzle, I have found. Few are as important as you, but I must make sure they succeed. Every thread creates a greater whole. If too many fall, then even you will fail." She leaned back against the pillows, her face pale, forehead beading with sweat. "I hope I can recover quickly. There's so much more to do."

"At least you're getting a better handle on contractions," I said, giving her a wink. "Your English is better every time I see you."

She laughed. "And I can even count better in English now." A sigh escaped her lips. "If only Arabic were not so hard to learn."

"Arabic?"

"Yes, among other languages. What is happening is very big, Justin. It makes me feel so tiny."

"You are tiny," I said, kissing her hand. "But you've got a lot of spirit." I stood. "Maybe I should let you rest."

"I am very tired," she said with a wide yawn.

I was about to leave when I remembered Cinder's question. "Oh, one more question."

She yawned. "Yes?"

"You know the gray men?"

"The golems?"

I nodded. "Uh, is it possible to turn them into real people?"

"Into humans?"

I felt stupid for asking the question. "Yeah. I kind of made another friend. A golem. But he's different than any golem I've met before."

Her eyes widened. "I do not know, Justin." She tapped her chin. "I am unfamiliar with how to make such beings. But Mr. Gray surely would."

"Somehow, I doubt he'd be willing to tell me."

"I agree." She grunted. "There is so much I don't know, and no one to tell me what to do. Sometimes, I feel so lost." Her green eyes turned sad. "I just hope I'm making a difference."

Hearing someone of her power tell me she felt lost did *not* inspire me. Maybe that was why people in her position usually confused their companions with vague half-riddles, giving the impression of knowing everything, when, in reality, they didn't know what the hell was going on either. Nightliss had some answers, but nowhere near all of them. I suspected not even Daelissa had all the answers. It both reassured and frightened the padooky out of me.

I took a deep breath to calm my nerves. Even if I couldn't save myself, I could ensure Felicia survived. "You are making a difference, Nightliss." I leaned down and kissed her forehead. "Whatever happens, I have faith in you. Without you, Vadaemos would have killed me. We all owe you our lives."

Tears glistened in her eyes. "It means so much to know you believe in me, Justin."

Taking one last look at the little angel who could, I turned and left the cabin. Elyssa was on me the second I stepped outside.

"What did she say?"

"She can help Felicia."

Her expression froze, as if waiting for me to continue. When I didn't, her lips parted ever so slightly. "And you?"

I squeezed her hands and tried to speak, but my throat went dry at the pained look on her face.

"No," she said, her voice dead. "No, please." Tears gathered in her eyes.

"She can't help me," I said, wishing more than anything else it wasn't true.

"Why?" She shook her head and jerked away. "It doesn't make any sense!" Elyssa headed for the door. "She'd better have a damned good reason—"

I looped an arm around her waist and pulled her back. "Elyssa, don't. She needs to recover."

"She needs to cure you, damn it!"

"She can't, okay?" I took her by the shoulders and looked into her eyes. "She can't, love. She can't." My hand moved of its own accord to tuck a loose strand of raven hair behind her ear. "Nightliss doesn't even know how the curse will affect me. And who knows? Maybe I'll fight it off since I'm not entirely human." A vile, cold feeling wormed its way up my leg as though the curse wanted a say in this conversation. "For now, I intend to help Felicia." I told her about our need for her sire.

"You're sick, possibly dying from the vampling virus, and you want to go for round two with Maximus?" She pushed me away. "What's wrong with you?"

"Aside from my general insanity? Nothing." My hands clenched at my sides. "Even if the curse kills me, I plan to help Felicia and kick Maximus's smug ass."

"That's your brilliant plan?"

I nodded. "Yep. Will you help me?"

Tears clouded her eyes, streaming silently down her cheeks. The anger in her face softened. She nodded. "You don't even have to ask." Her left hand took mine. Pressed it to her cheek. "I will be with you until the end, my love."

Her words brought back the image of that fateful dream, vision, or whatever it had been when I'd nearly died while Meghan used my blood to save Stacey from a festering hellhound bite. The angelic dream version of Elyssa had said that very thing. It burdened me with the foreknowledge of my own doom. And yet, it lightened my heart with comfort to know she would be there.

"What does your father plan to do about Maximus?" I asked, pulling my thoughts back on track.

"He's mobilizing. Michael," she said, her lip curling into a snarl at his name, "said Father had half of the Atlanta legion in Colombia to help with this assault. They're still performing perimeter duty to be sure the threat of a vampling outbreak is contained, but he's prepping to send them back to Atlanta today."

"Good. I hope he has plans for an urban assault. The area around Maximus's Atlanta lair won't be as easy to seal off. And if a news helicopter catches wind of a battle erupting, even the Custodians are gonna have a heck of a time containing it."

"It's tricky, but it's nothing new to my father."

"Was that a hint of pride I heard in your voice?" I asked, winking.

Elyssa rolled her eyes. "Maybe. He might be a crusty old bullheaded ass, but he's also pretty good at his job."

"Is Michael helping?"

She almost shuddered at the name. "I don't know."

Narrowing my eyes, I said, "Okay, spill the beans. What in the world is going on with you two? He used to be your fave, and suddenly you act like he's the world's worst brother."

Elyssa's mouth tightened. Her eyes looked away. "He's working for Underborn."

Surprise sprung my jaw open. "Say what?"

She told me all about a visit from Underborn and a hulking figure in black. How she'd fought him and figured out who he was. She also told me about the Key of Juranthemon and how she'd nearly stolen it from Underborn. I imagined a hefty steel key with a head shaped like a skull, twin rubies for eyes. It had to look pretty badass with a name like that.

Her story also kicked loose a suspicion I'd had about Michael but never been able to pin down. Now, I felt pretty certain what that tingling sensation had been. "I think your brother's been working for Underborn for quite a while."

She raised an eyebrow. "How would you know?"

"If I'm right, he saved me from moggy mutilation and a swarm of gray men."

"What are you talking about?"

It seemed so long ago, but, in reality, it hadn't been more than a couple of months. "When I didn't know what I was, I went looking for Stacey. One of her moggies jumped me and almost bit off my face. Someone whooshed past and sliced off its head." My chest pounded faster at the horrifying memory. "And when you and I were looking for Underborn in the Grotto and the gray men attacked, a big dude in black jumped down and sliced them to bits."

"I was unconscious, but I remember you telling me about it later." Elyssa gave a slow shake of her head. "I don't understand. Why would he work for that snake? Why would he betray me like that?"

"I think he did it for you."

Her forehead wrinkled. "You've gotta be kidding."

I shrugged. "Think about it. He's known for a while you and I were tied together. I'm sure Underborn let him read Foreseeance Forty-Three Eleven. Knowing the way that slime ball operates, he knew your brother wouldn't say no to an opportunity to protect you, especially with inside knowledge."

"But he could've done that without joining Underborn." She huffed out a breath. "He could've told me."

"First of all, I'm sure Underborn didn't tell him everything. He probably told Michael just enough and guaranteed him more if he gave his word." I chuckled. "I can guarantee you Michael didn't join Underborn to help me."

The hint of a smile brightened her face. "Thank you," she said, her voice wavering.

"For what?"

She gripped my hand and kissed me. "For making me feel better."

"Justin, I hope this is not an inopportune time to ask you a question," said a calm voice from a short distance away.

Elyssa and I jumped.

Cinder still sat on a bench twenty feet away, his form so still I hadn't noticed him.

"If this is one of those girlfriend things you mentioned, I can wait." His shoulders went up in a stiff shrug.

"Um, actually I do have an answer for you," I said, hoping the answer didn't break his little golem heart. "Nightliss doesn't know if you can become real or not."

He stood and nodded. After a brief pause, his lips turned down into a very glum frown, almost as frightening as his horrific smiles.

"Oh, god, make him stop," Elyssa said, looking away.

"Until I get you some soap operas to watch, maybe it's best if you lay off the body language," I said, feeling sorry for him.

His features snapped back to default. "Perhaps that is best, Justin. I don't wish to frighten anyone."

"We need to get a move-on," Elyssa said. "I'll find out what plans my father has. Maybe we can coordinate with him."

"I'll get the gang together."

"Uh, who would that be?"

"Bella, Meghan, Adam." I pursed my lips in thought. "I guess Fausta—"

"No," Elyssa said, voice firm. "First of all, she's bound to her unit here. Second of all, I can't stand that bossy bi—"

"And Fausta's off the list," I said, grinning. "How about Katie?"

"Now I know you're just testing me." She stuck out her tongue.

I laughed. "You've gotta admit, she's proven herself capable."

Elyssa nodded. "She might have actually graduated from being an irritating little bi—"

"Geez, babe, you're determined to use that word, aren't you?"

"If the shoe fits, wear it."

I shrugged. "Even though she helped rescue me, she's just human." It felt very strange to say those words, I realized.

"Yeah." My girlfriend tugged me toward the buildings in the center of the compound. "She wouldn't last long."

"Not without an automatic rifle at least." I motioned Cinder to follow us and we made our way toward the building with the briefing room in it.

By the time we saw the building, it was obvious something big was up. Templars and other personnel swarmed the area. Elyssa stopped a guy as he emerged from the building.

"What's going on?"

"Artemis Coronus is in there. He just ordered us to stand down."

Elyssa frowned. "He can't give an order like that. Not without—"

The man shook his head. "The Grand Master sent the order." With that, he stalked away, face grim.

We waded through the crowd of Templars until we could see inside the briefing room.

"Clearly, a military solution did not work," said a tall man in a long, red robe at the front of the room, his voice pompous. "Many lives were lost and the leader of this vampire rebellion escaped."

I studied the man, noting how his attire looked like he'd just stepped from the set of a movie about the Roman Empire.

"The Divinity has spoken. The Grand Master and the Synod have voted. The Templars are to stand down from this conflict. Our duty now turns to shepherding negotiations."

Christian Salazar stood from his seat at the side of the podium. "Honorable Knight, you do us great honor with your presence. However, Maximus has never responded to our attempts at diplomacy. His army represented a growing cancer in this city. We had to act before it metastasized."

Artemis nodded gravely. "Perhaps we should have stepped in sooner, Commander Salazar. The Synod feels confident Maximus will respond to us. Even the Divinity granted us clarity on this matter."

"If I may speak," Thomas Borathen said, standing.

The Templar Knight narrowed his eyes. "Despite your circumvention of the Synod's orders, and assaulting the vampires, I will allow your voice to be heard."

"First, the Synod's orders were never circumvented," Thomas said. "The vote had not yet been cast. Second, we have evidence the Divinity, an entity who goes by the name Daelissa, is directly involved with Maximus."

"Cease your blasphemies!" Artemis boomed. "The Divinity has guided our holy mission for thousands of years. I will not hear you speak of it this way."

"My daughter heard the truth of the matter straight from the Divinity's own lips," Thomas said, face defiant.

"The Divinity reveals herself only to the Synod," Artemis said, eyes glowing with anger. "To claim otherwise is blasphemy and untruth."

Anger boiled in my stomach. I felt my fists tighten. Heard my knuckles crack. This idiot didn't know what he was talking about.

"Should you continue to spout such lies, Commander Borathen, we may have no choice but to relieve you of leadership." The knight put a gloved hand under his chin. "The Synod is aware your daughter had—how to put it politely—psychological issues, which you deemed damaging enough to order her to take the White."

"It was an error on my part," Thomas growled.

"You have not made many command errors during your service," Artemis said, his voice taking on an insulting air of pity. "But where progeny are involved, it is easy to let one's judgment be clouded. Still, not every child of a Templar is sturdy enough to *become* a Templar."

"My daughter—"

"Your daughter proved reckless and immature." The knight sliced the air with his hand. "She let evil guide her and it sounds as though you have done nothing more to help her. Her morally corrupt—"

"You, sir, are a blithering idiot!" My face burned with rage.

All heads turned to me.

The knight turned to me, his eyes bright with outrage. "How dare you speak to me in such a manner, Templar."

"Elyssa Borathen is not evil or morally corrupt, *sir*. But I can tell you who is. The Divinity, aka Daelissa, aka the brains behind Maximus's operation and god only knows what else." Artemis tried to speak, but I cut him off. "Daelissa is using her influence to pit the Synod against the Templars now. She wants all the factions to be weak so when her people invade, the Overworld won't be able to resist."

"Blasphemy!" Artemis said, his face glowing red. "Who is this Templar?"

A thin man with stooped shoulders stepped from a dark corner in the front of the room and spoke into the Templar Knight's ear. Artemis's back went stiff at whatever he heard.

His finger stabbed toward me. "He is not a Templar. This *boy* is the demon spawn known as Justin Slade. He is the instigator of this sordid mess."

"Daelissa started it," I said. "Not me. But I sure as hell intend to finish it."

"You will finish nothing, boy." The knight pointed at me. "Arrest him."

Chapter 31

A sea of Templars turned my way.

I became acutely aware of my vulnerability in the midst of the tightly packed room. Even with my strength, I couldn't hope to fight my way free of this many trained soldiers, each one with supernatural abilities of their own.

"Arrest me? On what charge?" I said, my voice cracking like the time I'd had to read a love letter aloud in tenth grade English.

"Almost too numerous to list," Artemis said, his voice calm and cold. "The Divinity detailed your most heinous crimes to us. Hers is the absolute authority."

"Then name them." *Asshat.*

"He hasn't done anything wrong," Elyssa said, gripping my arm.

"So says the one most corrupted by him," the knight said. "You, child, are troubled. This boy has led you down a path of darkness and moral iniquity."

"I will hear no more slander against my daughter," Thomas said. "Not even from a Templar Knight."

"Then it pains me to do this, Thomas Borathen, but your judgment is obviously too clouded where your daughter is concerned." The knight scowled. "I am of the opinion you are no longer fit for command. By the power vested in me, I hereby relieve you of duty and assume command of your legion, effective immediately."

Shocked murmurs echoed throughout the room.

"I completely disagree with this decision," Salazar said, standing. "And I must also point out only the Grand Master and a complete vote by the Synod can relieve Commander Borathen."

The knight nodded. "True, true. But I do have the authority to place him on temporary leave and assume command until a vote is passed."

"If the Divinity has her hooks in you, it's pretty obvious how that vote will go," I said.

Artemis's face hardened. "Why is this boy still in here? Did I not order him arrested?"

Again, nearby Templars gave me uneasy looks, but nobody made a move to restrain me.

"Belay that order," Christian said. His eyes met mine. "Justin, it might be best if you leave."

"You cannot disregard my orders," Artemis said. "To do so invites your own suspension, Commander Salazar."

"You can try to suspend me all you like," Christian said. "But I doubt you'll find many takers here."

A loud cry went up from the assembled Templars. "Hooah!"

Or they might have said "Hoo-hah." I wasn't really sure, but the sudden uproar startled the crap out of me.

Christian raised an eyebrow and smiled. "Answer enough, Honorable Knight?" He stepped forward. "I call for an Imperator Concilium. The leadership of the Synod is in question."

Artemis's face went purple. "To do so would be an illegal order since you are no longer in command, Salazar!"

"You never gave the order relieving me of command, Honorable Knight. Therefore, I have the privilege to call forth a council of commanders." Christian smiled, baring his teeth. "Procedure and Templar law dictate that, should the Synod's loyalty to the cause come into question, the commanders must meet and vote on whether to dissolve the Synod and elect new members."

"This is an outrage," Artemis said. "You can be certain, reports of this treachery will be spread to the other commanders so they can see how poisoned this legion has become."

Grumbles and angry stares from the crowd turned on the knight.

"Poisoned, my ass," said a voice from nearby.

"I'm gonna stick my honorable foot up his honorable ass," muttered someone else.

Christian shrugged. "Since I took the liberty of recording this session, I'll be happy to pass it on to the other legion commanders. In the meantime, Honorable Knight, it might perhaps be best if you took your leave and reported back to the council."

Artemis seemed ready to launch another salvo when the thin man reappeared from the shadows and whispered into the knight's ear. Artemis scowled and straightened. "You can be certain the Divinity will not be pleased. Beware her wrath, Salazar." He stormed up the stairs in the auditorium, long red robe sweeping behind him, trailed only by the thin man. As he passed near me he stopped and glared. "*You* are the cancer, spawn. May the Divinity wipe your kind from the face of our fair Eden." With that sweet little pronouncement, he turned and left.

The thin man paused a moment. Looked at me, a greasy smile spreading across his face. His skin looked especially pale and doughy in the light. "Good day, Your Excellence," he said, flourishing a mocking bow, and leaving.

I stood, stunned for a moment by the odd behavior when it occurred to me where I'd heard that cockney accent and mocking salutation before. *Mr. Bigglesworth.*

"Stop that man!" I shouted, pushing through the crowd.

Unfortunately, while the crowd parted for the Knight Templar, it didn't for me, closing in behind the departing guest and making it a struggle to get through, despite my shouts to make way. After working our way outside, Elyssa and I watched as a slider disguised as a jet lifted into the air and flew away.

"Son of a biyatch!" I shouted, smacking my fist into my palm. "It was Bigglesworth."

"I knew the voice sounded familiar," Elyssa said. "Not to mention the attitude."

"When I catch that—that *thing*, I'm going to puree him in a blender, dump in a bunch of flour and bake his gooey ass into cupcakes."

Elyssa gagged. "That's disgusting."

A sudden flood of Templars formed an exodus from the auditorium, rushing in all directions with a sense of purpose. Elyssa and I waited for the crowd to disperse and went inside where we found Thomas and Christian huddled over an image on the conference table.

Elyssa went to her father and pecked him on the cheek.

Thomas Borathen, a man I'd never seen crack under pressure, looked almost alarmed at this sudden gesture from his daughter.

"Thanks for standing up for me," Elyssa said.

Thomas opened his mouth to speak, but Elyssa cut him off with a wave of her hand.

"But don't for a minute think I've forgotten about the White or all the hell you've put me and Justin through, Father. You have a long way to go before you make up for everything."

Her father's face regained composure. "I—" he stopped whatever he was about to say and shook his head. "You're my daughter. My own flesh and blood. Templar Knight Artemis made me realize something very valuable today. He made me realize what it's like when someone in a position of authority over you refuses to listen to reason and sees only what he expects to see." Thomas sighed. "I must have looked exactly that way to you, Elyssa."

She returned a stern nod. "Did he also show you how a pompous ass looks?"

Her father's lips curled into the faintest smile. "Indeed."

"The way I see it," said a female voice from behind, "you owe someone an apology."

I turned and spotted Leia Borathen, Elyssa's mother walking down the ramp toward us.

"Yes, you were right, Leia," Thomas said. "Right all along." He walked away from the table, face set in grim lines. "I have commanded loyalty from my soldiers, and gone without defeat for so long, I thought I was always in the right. My focus shifted. And when we finally had another family, I saw them only as Templars."

"*Another* family?" Elyssa said. "What does that mean?"

Leia shook her head. "We can discuss it another time."

Thomas turned back to us. "I let my own foolish pride and sense of self-worth stand in the way for too long. And because of it, we lost Jack." He took a deep breath. "I am so proud of you, Elyssa. Forgive me for not listening to you. Forgive me for not being the father I should have been."

Tears glistened in Elyssa's eyes. She nodded, and wiped her cheeks. "I forgive you, Dad."

John Corwin

Thomas Borathen, mighty warrior, commander of a legion of Templars, and the scariest, most overprotective dad a boyfriend could ever meet, hugged his daughter.

It was enough to make my eyes mist up.

When he pulled away, he cleared his throat and looked a little uncomfortable. I figured, within the last five minutes, he'd used up his emotional quota for the next century.

"There's still one apology left," Leia said.

Thomas looked at me, his eyes displaying what had to be pent up horror. "Surely, you don't—"

"Surely, I do," Leia said.

Elyssa's eyes went wide. "What's going on? Since when do you even like Justin, Mother?"

Leia smiled. "You have shown time and time again there is no force on this Earth that will keep you two apart." She shrugged. "Not even a mind wipe."

Thomas turned his glare on me. "I hoped you would drop off the radar as most of the boys who have met me have done. But after everything that has happened, I must admit, painfully and under duress," he shot a look at his wife and sighed. "You have proven yourself adequate."

It took everything I had not to respond to that backhanded compliment in kind. Instead, I simply said, "Thank you, sir."

He extended a hand. Not wanting to keep him hanging, I extended my own. Thomas shook it.

"You may be spawn, but you've proven yourself more a man than others." He leaned in closer, his grip tightening until I heard the bones crunching in my hand, and whispered, "And if anything happens to my daughter, there is no place safe on this Earth for you to hide."

I forced a smile as his grip relented. "Understood."

Thomas released my hand and grunted. "Now that this is settled, I believe we are ready to proceed. Correct, Commander Salazar?"

Christian, who, up until now had been pretending to read something very important on his phone looked up, and nodded. "We're nearly ready to ferry troops over to La Casona. The Custodians report that Maximus's compound is sterilized and there is no longer a need for the perimeter your people are holding."

Thomas pulled up the holographic map of the compound. "I'll have them report to La Casona. We can send everyone over in one wave to the Grotto and use my compound, The Ranch, as a staging area."

A rap came on the doorframe at the top of the auditorium stairs. Christian looked up and waved the man to enter.

"What is it, Hernandez?" Christian asked.

"Bad news, sir," the Templar said. "We received word from the Arcanes at La Casona—someone put a hex on the Obsidian Arch. We can't send anyone through it. Not until the hex is defused."

"A hex?" Christian said. "How long to defuse?"

The Templar shrugged. "They said it was so complex they'd have to send for outside help."

I groaned. "Dollars to donuts Daelissa did it."

Christian nodded curtly at the Templar. "Dismissed."

The man turned and left.

"This puts a wrench in things," Thomas said. "Even if I summoned our entire fleet of sliders, we wouldn't have enough to transport everyone to Atlanta in a timely manner."

"We only have one high-speed slider," Christian said. "The rest of ours are meant for local transport. They're too slow to ferry troops all the way to Atlanta."

"We have two high-speed sliders," Thomas said. "But each one only holds eighteen."

"How is it possible you guys don't have a big plane somewhere meant for troop transport?" I asked. "Aren't you the Overworld equivalent of the army?"

Christian shook his head. "We're more like local militias. That's why there are legions dispersed around the world, a legacy from the Roman Empire. The Synod never saw a use for aircraft since Obsidian Arches are usually sufficient."

I groaned. "God only knows what Maximus is doing in the meantime."

"Most of my forces are down here," Thomas said. He scowled. "I nearly ordered them to remain in Atlanta, and then received word of Artemis Coronus's intent to order off our attack against Maximus. I now wonder if Daelissa let me know this so I would divert more troops here."

"Webs within webs," Christian said. "And now Maximus has nearly free reign in Atlanta."

"Do you think that was the plan all along?" I said.

Elyssa shook her head. "Before Daelissa wiped my mind, she acted crazy half the time. For all we know someone else is pulling her strings."

"It won't stop us for long," Thomas said. "If I have to hijack transports from the Colombian government, we'll find a way back."

"There is a way," I said, a shiver running down my spine at the thought. "You'll need to contact the Arcanes near El Dorado for help."

"El Dorado?" Elyssa said. "What could possibly help them there?"

"Thunder Rock has a huge room full of arches. El Dorado might have one too." I shrugged. "It's not the best plan, I know, but—"

"It's suicidal," Elyssa said, crossing her arms. "Remember the hordes of husks and shadow people down there? And didn't you tell me there are more of those things in Thunder Rock?"

"Well, what about the arch in Maximus's compound?"

"Our people inspected it," Christian said. "The magical energy required to send through so many troops would be staggering."

"We could capture another leyworm," I said.

Elyssa's eyebrows shot up. "That's as crazy an idea as using El Dorado."

Thomas, looked at me with a strange light in his eyes. "Sending an army of Templars inside those caves to search for an arch room that may or may not exist could be disastrous, especially with enemies that cannot die by the sword." He shook his head. "No. Commander Salazar and I will weigh the options and come up with a plan."

I sighed, though I couldn't blame him. El Dorado was the last place on Earth I wanted to return to. "At least talk to the Arcanes near El Dorado. There's a whole town of them. Maybe they'll know how to deal with this hex."

"I agree," Christian said. "I have their contact information."

"Then let us proceed." Thomas looked at Elyssa. "I suggest you get some R and R in the meantime."

"Yes, sir," Elyssa said. She took my hand and we exited the building. The streets were clear, save for a harried Templar or two jogging past with some important duty awaiting them. Or maybe they'd just eaten spicy Indian food and were looking for the nearest latrine.

I brainstormed for possibilities as we walked back to the cabin. Inside, Nightliss lay sleeping on the bed, her face still wan and pale. I'd hoped she might, at the very least, have some useful information, or use her angelic powers to zap the Templar army north.

Not gonna happen.

Nightliss had been Plan C. As with most of my plans, I'd probably end up using all the letters in the alphabet by the time it was all said and done.

"Might as well pack," Elyssa said. "When Thomas and Christian make a decision, it'll come down the pipeline fast."

"I really need to wash my clothes," I said, grabbing my duffel bag. It was the same one I'd used when escaping hellhounds as they attacked the home I grew up in. After returning to the States from Colombia the first time, Shelton had given it back to me. Inside it were all my remaining worldly possessions and a few thousand dollars in cash I'd raided from my parents' rainy day fund.

I turned the bag upside-down over the table, emptying all my clothes into a heap. I picked up a pair of shorts and sniffed them. Tossed them back into the bag. Sniffed a pair of boxers. Wrinkled my nose and tossed them on the floor.

Elyssa laughed. "That's disgusting."

I gave her a sheepish grin. "I meant to wash all this stuff, but Shelton didn't have a washer or dryer in his hideout." Within a couple of minutes, I was left with two pairs of tighty-whities, cargo shorts, and a single sock. Everything else smelled or looked dirty.

"You're in luck," Elyssa said, opening a door to the side of the kitchen to reveal a washer and dryer. She eyed the pile of dirty laundry and grimaced. "I think I'll let you handle it from here."

While I shoved in the load, Elyssa emptied out the other compartments on the duffel bag to make sure I wasn't missing anything. The companion sock to the lonely one on the table spilled out of an end pocket. Two large bundles of cash, my wallet, and an old folded piece of parchment tumbled from the others.

"What's this?" Elyssa asked, unfolding the thick yellowed parchment on the table.

I shrugged. "Meghan found it on Vadaemos when we brought him back to Atlanta. I figured it might be something important, but forgot about it."

"It's a map," she said. "A really old map."

When fully unfolded, it formed a rectangle two feet by three feet. Black ink outlined streets and buildings in what appeared to be a small town, or maybe a portion of a town. For all I knew, it was a map of Disney World. A black dotted line ran from the edge of the map and intersected a house, terminating in an "X".

"Is that where the treasure is buried?" I said, touching the mark and tracing my finger along it. "I'd definitely like to know how to get there."

The lines on the map shifted. I jerked my finger back and stared. "Did I imagine that?"

Elyssa shook her head. "I saw it, too."

The black lines soaked into the parchment, vanishing altogether. As if by an invisible artist, the map redrew itself, showing crooked little streets, and birds-eye outlines of buildings, detailed down to shingles and ridges. Trees, shrubs, and other details sketched themselves into place. The black outline of a stick figure appeared within the outline of a house. The invisible pen drew a dotted line, running down a nearby street and vanishing off the edge of the map.

"Whoa, this is trippy," I said.

"Wait a minute," Elyssa said. "I recognize those streets." She grabbed the map and ran outside the house. Stopped beneath a tree, and gaped at the map. "This *is* trippy. Look!"

I stared with disbelief. The stick figure had moved outside the house and now stood beneath the outline of a tree. "What kind of map is this?" I said.

"Show me a wider view," Elyssa said.

The map redrew itself, showing more of the surrounding area.

"Show me all of Bogota," she said.

Nothing happened.

"Show me this entire city."

Again, the map redrew itself. Though almost too fine and cluttered to make out, Bogota was clearly the city.

"Show me where I am," I said, and watched as the map circled our location. I looked at the amazed expression on Elyssa's face, certain my own looked about the same. A light bulb flickered on in my head. "Show me where Maximus is."

Nothing happened.

"I've seen a lot of crazy things," Elyssa said, "but I've never seen a magic map like this one."

"You told me about the Key of Juranthemon," I said. "And that it required a map to create new connections from one place to another. What if this is it? Maybe Vadaemos was hoping to find the key so he could stay one step ahead of everyone."

Elyssa said an unladylike word. "And I was so close to stealing it from Underborn."

"Where's the key you stole from him?" I asked.

She dug in her pocket and pulled out an old-school skeleton key. It was made of thick steel with a head shaped like a skull. Two rubies glittered in the eye sockets.

"It looks exactly like I imagined it," I said, taking it in my hand.

"It definitely didn't look like that when I took it," Elyssa said.

Our eyes met.

"Where's the place Underborn used it?"

We raced to an ancient stone building not far from the cabin. I took out the key. Put it in the old rusted lock. Pulled the door open.

Instead of the inside of the tiny building, the broken ruins of something massive greeted us. Elyssa poked her head through and gasped. She jerked back, as if afraid it might get cut off.

"That's the Coliseum. In Rome, Italy."

Chapter 32

"We've got a way to take the troops back to Atlanta," I said. "Holy crap, can you believe it?"

Elyssa squeezed me in a happy hug. "Underborn lied. This *is* the key." She pulled away as a concerned look spread across her features. "But that would mean—"

"He's manipulating us," I said. "Do you really think he'd let you take something so valuable for nothing?"

She sighed and shook her head. "That weasel. I think I know how he's pulling our strings."

I raised an eyebrow. "Enlighten me, because I, for one, don't have a clue."

"What's the quickest way to make someone do something?"

"Uh, take over their brain? Show them your sexy legs?"

She punched me on the shoulder. "Oh, hush. No, the best way is to tell them they can't do it."

"You mean like your parents telling you not to date me?"

Elyssa snorted. "You could say that."

I made a sad face.

"Hey now, remember we started dating way before my parents told me not to." She pecked me on the lips. "Their disapproval has nothing to do with me wanting you. So get that look off your face before I have to do something evil."

"What you're saying is Underborn used reverse psychology on you, telling you that you couldn't have the key, he'd never give it up, and then allowed you to steal it so you'd use the key?" I wrinkled my brow and quirked an eyebrow to leave no doubt how confused I was. "Why not just give the stupid thing to you and then tell you what he wanted you to do?"

"Because then I would question everything about the situation."

"Maybe he was just pissed you actually stole the real key and didn't want to admit you got the better of him." I shrugged. "Men don't like it when a girl beats them at something."

"Oh, I know that all too well." Elyssa sighed. "Maybe I'm just over thinking things. Besides, how I got the key doesn't matter right now. What does matter is figuring out how to use it."

"That should be easy enough," I said, and closed the door. Twisting the knob again, I opened it to...the inside of a toolshed. I closed the door again and reopened it. Same thing.

"Isn't that just the inside of this shed?" Elyssa asked.

I glanced at the garden shears on the wall and sighed. "I imagined the door leading to Atlanta."

"Maybe the key doesn't recognize proper names." She looked at the map. "This thing didn't do anything when I asked for a map of Bogota."

"Show me Atlanta," I said to the map.

Nothing.

"Show me my hometown."

A moment later, the map displayed Decatur, Georgia.

"Show me the city I'm imagining," I said, squeezing my eyes tight and thinking of the Atlanta skyline on a clear spring day.

This time, it drew downtown Atlanta.

"So it figures it out by what you're thinking?" Elyssa said.

"Yeah, brainwaves or something weird like that."

"Oh, I have an idea," Elyssa said. "Map, this city is Atlanta."

We fooled around with the map for several more minutes and figured out that it could show us just about any place we could imagine in detail. I had to pull up images on my arcphone and focus on them if I wanted the map to display that location. Once we told the map a city or location name, it remembered it.

"Show me the door locations in Atlanta," I said.

The map drew a single circle on the east side. When I told it to zoom in, it redrew the area in greater detail, including rows of small rectangles.

"I know that place," Elyssa said.

"What is it? A parking lot?"

She shook her head. "No. A graveyard. It's where we just buried my brother."

I felt surprise light my face. "What kind of bizarre coincidence is that?"

"I don't know if I believe in coincidence anymore after all we've been through." Elyssa touched the map, as if to confirm it was real. "When I was in the Goths, we used to go to that graveyard and scare each other with ghost stories. We were so stupid. I never once thought I'd be burying my brother there. Never thought I'd lose Jack."

I squeezed her shoulder in what I hoped was a reassuring manner. "I'm sorry."

She shook her head as if she could shake off the memory. "Whatever. What's done is done."

"Try the key again?"

Elyssa nodded. Took it and opened the door. Hard-packed earth waited on the other side.

"You've got to be kidding me," I said, kicked at the dirt.

Some of it crumbled, spilling onto the ground, revealing a thick maze of roots and a worm or three.

I looked at the map again. "Show me a street view of the door." When that command failed, I tried again. "Show me the view of the door from ground level."

The parchment cleared and redrew the graveyard from a first-person perspective. By the time it was done, I realized what the problem was. The door was fifty feet or more underground. I had the map redraw the scene from different angles.

"There's an old crypt or something beneath the cemetery," Elyssa said. She traced a finger up a ramp. "Looks like it was buried."

I groaned. "Didn't you say the map could be used to make new connections for the key?"

"According to Underborn, yes."

We fiddled with the map, trying to get it to connect a door in an abandoned warehouse near Elyssa's house, aka the Templar compound known as Big Creek Ranch, or The Ranch for short. The map ignored our pleas. We tried different doors, all to no avail, and finally gave up. I searched the interwebz on my phone for more information about the map, but came up with zilch. Either Underborn had lied about the name, or it was so old, it had already passed from legend, to myth, to oblivion.

"The only person who might tell us how to work this thing is the last person I want to know about the map," I said. "And I don't plan on giving Underborn the key. That leaves one option."

"We dig?" Elyssa said.

I nodded. "We dig."

"Justin, may I help?" Cinder said from behind us.

I almost jumped out of my skin. "Geez, dude, do you have to sneak up on me all the time?"

"My apologies," the golem said. "I had no intention of a stealthy approach, Justin."

"Can you use a shovel?" Elyssa asked.

Cinder's eyes went distant. "If you show me how, I am certain it is within my grasp."

Elyssa closed the shed door and reopened it without the key. She went in, grabbed a couple of shovels, an axe, and a few other items, then stepped back out. Shoved the key in the lock and reopened it to the wall of dirt.

"It's easy," she said, demonstrating. "Just shove the tip in hard, wiggle it around, and then pull out a load."

"That's what she said." I said with a wide grin.

She threw a clod of dirt at me.

Cinder took to the task without another word.

"I'll go tell Thomas," Elyssa said. "Why don't you round up the gang?"

Within twenty minutes I returned to the shed with Bella and Katie in tow. Adam and Meghan promised they'd be over soon. A crowd of Templars stood near the shed watching Cinder work. The door was a little wider than a normal one but didn't offer much room for more than one person. As Cinder worked his way forward, Templars formed a chain, using wheelbarrows and buckets to move dirt.

"This is amazing," Bella said, looking at the map. "This isn't the first magic key or map I've heard of, but one that can transport you from one side of the planet to the other is simply unheard of."

"You couldn't figure out how to make it open to another door?" Katie asked.

"No. Maybe it requires some magic words or sacrificing small animals, for all I know."

"Does Nightliss know?" Bella asked, her eyes wandering toward the cabin.

"She's still unconscious," I said.

Meghan and Adam appeared around the corner of the cabin. The blonde Arcane waved me over, so I excused myself and jogged to them.

"Nightliss is awake," Meghan said. "She's asking for you."

I sped back inside. The petite angel still looked sickly, her cheeks gaunt, eyes hollow.

"Feeling better?" I asked as I sat on the side of the bed, thinking she looked worse than ever.

She smiled. "A little."

"Have you ever heard of the Key or Map of Juranthemon?" I asked, before giving her a chance to get out another word. I pulled them out and showed her how the map worked.

She gazed with wonder at the map. "This is amazing."

"That's what Bella said."

"I have never seen these before." She inspected the key. "And you say it can create portals between doors?"

I nodded. "Yeah." I told her about the first time I'd seen it used by Phissilinth, one of Underborn's henchmen. "Well, that stinks. I was hoping you could tell me how to connect another door."

She handed me the key, an uncertain look on her face. "Justin, my people have made many wondrous things. The arches are one of our greatest achievements. If this map and key can do what you say they can, this is magic on another scale altogether."

My mouth dropped open at this new information. "You're saying this is even more powerful than what angels can do?"

"Unless I've forgotten something, the map and key are not something my people created." She shrugged. "The Obsidian Arches require a great deal of magical power to operate. From the way you describe it, this key requires none of that."

"I'll bet the Arcanes who charge a bundle to travel via arch would be ticked if something like this were available for general use," I said.

"Indeed." A wracking cough hit her, shaking her frail form until she lay back against the pillows, exhausted. "It appears my recovery will take longer than I thought." A weak smile glimmered on her face.

"Why did you want to see me?" I asked.

"Remember when you told me how others have seen me around the world, but sometimes they saw a blonde angel?"

I nodded. "Was it Daelissa causing trouble?"

"No." She took my hand in her weak grip. "I was in those places too, Justin. I caught a glimpse of this other angel, and it was definitely not Daelissa."

"Wait, are you saying there's another crazy blonde angel running around? Are you even sure this other woman is one of your people?" I thought back to the clump of blonde hair Cinder had found, and wondered if it belonged to Daelissa after all.

"I can usually sense when one of my people is nearby," Nightliss said. "Twice I went to help someone only to sense another presence. When I arrived, I discovered this other angel had already helped them." She sighed. "I only know about this sense from being close to Daelissa a few times. This other person felt…different. Not as pure or strong, perhaps." She paused, mouth partway open as if searching for a better way to say it. "Perhaps the sensation is different with other angels. I do not know for sure."

I realized how close I was leaning in to hear her every word, and straightened. "So she's probably good we hope?"

"I think so."

"Man, I just wish you were feeling better!" I squeezed her hands. "We need your help so much right now." A tingle grew in the back of my mind. My essence extended, and the view filled with floating motes of magical energy. I suddenly knew with great certainty I could heal her. Somehow, it had to be possible.

Nightliss's eyes grew wide. "Are you channeling magic?" she said.

"I can help you," I said.

"Justin, attempting to heal me could be very dangerous if you don't know what you're doing."

"I can do it. I *know* it."

"No." She pushed weakly at my hands. "Stop it. You will hurt yourself."

My leg went ice cold. The vampling wound throbbed. My pulse hammered against my temples and the sense of magic slipped from my grasp. I felt my back thud against the floor. Rolling in pain, clutching at my wound, I squeezed my eyes tight and wished for the agony to go away.

Maximus and Dash flash into my view. Dad, shackled in a crypt, weak, and starving while a filthy girl whimpers nearby. I slam against the barred door, unable to open it. I'm weak. Tired. The scraping, moaning sounds of vamplings as they shamble toward me pull my attention away from Dad. I see a still figure lying on the floor, blood puddling beneath her. It's Elyssa! A scream of grief roars from my throat, deepening to a guttural throb, a demonic howl of anguish. I will kill them all!

"Justin!"

I jerked. Sucked in a deep breath. Nightliss's face appeared above me over the side of the bed.

"You must fight it," she said.

Something wet hit my cheek. It was a tear from Nightliss's eye. "I will find a way to cure you. I promise I will. You're too important."

I sat up and looked at her, hopelessness and fear tearing me up inside. "I'm not going to make it much longer," I said. Pulling up my pants leg revealed the truth. Blackened veins pulsed around the wound. The curse was spreading.

Time was running out.

Chapter 33

I tucked Nightliss back into bed. Kissed her on the cheek. "Thanks for all you've done."

She nodded, her eyelids drooping as she tried to speak. Sleep claimed her before she could say another word.

A shout of victory went up from outside. I raced around the cabin and toward the shed as Cinder, covered from head to toe in dirt, emerged from the doorway. A couple of Templars patted him on the back. Cinder smiled awkwardly, and I had to admit his attempt didn't look nearly as frightening as the first time, though one Templar jumped back when he saw it.

"They're through," Elyssa said, taking me to the door and pointing up a long sloping tunnel. Some forty feet in, a patch of daylight slanted in. "Looks like the earth simply swallowed it up centuries ago, so there's no direct access to the surface. Your golem kept digging up at a slant until he found the top."

"Did anyone make sure it's the right place?" I asked.

"Yeah, they sent up a scout. He confirmed it's in the graveyard."

"Awesome! When do we move out?"

"My father is coordinating with Christian on the best way to move in the troops. Either way, it'll take a while to move so many people through in single file."

"We'd better go through first," I said.

Elyssa crossed her arms. "You're not planning on anything rash are you? Maximus might be wounded, but he's far from done."

"No, but I don't want to be stuck waiting behind hundreds of Templars either."

"Hmm. Good point." She winked and walked back toward the cabin, leaving me alone.

Beck Andrews sauntered over from the group of Templars, an amused look on his chiseled face. He looked like a male model, and seemed to dress accordingly, with fashionably tortured jeans and an untucked, button-up shirt. "Dude, where do you find these people?" He jabbed a thumb at Cinder. "You're like a traveling circus."

I felt anger stir inside me at the sight of him, remembering how he'd prematurely led Thomas Borathen to us, after we'd captured Vadaemos Slade, just to get brownie points. Apparently, I hadn't completely forgiven him yet. "That's funny, Beck. You're like a travelling douche yourself."

He laughed. "Aw, c'mon. Don't tell me you still have hard feelings—"

I got in his face so fast, I didn't even remember crossing the distance. My leg throbbed with pulsing cold. "If I had hard feelings, you'd be a puddle of red mush right now." I felt a cruel smile spread across my lips. "Luckily, I'm a forgiving guy."

For once, Beck actually looked a bit scared, wide-eyed and back on his heels. "Crap, dude, I'm sorry, okay?" He took a step back. "I shouldn't have done it, I see that now."

"Oh, really? I wonder how all the Templars who died that day feel about it." The cold anger inside me swelled like an alien presence, choking my heart with thorny vines. "I wonder how Elyssa's dead brother feels about it."

His face went white, and his mouth hung open. "I—I didn't think—"

"That's right, you didn't *think*."

Beck's eyes flicked to the ground. "Do you know how hard it is to make a name for yourself when your father is a screw-up? How everyone talks about the screw-up's kid behind his back? How nobody gives you a fair shake just because of who your dad is?" He blew out a ragged breath. "My dad didn't get transferred because I kissed Elyssa. I only wish it was that simple. No, you see, Commander Borathen didn't want my dad because he sucked at his job. I just wanted to prove myself to the Commander. To show that I was better than that."

The comment about his father struck me hard, reminded me of the prejudices I'd suffered because of my lineage. I forced down the irrational anger boiling in my chest. Forced myself to ignore the cold ache in my leg. Then I took a deep calming breath. "And you thought hogging the glory would do that."

"Yeah, I did." His shoulders sagged. "But you're right. Because I called the Commander, all those Templars died. Jack died." He looked me in the eye, his face screwed up in pain. "I'm responsible for their deaths."

Now, I was the one who felt bad. Beck was no more to blame for those deaths than I was, but I'd wanted to hurt him. *Mission successful, jackass.* "Look, Beck, you're a special kind of asshole, but even I don't really blame you for those deaths. Daelissa freed Vadaemos. If it hadn't been for the extra Templars Thomas brought along, the rest of us might not have survived the hellhound attacks that followed." I shrugged. "In a way, you might have saved the rest of us."

His gaze seemed to focus on something in his mind before he looked back at me. "Do you really believe that?"

"Yeah. Much as I hate to admit it, I do. Just don't let it go to your head, okay? It's already big enough."

A wistful smile crept over his lips. "I'll try."

Elyssa called my name. I looked at her over my shoulder and turned back to Beck. "Well, I gotta go get ready. Are you going to Atlanta?"

He shook his head. "Nah. I've got to do cleanup here." He held out a hand. "Good luck."

I resisted the urge to say something snarky, and gave his hand a firm shake. "Just try not to be a douche in the future, okay?"

He laughed. "I'll do my best."

I turned, and Elyssa motioned me to the cabin. It was time to get ready.

Bella, Adam, Meghan, and Katie were ready in ten minutes. Elyssa and I grabbed our bags and met them while Thomas and Christian lined up the troops.

Thomas grabbed my arm and took me aside before we went through the door. "The Arcanes at The Ranch added an extra charm to our Nightingale armor that should keep Maximus's cursed bullets from penetrating."

"Really? That's great news," I said.

261

"Except it'll take a week to upgrade all the armor." Thomas glanced back at the milling troops. "I've authorized you and Elyssa for the upgrade."

"What about the rest of my team?"

His jaw tightened for an instant. "Your team?" He seemed to struggle internally for a moment before continuing. "I know my orders have never stopped you before. I expect you'll continue to leap before looking no matter what I say." His expression softened. "Mr. Slade, I would appreciate it as a father if you thought twice before taking my daughter in harm's way."

My mouth went slack at his sudden change in tone. "Sir, I can assure you there is nothing on this earth I value more than Elyssa. You think I'm hard to control? Elyssa makes me look like a puppy on a leash."

A smile broke through his grim façade. "That's one thing we can agree on." He pulled out a phone and tapped in a message. "I've authorized your...*team* for upgrades. Good luck." He turned and went back to Christian, talking to him as if our conversation had never taken place.

I rejoined Elyssa at the door.

"What was that about?" she asked.

"Uh, you know. He wished us good luck and all that jazz." I hurried through the door.

Elyssa tugged on my arm. "How about you tell me what he really said before I jerk your arm out of the socket?"

I looked up the ramp where the rest of our group was already exiting and sighed. "He told me the Arcanes figured out how to block the cursed bullets and are upgrading the Nightingale armor. He wants me to make sure we all grab a set before embarking on anything crazy."

"Figures," she said, her lips curving into a pleased smile. "Overprotective to the core."

"And you're eating it up."

She pinched her brow. "After years of him treating me like nothing more than a tool to be honed and shaped for the Templars? Hell yeah. It's about time he started treating me like a daughter."

I squeezed her hand and walked up the ramp toward daylight. "All my life I thought I had the perfect family." My heart sagged.

"And in the space of a month, the fantasy shattered. My mom left me to be with Ivy and her family. My dad is marrying a succubus. My sister thinks I'm evil." I forced a smile and looked at Elyssa. "Your family was never close. Your dad sounds like he's always been the commander in chief of the family while the rest of you were trained like monkeys. But now you have a chance. Maybe you'll get the great family after all."

Elyssa stopped and pressed a hand to my cheek. "Oh, Justin, I'm sorry. Even if my family hasn't always been the greatest, I grew up with great brothers." She squeezed her eyes shut. "Jack and Michael were always there for me when my parents weren't." She opened her eyes, wiped a tear away. "We have each other now. We have our own future to make."

I kissed her softly on the lips and smiled. "I know, babe. I just wish—I wish we could have it all. Great families. Huge gatherings for the holidays. No insane angels threatening to invade the world."

She laughed. "One step at a time, honey boo-bear." She pecked me on the nose and we resumed our climb into the light.

We emerged in an area devoid of graves. I looked around the area and spotted Jack's grave in the distance. The large Conroy headstone loomed not far behind it. This insane roller coaster ride had started here. My sister had contacted me here. Deep down, a question still burned in my guts.

Had Ivy been the one to lie about Maximus kidnapping her? Had she sent me into Maximus's ambush?

Another figure emerged from the tunnel. Cinder, still filthy, approached. "I hope it is okay for me to come with you, Justin."

I nodded. "Until the bitter end, buddy."

He tilted his head. "Buddy? Does this mean you consider me a friend?"

A wince almost crossed my face before I stiffened my expression. This man—this thing was a golem. It wasn't even alive. And here I was acting like it was just one of the gang. It wasn't a friend. It wasn't an enemy. It was just a construct of metal and fake flesh, nothing more.

Katie stepped forward and took Cinder's hand. "You're my friend. You kept me safe after we busted out of Maximus's place. You dug that tunnel all the way from one end of the planet to the other so we could get here."

Bella took his other hand. "You were created a slave to serve the purpose of an evil master. Somehow, you've thrown off those chains and taken control of your own destiny, Cinder. You may also call me friend."

They were right. I knew it. More importantly, I felt it. This being had no choice in his creation, no choice in who or what he was. What mattered was what he did now, and as far as I was concerned, he was doing the right thing. I patted him on the shoulder, and nodded. "Yes, Cinder. You're my friend."

Elyssa raised an eyebrow, but apparently wasn't quite ready to give the golem a friendship bracelet just yet.

Cinder nodded solemnly, though he probably didn't know any other way *to* nod. "I am grateful for the friendship you have entrusted me with, Katie, Bella, and Justin. If it is within my abilities, I will not let you down."

Templars began emerging from the tunnel in single file. People at a nearby funeral looked our way, confusion plain on their faces as more and more figures poured from the tunnel.

We made our way to the cemetery exit where a convoy of Templar vehicles waited. I surveyed the nearby streets and buildings, body tensed in anticipation of a fireball and a horde of vampires. Even when nothing happened, I didn't relax until the driver pulled onto the road and headed out. The others looked tense as well, crowded as we were into the back of a large SUV.

"Well, I guess Daelissa doesn't know about our new mode of transport," Bella said, offering a smile.

"My father asked us to hand over the key and the map," Elyssa said.

Alarmed looks met her statement.

"Obviously, I told him no."

"And he didn't argue?" I asked, surprised.

"Oh, he argued, alright. But I told him Nightliss made it clear Justin was supposed to use them."

My forehead went tight. "She didn't say that."

Elyssa grinned. "I know that. But he doesn't."

"*Elyssa*," Bella said in a scolding tone. "Lying to your father is not nice."

"Oh, give me a break," Elyssa said, rolling her eyes. "After all he's done to me, he deserved it."

Bella's eyes twinkled. "I have the feeling this is just the beginning of your revenge on that poor man."

I checked my phone. It was three in the afternoon the week before Christmas. I could hardly believe how little it felt like the holidays to me. Everyone else would be doing last-minute shopping and preparing to put on the ugliest sweater in their wardrobe for a special visit to a relative. I wondered if the Conroys or the Slades celebrated Christmas. It was almost laughable to think of demon spawn or my evil grandparents putting up a tree and festive lights in their yards.

I chuckled as another thought occurred to me.

"What is it?" Elyssa asked, nudging me in the ribs.

"Every time this year, me, Harry, and Mark used to get together for a huge sci-fi marathon. We'd drink tons of hot chocolate and eat obscene amounts of candy."

Elyssa's mouth twisted sideways. "Do I even want to know what you watched?"

"Now that I think about it, all that make-believe stuff on T.V. seems pretty normal compared to my reality."

She laughed.

I shook my head. "It was so stupid, in retrospect, but I guess I kinda miss it."

"You miss your nerd friends, and running around with a foam sword?" Elyssa said, a smirk still on her face.

I nodded. "Remember the time you joined us and kicked ass?"

"You were into LARPing?" Adam said from behind.

"What in the world is a LARP?" Meghan asked.

Now they were into my area of expertise. "Live action role playing." I turned my head to face them. "We dressed up like fantasy creatures and beat the crap out of each other with foam swords and shields."

Adam nodded. "I used to LARP myself, back before my parents..." He looked out the window. "It was fun just being a kid. Not a care in the world."

My childhood was so far back in the rear-view mirror, it wasn't even funny.

The SUV pulled up a long driveway and stopped at The Ranch. I stepped outside and looked at the horses grazing in the pastures nearby. I briefly wondered if they bred unicorns here, too. Of course, it was all a cover to give the Templars a base of operations in a sprawling metropolis. My childhood home wasn't far from here—or at least what was left of it. Since the day hellhounds had chased me from it, I hadn't returned to see.

Katie tugged on my arm when we got out. "Justin, will you do me a huge favor and contact Ash and Nyte?"

I grimaced at the thought of my Goth friends. Besides Elyssa, they'd been the only other people at high school who'd taken me in after all my troubles had started. Katie had been one of those troubles. I'd crushed so hard on her I'd lost sight of everything else, and managed to alienate my friends and everyone else in school to the point where nobody else would have anything to do with me, not even Andy Dudowitz. Nathan Spelman and his gang of bullies had made things worse, once shoving Ash down a row of bleachers.

Now they needed me, and I hadn't done a thing to help. They had no idea what they were getting into with Maximus.

"Yeah, I'll call them right now," I said.

Nyte answered on the first ring. "Justin, oh my god, dude, where have you been?"

"Uh, travelling a lot."

Nyte chuckled. "You're never going to believe what Ash and I have been up to. Where we've *been*, man."

Another voice came on the phone. "Justin, it's Ash! We thought you were dead after that bus plowed into you, but the cops never found a body or anything. Are you okay?"

I smiled at hearing their voices, feeling a flood of relief. "I'm fine. In fact, I'm with Elyssa right now." I tried to think of a way to gauge their knowledge, though, from what Katie had said, they probably knew all about the Overworld. "Why don't we grab a bite to eat tonight?" I knew for a fact I wasn't ready to ram through Maximus's front door just yet. Besides, if Ash and Nyte really were considering joining him, maybe they'd have valuable intel. I could fill them in on how big a douche Maximus was and maybe come up with a plan of attack all at the same time.

"Definitely," Ash said. "We have a huge surprise for you."

A wave of dread filled me at the prospect.

We arranged to meet at a pizza place near my old house and ended the call.

"Thanks, Justin," Katie said. "Is it okay if I come, too?"

I shrugged. "Sure."

We swung by the armory and grabbed the upgraded Nightingale armor and supplies before heading into the main house. Elyssa had someone give Cinder his own private room and a new set of clothes, along with the stern order to shower.

"We'll be back later," Adam said as he and Meghan went outside to a waiting car, the tailpipe steaming in the cold air. "I just want to take a nap in my own bed."

The rest of us grabbed seats in the kitchen while I made hot chocolate.

"I do so love this time of year in this part of the world," Bella said. "The weather just doesn't feel right in the south for Christmas."

Harry Shelton walked through the kitchen door, wearing his standard leather duster, jeans, and cowboy boots.

"Harry!" Bella said, meeting him halfway with a hug, and a kiss to both cheeks. "It is good to see you again, dear."

Shelton's face flushed bright red. "Yeah, yeah, darlin'. Good to see you, too."

She laughed. "Don't be embarrassed."

"I'm not—" he huffed out a breath. "Oh, whatever." He walked over to the counter. "You got any coffee brewing?"

I gave him an exasperated look. "Good to see you, too, Shelton."

"Glad you made it out of there alive, kiddo."

"I'm glad *you* made it out alive," I said, resisting the urge to pelt him with questions.

Shelton grabbed a mug and sniffed at the dark liquid in the decanter on the industrial coffee machine. Shrugged and poured a cup.

"It's fresh," Elyssa said.

He took a sip and grimaced. "Weak." He sat on a stool and looked at us, his eyes settling on Katie. "What's she doing here?"

"Polite as the last time we met," Katie said, crossing her arms and staring him down. "If you can't afford etiquette school, I'd be willing to work two jobs to support you."

Shelton laughed. "You're not the scared little girl I remember."

"She helped rescue me from Maximus," I said. "I think we've all done some growing up in the past few days."

"Amen to that," Elyssa said, before taking a sip of hot chocolate. "You can add my father to that list."

"Sounds like I've missed out on a lot," Shelton said.

"You have no idea." Bella grabbed her own mug. "I emailed you a couple of times to fill you in, but I think I did something wrong."

"Heaven help this poor woman with technology," Shelton said, a grin spreading on his face. "You typed everything in all caps for one thing. And your email ended in the middle of a sentence."

"Yes, I somehow deleted part of the email and couldn't figure out how to get it back, so I sent it to you, hoping the program would recover my missing text." Bella shrugged. "I suppose it didn't work as I'd hoped."

I took in the perplexed look on the petite Arcane's face and burst into laughter. It didn't take long for the others to join in. After the laughter died down, we took turns giving Shelton the detailed story. By the time we finished, it was almost six and all the hot chocolate was gone. Shelton, I noticed, didn't say a word about his abrupt departure, or what problems he'd encountered during his brief stint in Colombia.

"We need to get ready if we're meeting Nyte and Ash," Elyssa said.

Shelton stood. "I'm headed back to my place. I say we meet there to plan the next move."

"I'll go with you, Harry," Bella said. "Assuming you haven't kicked me out of the guest bedroom."

"Nah, sweetheart, the bed's still unmade and your underwear is still all over the floor where you left it."

Her face went scarlet. "I—but I picked up all my underwear before I left!"

He laughed. "Oh man, you are too easy."

She slapped him on the shoulder. "You are so mean sometimes."

I looked at the two of them, thinking back to Bella's questions about Shelton. Did she really like him? Bella really was a sweetheart, at least as far as I knew, but she'd need some heavy duty magic to make Shelton behave.

Shelton's face grew serious as he looked back at me. "You've made some impressive gains in the magic department. A few tweaks, and you'll be casting spells like a pro." He stood back and gauged me. "What do you think, Bella, six and a half feet?"

Bella looked me up and down. "I think it would be perfect."

"What would?" I asked, confused.

Shelton clapped me on the shoulder. "I think it's time we got you a staff. You're ready for the big leagues now."

John Corwin

Chapter 34

"My own staff!" I said for at least the tenth time, so excited I couldn't stop rubbing my hands together.

Elyssa snorted and glanced over at me. "Don't have a nerdgasm in the car, hot stuff." She took a left turn and pulled into the parking lot of the pizza place.

"Is a staff a big deal?" Katie asked from the back seat.

"Don't even get him started," Elyssa said with a grin.

Nyte and Ash stood near the front door of Ghetto Pizza, their eyes already locked onto us. Elyssa opened the door to get out, but Nyte jogged over. In place of his usual Goth attire, he wore designer jeans and a leather biker jacket. He wore only a couple of earrings in place of the metric ton of metal he used to wear in his nose, eyebrow, and numerous other places on his face. His red hair was shorter and worn stylishly. He looked really good.

I leaned over so I could look at his irises, and breathed with relief when I saw they weren't red—a sure sign of vampirism.

"Don't come in," Nyte said, looking around conspiratorially. "We grabbed some pizza to go. Thought we'd eat it at Spooky House for old time's sake." He winked at Elyssa. "You cool with that?"

She smiled. "Wow, I haven't been there in ages." She looked at me. "You're not scared to go are you?"

I laughed. "I'm petrified. Let's do it."

"I'm in," Katie said, an uncertain look on her face.

"Sweet!" Nyte slapped the top of the car and jogged over to Ash's tank-like, periwinkle Ford, a car that looked like something out of a seventies film.

"What's this Spooky House?" I asked.

270

Elyssa rolled up the window and made a U-turn out of the parking lot. "It's this old antebellum house just down the street. Nobody's lived there for years. Remember how I told you about our ghost stories in the graveyard?"

I nodded.

"This is just another place we used to go to scare each other and party." She smiled. "Not just us, but a bunch of other Goths, too. It's a cool place."

"You used to party? Like drink and all that?" It was hard to imagine Little Miss Templar as a party girl.

Her lips curled into a lopsided grin. "Yeah. Alcohol doesn't affect me that much thanks to my dhampyr–enhanced metabolism." She gave me a sideways look. "I suppose I could lie to you and say I did it as part of my undercover duties as a Templar, but truth is, I actually had a lot of fun." She sighed. "I miss those days sometimes. Now everything is so serious."

"Well, maybe we *can* have fun tonight. Doesn't look like our friends are vampires."

"You looked at his eyes, too?" Elyssa glanced at me as she stopped at a stop sign, and looked both ways.

"First chance I got."

"Thank goodness," Katie said. "I was so worried we were too late."

"We might have gotten lucky." *Hopefully.* I looked out the window at the neat little houses with their porches and tiny front yards. We were in Kirkwood, not far from East Atlanta Village, so the houses were smaller and tightly spaced.

Elyssa parked on the road before a crumbling stone wall. Behind it loomed the silhouette of a house. Darkened windows and a thick overgrown lawn told me it had been abandoned a long time.

"Whoa, this is a spooky house," I said, peering out the window. I looked at Elyssa. "Does it have ghosts?"

She laughed. "Probably." We got out of the car. "Looks like they're inside already."

"The ghosts?"

"No, Ash and Nyte, silly."

Katie regarded the house, an uncertain look on her face, but said nothing.

The three of us squeezed through the gap in the rusted, iron gate and waded through a footpath overgrown with weeds, brambles, and ivy. Large columns supported a wide porch. At one end, a broken bench swing hung by a chain. A gentle breeze caused the swing to scrape against the deck, sending a chill up my spine. Skeletal branches from the oak tree slapped against a window. Despite all the horrors I'd seen, something about this place creeped me out. The porch groaned when I stepped on it. Cracks and holes showed where other people had found weak spots in the flooring.

Something thudded against a wall inside the house, followed by a muffled cry.

Elyssa and I looked at each other with alarm. She burst through the front door. I'd actually planned to run *away* from the house, but steeled my balls and rushed in after her. We paused in the silence at the bottom of the main staircase and listened. Katie plowed into me in the darkness as she caught up. Another thud boomed against the floor upstairs. Dodging broken spots in the stairs, we ran up them. The space upstairs consisted of one large room with a few wooden supports holding up the ceiling.

Old paint buckets and broken scaffolding leaned against a wall. It looked like the previous owners had tried some renovating before leaving the place to rot. Dim light from a streetlamp glowed through a broken window. A cold breeze ruffled the tattered curtains. My night vision flickered on. A figure writhed against the far wall.

"How's this for OP?" Nyte shouted and tossed a something across the room toward the figure on the floor.

Ash laughed as another body thudded against the hardwoods. "Dude, that is so IMBA." He flashed across the room in a blur and leaned over the person. "How does it feel to be on the receiving end, Nathan?"

"What in the hell is going on?" Elyssa said, eyes wide with shock.

"What? What is it?" Katie said, picking her way up the stairs carefully. I'd forgotten about the poor girl not having night vision. "I can't see a thing!"

Ash and Nyte flashed over to us, huge grins spread on their faces.

"Surprise!" Nyte said, flashing his teeth, and revealing sharp fangs. "Guys, you're not going to believe this, but vampires are real."

"We're vampires," Ash said. "Can you freaking believe it?" He ran across the room to a wall. "Watch this!" He reared back a fist, and punched a hole in the wall. Held out his hand. "And it doesn't even hurt."

"And if that's not enough proof," Nyte said, flicking across the room and grabbing a bulky figure off the floor. "Look at this." He flashed over, holding the form of Nathan Spelman over his head with one hand.

Nathan's eyes bulged. Duct tape wrapped around his head muffled his screams.

"Put him down this instant!" Elyssa said, eyes wide with horror.

"But—"

"I said, put him down." Her violet eyes blazed to life in the dark.

"Whoa," Nyte said. "Your eyes…" He set Nathan down.

"Who's the other one?" she asked, nodding her head toward the other figure. "Bring him here."

Ash and Nyte, eyes downcast, brought two more squirming figures and dropped them next to Nathan.

"Adam and Steve," I said, recognizing Nathan's buddies, both linebackers from the football team. I couldn't remember their last names.

"Were you wearing contacts earlier?" Elyssa said, looking into the eyes of our friends, now flashing the red of vampires.

They looked at each other and nodded.

"We knew our red eyes would freak people out," Ash said. He looked from Elyssa to me to Katie. "But you guys don't even look surprised."

"Or happy." Nyte grabbed Nathan by the hair. "Don't you remember how evil these assholes were to us? Remember when they shoved Ash down the bleachers? And when Nathan punched you in the face?"

"Why do you look so mad?" Ash said, a plaintive note in his voice.

"What's going on?" Katie said again. "Who's a vampire? I can hardly see a thing."

Elyssa spotted some battery-powered lamps beneath a tarp and turned them on, casting shadows across the large room.

Katie's eyes went wide with shock. "Oh my god, oh my god! Ash, how could you? I can't believe you'd beat someone up like that!"

Ash's face fell. "B-but I can protect myself now. I'm strong. Isn't that—"

"Just because you're strong doesn't mean you can go around beating up people who are weaker than you." She took a step back. "And to think—I thought you were different. I thought you were better than that."

Pain entered his eyes. "I only wanted to..." His voice trailed off midsentence and he looked away.

I squeezed my eyes shut and rubbed my forehead. "Oh, *brother*." My guts knotted. I pulled Elyssa aside and whispered, "What are we going to do? We're talking kidnap, assault, and hell, I don't even know how many other laws they've broken."

Elyssa sighed. Leaned down and unwrapped the duct tape from Nathan's mouth and hands, freeing him.

"Oh, god, please don't kill me," the meaty football player cried out in a hoarse voice. "Don't suck my blood, please!" Tears poured down his face as he fell at my girlfriend's feet. "I swear to god I'll never tell anyone about this. I swear!" He grabbed my foot. "Justin, we're friends, right? You gotta help me, man. Please!"

My stomach rumbled. I felt like I was going to be sick. I backed away. "Ash, Nyte, I—I can't believe you would do this."

"Nathan and his goons are nothing but animals," Ash said. "They took our dignity and dragged it through the mud. Nathan even tried to rape Katie and if you hadn't been there to save her, he probably would've gotten away with it."

"I know, I know." I bit the inside of my lip and stared.

Katie's face went white. She looked away from Nathan as a tear trailed down her face. Ash looked stricken. He took a step toward her, but she backed away, throwing her hands up in the air, palms out. "Don't touch me!" She took in a long shuddering breath. "Being a bully like Nathan would destroy anything attractive I ever saw in you. Don't you get that?"

"It's too late to send them back, and pretend nothing ever happened," Elyssa said, face blank.

"Oh, god, no!" Nathan cried, gripping me by the feet and holding on for dear life. "Don't kill us, please! I'll do anything you want.

274

Anything." He looked at Katie. "I'm sorry. I was so stupid. Please, Katie, don't let them kill me."

Katie didn't meet his eyes.

"We're not going to kill you," Elyssa said with a sigh. "I think we'll have to send them through the Overworld orientation program."

I pried Nathan's meaty hands off my legs. "Stay there, and don't move an inch. You saw how fast my friends are, so don't even think about running. Your life is in my hands."

He looked so pathetically happy through the tears and snot bubbling out of his nose, I almost laughed. I motioned the others to another corner of the room.

I shook my head sadly, looking from Nyte to Ash. "We need to have a serious conversation. But not now."

Katie didn't say a word, though the shock and anger was plain in her eyes.

"I am so disappointed in you two," Elyssa said. "Kidnapping and assault? Really?"

I touched her arm. "We'll get to that later. As for what to do about those bozos, I think I have a better idea than sending them in for Overworld orientation."

Elyssa crossed her arms and glared at me. "And what would that be?"

"Look at the bright side—Nathan and his buddies are about to crap themselves."

Nyte sniffed the air. "Actually, I think one of them already did."

I gagged and jabbed a finger at him. "Not another word until I'm done."

He nodded solemnly. Ash, for his part, looked as ashamed as a dog who'd been caught eating the kitty treats, and kept sneaking furtive glances at Katie.

I continued. "Let's use their fear to our advantage. Heaven knows they've kept the nerd population in a state of constant panic and turmoil with their bullying."

"You want to let them go back to school, knowing what they know, and hope they'll be too frightened to say anything?" Elyssa said, skepticism plain in her voice.

"More than that." I grinned.

275

By the time I explained myself, even Elyssa and Katie couldn't help but smile.

We approached the victims, unbound the three of them, and lined them up. Aside from scrapes and bruises, none of the captives seemed to have broken bones. Nyte, Ash, and Elyssa gave them slow grins, extending their fangs. Ruby red irises glittered from Ash and Nyte's eyes. Elyssa's glowed violet. I still hadn't figured out how to make my eyes glow on command, but figured it wasn't necessary.

Nathan gulped. Steve whimpered. Adam shrank against the wall.

Nathan opened his mouth to speak.

I put a finger to my lips. "No talking. I want you to listen very closely."

They nodded.

"There are horrors in this world you have no clue about. Nightmares that will eat you alive and spit out your bones." I leaned in closer. "No mortal should know about our existence, but as you can see, it's too late for that." I paced in front of them. Paused and gave them a sideways glance. "There are those among us who'd like to suck you dry and throw your bodies in a ditch."

Adam's teeth chattered. All three football players shrank together against the wall.

I offered them a condescending smile. "Cooler heads have prevailed, however."

"I still think this is a horrible mistake," Elyssa said, growling in her throat. "And I haven't had a good meal in days."

"Oh, crap. Oh, crap!" Steve said, trying to hide behind Nathan even as the bigger guy fought to hide behind him.

I might have laughed if I didn't feel so guilty. "Here's the deal, *boys*. No more bullying. If you pick on anyone else for the rest of your life, you're dead. In fact, it is now your sworn duty to protect those who cannot protect themselves. If you see someone else picking on *anyone*, nerd or otherwise, you have to step in and protect them. Do I make myself clear?"

"Y-y-yes," Adam said, his teeth chattering even harder.

Nathan nodded like a bobble head doll. "I swear to god, man!"

"Yes," Steve said, voice hoarse.

I stared them down for several long seconds before saying, "We'll be watching. If you slip up, we'll be ready." I was just about to tell them they were free to go, when one last indignity occurred to me. "One last thing."

"Anything, man, please just let us go!" Nathan hugged himself like a little kid, staying as far from Ash and Nyte as he could.

"You must join the Chess Club at school."

The three guys looked flummoxed, but not a one of them protested.

"Good, now—" A sudden throb of cold raced up my leg.

Maximus's face hovers over me, blood flowing down his face. He grins. Licks the blood. "You're mine, Slade. You and your little sister." He throws back his head and laughs as he pulls Ivy from the dark. Like a viper, his head strikes forward, and his fangs clamp on her neck. Blood spurts. Eyes wide with fear, she screams.

I squeezed my eyes shut as rage boiled into me. *It's just a hallucination*, I thought, desperately trying to return to reality. Pain cracked into my skull like a sledgehammer. A guttural growl rumbled through my chest. The world seemed to vibrate. Energy crackled around me, lancing my body with white and black bolts of energy. The world was breaking around me. Shattering to pieces.

I roared.

Someone squealed like a pig and a rotten odor drifted into my nostrils.

"Justin!" Elyssa said, gripping my arm.

I snapped out of my trance. Nathan and his pals were literally shaking in their shoes, huddled tight in the corner next to the window. One of them whimpered as a puddle formed at his shoes.

My voice, deep and inhuman, growled, "Do as I say, or die."

They screamed.

I made a slashing motion with my hand and walked into a dark corner as the world around me wobbled. Ash and Nyte herded the captives downstairs and outside. Elyssa appeared beside me.

"Justin, are you okay?"

I nodded as the sick feeling in my stomach subsided, and the cold bite of the vampling curse faded in my leg. "It's getting worse. The visions. The anger. We've got to get to Maximus and stop him before

I go over the edge." The small horns on my forehead clattered to the floor as my body reverted from its half-demon form to normal.

She leaned her head on my shoulder. "We will." Her arms wrapped tight around me and we held each other in the darkness.

Chapter 35

Nyte and Ash returned later, having dropped Nathan and pals at a bus stop. They had hot pizza with them, probably hoping it would serve as a peace offering and save them from mine, Katie's, and Elyssa's wrath. While we were shocked at the abrupt change in our friends from Goths to vampires, it was hard to blame them for wanting payback for all the cruel things Nathan and his goons had done to us. So instead of yelling or making a big deal out of the whole kidnapping, assault, and revealing the secrets of the Overworld to noms, we accepted the pizza.

Besides, it had mushrooms and olives on it—my favorites.

"I don't even want to think about how many times they crapped themselves," Nyte said, laughing as he passed out paper cups.

Ash giggled like a little kid. "Join the Chess Club? Classic! Can you imagine those morons trying to figure out how to play?"

Elyssa wiped her mouth with a napkin. "I think making them protect the other nerds from bullies was a nice touch. But do you really think they're going to keep it up?"

Nyte looked at me with wonder. "Man, if growing horns out of your forehead and roaring like a demon doesn't keep them straight, I don't know what will."

"Yeah, about that," I said, scratching my forehead where the aforementioned horns had been. "I guess it's time to tell you two everything."

"All this time you've been holding out," Ash said. "Not cool, guys." He looked at Katie. "And you knew?"

She nodded. "I found out by accident. But I was sworn to secrecy." Her green eyes regarded him, traces of hurt or disappointment still evident.

"We had our reasons to keep it quiet." Elyssa gave them pointed looks. "Maybe you'll agree once we're done explaining."

We gave them the short version, taking turns, from the time I'd discovered my incubus abilities, to Elyssa's duties as an undercover Templar, sent to apprehend vampires preying on unsuspecting noms at our high school. It was hard to believe all we'd been through in the past few months.

Ash and Nyte looked absolutely flummoxed.

"Whoa, whoa, wait!" Ash said, a horrified look on his face. "Are you saying we joined the bad guys?"

Nyte's eyes grew worried. "Did we go to the dark side?"

"How did Maximus turn you?" I said, my heart chilled at the thought the rogue vampire might have infected them with the vampling curse.

"We injected ourselves." Ash pulled out two vials of a clear red substance with a bluish glow. "The recruiter told us we'd made the final cut and gave us vials like this. He had a bundle of them, so Nyte distracted him while I stole a couple, thinking we'd give them to you guys." He shrugged. "Obviously, you don't even need them."

I took one of the vials and examined it in the dim light. "Why is it glowing blue?"

"Oh, god," Elyssa said. "Maximus had time to make a batch with your blood, Justin." She peered at Nyte's eyes. "I knew something was off. Look at their irises."

I leaned in and spotted the anomaly right away. Although his and Ash's eyes had the standard red irises of vampires, they were edged by a soft blue tint. "Let me see your hand," I told Nyte.

He raised an eyebrow, but held it out. His hand was warm. I motioned for Elyssa to touch it.

She gasped. "Most vampires have a low body temperature. They're not cold, but they definitely aren't warm." Her eyes met mine. "But they aren't like dhampyrs either. This would explain why we didn't sense them as vampires."

"Dhampyrs have violet eyes?" Ash said. "And I always thought you were wearing contacts."

Elyssa squeezed his hand. "Have you had human blood yet?"

Ash and Nyte looked warily at each other.

"This is important, guys," she said. "Have you drunk blood from a human?"

Nyte winced. "Well, not exactly *from* a human. We drank from some blood packs right after, because the recruiter didn't want us jumping any classmates. We were supposed to go to an orientation tonight where they'd teach us how to hunt properly, you know, without killing people."

"Oh, and how to control blood urges, and what to do if we get the munchies," Ash added.

"How does daylight feel?" Elyssa asked.

"Uh, normal." Ash shrugged. "The recruiter told us we'd feel sluggish and tired in daylight, but he was wrong."

Nyte nodded. "I'm just glad I don't have to worry about bursting into flames or having a hot girl stab me in the chest with a stake."

"So they're not normal vampires?" Katie said, looking somewhat relieved.

"Not entirely," Elyssa said. She asked them several more questions, probably straight out of the Templar handbook for identifying vampires, and mulled over their answers before asking one last question. "And how many vials did you say this guy has?"

"Probably thirty or forty," Ash said. "No telling how many others he's already juiced with the stuff."

Elyssa stood and brushed the dust off her jeans. "We've got to get those vials."

"The orientation is at the same place they took your dad," Ash said, looking at me. "The dude gave us a pass phrase to get in the front door. Supposedly, we're gonna meet Maximus, too."

"Has he added any security?" I asked.

"We only went one time before," Nyte said, an apologetic look on his face. "The recruiter took us in to meet a British guy. We didn't think to look for cameras or anything."

"We didn't even know they *were* vampires," Ash said. "They told us the meeting was about finding new meaning or some crap like that. The British guy asked us a lot of questions."

Nyte shuddered. "And he shook our hands in a really creepy way, too."

"Did he have a monocle and an oiled mustache?" I asked.

Nyte gave a vigorous nod. "Yeah, exactly. Accent like Sherlock Holmes."

"The Master," I said. "Maximus's sire."

"Didn't you say Felicia needs Maximus's blood?" Nyte said.

"She needs the blood of her sire, whoever that is," I replied. I flicked my gaze to Elyssa. "It must be the Master, right? I mean, who else could it be? Unless Maximus has more than one elder vampire helping him."

Elyssa pulled a ring from her pocket, crowned with a tiny red gem. "Meghan made this to help. She charmed it with Felicia's blood so when we're within a few yards of her sire, it'll glow. The closer we are, the brighter the glow."

Nyte oohed. "A magic ring?"

She smiled. "Yep. Not much else to it, though."

"I wish I could do magic," Ash said, looking glum.

I stared at the ring, my mind wandering in a thousand different directions.

"You've got that look," Elyssa said, crossing her arms.

I turned to Nyte. "When is the orientation?"

He checked the time. "At midnight, a couple of hours from now."

"Please tell me you're not thinking what I think you're thinking," Elyssa said, a note of alarm in her voice.

"Your father won't even be ready to attack for a couple of days," I said. "By then, it might be too late for Felicia." I sighed. "It might be too late for me."

"We'll do whatever it takes," Ash said.

Nyte nodded. "No matter what, guys, we'll help."

"If I can help, I will," Katie said, giving Ash a concerned look.

I took Elyssa's hand. "Trust me, babe, I have a plan." My stomach, heaved. Apparently, it didn't think my plan was so great. I grinned to cover my nerves. "Where's a good Goth store?"

An hour later, I stood before a mirror, a man transformed. My eyes gleamed red. Fake fangs protruded beneath my lips. But the biggest difference was my hair. Elyssa's mom, whose day job was hair styling, cropped my hair close and bleached it blonde. By the time I put on the designer jeans and long-sleeve button-up shirt, I looked like a vampire who'd escaped a steamy romance novel.

"Your father doesn't like this plan one bit," Leia said, looking me over, and preening my eyelashes.

Elyssa took a towel and brushed something off my ear. "We don't have time to wait for him to be ready."

Leia looked at her daughter. "He promised not to get in your way, but he is sending a squad of his best people to go along."

"As long as he doesn't storm the castle," I said. "We don't need a bloodbath."

"Why do you think he hasn't gone in already?" Leia said. She took Elyssa's hands. "I'm not saying the plan is a bad one. Just be careful."

Elyssa offered her mother a smile. Nodded. "We will."

Her mother turned to me. "Bring my daughter back, Justin."

It was hard meeting her eyes, but I forced myself to do it. "Yes Ma'am."

Someone knocked on the door. Elyssa opened it. Adam Nosti stood outside, tablet in hand.

"I did some digging and found some background on Maximus and the Master." He stepped inside. Gave a nod to Leia. "Want to see?"

"Let's save it for the group," I said, motioning toward the door. "No sense in repeating it."

"You don't look half bad as a blonde," Elyssa said, running a hand through my short hair as we stepped into the hallway. "Will you be able to mask yourself from the vampires?"

"I did it the last time," I said. "Considering all the freaks after me, it's a matter of pure survival."

We made our way to the main hall where the rest of my so-called team waited. As my eyes wandered over the assembled crowd, I found it hard to believe how large the group had grown. Cinder sat isolated in a chair near the corner of the room, his gray eyes never leaving the motley crew. Katie also sat somewhat apart from the group, her uncertain eyes regarding Ash. She'd been through a lot. Seen a lot. And she'd killed. I knew from experience how bitter a pill that was to swallow.

I also wondered how deep her emotions ran for Ash. Had his change from gentle Goth nerd to vampire changed her feelings? No telling. Trying to understand women was like—well, like trying to understand something that's super hard to understand. But maybe things would work out. I spotted Ash where he stood next to Nyte, taking in the motley crew. But I also caught his furtive attempts to look at Katie, worry on his face.

Man, I knew the feeling.

I still felt the weight of my mental scars after seeing Brad Nichols and others die as a result of the vampling curse. I had also killed people. Some people needed killing, but it didn't make me feel any better about it.

Most of this crowd had fought together. They knew each other. While they'd never be the perfect, happy-go-lucky bunch I'd seen in sitcoms, I still considered them family. A wonderful, bizarre, dysfunctional family. At least I knew what they were, rather than the lie of a perfect family my parents had smothered my childhood with. For all I knew, my mom had blurred out all the negative memories, leaving me with only positive ones.

It doesn't matter anymore.

My parents might as well have been dead.

Nyte was speaking with animated gestures to Shelton and Bella, probably begging for magic tricks. He'd already extracted a promise from Ryland to transform into a wolf, though I expected he'd hovered close to the lycan so he could gawk at Stacey's shapely form.

Meghan stood near the roaring fireplace, while Adam took up a position in the center of the room, his tablet ready with whatever information he'd gleaned. His face looked pale. I had to assume he was worried sick about his sister. Meghan's eyes locked with mine and held contact for the space of a couple of seconds. If she was trying to tell me something, I didn't get it.

"Oh, lamb," Stacey said, walking a circle around me, a purr in the back of her throat. "You look absolutely delicious." She glanced at Leia. "I really must have you style my hair sometime. You do a marvelous job."

"A Templar hair dresser?" Shelton said from his position on a leather sofa to the left of the table. "I don't get it."

Leia shrugged. "It started out as a cover for one of our operations many years ago. By the time we were done, I realized how much I enjoyed styling. So I continued."

"If you'd ever take off that cowboy hat, maybe she could gussie you up," Ryland said to Shelton with a wolfish grin.

Shelton grunted and pulled off the hat to reveal his close-shorn head. "For one thing, wolf man, this is a fedora, not a cowboy hat. As for hair—" He gave a disdainful look at Ryland's thick head of long, unruly hair. "I got a pair of hedge trimmers that might improve that mess."

Ignoring the verbal jousting, I set my arcphone on the table in the middle of the room. "Before we start talking about waxing body hair Brazilian style, maybe I should go over the plan." I spoke some magic words to pull up a holographic image of Maximus's crib. Unless the rogue vampire had changed things up, the map appeared accurate, including the location of the crypt where he'd kept my father deep beneath the old building. As I looked it over, apprehension settled over me. Never in my wildest dreams had I imagined setting foot back in the place where Elyssa had almost died. The place where I'd first manifested into demon form and annihilated a mob of vamplings. The place where Felicia had sicced those very vamplings on me and Elyssa. How ironic it was, going back into that place to save Felicia.

"Are you okay, Justin?" Bella said, concern etched in her face.

I shook my head. "Yeah. Sorry." I covered my worry with a smile. "Just some bad memories of this place." I glanced at Nyte, whose eyes were glued to Stacey's backside as she prowled about the room. I cleared my throat. "Anything you and Ash want to add before I go over the plan, Nyte?"

Ash looked away from Katie, a guilty expression on his face. "No?"

Nyte wiped the corner of his mouth and jerked from his ass-induced trance. "Uh, no. I wish we had more inside info."

I waved to Adam. "Want to show us what you found on Maximus?"

The gawky Arcane came to the table and set his tablet on it. Flicked a finger across the surface. The black-and-white image of a man with a monocle and an oiled mustache flickered into the air. "Meet Simon Barclay, aka The Master. This is the vampire turning noms for Maximus."

"What a horrid moustache," Stacey said, wrinkling her nose.

Adam smiled, though it didn't look like his heart was in it. "Barclay isn't ancient by vampire standards, having been around only since the fourteenth or fifteenth century, but from all the information I was able to find about him, he's anti-establishment."

"He doesn't like the Red Syndicate?" Ryland asked.

Adam shook his head. "Back before vampires modernized to the Syndicate, they ruled with an elder council. Barclay thought vampirism was a gift they should spread to the masses. The elders disagreed. Said it was reserved only for a chosen few."

"Populist versus the elitists," Shelton said. "How quaint."

"Barclay formed his own cult and tried to create a vampire army. At the time, he wasn't old enough and, instead, wiped out an entire village in Northern Ireland with the vampling plague." Adam changed the image to that of old drawings, showing zombie-like vampires in the act of killing screaming victims. "Sound familiar?"

"Obviously, he's old enough to turn noms into vampires now," Bella said. "But why did he wait centuries before trying this again?"

"Apparently, the elders ordered Barclay executed. I couldn't find any historical records about the results, but I think it's safe to say they failed. Barclay went underground for centuries. When he came back, he must have started by turning Maximus, using him as a proxy instead of coming out of the shadows himself."

"Because the Syndicate would kill Barclay," Elyssa said.

Adam shrugged. "Far as I know, a number of the elders from those days are still around. I'm sure they haven't forgotten." He switched to the black-and-white image of a group of vampires posing with fanged grins before what looked like an old Ford Model T. Using his finger, he circled a familiar face on the far left. "Say hello to Herbert Lipschitz, aka Maximus, shown here shortly after his transformation to vampire."

A few chuckles went up around the room.

"Are you serious?" Stacey said, raising an eyebrow. "His bloody name is Herbert?"

"I kid you not," Adam said, zooming in to show Maximus's face.

"No wonder he changed it," Ryland said with a grin.

Adam moved the focus to another familiar face, at least to me. "As you can see, Barclay is in this picture as well. According to the writing on the back, this photo was taken a couple of days after he turned this group of men into vampires."

"So we know for sure Barclay is Maximus's sire," Bella said, leaning in to examine the hovering image.

"I couldn't find much more about Maximus's history, but he was supposedly abandoned by his immigrant parents when they arrived in America. A rich Jewish couple, the Lipschitzes, found him abandoned at a warehouse by the docks and raised him as their own. Sometime after this picture was taken, his adoptive parents were found murdered in an alley, supposedly mugged, and Maximus took over the family fortune."

"Did he kill them?" Katie asked.

The Arcane shrugged. "From the old newspaper articles I dug up, plenty of people suspected as much, but nothing was ever proved." He glanced back at me. "Anyway, that's all I got."

Shelton raised his hand. "One thing I gotta know."

Adam raised an eyebrow. "What's that?"

"How in the hell do you say Lipschitz with a straight face?"

After the chuckles died down, I spoke. "The plan is simple. Elyssa, Nyte, Ash, and I will go in Maximus's front door and act like we're there for the orientation." I held up a tiny glass ball. "Along the way, we'll drop these flashers Shelton gave me. Once we identify Felicia's sire using the magic ring from Meghan, I'll shout out the magic word to activate the flashers. That should stun or knock out most of the vamps. We'll grab Barclay and Maximus and head out."

"Whoa," Shelton said. "Do you know how much sunlight I concentrated into those flashers? A lot. Last time I checked, your pals there are vampires, so you'd better plan on toting them outta there, too."

"I don't think the flashers will work on Ash and Nyte," I said, and told them about the serum Maximus had made from my blood. By the time I finished, those who hadn't heard about the stuff looked shocked.

"The bloody fool can inject people now?" Stacey said. "And make super vampires?"

I nodded. "We have to stop him before he turns more people."

Shelton didn't look convinced. "Alright, so you set off the flashers, scoop up our good buddy, Herbert, and then what? You make a break for it?"

I nodded. "The flashers should knock out most of the vamps. Then it'll be up to the rest of you to clear out the vamps outside."

"Don't this just feel like déjà vu all over again?" Shelton commented dryly. "After the can of whoop-ass the Templars opened on Maximus down in Colombia, do you really think you'll just be able to march in there with your fancy blonde hairdo and fake fangs, and manage to drag Lipschitz out of there?"

"He has a point," Ryland said. "A snatch and run ain't a half-bad idea, but I'd be willing to bet Max has a few more tricks up his sleeves."

"What about guns?" Katie said. "What if the place is surrounded by armed vampires?"

"Thomas has provided us with upgraded Nightingale armor," I said. "It'll stop the bullets."

"I'm gonna look ridiculous in that black unitard," Shelton said with a grumble.

"You can wear it under your clothes," Elyssa said, rolling her eyes. "It's skin tight and nobody will notice."

He groaned. Looked at Meghan. "How long does geek-boy's sister have before—uh—you know?"

Her lips tightened. "Not long. Hours at most, the last time I checked."

"And she's the same crazy vamp who helped kidnap your father?" Shelton said, shaking his head.

"I seem to recall a certain Arcane who tried to kidnap him, too, Shelton. Just before Felicia and her gang showed up."

"Man, you're never gonna let me live that one down, are you?" Shelton shoved the fedora back on his head, and stood up. "Guess I need to go put my bulletproof undies on."

I looked around the room. "Look, it's not the best plan in the world. We don't have any recon on the place, or certainty that Maximus and Barclay will be there. If anyone wants out, I won't blame you."

Ryland grinned. "Why would I want out? This is gonna be fun."

"I wouldn't miss it for the world," Stacey said.

A chorus of agreement went up from the others.

Elyssa took my hand and held it tight. "Guess we'd better get moving so you can be back in time for your sci-fi marathon."

I couldn't help but laugh.

It was go time.

Chapter 36

We piled into SUVs outside.

"I am pumped!" Ash said.

Nyte bumped his fist and said, "Dude, we're gonna show them what OP is."

Ash grinned. "Totally IMBA."

"What does that even mean?" Elyssa asked, climbing into the passenger seat.

"Gamer stuff," I said, wondering if I'd ever get to play a video game again. "OP stands for 'over powered', and IMBA is 'imbalanced'."

"And you're using this terminology in real life?" Katie said, sliding in next to Ash. "Kind of nerdy." She caught my eye in the rear-view mirror as I adjusted it, and winked. "Then again, I guess I'm surrounded by nerds."

Ash suddenly looked self-conscious as the cute blonde sidled up next to him. "Uh, yeah."

Adam and Meghan climbed in the third-row bench seat, closing the side door behind them.

"Ready," Adam said.

The door opened again, revealing Cinder. "May I ride with you, Justin? I believe my presence may cause discomfort to the others."

Adam slid over. "Come on in."

"Let's kick some ass!" Ash said pumping a fist in the air as Cinder took a seat.

"Woot!" Nyte shouted back, as the two performed a complicated series of fist bumps and handshakes.

I turned on the engine. Shifted into gear.

"Oh, wait," Ash said, a sheepish look on his face.

"What is it?" I asked.

"Can I run in and use the bathroom real quick?"

A few minutes later, we were finally ready to go.

The drive to Edgewood seemed to take forever, though it was only a few miles. We arrived about fifteen minutes before midnight. What used to be a school loomed large in the hipster neighborhood, its Gothic architecture practically shouting, "Vampires R Us." It lurked across the street from a popular bar and just down the road from a number of other popular restaurants.

As usual, crowds of late-night revelers wandered about, some in drunken hazes, while smelly bums and street artists competed for the spare change of passers-by. If anything went wrong, at least the Custodians might be able to convince any eyewitnesses it had been an alcohol or drug-induced hallucination.

The moment I stepped out of the van, déjà vu punched me. Fear gripped my chest. I felt claustrophobic. The memory of straps tightened around my body, of being held helpless to the depravities of Maximus and his ilk replayed in my mind. *Never again.* A hand touched mine. I jerked. Saw Elyssa's concerned gaze. Only then did I realize how hard my heart beat in my chest. How tight my lungs felt despite my rapid breaths. Her concern softened to understanding, and yet she said nothing. Instead, she smiled.

The weight in my chest lightened, and a deep breath cleared the fear and apprehension.

I smiled back.

My senses tingled. There were vampires nearby, of course, but they weren't the only ones. It didn't take long to spot random people who looked out of place in the buzzing night life, their faces too serious and too sober to be anything but Templars.

"Looks like my father isn't taking any chances," Elyssa said. "This place is surrounded by Templars."

"So I noticed."

Ash and Nyte climbed out, faces somber, eyes nervously glancing around at the crowds. I knew how they felt. Elyssa had inserted red contacts into her own eyes, and braided her hair. Underneath her skinny jeans and a tight long-sleeved graphic T-shirt, she wore the upgraded Nightingale armor like the rest of us.

291

I was just thankful it didn't bunch up in the crotch.

Even with the armor as a security blanket, I still didn't feel all that secure. I stared up the long driveway at the looming headquarters of Herbert Lipschitz, aka Maximus. Anger and determination filled in the cracks left by uncertainty and slowly overwhelmed the sense of doom. It was time to pay this jackass back for everything he'd put me through. For what he'd done to Felicia. For all the innocent lives he'd taken with the vampling curse in his narcissistic quest to become a big shot.

Bella and Shelton walked across the street to us.

"Put this in your ear," Bella said, handing me something.

I nearly shouted as the thing she put in my hand squirmed. A small worm wiggled in my palm. "Are you kidding me?" I said. "I'm not putting something alive in my ear. Haven't you ever watched horror movies?"

"We thought about going with a standard earpiece," Shelton said. "But when we got here, Bella and I ran a few tests. Maximus has this place warded against electronic eavesdropping."

"Dash Armstrong probably warded this place to the gills," I said. "I guess the magic doesn't go away when you die, huh?"

Bella shook her head. "I know it's undesirable to put a worm in your ear, Justin, but it's quite harmless. It will coil up near your eardrum and stay there and will come out when we're done. We'll be able to communicate with you then."

"It won't control my mind or anything nasty?"

Shelton laughed. "Kid, this ain't no mind-control worm, alright? I save those buggers for people I really hate."

My face wrinkled with disgust as I put the wriggly little dude into my ear. The feeling as it slithered inside was almost unbearably creepy.

"Please don't make me put one in my ear," Ash said.

Nyte's horrified expression indicated his agreement to the sentiment.

"Have one for me?" Elyssa asked.

"We only had time to charm one of these," Bella said, an apologetic expression on her face.

Shelton nodded. "That, and it requires a specific kind of worm." He looked thoughtful for a moment and said, "Although maggots work. I could probably find one in a dumpster—"

"No," Elyssa said, recoiling with a grimace. "I think I'll be fine, thanks."

Bella and Shelton shared amused looks.

"Can you hear me?" Bella said, speaking into her wand as if it were a microphone.

Her voice echoed in my ear at a normal volume. I nodded. "Loud and clear."

She gave me a hug. "Good luck, dear. You're going to need it."

Shelton shook my hand. "Try not to get yourself killed, all right?"

Katie kissed Ash on the cheek. Smiled. "Please be careful, okay?"

Ash looked like he was going to pass out. "Y-yes." He took a deep breath. "Maybe after this is over we can, uh, like maybe see a movie or something?"

A smile lit her face. "I'd love to."

His chest seemed to swell, and pleasure flushed his skin. "Sweet!"

Ash, Nyte, Elyssa, and I walked up to the tall iron gate surrounding the building.

"Hold it there," said a man in a black suit as he came out of the guardhouse. "What's your business?"

"Seeking higher purpose," Nyte said, giving him what I assumed was the pass phrase.

The man looked us over. Motioned for a woman to come out of the gatehouse. "We gotta frisk you."

He approached, pulling on latex gloves as he did. "I will now check non-sensitive body areas." He ran his hands along my arms, chest and legs. "I'm about to touch you with the backs of my hands in the sensitive buttock region," he said, and then proceeded to do so. He stood in front of me. "I will now touch you with the backs of my hands in the sensitive groin area."

Since when did vampires hire politically correct security guards?

Ash snorted, despite his best efforts not to laugh.

Backs of the hands or not, my manhood tried to crawl inside my body at the mere thought of this dude feeling me up.

By the time we made it through the gate, I felt thoroughly degraded, and figured everyone else felt the same way by the disgusted looks going around.

"Those guards are noms," Elyssa said in a whisper as we made our way up the long winding driveway.

I extended my senses and found other male presences nearby, unmasked, and definitely not vampires. Pretending to tie my shoelace, I glanced into the shadows to either side of the unlit driveway. The sight of a pair of night-vision goggles looking back from fifty feet away almost made me fall over backwards. The owner of the goggles held what looked like an M-16 diagonally across his chest with the muzzle pointed at the ground.

As I casually looked around, I spotted more and more such people. "Good god, they've got a small army here," I said, standing and brushing the knees of my pants off.

"They look trained." Elyssa pursed her lips. "And since they're not vampires, the flashers won't knock them out."

"They have on NV goggles," I said, taking out a few of the flashers and flicking them into the dark. "At least they'll blind them for a little while."

"True." She flicked a few in the opposite direction. "I just hope they do some good."

By the time we reached the front door, it was evident my estimation of a small army wasn't all that far off. At least thirty heavily armed people patrolled the grounds, and half a dozen stood at the entrance to the building. There were probably plenty more we hadn't seen.

The man inside the door, however, was definitely a vampire. He wore a confident smile on his pale, handsome face. His pants, vest, and shirt looked tight, probably fitted, and his hair was sculpted into a spiky mess. Somehow, he still looked fashionable and oh-so metrosexual. "Sorry about all the fuss, but you can never be too careful these days." He held out a hand. "The name is James."

Nyte took his hand and shook it. "I'm Nyte. This is Ash, Wilma, and Roger."

James shook each of our hands. "How odd," he said, pausing mid-shake with my hand in his grasp. "You look familiar. Have we met?"

A cold feeling prickled up my spine. "No, I don't think so."

"Who was your recruiter?"

My mouth froze half open. I hadn't even thought about asking for that information.

"Joseph," Ash said hurriedly. "Short guy with curly brown hair."

"Yeah," I said, nodding.

James's lips curled into a lazy, fanged smile. "Ah, yes. Ever since the vampling incident at Edenfield High, we've been much more cautious in our selections."

"Best of the best," Nyte replied, a grin on his face.

James narrowed his eyes and gazed at me a moment longer. "There is definitely something very familiar about you, Roger." Without releasing my hand, his eyes swung to Nyte. "And your hands are so warm."

My muscles tensed. We hadn't even thought about body warmth. Then again, I hadn't expected someone to shake my hand at the entrance. *It's the little things that count, you idiot!*

Nyte and Ash froze. Elyssa's looked calm as ever, though I felt certain she was figuring out who to kill first to get us out of there.

James released my hand and gave a noncommittal shrug. "Don't look so worried, Roger. You're not the first of Maximus's new recruits to come through here with a higher body temperature. It appears the new serum has some interesting side effects."

I felt myself sag in relief.

The vampire motioned us to follow. "You're a bit early, but never fear. There are drinks and snacks waiting." He led us down a familiar hallway to a door I recognized.

It was the same door leading down into the basement. I couldn't stop the shudder as we began a long descent down the stairwell. Loud music boomed up the corridor. When we reached the bottom, I saw the source—huge speakers and a towering projection screen dominated a wall at the far end where a group of vampires competed in a dancing video game. It was the same exact game they'd been playing the last time I sneaked into this place to rescue my dad.

"Sweet setup," Nyte said, ogling the massive entertainment system.

"Knowing how to dance comes in handy as a vampire," James said. "We do so love our nightclubs."

The large basement was divided by cubicle partitions into sleeping areas. I looked across the way where a divider blocked my view. Behind it, somewhere, was a door leading down into the crypt. I wondered if there were more vamplings down there or not. I noticed Elyssa flicking a few flashers toward the dancing vampires, and dropped a few of my own into the middle of the space between dividers where they rolled into the cracks of the stone flooring.

James led us away from the music and to the other end of the sprawling space where a harried-looked vampire lined up chairs in front of a podium.

"Where are the rest of the chairs?" the organizer said, turning her red eyes on James. "I told those idiots we needed at least fifty more." She threw her hands up in the air. "Why do I even bother? We should just make the newbies stand."

"Now, now, Erin. We wouldn't want our guests to feel unappreciated, would we?" James put an arm around her shoulder and led her a short distance away as he spoke in calming tones.

"Look at all these chairs," Elyssa said, her gaze running up and down the rows. "There must be over a hundred of them."

"Maybe it's for everyone here," Ash said, uncertainty plain on his face.

I glanced back at the crowd of vamps raising the roof in sync with the game. Cold apprehension gripped my insides. If every chair represented a super vamp, unaffected by flashers, we'd have our hands full. Coupled with the armed noms patrolling the grounds, I wasn't sure our plan had a good chance of succeeding. "Do you see Max or Barclay?" I said, scanning the area.

Elyssa shook her head. "Not a sign."

"Maybe they're upstairs?" Nyte said.

I glanced at James. He and Erin had wandered further away. "Let's check out the vamps at the other end. Act casual."

A long table bore cups of red liquid and an assortment of chips and dips. Nyte picked up a cup and took a sip. He laughed. "Kool-Aid."

I tried a tentative sip myself. It was cherry flavored. "You've got to be kidding me." I piled a plate with chips along with the others and we moseyed down to the dancing vampires, doing our best to act like casual observers.

While Nyte and Ash watched two vampires do the Running Man in time with the music, Elyssa and I looked at the faces of the participants. One or two looked vaguely familiar, probably because I'd fought or run from them at some point over the past few months. One thing was clear—neither Maximus nor Barclay were in the room, unless they were hiding in one of the partitioned areas. Elyssa seemed to be a step ahead of me. She motioned toward the haphazardly arranged dividers with her head, and moved down the row, looking in each one she passed on the right.

I followed her lead, taking the ones on the left. As I passed by the area where the corridor down the middle of the room intersected with the door leading back upstairs, I saw a man hurry past, heading straight across the room toward the entrance to the crypt. Unlike most of the fashionably attired residents, this man looked disheveled. Something about his clothes seemed wrinkled. Or maybe they just seemed to hang unnaturally on his pale, doughy—

"Holy crap," I hissed, making a beeline for Elyssa.

She turned from inspecting a cubicle and raised an eyebrow. "What?"

"Bigglesworth just passed through here." I motioned my head toward the crypt door. "He headed downstairs."

"Are you sure it's the same guy? Wasn't he with Artemis in Colombia?"

"Unless he has a twin with the complexion of a marshmallow, yeah."

She put a hand to her chin. "He's spreading himself pretty thin."

"Considering he's really just a ball of goo, I guess he's capable of handling it." I edged toward the divider hiding the crypt door, looking up and down the center aisle for James or any suspicious vampires.

"Justin, this is Bella," said a static distorted voice in my ear. "Can you hear me?"

I resisted the urge to put a finger to my ear and said, "Yeah, but barely."

"—move…new position. –thing interfering…very powerful….careful!" came the garbled reply.

"What?"

No response. I spotted Ash and Nyte looking around the room. "We can't go without telling them where we are," I told Elyssa. "Hang on." I sauntered up to my friends, trying to look casual.

"Dude, this is the best party ever," Nyte said when I reached him. "I think I'm actually going to do it, man."

"Do what?"

"Compete in a dance-off."

I groaned. "Seriously? We're not here to party, in case you forgot."

His expression sobered. "Oh. Yeah."

Ash gave me a serious look. "So, what's next?"

I glanced around, certain with all the sensitive vampire ears around me, it would have been impossible to say anything privately without the insanely loud booming of the dancing game. "Elyssa and I are going into the crypt to check something out. You two stay up here and watch our backs. If anything happens, you have to get out of here and warn the others. Bella's little worm radio trick isn't working very well, so I might not be able to use it."

The two nodded.

"And if you can find out how many people they've given the vampire potion to, that'd be huge."

"We'll ask around, casual-like," Ash said.

I locked eyes with Nyte. "Look, I know how tempting it is to cut loose. These guys look like a barrel of laughs, but they're not. We're in the middle of enemy territory, and the door we came in through is the only way out."

My friend's face paled even more than usual for his ginger complexion as he looked to the door leading up and out of the house. "Don't worry, Justin. I won't let you down."

"Be careful," Ash said, his eyes big and worried.

I flashed a quick grin. "Ah, we'll be fine. Just do what I said, and everything will come out peachy keen." I didn't, for a moment, believe a word of what I'd just said.

Elyssa waited behind the divider at the door. The keypad was still fried, probably from the last time I'd been through here and knocked power out in the entire building with a flubbed attempt at using magic to get through the electronic lock. She looked down the dim passage beyond the metal door. Back at me.

Dread Nemesis of Mine

It was time to enter the belly of the beast.

Chapter 37

Elyssa took a step inside. Paused, and turned to me. "You know this could be a trap. Once we're down there, there's nowhere else to go."

My guts felt like a wildcat was trapped inside and trying to get out as I stared down the spiral staircase. Terrifying memories coiled around my mind. I froze at the first step, fear riding my back. Elyssa looked at me and nodded.

"I feel it too," she said. "God knows I almost died down here." She took my hand. Squeezed it. "But my hero saved me."

I blew out a breath. "Well, your big hero is scared." With an effort of will, I pushed myself across the threshold. Kissed her hand. "Let's kick some ass." My bowels still didn't appreciate being thrust into danger, but I was the boss of them, dagnabbit, and there was no way I was going to let them mess up a nice pair of jeans.

We crept our way down the winding staircase and reached the crypt—or what used to be the crypt. Instead, the area, where before there had been tombs, skeletons, and all sorts of other creepy stuff, was a bare dirt floor and building supplies. Crates of floor tiles, bundles of lumber, and an assortment of tools like nail guns and power saws sat in neat piles. Someone had strung up lights on a wire leading around the corner and presumably into the cave beyond. Despite the new construction, a musty, dank odor still hovered in the air—a smell I much preferred to the fresh aroma of rotting vamplings we'd encountered the last time.

Elyssa crouched and peeked around the corner. Motioned me to follow. The corridor beyond was clear of coffins up to a point. Beyond lay a pile of rotted wood, stone, and skeletal remains. Her face went livid. "That son of a bitch. Clearing out the dead like they're trash."

I pointed to a tall stack of wooden crates, some stamped with "Property of United States Military" on them. "He's trying to build an armory. Just like in Bogota."

Voices echoed from farther down. While I couldn't make out what they were saying, it was evident someone was seriously ticked off. We skulked onward, using crates and refuse piles as cover until we reached a place where the old crypt ended and the natural environs of a cave took over. Several figures gathered in front of an outbuilding I recognized—the one Maximus had used to imprison my father. The string of construction lights hung to the sides of the cave, illuminating the small group.

A tall man in a top hat and suit, appearing like someone out of a classic movie, stood with his back to me, an ivory cane in one hand. Beside him stood the pale form of Bigglesworth.

"I daresay you have failed us most miserably, Maximus," the man said in a southern genteel accent. "If not for the patience of our patroness, I would have already ended your little rebellion."

"Patience?" Maximus spat. "You mean insanity. That crazy bitch doesn't know her head from her ass half the time."

The man stiffened. "I suppose I should expect such disrespect from your ilk."

"You want I should teach him some manners, sir?" Bigglesworth said, his fist swelling to grotesque proportions as he pressed it into his hand.

"No, Mr. Bigglesworth. I believe it would be a waste of time."

Maximus showed his teeth. "I'd like to see you try, goo-ball."

The man rapped his cane against the floor. "Did you ever stop to think what a vampling plague would do to the mortal realm?" He paused for a second. "Centuries of planning wrecked because you couldn't control your ego, sir. Humanity reduced to worthless rotting corpses. What use would the Brightlings have for the walking dead, I ask?" He didn't wait for an answer, instead, lashing out in a blur with his cane to smack Maximus in the head. The end of the cane rapped against the floor again. "Why, no use at all, *sir*."

Maximus reeled from the attack as dark blood welled from a cut on his cheek. He growled. Lunged. His body smacked against an invisible barrier, the only evidence of its existence a ripple in the air.

"What in Heaven's name is this about?" said a voice to the side of us.

I nearly had a heart attack as Barclay strode in from our left. Had he not been so focused on the unfolding drama between Maximus and the rebel South, he would have seen Elyssa and me before we dropped flat on our stomachs behind another set of crates about twenty feet to his right. The vampire wore a bowler and a suit which matched the other man's in that it looked out of an era long past. He adjusted his monocle as he slowed his stride to a saunter.

Barclay stopped a few feet from the other man, tweaked his oiled moustache, and said, "Mr. Conroy, I will know the meaning of this visit and why you're provoking my protégé."

I almost gasped out loud, instead, sucking in a breath, an even bigger mistake as dust went up my nose thanks to the close proximity of my face to the ground. Pinching my nostrils in an attempt to prevent a sneezing fit, I looked to Elyssa with watering eyes. Her mouth hung slightly open, eyes tight with apprehension.

Somehow, I avoided the classic sneeze and give away your position scenario and climbed cautiously back to my knees to peer over the crates as Barclay took up a stance to Conroy's left.

"Mr. Barclay, so *good* of you to put in an appearance," Conroy said, turning to present his thin profile to me. He wore a graying mustache, long goatee, and a pair of round spectacles on a nose of generous proportions. He immediately made me think of Mark Twain. I figured my mom must look like Mrs. Conroy, because she looked nothing like this guy.

Barclay ignored the jibe. "Again, I ask you, sir, what is the meaning of this intrusion?"

"I believe that to be rather evident," Conroy said, spreading his arms. "My disciples have spent countless days cleaning up the messes left behind by this fool. Already, we have quashed five different outbreaks of vampling plagues where he has attempted to convert people into vampires despite his obvious inability to do so." He shook his head as if to exaggerate his disappointment. "And let us not forget Bogota. Had a plague descended upon such a large populace, the results would have been catastrophic." He leaned forward on his cane. "Just what, may I ask, do the vampires intend to use as a food source should humanity fall victim to such a plague?"

"I believe our original deal with Daelissa was to sow chaos, Conroy." Barclay took off his monocle and polished it on a handkerchief. "I fail to see the problem."

"I'm rather surprised a vampire of your age doesn't grasp the obvious, sir. We have cautioned you to keep your protégé under control. We have, time and time again, told you a vampling plague is unacceptable. You then created a serum and used it willy-nilly in the mortal population without properly testing it to see the results, ending up with a massacre at a high school when your recruiter turned into a vampling."

"Blah, blah, blah," Maximus said. "How was I supposed to know the serum would have that effect? Besides, no lasting harm came out of it."

"Oh, I disagree," Conroy said. "An unknown third party with access to quicksilver cleaned up the mess. I even found out from police reports my grandson was party to this debacle."

Grandson? It felt so bizarre hearing this man I'd never met—or at least remembered meeting—spoke of me like a family member. Hearing a third-party recounting how poor Brad Nichols had been infected with the vampling curse seemed even stranger.

Barclay flicked aside the criticism with a hand. "Yes, well, with any great undertaking, mistakes are bound to happen, Conroy. How do you Americans say it—ah, yes. To make an omelet, you must first break some eggs."

"Exactly," Maximus chimed in. "And don't forget it was you people who asked us—" he jabbed a thumb at his chest, "—for help. Your crazy angel chick begged us to help her. And that's what we've been doing."

"Daelissa never begged, boy. Your organization was starved for money and you, Mr. Barclay, feared for your life." Conroy sighed and shook his head. "No, I'm afraid the experiment is over. We have fingers in enough other pies that your organization is no longer needed. If anything, it has become a threat to the greater good."

"Then, by all means, Mr. Conroy, take your leave, and consider our business concluded," Barclay said, waving a hand toward the exit. "I think you can see yourself out."

Conroy put both his hands atop his cane and smiled. "Perhaps you misunderstand, gentlemen. Your organization is far too dangerous to leave to its own designs. The Red Syndicate, despite its many flaws, does an excellent job keeping youngsters from trying to spread their gift prematurely, if at all. Not only do you two not care about the dangers, but you have done nothing to educate your group of renegades about the dangers of the vampling plague." He put hand on his chest. "I feel we bear some responsibility for not seeing that potential pitfall."

"Are you threatening us?" Barclay said.

"You've got one way out of here, old man," Maximus said. "And that's through me and my people. So why don't you shut your mouth and haul your old ass out of here before I call down a hundred vampires to tear you and pudding boy to shreds?"

Conroy took off his spectacles and stowed them inside a front pocket. "I do apologize for the necessity of this, Barclay, but we have recognized the error of our alliance with you and have decided an amputation and cremation is the most effective solution."

Elyssa and I exchanged horrified glances. What the hell did this mean?

Barclay's calm composure faltered. "Surely that's a bit extreme. W-w-we could come up with procedures to alleviate your concerns."

"Oh?" Conroy leaned back and regarded the other man. "And if I told you the only way we would consider your proposal is if you handed us your associate's head on a plate?"

Maximus tensed, his burning red eyes going back and forth between Barclay and Conroy. "You aren't seriously listening to this jerkoff are you, Master? He's bluffing us."

"I'm sorry, son, but these people do not bluff." Metal rasped as Barclay whipped a long blade from his cane and flashed it at Maximus's neck.

Elyssa and I both gasped.

Maximus blurred. An explosion boomed through the cavern. Barclay's head turned into red mist. The sword dropped from limp fingers as his headless corpse tumbled to the floor. The big pistol in Maximus's hand snapped to Conroy.

It boomed several more times until clicking empty. Half a dozen smashed bullets hovered a foot from Conroy's face before dropping harmlessly to the ground.

Maximus roared and dove at the Arcane, pressing ineffectually against thin air. Apparently realizing the futility of this, he did a one-eighty and ran for it.

"I'll get him, Bigdaddy," said a girlish voice. Maximus jerked like he was on a rubber band and popped backwards, sliding across the rough stone floor to stop at the feet of a blonde girl.

At the feet of my sister, Ivy.

Chapter 38

Maximus pulled out what looked like a phone and tried to speak. The device shattered in his hand. He lashed out at Ivy with his fist. I flinched. Felt myself jerk to my feet. A steel grip grabbed my belt and tugged me back down to the floor.

"Stay down!" Elyssa hissed.

When I looked back, I realized it was no contest. Maximus floated helplessly in the air before my sister. Foam flecked his mouth as he screamed in impotent rage.

"Very good, sweetheart," Conroy said, patting Ivy's shoulder and smiling.

"Can I do the spell?" she said. "Please Bigdaddy? Please?" She bounced on her toes and clasped her hands together.

He pulled the spectacles back from a pocket and put them on. "I do believe you're ready, young lady." Cane held out to his side, he tapped it twice on the ground. The ends popped out, extending it into a long ivory staff with the bust of a winged angel atop it.

Ivy took the staff, and pulled out what appeared to be an arcphone. Holding the staff before her, she rotated slowly before stopping. "There's a large ley line underneath us like you said, Bigdaddy. I should have all the power I need." She giggled. Calmed herself and took on an expression that seemed far too serious for a girl her age. She set the arcphone on the ground and touched a finger to it. The air around her flickered, tiny particulates of smoke or fog rising from the ground to form complex patterns and symbols circling in the air around her.

Maximus's eyes went saucer-shaped as the patterns took shape. He squirmed and thrashed, all to no effect.

Conroy motioned to the doughy man beside him. "Mr. Bigglesworth, why don't you run upstairs and make ready for our departure?" He retrieved a pocket watch from his vest and looked at it. "It shouldn't be long."

"I'm on it, guvnah." On his way out, he leaned down and picked up Barclay's brain-spattered bowler off the floor. Brushed it off, and perched it atop his head.

I peered closer, focusing on one of the large symbols floating around Ivy, and felt my chest contract. "Oh crap."

"What is it?" Elyssa asked, crouching.

"She's using the mass kill spell. The one that'll wipe out every vampire in range."

"How wide of a radius?"

I shook my head. "I have no idea." Panic rose as I thought of Ash and Nyte upstairs. "For all I know it could take out every vampire in Atlanta."

More of the misty substance swirled from the ground in a torrent, some of it forming a mosaic of symbols in the air, while Ivy seemed to absorb the rest into her body. It took me a moment to realize what the mist was. It was magical energy. I shifted into incubus mode, using the alternative eyesight it gave me. Motes of energy drifted around the room, just like I'd seen while Maximus's prisoner. The energy pouring into Ivy was almost too bright to look at.

Cutting off the sight, I turned to Elyssa. "Do you see the white mist?"

She nodded. "Why? What is it?"

"Magical energy." I let out a breath. "She's drawing in so much, even you can see it."

"What do you want to do?" Elyssa's troubled gaze bore into mine.

Uncertainty clouded my mind. My mouth opened to speak, but nothing came out. I had absolutely no idea how to approach this. Conroy and Ivy had made Maximus their little bitch. Against the two of them, I had no chance. But if Ivy completed the spell, she might kill my friends, not to mention a lot of freshly minted vampires. My heart felt like lead. How could my little sister commit such an atrocity? This was mass murder! What kind of monster had my grandparents turned her into? For all I knew, she'd finish the spell within seconds and it would be too late to do anything.

Power and energy coalesced around her, white and humming and violent. The cavern buzzed like a million bees in my head. The vampling infection in my leg throbbed like an alien organism, pulsing in time with the massive energies racing toward destruction.

There was only one thing I could do. Only one thing.

I turned to Elyssa. Gripped her shoulders, and took in her face one last time. "You have to get everyone out. Tell them to run as far and as fast as possible." A shuddering breath worked through me. "I'm going to buy them time."

Her face blanched. "Buy them time? Justin, you can't—"

I shook my head. "I have to. Don't argue with me, Elyssa."

"But—"

"We don't have time." I kissed her, pulling her hard against me. Savoring the feel of her soft lips against mine. Wishing to god I didn't ever have to let her go. Before she could say another word of protest, I dashed down the right wall of the cave, keeping low and circling around behind dear old Granddad and my sister.

I grabbed a couple of rocks off the floor. Conroy stood behind Ivy and to the side. If, by some miracle, I could conk him on the head, I might be able to knock out Ivy as well. I hated the idea of hitting a little girl, but I was out of options. I caught a glimpse of Elyssa slipping away, hugging the wall, and heading upstairs. This was it. All or nothing.

I sneaked as close as I dared, about twenty feet behind my grandfather. Cocked back my arm. Aimed. Whispered a prayer, and threw. The rock blurred toward his head.

The man tensed, his back going straight. The projectile bounced off the air, leaving a gentle ripple. He turned, an amused look on his face.

"My, my, what a surprise." He regarded me for a moment. "You certainly have a way of turning up most unexpectedly, boy."

My body stiffened in anticipation of retaliation, but I still had the presence of mind to do what I could to stop this. "Ivy, don't do it! Don't murder all those people!"

Though her back was to me, I could heard her chanting something, almost under her breath as she guided the staff through an intricate series of patterns. The nimbus of energy brightened around her, swirling. One of the complex runes in the air flashed red and magical energy soaked into it, drawing off the waist-high vortex of energy around her until it was gone. The rune stayed bright, humming and vibrating the air like the deepest note on a string bass.

She paused, taking a deep breath, and wiping sweat from her forehead. Turned and faced me. A smiled lit her face. "Justin, you came to watch!"

I felt an incredulous look yank my eyebrows up. "Don't kill those people Ivy. This is wrong. It's not a game."

She snorted and waved off my statement like a pesky fly. "People? They're *vampires*, Justin. Bloodsucking demonic parasites. And if they start a vampling plague, that'd be a bummer."

"They're not all evil."

"Listen to him, kid!" Maximus said, flailing against the invisible forces holding in in the air. "Vampires are people, too!"

Ivy wrinkled her nose. "You want to protect *him*, Justin?" She grimaced, as if she'd just bitten into a lemon. "It's so sad." Her blue eyes softened. "You're evil, too, and you can't even admit it. Maybe that's why you want to protect them."

"Excellent line of reasoning, my little dumpling," Conroy said, smiling with what seemed genuine affection. "Now, why don't you get back to the task at hand?" He checked his pocket watch again. "Your grandmother is making some of her famous angel food cake for dessert tonight, and I am famished."

My sister's eye went wide with delight. "Oh, I love angel food cake, Bigdaddy!" She turned back to the hovering symbols, eyes focused on another rune, and began chanting again.

"You stupid son of a—" Maximus's mouth slammed shut. His eyes bulged, but he seemed incapable of saying another word.

"I will not have your foul mouth running off in front of my granddaughter any longer," Conroy said.

While Conroy seemed distracted with Maximus, I mustered every last ounce of speed I had, and blurred toward Ivy. I hadn't gone five feet when something yanked me off the ground, and jerked me back, suspending me in the air like Maximus.

"Haven't you caused enough trouble in the past few months, boy?" Conroy said.

"Me?" I said, pinching my forehead. "Now, that's the pot calling the kettle black." I wriggled, and only succeeded in spinning myself upside down. It was like floating in space—a sensation I might have appreciated at another time.

"I suppose our little plan to deliver you into Maximus's hands wasn't the best we've ever come up with," Conroy said, regarding me as one might an interesting zoo specimen.

My heart almost broke. "Ivy helped?" I asked, a bitter taste in my mouth.

"But of course she did, boy."

I looked to Ivy, but she was too busy powering the next rune.

Conroy shrugged. "If it's any consolation, she didn't want us to outright kill you." A frown tugged on his lips. "Truth be told, even if you are one of those filthy spawn, you *are* my"—he shuddered—"grandson."

I didn't know what to feel. Rage, grief, and fear swarmed through me, leaving my insides a conflicted mess. The dark poison inside my leg ached and burned, tingling all the way down my toes and up to my waist. No matter what happened here today, I suspected I didn't have much time left.

"You do realize Ivy has the same parents, right?" I said, mustering some venom. "She's as much spawn as I am."

He chuckled. "In that, you are quite mistaken, boy. She takes after her mother." His gaze turned to Ivy. "I do believe our conversation is at an end." He flicked his hand toward me and something clamped my mouth shut. I could still breathe through my nose, but no matter how hard I tried, I couldn't pry my jaws open, not even using my hands.

The time for pleading was at an end. Now I had to do something. But what?

Anything physical was out of the question. Even if I managed to build up enough rage to manifest into my demon form, all the strength in the world wouldn't matter if I couldn't touch the ground or move.

It occurred to me I might have one powerful tool at my disposal, and extended my incubus senses, hoping I might be able to upset her concentration at the very least. My essence reached toward her aura. The swirling energy around her masked, it but I knew it was there. But as it reached her, it found only a void. Every attempt I made to latch on was like grasping at thin air. She was either shielded, or had some way of protecting herself. I grunted in frustration and withdrew my tendril.

No good, damn it!

The only avenue left to me was magic. Considering the amount of raw power my sister wielded, and how effortlessly Conroy had snared me, I knew, without a doubt, I had very little chance of pulling off anything. If I was lucky, I might manage another fireball. But I had to choose a target. A fireball would undoubtedly burn the hell out of whoever it hit, but it was likely Conroy still had a shield around him. If dear old Granddad did have a shield, the element of surprise would be lost. I wondered if he might also be shielding Ivy. I wondered how terrible I'd feel for burning my sister. She was still so young. The Conroys had brainwashed her all her life, twisting her into a little monster. I didn't want to be responsible for destroying her physically.

I don't have a choice.

Peering hard at Conroy, I tried to see if the air was rippling around him. I switched to incubus view, but the brightness of the swirling energy overwhelmed everything else. I could just barely make out the outline of something around me, but only because it was so close. I suspected it was whatever force Conroy had used to keep me in place.

Extending a tendril toward the vortex of energy around Ivy, I opened myself up to it. The shock of so much raw power hit me like a wall. I blacked out for a second. My vision flickered. Nausea churned up my throat. Puking would be the worst thing possible with my mouth clamped shut. I withdrew my probe, cutting off the flow with a gasping snort. Something wet dribbled on my lips. I touched a finger to them and saw blood.

Power pulsed in my veins. I felt as though I might explode with energy. I tried to concentrate on Ivy, but my vision swam. My head lolled to the side and my eyelids fluttered. I was drunk on magic, or else so sick with it, I wanted to spew.

No, dammit. Concentrate! Do it!

I clenched my teeth tight. Balled my hands into tight fists. Glared at Ivy. Imagining a fireball was easy. Imagining it engulfing the lithe figure of my little sister was hard. So damned hard. God, I didn't want to do this. But I had to. I had to.

Using every last shred of willpower, I imagined the fireball, white hot, and laser-fast blasting Ivy to the ground. Something built inside me. My head roared with power. And then the next rune sucked in the vortex of energy around Ivy. As the air around her cleared, a faint bluish ripple became visible. I looked to Conroy and, without the blinding energy present, could see the same thing around him. They were definitely both shielded.

Relief spread through me, so powerful it almost erased the sick churning feeling in my stomach. At the same time, despair took hold. This was hopeless. I couldn't do anything to stop her.

I was done.

Chapter 39

Fighting back useless anger, I looked at the symbols in the air, my incubus senses still highlighting the magical energy in the room. Ivy wiped her forehead. Her face looked pale. Dark rings underlined her eyes. The effort of casting this spell seemed to be wearing her down. I dared to hope she might be too tired to finish it, but even that was false hope. Our grandfather wouldn't have a problem taking over and completing it.

As I stared at the last remaining rune, I realized it was the one Adam had identified as the killing rune. The other symbols floating in the air flickered. I had the strangest sensation I could read them, if only I looked at them a certain way. They had to be Cyrinthian. My demonic side seemed well-versed in the language. Unfortunately, I didn't have a way to summon those lingual abilities at will.

A thought occurred to me. The desperate thought of a person who has run out of time and with nothing left to lose. Reaching inside me, I let the anger and frustration free. I let the incubus within loose. Focusing on Conroy, I reminded myself of all he'd done. Stolen my sister. Brainwashed her. Betrayed me to Maximus. Anger piled upon hate and grew to rage. Blinding red fury washed across my eyes and a skull-piercing headache cracked into my head with all the force of a boulder. I touched my forehead and felt the tiny points of horns.

My eyesight shimmered as I crossed the threshold from somewhat human to demonic. Some of the symbols suddenly held meaning for me, clear as reading about Dick and Jane. But there was so much to read. My gaze locked onto the last rune. Even with this new understanding, it looked like a mass of gibberish. As the spell rotated around Ivy, I realized with a start, I had been viewing the rune from the back. With it facing me from the front my vision zoomed in until I could see the hundreds of tiny symbols creating the pattern, almost like ASCII art.

It was like looking at a picture with two different images hidden inside it. Like seeing a face on the surface of the moon. The meaning of the pattern clicked inside my head. I traced the symbols until I found one tiny part that held the meaning of the rune together and defined it. I willed it to vanish, but the single character was bound by the symbols around it, held into form by the magic used to create it in the first place. Digging inside, I pulled up every shred of energy I'd absorbed, but no matter how hard I tried, I couldn't erase any part of it. Doing so would erase the rune and cause a vacuum, some part of me realized. There was too much energy bound in the spell to allow it.

But there was an alternative. One thing that might work. Instead of erasing the tiny symbol holding the rune together, I could add a tiny slash through the center, like changing the letter "C" to an "E". It took everything I had just to make one tiny mark. As my will finished adding the slash, I collapsed—or at least would have if I hadn't been held captive in Conroy's anti-gravity field.

Ivy was already summoning more energy, renewing the vortex around her as she started the incantation to power the last rune. To commit mass murder. As exhaustion took hold of me, my demonic sight flickered off. Tiny nubs fell from my forehead as my manifestation aborted itself. I had done all I could. I hoped.

Knowing my luck, I'd come up with an even better idea after the fact and curse myself. Like the time Phyllis Jenkins had called me a loser during recess in eighth grade, and by the time I came up with what I should have retorted, it was already lunchtime.

I wondered how Elyssa was doing and prayed she'd been able to evacuate the place in case my plan failed.

The last rune burst into red light. Energy washed across the cavern as the powered runes glowed with the brilliance of a small sun. Ivy, a look of triumph and pride on her face, placed the staff in the center of the runes and shouted a word. Bolts of white energy speared into the staff. A sphere of power gathered atop the ivory shaft, growing larger and larger. It floated up into the air, gathering size until it was the size of a watermelon.

It exploded.

A wave of energy washed over me like the mother of all static electricity charges. The hairs on my arm and head prickled straight up with the sensation of needles all over my skin. The prickles across my lower regions made me glad I at least didn't have back hair to add to it.

Light bulbs exploded. The air thundered. Whatever had been supporting me cut out and I tumbled to the ground, my jaws suddenly free.

For a moment, there was only darkness. Then some of the surviving light bulbs flickered back on. Ivy lay in a heap in the middle of the floor, the staff beside her. Conroy noticed I was free, and flicked his hand, sending me back up in the air again. He scooped up Ivy, his staff, and her arcphone.

She lifted her head. "Did I do it, Bigdaddy?" Her voice sounded tired.

He smiled. Kissed her forehead. "Yes you did, my little angel. Yes you did."

"Can I have cake now?"

Conroy laughed. "All you want, honey." He looked at me. "Well, boy. I just don't know what to do with you. I hesitate to leave you alive, lest your mischief completely derail our plans, and the Foreseeance—" He broke off as if coming to a conclusion. Sighed. "It pains me to do this. Truly it does. But I see no other choice. I know you're an abomination—all your kind are—but this is the only way." He regarded me for a long moment, and then chanted something.

My jaw clamped shut again. My nose pinched tight. I couldn't breathe. Couldn't draw another breath. Terror slammed into me and my heart raced.

"Your kind is very difficult to kill, but even if you somehow manage to survive without oxygen, I suspect you'll be too brain damaged for even your remarkable healing abilities to fully repair the damage. I know it's a terrible way to go, but I much prefer it to— ahem—other methods."

He made a motion with his hand like tying a knot. "Rest in peace, boy." He turned and left, leaving me suspended in the air.

I knew from experience I could hold my breath for a long time, having performed an underwater tour of terror at Thunder Rock, holding my breath for minutes. But I had the sinking feeling this spell wouldn't free me until I was stone-cold dead. Drawing upon the final shreds of will I had left, I extended my incubus senses so I could see the magical energy.

Ghostly patterns hovered before my eyes. I could tell they covered my nose and mouth, but when I touched my face with my hands, they went through the insubstantial binding magic. I tried to soak in the energy around me, but spots danced before my eyes, and dizziness made it impossible to concentrate. Again and again I tried to will the spell off of me, but nothing I did had any effect.

Time slipped from seconds into minutes.

Consciousness left me little by little.

I was going to die, and there was nothing I could do about it.

Goodbye, Elyssa. I love you.

A bright flash startled me. Arms enfolded me and pulled me to the ground. I looked up with blurry vision and saw bright blonde hair cascading down from a face I couldn't make out.

The pressure on my nose and mouth abruptly vanished. I sucked in a long breath of air, gasping and panting for precious oxygen as my brain screamed and pounded with pain.

When my eyesight cleared I looked into clear blue eyes and the concerned face of my mother.

Chapter 40

"Mom?" I said, rubbing my eyes and looking again to be sure I was really seeing her and not some hallucination brought on by brain damage from oxygen deprivation.

She nodded, tears clouding her eyes, and pressed her hand to my face. "I'm so sorry, Justin. So sorry." She sobbed harder. Tears dripped onto my face.

I sat up. My head hated me for it, throbbing with pain, but I let it wash right through me. "What—how—why?" I had no idea what to ask first. The last time I'd seen her she told me that Dad and I were no longer part of her family. That she never wanted to see us again.

She shifted into a kneeling position, wiping away the tears, and pulling a tissue from a pocket in the pants she wore. "I wish I could answer those questions, Justin. But I can't." She leaned forward and gripped me in a tight hug, kissing my cheeks and holding me for so long, I wasn't sure she'd let go.

Without thinking, I returned the hug and felt tears burning in my eyes.

She does love me. She really does.

"I can't stay, darling," Mom said after a long moment. "I'm risking too much by coming here, but I couldn't stand by. I just couldn't." She planted another kiss on my forehead. "Just know that no matter what you hear or find out, I love you with all my heart, and I'm proud—so proud—you're my son."

"Please don't go, Mom," I said my voice sounding like a little kid. "Dad's going to marry Kassallandra, and Ivy is brainwashed, and—and I don't know what to do. I don't know how to stop it all. Everything is crazy and the world doesn't make any sense!"

A smile shined through her tears, and she laughed. "Honey, if I knew the answers any better than you, I wouldn't hesitate to fix everything for my little boy." She caressed my cheek. "Everything I've had to do has been so hard. To see the way you looked at me that day—" she choked up. Turned her head away. "I'm afraid it won't get any easier from here, and I don't want you relying on me." She put a finger on my chest. "You have all the power you need right here, son. No matter what anyone else tells you, I believe you can do anything once you put your mind to it."

"Considering all the school I've missed, I'll probably have a really bad report card, though."

Another laugh escaped her lips, and she shook her head. "You and that sense of humor." She sighed. Kissed me on the cheek. "Good bye. For now."

Light flashed, blinding me for a moment, and before I could say another word, she was gone. I looked around the dim cavern. At the flickering lights. Maximus's body lay feet away. Aside from that, I was alone.

Stumbling forward, I found Maximus's pistol lying on the floor and picked it up. The magazine was empty. I wasn't sure what lay upstairs. For all I knew the armed men outside had stormed the place. For all I knew, dead vampires littered the ground.

A cough echoed in the cavern. A groan. Maximus rolled over onto his knees and pushed himself up. He saw me and his eyes went wide. Without pause, he sprang at me with, well, natural speed. Tripped, and fell flat on his face. When he looked up at me again, I saw brown irises glaring at me.

"What the hell?" he said, climbing to his feet and touching his face, his teeth with his hands. "What's wrong with me?" He charged at me again. I grabbed him by the arm like a little child and dragged him after me.

"Just shut up," I said, feeling a giddy delight. It had worked. Holy crap, I'd done it!

I pulled the screaming, cursing, sputtering non-vampire up the spiral stairs after me toward the booming music from the sound system upstairs. When I stepped into the main sleeping chamber, I saw unconscious bodies lying all over the place. I saw James lying in a puddle of drool and leaned down to touch him. He was warm, and a pulse beat in his neck.

The vampires around the dancing game were all out, too. The music shifted from some kind of rap music to a song I remembered from a movie I'd seen during an eighties movie marathon. As the words, *Every time you go, away. You take a piece of me with you*, rang out in the otherwise quiet hall, Elyssa, tired, hair mussed, and with a very concerned look on her face, appeared at the doorway. Blood crusted her ear, and she had an automatic rifle in her hand.

The song seemed oddly appropriate, because a missing piece slid back into my heart at the sight of her.

Maximus squirmed in my grip. "Let me go you mother—"

I popped him on the side of the head and let his unconscious form fall hard on the floor.

Elyssa's eyes grew wide. She dropped the rifle. Raced for me, slamming me against one of the dividers, and kissing me until I gasped for breath.

"I thought you were dead," she said, tears brimming, and in between her kisses, said, "I tried so hard to get everyone out, but none of the vampires would listen. And then the noms with guns locked the place down, and all hell broke loose. Shelton and the others took out the noms guarding the perimeter, and secured them. Then I came back for you, but this bright light blinded me, and all the vampires just dropped dead." She took a breath and glanced at Maximus. "But if Maximus is alive, then—"

"I changed it, Elyssa. The spell—I made it so it wouldn't kill the vampires, just take away the bit that makes them vampires in the first place." A sudden terrible though occurred to me and I looked at her eyes. They burned with their usual violet intensity. "Do you still have fangs?"

She extended her fangs, and touched one. "I guess the spell didn't affect dhampyrs."

I breathed a huge sigh of relief, having completely overlooked that major detail. Even so, the terrible image of losing Elyssa washed over me. The cure to that awful thought was another kiss.

"Haven't we done this all before, love?" said a sultry voice from the doorway.

I turned to see Stacey, a wicked smile lighting her face. "It feels like it, doesn't it?" I shook my head, feeling like everything had come full circle. But I knew we were a long way from the end of all this. I thought of Mom, and my heart nearly burst with the desire to tell everyone. Now wasn't the time. "Ash and Nyte?" I asked Elyssa.

"They tried to run, but the other vampires pinned them down." Her gaze flicked about the large room. "I barely got out to warn the others." She saw something and raced toward the speakers near the huge television. Knelt beside a limp form.

A groan sounded nearby, and one of the vampires—former vampires—sat up, a dazed expression on her face, and looked at me. She sprang to her feet and promptly face-planted against a divider when her legs betrayed her. "Wha—what's going on?"

Seeing her reminded me of the task I'd come here to complete. I ran to Elyssa. Ash and Nyte were slowly coming to, confused expressions on their faces. "Elyssa, can I have the ring?"

She gasped. "In all the excitement, I completely forgot!" Pulled the ring off her finger and tossed it to me.

"What's the problem, darling?" Stacey asked as I ran back for the door to the crypt.

"Uh, keep an eye on these people," I said. "I'll be right back." I flitted down the stairs and back to the corpse of Simon Barclay. My stomach tried to turn inside out at the gruesome scene. Half his head was obliterated, and I didn't even want to think about the bits and pieces lying around. I took out the ring. Held it over him. It didn't so much as flicker.

"No," I said, horror swelling in my chest. "Who else could it be?" I took out one of the diamond-fiber vials Meghan had given me and held it beneath the dripping wound. I heaved. Felt bile climbing up my throat. I'd seen so much horror, it surprised me I still felt this repulsed by a gaping head wound. Then again, maybe that was something I should be happy about.

The vial sealed itself automatically after filling, and I tucked it in my pocket. Wiped excess blood off my hand onto a clean part of Barclay's suit.

Racing back upstairs, my mind hunted for answers. If Barclay wasn't Felicia's sire, who was? I found Maximus's unconscious body lying where I'd left him. Held the ring over him. Nothing. This couldn't be right. I staggered upright, looking about the room, feeling disoriented and clueless. As far as I knew, there weren't any other vampires in Maximus's rebellion who were capable of siring vampires.

Black-suited Templars appeared along with a team of Custodians. Within an hour they had all of the former vampires lined up in the middle of the room. The human security force was taken elsewhere, probably to find out how much they knew about the Overworld.

Ash and Nyte looked unharmed, though their eyes were back to a normal hue, and their fangs, like everyone else's were gone.

Nyte dropped into a chair and propped his chin on his hands, face glum. "Man, this sucks."

"Tell me about it," Ash said, and slumped on a couch.

Someone grunted.

Ash jumped up in surprise as a man burst from his hiding place beneath the sofa cushions and raced for the exit. Nyte bounced to his feet, grabbed the man by the arm, and flung him skidding thirty feet down the center of the room. His eyes went wide as he regarded his hand.

"What the—" He punched a hole in a divider.

Ash tested his strength on another divider. They both hooted with joy.

I looked at the former vampires, a terrible realization hitting me. The spell must have only temporarily taken away their powers.

Bella stopped what she was doing and approached the two of them. "Come here, young man."

Ash gave her an uneasy look, but did as she asked. "You're not going to take it away are you?"

She ran her wand up and down. Her forehead scrunched in confusion. "How odd." She motioned for Meghan to join her. "Can you scan him and tell me what you see?"

The other Arcane twirled her wand. Ash winced as a globule of blood squeezed from a pore. The blood whirled rapidly, separating into plasma and other fluids. Meghan directed her wand at the plasma and made a swishing motion. A gentle blue glow surrounded the plasma. "The serum," she said in a wondering voice. "It used Justin's blood. The spell must have removed the vampirism, but left some incubus enhancements."

"I can seduce women?" Ash said, a hopeful look in his eyes.

Nyte's mouth dropped open, and I could practically see his head filling with the possibilities.

Meghan shook her head. "No, I don't think so. You would have shown signs of it before now. Aside from the obvious strength you've gained, I can't be sure until I run more tests."

Ash backed away a step. "Tests?"

Bella grinned, holding her wand in a tight grip. "Oh yes. And anal probes."

Nyte and Ash went white as ghosts.

Meghan rolled her eyes. "Really now, Bella. Why would I use something small as my wand for anal probes? I use my staff for that."

I wanted to laugh and enjoy the feel-good moment, but I couldn't. Felicia weighed far too heavily on my mind. I pulled Meghan aside. "The ring. It didn't light up around Barclay or Maximus." Her grin vanished. "But who else could it be?"

I looked up and saw Adam coming our way, his face daring to express hope. My heart sank at the thought of dashing his fragile hope to pieces. A buzzing in my pocket startled me from my thoughts. I pulled out my phone and saw *Unknown Caller* flashing on my screen. I answered.

"I see you're staying on task, Justin," said a very creepy, very familiar voice.

My body went rigid. I held up a finger to the others, and walked closer to the booming speakers. "What do you want, Underborn?"

"First, congratulations. Yet again, you've proven yourself quite worthy, young man." I could hear the smile in his voice.

"Get to the point. Elyssa told me all about your offer to her, and how you backed out."

"Yes, well, I gave her certain conditions, and she couldn't meet them in time. I'm sure you understand."

"And you dragged Katie into this mess?" I huffed out a disgusted breath. "Used her feelings for Ash and Nyte to get her to spy for you? And then you didn't even lift a finger to help. You're a slimeball. A cowardly piece of sh—"

"Now, now, Justin," he said, the amusement gone from his voice, replaced by a calm, cold tone. "Perhaps you've forgotten the key."

"You didn't mean for Elyssa to get that," I replied. "And when she did, you lied about it."

"Actually, I knew if I gave it to her, she would be suspicious of the gift."

"Damned right."

"But my reasons were not entirely selfless, I must admit." Underborn chuckled, as if he'd just cracked an amusing joke. "You see, the Relics of Juranthemon sense each other. They're drawn to each other. But they also have minds of their own, it seems. Though I knew another of the relics was near, the key refused to draw me any closer. I suspected you had found another Relic. The one I have been hoping to find for years. You have the map."

I almost laughed into the phone, and pulled a "Nyah nyah, you can't have it" on him, but miraculously stopped myself. "The only map I have is from Triple-A. I know which map you're talking about, though. Elyssa told me all about your little conversation." It occurred to me that Underborn hadn't just made idle conversation about the map. He had *known* it might be nearby thanks to the key. That bastard did everything for a reason.

Underborn sighed. "Justin, I know you have the map. And even if you have another of the relics instead, they will lead me to the map eventually." He paused. "I would like the ey back and the map."

This time, I did laugh. "Screw you. You gave Elyssa the key. She's keeping it."

"I propose an exchange."

"Can I have my life back?" I asked. "Or how about a scholarship to MIT?"

He chuckled. "The second could easily be arranged, though I doubt you'd have much time to enjoy a higher education. No, I have something far more valuable, but time is ticking away before the value of this gift expires."

"Did you buy me an ice cream cone?"

"As usual, young man, I have something far more valuable. Information. But this time, I went a step further. The item my information would have led you to is here. If you meet me in five minutes, I will give you that which you seek."

"And what is that?"

"Felicia's sire."

Chapter 41

My grip tightened around my arcphone. Thankfully, it was a lot stronger than the nom version, and didn't crack under the strain. "Who is he?"

"The correct pronoun would be 'she', Mr. Slade. I will send you a text with a location. You have five minutes to reach the location with the map and key. If I see anyone besides you and your girlfriend, I will vanish. Your friend Felicia will die. Do we have a deal?"

I wanted to roar with frustration.

Instead, I pulled the map and key from my pockets. Stared at them. Using them, figuring out how to make them function together could give us a huge upper hand. We could strike at the enemy from any direction. Go straight where they lived and stop them in their tracks. Each one was priceless. Together, they were even more priceless-er. I glanced over at Adam. Saw the pain in his face as Meghan spoke with him. Saw the hopelessness take the life right out of his expression.

I could just keep the map. Never tell him about this conversation with Underborn. Dammit, we needed every advantage in this conflict, war, whatever the hell you wanted to call it. Giving up the relics meant doing things the hard way. But saving a life—saving Felicia— that would be doing things the *right* way.

"Deal," I said, my voice rough with anger.

I hung up and went over to Elyssa.

Adam, his eyes red, put a hand on my shoulder. "Thanks, Justin." He choked up. "You—you put it all on the line for Felicia, and I'll never forget that." He turned and punched a divider. Dropped his forehead against it. "If I had listened to her. Talked to her, I might actually know who her sire is. I could have saved her. Now it's—it's over."

I gripped his shoulder. "Don't give up just yet. I might have a lead."

He spun, the barest flicker of hope in his eyes. "What is it?"

My phone buzzed with Underborn's text. "No time to explain but I have an option. A deal. Wait here, I'll be right back." I looked at Meghan. "Where are Felicia and Nightliss?"

"At The Ranch. I had them relocated.

"Meet me there. Make sure Nightliss is awake and ready to go."

Meghan gave me a curt nod. "I'll be ready." She handed me a vial. "Just hold this against the sire's skin and it'll draw blood."

"I'm going with you, Justin," Adam said.

I shook my head. "Can't. If anyone but Elyssa is with me, deal's off. Understand?"

He looked like he had plenty more to say, but backed off. Nodded. "I'll be waiting with Meghan." The look of hope in his eyes made me hurt inside.

I looked at the text on my phone. Set my GPS to give me walking directions. Grabbed Elyssa's hand. "Let's go."

We blurred out the back door. The time on my GPS dropped from a one-hour walk to four minutes at the speed we were going. I was going to need every second.

The address was an abandoned building once owned by a power utility. A train rumbled past on tracks less than a hundred feet away. A row of houses lined the curving road on the other side while a chain-link fence with numerous holes provided a weak defense to the red brick structure.

We sped inside. Underborn stood in the middle. Alone.

"The relics, please," he said, holding out a hand.

"Felicia's sire first," I growled.

Underborn paused. "Phissilinth informs me you have come alone." He smiled and my blood went cold. "It's heartening to see you adhering to the terms of our agreement." He motioned with his fingers and a masked man shoved a hooded figure from behind a column.

I pulled out the ring and noticed a dim ember burning inside the gem. As I stepped closer, it brightened until the entire gem glowed.

"She's drugged," Underborn said. "And she won't offer any resistance."

"How did you know we needed Felicia's sire?" I said. "Did Michael tell you?"

He smiled. "No. Naturally, he is not my only resource."

"Then—"

His hand went up in a halting gesture. "I will say nothing more on the matter. I suggest you give me the relics, and return with your prize."

I pulled the map and key from my pockets. The pleasure on his face at seeing the map made me want to punch it right off his stupid head. My leg throbbed as the anger simmered in my blood. An icy stab of fear at having an episode right now drove the anger back into its cave.

Underborn took the relics, and motioned with his head toward me. His helper guided the wobbling form to me. I pulled Meghan's vial from my pocket and pressed it to a bare patch on the captive's arm. Blood welled inside, filling it. I handed it to Elyssa.

"Get back to The Ranch. I'll be right behind you, but don't wait up."

"No need to walk," Underborn said, walking through the door and outside. He pulled a dark green tarp off a humped shape to reveal a red Mini Cooper beneath. "I thought it only polite to provide transportation since—" he check his watch, "—time is ticking." He tossed me the keys. "I recommend, however, you not use it as a daily driver since the previous owner might report it stolen come morning."

A slew of nasty replies popped into my head. "You realize by taking away the relics you're making things a lot harder on me. They would have tipped the balance in our favor."

"Indeed." He rolled his shoulders in a shrug. "You should go. Tick, tock. Tick, tock."

Elyssa climbed into the driver seat. I shoved the captive into the back, took shotgun.

As we sped to The Ranch, my mind spun in an endless circle of reasoning. Why was Underborn doing this? Did he want the relics for his own personal power? Why had he even "helped" me before—if marking my father for death to put me through an elaborate test was considered helping. He seemed to give with one hand and take with the other. He wasn't working for the other side, or I felt quite certain I would be dead or in captivity. He definitely wasn't working for our side either—whatever side that was.

I still couldn't figure it out myself. But I knew I had a decision to make. A very important one.

"You did the right thing," Elyssa said, eyes never leaving the road as she screeched around corners like a banshee, the scenery blurring past. "You've always tried to do the right thing." She made a hard turn and skidded onto the long driveway to Big Creek Ranch. Screeched to a stop in front of the house and turned off the car. Her eyes met mine. "And I love you for it."

Meghan and Adam rushed outside. Elyssa gave Meghan the vial and the healer rushed inside. I grabbed the captive vampire out of the back and hauled her through the door. Nightliss was awake, though bleary-eyed and offered me a gentle smile.

"Are we in time?" I asked, looking at the slumbering form of Felicia on the bed where she lay with only a towel preserving her modesty. Blackened veins claimed her arms and legs, and had snaked up her neck, reaching into her chin. She looked dead.

"We will see," Nightliss said.

I pulled the hood off the vampire. Dark hair spilled across her face. I pushed the hair back to reveal the face of a woman I didn't recognize.

"Please, I need to be alone with her," Nightliss said.

I nodded, and left the drugged vampire lying on the floor. Adam, his face a mix of hope and fear, leaned over and kissed his sister on the forehead before following us out.

As we left the bedroom and headed downstairs, the constant tension gripping my body finally let go. My body ached with the release, and I faltered, almost tumbling down the stairs before Elyssa caught me. A sick feeling churned in my stomach. I rushed into a bathroom and emptied my stomach into the sink, heaving and straining until I collapsed to my knees in exhaustion.

Elyssa knelt, her face inches from mine, eyes full of concern. "Are you okay, babe?"

I gave a weak nod. "Wow, you really must love me," I said, trying not to breathe in her direction.

She smiled. "Whatever gave you that idea, silly?"

"I just puked my guts out, and you're not even complaining about my breath."

A laugh burst from her. "You've smelled far worse, believe me."

"You didn't like my vampling perfume?"

"It was wonderfully aromatic." She combed my hair with her fingers.

A pleasant chill rose on my scalp where she touched me. I curled up and rested my head on her knees, right there on the bathroom floor. "I'm the happiest man in the world right now," I said. "My sexy ninja girl."

I jerked awake with a start. Sat up, and looked at the couch. At the blazing fire in the fireplace.

"Welcome back, sleepyhead," Elyssa said.

I turned and saw her sitting behind me, a pillow on her lap, a book in her hand. "How long?"

"Oh, an hour or so," she said, looking at a clock on the wall. "I had to carry you in here." She set the book aside and touched my cheek. "Are you feeling better?"

I nodded. "I don't feel like barfing, if that's what you mean."

"Meghan checked on you. Said it was magic poisoning."

The healer walked around the corner, a steaming mug of something in her hand. "I thought I heard you." She set her cup down on the coffee table and took a seat in a divan across from the couch, a serious look in her eyes. "Justin, we have to talk."

"Do you know how many times I hear that in a day?" I asked, sitting up straight and rotating my legs off the couch. "When I'm not fighting vampires, someone is giving me bad news." I ran a hand through my hair and sighed. "What's the crisis now?"

She almost smiled, but something like concern tugged the corners of her lips back down into a neutral expression. "It's about the magic poisoning. Can you tell me exactly what happened in the crypt?"

I shrugged. "Sure." I told her all about the encounter with Conroy and Ivy, including how I'd managed to change the spell, altering it to remove the magic intended to make a person a vampire. Try as I might, I couldn't recall how I'd known it, only that the demon side of me knew the lingo.

And then I reached the part about Mom. I hadn't told anyone yet, not even Elyssa. Just thinking about it choked me up with sadness and happiness at the same time. But as I told them, the tears evaporated. I felt...happy. It was strange to feel that way when talking about my dysfunctional family.

"After she told me that, she just *poof*! Vanished into thin air," I said, recounting the last bit of the saga.

Elyssa gasped, a beautiful smile on her lips. "Justin, she was trying to protect you. I couldn't believe a mother would abandon her child like your mom did."

I grinned. "Just when I was ready to give Mom and Dad the 'World's Worst Parents' award." The thought of my dad robbed some of my joy. Either he didn't know about Mom's plans, or didn't care. Far as I knew, he still planned to marry Kassallandra. Damn it, if I'd only had a little more time with Mom. There was so much to tell her and so many questions to ask.

Meghan wore a faint smile on her lips, or maybe it was a joyless smile, because it turned back into a frown. "Justin, when I was examining you closely while you were asleep—"

"You didn't anal probe me with a staff did you?" I said with a wink, trying to lighten her mood.

Again, she gave me a brief, but fleeting smile. "While spawn are capable of using magic, they're usually less powerful than human Arcanes. This is true of other supernatural species who are capable of magic. Why, exactly, that is, I don't know." She rolled her wand between her fingers, looking down at it. "What you and your sister Ivy were doing required a great deal of magic. Channeling that much energy would burn out all but the most powerful Arcanes."

I sat back, confusion pressing in on me. "Well, my mom is supposedly a pretty strong Arcane."

"The Conroys are probably the most powerful Arcanes alive," Meghan said, seeming to agree. "I'm sure they could have channeled this spell. In terms of raw brute force, Shelton might even manage it."

"Shelton?" I glanced at Elyssa. "Is he really that powerful?"

Meghan nodded. "He has, shall we say, potential to be great. But his rogue tendencies and lack of attention to fine control are his undoing." She waved a hand in the air. "But that's not what I want to talk about. The thing is, when I measured your *well*—the nonphysical place in your body where you store magical energy—I discovered you haven't even yet tapped its full potential."

"And this is separate from where I store all my evil incubus power, right?"

She nodded. "Completely separate, as far as I know, although it is a matter of some debate in high circles. Think of it like lungs. You can draw in only so much air. By training your lungs, you can increase their capacity and efficiency." She stopped fiddling with her wand and looked me in the eye. "What I'm getting at, is as you pull in more magic, you'll continue to get these sick spells until your body becomes used to it. But even without reaching the full limit of your well, you've already far exceeded how much energy *I* can draw in all at once."

I arched an eyebrow. "I can suck in more magic than you?"

"It's difficult to quantify the depth of a well. I can only sense its depth, like dropping a stone down a shaft and listening for it to hit bottom."

"So how long is my shaft?"

Elyssa gave me an amused grin.

"Get your mind out of the gutter," I told her.

Meghan cleared her throat. "Perhaps I should skip to the point. From what I can sense of your current ability, your well is at least three times larger than the most powerful Arcanes I have ever treated."

Shock at the revelation drew both eyebrows up my forehead. Pleasure at hearing my own potential curled my lips into a smile. "So, I'm a badass?"

"Justin, the only person I've treated who has that much ability is in the room with Felicia."

I looked around. "Who, Adam?"

Meghan groaned. "No, I'm talking about Nightliss."

I was on my feet before I knew what was happening. "Huh? I have as much power as Nightliss? But that's impossible. She's a freaking angel!"

"Nightliss still has far more power than you, but that's only because you haven't yet found the depth of your ability." She motioned for me to sit down. "What I'm about to tell you next may come as even more of a shock."

I dropped onto the couch, hands in my lap. If I'd had a seatbelt, I would have put it on. "Oh, god," I said. "What is it?"

She looked from me to Elyssa, and chewed on her lip, as though trying to figure out how to say something. Finally, she said, "I'm almost ninety-nine percent positive your mother is not an Arcane."

I laughed. "Of course she is. She freed me from Conroy's spell, and poofed herself out of there."

"Yes, and there's a very good reason why she could do such things. Your mother is like Daelissa and Nightliss. She's an angel."

John Corwin

Chapter 42

I reeled back like she'd just hit me. "Impossible. That would mean the Conroys are angels too. It would mean me and Ivy are—" I couldn't finish the statement.

"You're both part spawn, part angel," Elyssa said, wonder in her voice.

Meghan nodded. "It's impossible to measure the division of your magical heritage, Justin, but considering how developed your spawn side is, and how powerful your magical side is, you've inherited a great deal from both sides of the family. Ivy is obviously extremely powerful considering her age and the ability needed to pull off the spell. Adam measured the shockwave from the anti-vampire spell and told me it went out in about a one-mile radius. If she'd performed it above ground, it's possible it would have extended much farther."

"But if the Conroys are angels, why do they need Daelissa?" I said. "It doesn't make sense."

Meghan stood, tucking her wand into a pouch. "There's a lot that still doesn't make sense. But all the evidence points toward my hypothesis. It's more vital than ever Shelton and Bella train you. Drawing in that much energy without the training to properly focus it is dangerous."

"How could it be dangerous?"

"You know the fireball you shot off while Maximus's prisoner?"

I shrugged. "Yeah."

"Imagine if you'd used enough power to engulf the place in fire, or detonated it like a bomb. You don't know your own potential or the danger you pose to yourself and others, Justin. I suggest you get it under control." She picked up her mug. Took a sip and grimaced.

Took out her wand and stirred the liquid until steam rose from it. "You know, the spell I just used to heat up my tea takes a very precise amount of control and power. Otherwise my tea would evaporate, or the ceramic mug might explode in my face, cutting it to shreds. Or—"

I held up a hand. "Fine, fine, I get it. I'll train." I sighed. "Just what I wanted to do with my free time."

She smiled. "I thought you might see it that way." Her eyes locked onto something behind me, and a genuine smile of happiness split her lips.

I turned and saw Nightliss and Adam walking down the stairs. Adam guided a pale and tired looking woman down the stairs. Felicia. She saw me and smiled, tears sparkling in her eyes. I met them at the bottom of the stairs, giving Nightliss a big hug. Felicia sobbed, and wrapped her arms around me.

"Thank you, Justin. Thank you." She let go, tottering backwards.

I caught her at the same time Adam did. "Whoa, take it easy."

She let Adam help her to the couch. "I don't have much of a choice." The blackened veins had left her skin for the most part, though her pale flesh still looked bruised in places.

Elyssa stepped into the kitchen and returned with a couple of blood bags. Handed them to the recovering vampire. "Drink slowly. I don't want you throwing up blood on the couch." She smiled. "I've had enough with people throwing up today."

"Maybe I should brush my teeth," I said, sticking out my tongue at her.

Meghan took Nightliss aside and spoke with her in quiet tones. The petite angel's eyes went wide and turned to me. I didn't have to hear the conversation to know what they were talking about. They approached me.

"I—I cannot believe this," Nightliss said, touching me as though I might disappear in a cloud of smoke at any moment. "Your mother is one of my people? And you—you're like us too?" A smile of pure joy lit her cute face. "I am not alone with only my crazy sister on this world?"

I cleared my throat. "It doesn't look that way. Now you have crazy old me and *my* insane sister."

"It makes so much sense now," the angel said, mouth widening as if a thought had just occurred to her. "The blonde angel who helped

333

me. Who's been helping others. It must be your mother. Daelissa would never help anyone unless it was part of her goals."

My mouth dropped open. "Whoa." After it had passed, an obvious question hit my brain. "Can you train me, Nightliss? I mean, if you're one of—I mean if I'm one of you, wouldn't it make more sense for you to train me than Shelton and Bella?"

A sad look hijacked her smile. "I cannot be your teacher, Justin. I still have so much to do, and even though I am recovering, I still don't understand some of my own abilities. Understanding comes to me in moments of clarity. Other times, it feels as though I'm surviving on pure instinct. I do not even know how to begin to teach you."

I blew out a sigh, thinking how I'd relied on demon instinct to accomplish things without really knowing how. "I totally know where you're coming from."

A knock sounded on the door. Stacey came through a second later followed by Ryland. He held a grocery bag brimming with food in one arm, and wore a T-shirt with three wolves howling at the moon.

"Sweet shirt," I said, stifling a laugh at the ridiculous thing.

Stacey snorted and covered her mouth.

Ryland seemed unfazed. "Ain't it just the cat's meow?" He traced a wolf with his finger. "Seems my lovely gal decided I needed a T-shirt to illustrate how much testosterone flows through this manly body of mine."

Stacey couldn't hold it any longer and howled with laughter. "I do believe it more than makes up for the leopard print tights you purchased for me, darling."

Ryland's eyes met mine and he winked. "Looks like we all survived again. I'd say this calls for a proper celebration." His gaze moved to Elyssa. "Show me the kitchen?"

Elyssa laughed. "Let me show you the way."

Stacey regarded me a languid smile as her laughter died down. She prowled over to me and kissed me on the cheek. "Hello, handsome."

"Hello yourself, uh, kitten," I said, trying to come up with something witty, and failing.

She looked around the room. "Might I have a moment in private?"

334

I gulped. "Stacey, I have a girlfriend, and, uh, I mean Ryland—"

"Oh, you are such a dear," she said laughing. "I have no plans to sexually assault you, yummy though you are." She purred. "My wolfykins is more than enough to sate my appetite."

My face burned. "Uh, okay."

She led me further back into the house to a large dining room. Closed the door. Her usual confident sultry smile faltered. "Justin, I—this is not easy for me to say."

My heart locked up with apprehension. "What is it? What's wrong?"

She shook her head, eyes downcast. When she looked up, tears rolled down her cheeks. She took my hand and smiled. "Absolutely nothing, darling. I just wanted to say thank you."

"For what?"

A laugh broke through her tears. "You are so lacking in clues at times, you dear, sweet boy." She took a tissue from a pouch at her side and wiped her face. "Before I met you, I was alone. I have wandered this Earth for so long, always so lonely except for my feline companions. I have made friends along the way, true. Bella, as you know, is quite an old friend. But after I met you, things, well, they changed."

"Yeah, if you count me dragging you off into dangerous encounters with people who want to destroy the world."

"Oh, it is quite exciting," she said, nodding. "And I enjoy fighting for a cause. But what I mean by change is so much deeper, love. You brought me in, a lonely stray whose only thought was of living day-to-day. You accepted me. You made me a part of your—dare I say it?—family. I had forgotten what it was like to be loved and cared for. You risked your own life to save me. And without you, I might never have met my love, Ryland." Her face lit up at his name. "Oh, he is a scoundrel, and our relationship is by no means perfect." She purred. "He is a wolf, after all. A very naughty—"

"Uh, I don't think you need to get any deeper into the naughty bits," I said, smiling while my heart swelled to bursting with affection for this crazy woman. "Maybe it's a good thing you assaulted me at the gym."

"Oh, the things I planned to do with you," she said, sniffling into a tissue. "But I'm rather glad things turned out this way. It seems

335

every time I've built up the courage to tell you this, Justin, something comes up, or I falter. I'm not very good at trusting people with my heart." She touched my chest. "But you have a good one, and I trust you. Know that you have my love as much as any brother of mine would have had. If you ever need me or Ryland, we will always be there for you."

I tried to speak, but my throat was suddenly choked up. The sting of tears in my eyes left me wiping furiously at them.

Stacey offered me a tissue.

I took it, sucking in a deep breath to keep the tears at bay.

"Just because you are a super hero doesn't mean you dare not cry," Stacey said, her usual mischievous grin returning. "I promise not to tell anyone."

A laugh broke through the blockade in my throat and a couple of tears pulled a jailbreak, rolling down my cheeks. I pulled her in for a hug. Kissed her on the top of her blonde head. "I love you too, sis. If you weren't older than me, I'd adopt you as my little sister."

"I believe you already have a little sister," she said, her grin fading. "I hope we can help you with that someday, *brother*."

We rejoined the others in the den. The crowd had swelled to include Shelton and Bella, both of whom were apparently trading the day's adventures with Elyssa's mother, Leia. Cinder stood in a corner, hands straight by his sides as he watched the festivities.

"Are you okay?" I asked the golem. "I didn't mean to abandon you at Maximus's place, but Elyssa and I had to get back here."

"I understand, Justin." He attempted a smile, but the result only startled me. His lips snapped back to neutral.

"This guy was a whirlwind," Shelton said, appearing to my side, and clapping a hand on the golem's shoulder. "He disarmed about ten guys before I even cast my first spell."

"I was glad to be of service," Cinder said. "Do you happen to know of any magic spells that could make me real?"

Shelton seemed at a loss for words, glancing back and forth between us.

"I'm sorry," Cinder said after an uneasy moment of silence. "That was meant to be a jest, but the attempt obviously failed."

Shelton and I burst into laughter.

"Or perhaps my attempt succeeded after all," the golem said, tilting his head like a curious puppy. "I must be, as you say, 'getting a handle' on humor."

I turned away from the two, and the laughter faded from my lips. Thomas stood in the kitchen doorway, beer in hand, looking on as Ryland worked his cooking skills. It reminded me a little of the last time I'd had Ryland's cooking. We'd been cooped up in one of Shelton's hideouts, on the run from hellhounds and one of my dad's sisters. Underborn had put a death mark on my dad, and Elyssa and I had gone through hell trying to get him to remove it.

Ah, the good old days.

I looked at today's date on my phone. The good old days had only been a few weeks ago. I really needed a vacation. It also reminded me of a promise I'd made to a certain young lady. A promise I had yet to keep.

Thomas looked over from where he stood. Met my eye. Nodded.

I nodded back.

'Nuff said.

The next night, after a full day of rest and relaxation, I pulled on my best clothes and regarded my short blonde hair in the mirror. I looked pretty badass, I had to admit, even if the coloring looked a bit fake. Oh well, it'd grow out. I stepped into the hallway and walked to the bottom of the stairs. It felt very strange to be staying in the same house as Elyssa's parents.

Elyssa stood at the bottom of the stairs looking stunning in a short, purple dress and high heels threatening to make her taller than me. When I came closer, I realized how perfectly the dress complimented her gorgeous eyes. She even wore makeup that wasn't Goth, enhancing every facet of her face. I felt my mouth hanging open and clamped it shut before drool happened.

"You are so beautiful," I said, taking her hands in mine. I opened my mouth to say more, but couldn't think of a strong enough word to express how I felt at that moment. I loved her so much it hurt.

"Have her home at ten," said a stern voice from behind.

I spun to see Thomas Borathen, cold blue eyes staring at me, and gulped.

"I'm sure ten-thirty would be fine," Leia said, coming up behind him and leaning on his shoulder. "After all, they were out way past midnight last night."

Elyssa rolled her eyes. "Mom, Dad, seriously? Are you trying to give him a heart attack?"

Thomas let out a booming laugh.

Everyone else went wide-eyed with shock.

Elyssa actually looked like she might run for the hills. "Mom, someone's kidnapped Commander Borathen and replaced him with an alien!"

Thomas abruptly stopped laughing. "Eleven o'clock." He pursed his lips. Narrowed his eyes. "Have fun, kids."

Elyssa and I left, chuckling as we made for one of the black Templar SUVs. I drove to the Grotto and led her to Ancient Chinese Secret, one of the nice restaurants I'd seen the last time we'd been there. Supposedly, they had fresh ingredients delivered via the Obsidian Arch every day, and the ratings I'd read on the *Howl* app on my smartphone indicated it was a cool joint.

"I *cannot* believe my dad laughed," Elyssa said for at least the third time as she used chopsticks to shovel lo mein into her mouth. "He probably hasn't done it for at least two centuries." She took a sip of oolong tea and gave me a look. "You have this very mind-bending effect on people. It's like you change them just from being in the vicinity."

"Incubus pheromones," I said, winking. "Not even the men can resist."

She threw a noodle at me. "You'd better not be using those pheromones on anyone but me, Mister."

I laughed. Bit into an eggroll. "This place is really good," I said. "I've eaten a lot of Chinese food, but this place is tops."

Elyssa's eyes turned serious. "My dad said he's sending all the vampires you turned back into noms to the same kind of rehab they usually reserve for noms who accidentally find out about the Overworld. Some of them were suicidal when they found out they were noms again."

"I feel kind of bad about it," I said. "Although, the world is probably better off without a bunch of juvenile vampires gallivanting

338

around without strict guidance. I wonder how many ended up like Ash and Nyte."

"Dad said they rounded up at least twenty, but he's certain there are a lot more. He doesn't even know what to do with them. It's like a whole new class of super."

"Well, they don't need blood, and they don't need to seduce women for food." I shrugged. "Maybe he could train them as Templars?"

"That's one idea. He doesn't want to just cut them loose without guarantees they won't abide by Overworld law." She sighed. "It's a huge mess. I don't even want to think about the ones who weren't in range of the spell."

"Not to mention anyone else Maximus turned that we don't know about."

"With him in prison, there are plenty of vampiric orphans out there. Most of them probably don't know a thing about Overworld law or the Red Syndicate." Elyssa shrugged. "Guess we'll have to deal with them as things happen."

"Any idea how many we're talking about?"

She shook her head. "The Arcanes are digging through Maximus's records for clues. Dash Armstrong put wards on his files, though, so breaking into them will take time."

After dinner, we headed to Arcanus Apparatus, a popular night club. Music boomed from inside, and I was thankful I'd instinctually figured out how to lower the sensitivity of my super hearing so I didn't get a migraine. When we stepped through the vestibule, I gasped at the sight of the dance floor. People our age were boogying in what looked like a magic forest, while unicorns and little glowing fairies zipped through the air, touching magic wands to some couples, causing them to float off the floor with hoots of enjoyment. I saw werewolves and vampires bumping and grinding, and even a couple of supernatural types I didn't recognize.

"Fairies are real!" I said. "And unicorns, oh my god, I want one!"

Elyssa laughed. "This is all illusion, silly." She put her hand up in front of a fairy, but it went right through like a ghost. "And I've already found my unicorn." She gave me a naughty wink before pulling me close for a kiss.

We danced for hours, enjoying the freedom to let go and just be kids again. Somehow, I managed to forget about everything, at least for a little while. When the lights came on and the illusions shut down to reveal a large white room, everyone groaned. I checked the time and almost had a heart attack when I noticed it was almost two in the morning.

A cold ache had settled into my leg, but I did the best to ignore the cancerous curse in my body. For now, it seemed to have stopped spreading, or at least slowed its march through my system. I wondered if my dual nature might afford me some protection from the inevitable, or if I was doomed to watch, helpless, as it consumed me.

Elyssa seemed to catch my change in mood, and her violet eyes filled with concern. "Are you okay?"

I smiled. There was still plenty to be happy about. Plenty to look forward to. "Yep. Just wondering if your dad was serious about that curfew."

She laughed.

"'Scuse me, Your Highness," said a very familiar voice as the crowd squeezed through the doors outside. A hand pressed into my pocket. I tried to grab the hand, but it slipped away like greased putty.

As we stood in the darkness outside, our breaths steaming in the cold night, I looked at what the hand had left. It was a piece of paper. I opened it.

Bigdaddy found out what you did to my spell, bro-bro. Not nice at all! I know you can't help being evil. That means, I gotta stop you. >:(
smoochies -Ivy

Elyssa scowled as she looked at the note. "Well, I guess you'd better start training."

I balled up the note and tossed it into one of the magical trash cans nearby, which incinerated it the moment it landed inside. Grabbed Elyssa's hand and twirled her around as we waited on the next trolley to take us to the parking deck. "My twisted little sister can wait her turn," I said, and pulled her in for a kiss. "For now, I plan on making this a night to remember."

She bit her lower lip. Leaned into my ear and whispered a suggestion that almost caught my pants on fire.

True, my sister and evil grandparents were out there plotting with an insane angel. My dad was about to marry his demon princess. And my mom might be an angel. Stranger things had happened. Or maybe they hadn't. I didn't care.

Because the night was still young, I had my beautiful girlfriend, and saving the world could wait another day.

###

Section A
MEET THE AUTHOR

John Corwin has been making stuff up all his life. As a child he would tell his sisters he was an alien clone of himself and would eat tree bark to prove it.

In middle school, John started writing for realz. He wrote short stories about Fargo McGronsky, a young boy with anger management issues whose dog, Noodles, had been hit by a car. The violent stories were met with loud acclaim from classmates and a great gnashing of teeth by his English teacher.

Years later, after college and successful stints as a plastic food wrap repairman and a toe model for GQ, John once again decided to put his overactive imagination to paper for the world to share and became an author.

Connect with John Corwin online:

Facebook: http://www.facebook.com/johnhcorwinauthor

Blog http://johncorwin.blogspot.com/

Twitter: http://twitter.com/#!/John_Corwin